CW01217572

The Masada Affair

Michael J. Metroke

outskirts
press

The Masada Affair
All Rights Reserved.
Copyright © 2021 Michael J. Metroke
v3.0

This is a work of fiction. Names, characters, businesses, places, events, locales, and incidents are either the products of the author's imagination or used in a fictitious manner. Any resemblance to actual persons, living or dead, or actual events is purely coincidental.

The opinions expressed in this manuscript are solely the opinions of the author and do not represent the opinions or thoughts of the publisher. The author has represented and warranted full ownership and/or legal right to publish all the materials in this book.

This book may not be reproduced, transmitted, or stored in whole or in part by any means, including graphic, electronic, or mechanical without the express written consent of the publisher except in the case of brief quotations embodied in critical articles and reviews.

Outskirts Press, Inc.
http://www.outskirtspress.com

Paperback ISBN: 978-1-9772-2905-2
Hardback ISBN: 978-1-9772-3330-1

Cover Photo © 2021 www.gettyimages.com.. All rights reserved - used with permission.

Outskirts Press and the "OP" logo are trademarks belonging to Outskirts Press, Inc.

PRINTED IN THE UNITED STATES OF AMERICA

For my wife MARCIA METROKE

Chapter 1

"**Artificial intelligence** The ability of a computer program or a machine to think, learn and perform tasks normally require human intelligence."

"**Android** A robot equipped with artificial intelligence and a human appearance."

From the *New Federation Wiktionary*

HESPERIA PLANUM, MARS—EARTH YEAR 2158

Vaccaro's workplace view of the Martian plain often reminded him of his home on the Iberian plateau. With his two-year tour of duty nearly over as the research colony's chief administrator, he looked forward to seeing his family's homestead on the western edge of Madrid again. The appearance of Keith Sinclair, his lead researcher, brought him back to the business at hand.

"How are our preparations progressing for the asteroid flyby, Keith?" Vaccaro asked.

"We're waiting for Earth astronomers to tell us the asteroid's final trajectory, Chief Administrator," Sinclair said. "They continue to believe the rogue asteroid will pass directly over our research colony."

"Are they still estimating the asteroid's diameter as five hundred meters?"

"Maybe larger. We won't know for certain until our Mars orbital satellites can accurately measure the asteroid's dimensions. The flyby represents a rare front row opportunity for our researchers to observe up close an object of this size from the asteroid belt."

"We don't get many chances to impress the Earth authorities. If we do our job right, the publicity from transmitting our data back to Earth will remind them of the value of our off-world research."

"We do face several challenges. Our asteroid tracking team has expressed concern about the lack of maintenance of our observatory equipment."

"Our entire infrastructure has lacked routine maintenance and repair ever since our androids disappeared."

Rumors are going around the colony our survival is at risk. Without those nineteen androids constantly keeping the base running smoothly, sooner or later, we'll face a major system failure."

"What's worse is we're not trained to do those tasks. It will take us years before we can match those androids' knowledge and skills."

"If the androids don't return soon, I'm afraid we may face the possibility of an emergency evacuation."

"Our problems wouldn't exist if the Earth authorities hadn't ordered me to deactivate the androids."

"You tried your best to convince the Earth authorities to revoke the order. It's too bad they failed to listen to you."

"It doesn't make up for the mistake I made. I should've informed the rest of you about the order before telling the androids of their fate."

"No one in the colony holds you personally responsible for their disappearance, Chief Administrator."

"At the time, I'd thought a private meeting with the lead android engineer, Camus might smooth over any difficulties with their deactivation. When I finished explaining what must be done, Camus offered words of comfort despite the drastic implication to him and the other androids."

"We've always held our androids in high regard. You did what any of us would've done."

"It's how I felt too. By Earth standards, our Mars androids are a special breed apart from other models made by the Android Manufacturing Consortium. I still have difficulty believing these same androids are the original vanguard which engineered and constructed this entire base decades ago."

"Our androids' ability to work in the harsh Martian environment has been a great asset to our ongoing research. Without their assistance, many of the planet's complicated geology would never have been properly surveyed."

"They'll be missed by many of us for other reasons too. I often sought out their advice on decisions affecting the colony's welfare. Their support often made the difference in my implementing the right decision."

"The entire colony felt a deep affection toward them. Our children saw the androids as family members."

"It's why I gave Camus a one-day reprieve to prepare the others. When they didn't appear, I assumed they needed more time. Only until I received reports of androids missing work assignments did I realize Camus had used the extra day to avoid their deactivation. I let my respect for them blind me to the real reason he had asked for the delay."

"The androids used the time well to plan their escape. Our search in and around the base perimeter discovered no signs of their escape. What's amazing is they took none of our terrain vehicles."

"It's also strange our drone and orbital satellite surveys came up empty-handed. How could those androids managed to disappear into the Martian night? When I told the Earth authorities what happened, I thought I'd be ordered back to Earth."

"The Earth authorities had no grounds to dismiss you. Their actions caused the problem in the first place."

"I don't fault them for complaining about my lack of foresight. Their anger did subside once I reminded them the land surface of Mars is equivalent to Earth's. With this planet's countless geological surface formations, they grudgingly conceded the androids had too many hiding places."

"It didn't make them sympathetic to your request for android replacements."

"How else could they've responded, Keith. The self-destruction of Earth's quarter of a billion androids left them and us with no choice. Either we fix the problem by retraining ourselves or face the prospect of closing this base."

"Even if they had android replacements, they wouldn't arrive for a long time. With all the Mars class cargo and passenger rockets sitting on our launchpad, a round-trip to Earth would take a minimum of fourteen Earth months. I'd give a year's worth of pay credits to see Camus and the other androids again."

"Let me know when you receive more data about the asteroid, and we'll talk again about our preparations for its arrival."

Michael J. Metroke

The Midlands, North America

Fall semester with its sounds of first-year coeds chattering about classes, new roommates and the possibility of engaging others of the opposite gender brought back pleasant memories of a not-too-distant past for Whitmore. *Before the android suicides and my wife's death.*

As he crossed the south campus, Professor Jonathan Whitmore, or Jay to family and friends, started his late-afternoon stroll home from his Chicago-area university research office. No sooner had he left the confines of the campus did his thinking return to the current global android crisis.

What once seemed a good solution to an age-old problem of educating each new generation has now become a catastrophe of epic proportions, Whitmore thought. *The mass destruction of Earth's android professional classes has exposed the global society's dependency on them for its knowledge workers. Overnight, practically all of Earth's android doctors, lawyers, engineers, teachers, accountants and others in highly technical occupations no longer exist.*

When first introduced, most people believed the benefits of an android workforce overshadowed any costs to society. Once a single android model had been programmed with the proper knowledge and skills, copies could be easily replicated at little additional cost. Within two generations, the public saw little need to require their offspring to waste years undergoing the rigors of a formal education. In less than a half-century, society had turned its back on higher education as a rite of passage into adulthood. Until the recent crisis, few federation citizens disputed this logic.

For its critics, the social and economic disruption caused by the android revolution outweighed any obvious benefits. Bright, young people faced a future of little or no lifetime challenges. Too many federation citizens now fritter away their lives playing meaningless virtual reality games with strangers and artificial intelligent programs.

Despite these criticisms, many people continued to prosper by joining the ranks of artisans and scientific investigators. Their efforts produced an outburst of creativity not experienced by humanity in the previous hundred years. Reports of new scientific discoveries and medical breakthroughs appear almost weekly on the NET news services.

A product of the android revolution, Whitmore had entered the field of psychology, specializing in the sources of human personality disorders. Over his twenty-year career, his research endeavors had brought him a great deal of professional recognition and personal satisfaction. Now in his late forties, his contributions to understanding how human mental disorders evolved throughout a person's lifetime made him a much sought-after speaker on the world lecture circuit. *It's how I met the love of my life and learned of her passion for androids.*

At his home, Whitmore found the usual group of teenagers clustered along his sidewalk. Their presence meant his late wife's experimental androids' afternoon jamming session had already started. Whitmore no longer remembered a time when their music did not attract the neighborhood children's curiosity.

His home's forlorn appearance reminded him the overgrown ornamental plants hadn't been pruned, and now hid his front windows. *I need to make a mental note and hire a teenager to prune them back.* Whitmore also noticed several large boxes of various sizes and shapes had been neatly stacked at his front door.

When he attempted to move the boxes away from his front door, Whitmore discovered each box's size disguised its uneven weight distribution. Now curious about their contents, he opened the largest box, and found an antique cello wrapped carefully in packing material. *Not a cello any human could ever play. This older style musical instrument incorporates an early version of artificial intelligence and mechanical means to play itself.*

Another box held an antique artificial intelligence guitar. Two more boxes revealed antique violins with similar features. The last box contained an artificial intelligent tenor saxophone. which surprised him with a friendly toot.

Convinced Laura had ordered them as part of her musical android experiment, Whitmore decided to determine what the three androids knew about their purpose. As he approached the kitchen door leading into his garage, the sounds of androids' whispering stopped as he opened the inner garage door.

"Hello, everyone," Whitmore said. "I didn't mean to interrupt your practice session."

"We're always eager to play for you," the android vocalist AMI said. "Would you like to listen to the latest addition to our repertoire? It's one out of Janice Joplin's songbook called 'Me and Bobby McGee.'"

"Her rendition of Kris Kristofferson's classic had been released posthumously," Whitmore said. "But before I hear you sing, I've a question. At the front door, I found several large delivery packages containing items I don't recall Laura requesting. Did my wife ever mention ordering an assortment of antique musical instruments?"

The sly look on each android's face told Whitmore an answer to this mystery would soon be forthcoming.

"We wanted to surprise you, Friend Jay," the percussionist android Bang said. "We're the ones who ordered those musical instruments off the NET."

"You ordered them?" Whitmore asked. "Why on Earth did you do so? And, how did you expect me to pay for them?"

"We do apologize for not keeping you informed," the android keyboard specialist KB said. "We thought you wouldn't want to be bothered by such trivialities."

"Until I understand what this is all about, your apology is only conditionally accepted by me," Whitmore said.

"We've a logical reason for our actions," Bang said. "A month after Friend Laura's passing, we posted a few of our songs on the NET for others' enjoyment. Our listeners requested we post more of our songs. A short time later, a music publisher contacted us."

"This publisher also liked our music, Friend Jay," KB said. "He liked the music so much, he proposed we enter into a recording contract with his organization. In return, this publisher promised us royalty payments each time someone listened to our songs."

"The publisher also agreed to set up a bank account to automatically deposit payments owed to us," AMI said. "We knew androids are forbidden to have bank accounts. Our problem went away after we made you our business agent, and put your name on the account."

"With the credits in the account, we could afford to purchase the musical instruments," Bang said. "There's no need for you to worry about paying for them."

"Those antiques you ordered don't come cheap," Whitmore said. "How many credits have you earned selling your songs?"

"Last time we checked, our account had over one hundred thousand credits," AMI said. "The publisher expects larger royalty payments once we record songs beyond the four languages we now know."

"I'm having trouble getting my head around all this music business," Whitmore said. "Why would a publisher enter into a recording contract with androids?"

"He didn't ask us this question," Bang said. "And, we didn't volunteer this information about ourselves."

"Neither do our fans know we are androids, Friend Jay," AMI said. "We act as if it doesn't matter."

"You have fans too?" an incredulous Whitmore asked. "If you're doing so well, why do you need these antique musical instruments?"

"We researched the original music, and identified other musical instruments playing in the background," KB said. "We thought by adding their sound, they'd make our music more authentic."

"You'll want to add several more instruments to create a brass section," Whitmore said. "I suppose you'll want me to unpack and set them up in the garage."

"Since we're without legs and not mobile, Friend Jay, your assistance would be greatly appreciated by us," Bang said. "You'll need to turn on their wireless power connections too. We can manage from there."

"You better hope my back doesn't give out lifting these boxes," Whitmore said. "And I'm not sold on this idea of becoming your business agent. I've plenty of work to do at the university."

As Whitmore carried each musical instrument into the garage, he pondered whether his wife had left him a Pandora's box. *Still, if the androids do have the means to pay for these musical instruments, what harm have they done? Who'd have thought people would pay to listen to old-fashioned music from the twentieth-century I like? I'm glad they didn't order an early Keith Emerson Moog synthesizer. Lifting one could easily throw out my back.*

YANKEEDOM, NORTH AMERICA

Unable to concentrate on his bureau work this morning, Chief

Michael J. Metroke

Investigator Greg Davidson's thoughts fell again into daydreaming about his retirement. *In a few more years, Sandy and I can move to a warmer climate, and leave these New England winters behind. An expensive cube retirement is out of the question, but it won't mean we can't live comfortably. We ought to be able to afford a place in Central America or an older cube in the El Norte region. If I had only known about the android suicides, I'd have not spent so much, and put more credits aside for retirement.*

Davidson's biggest daily challenge involved overcoming his job's bureaucratic routine and tedium. The major exception involved his assistant, Jana Gaspar. A bright, attractive woman in her early thirties, Gaspar came across to him as a social climber hell-bent on becoming his replacement. *The woman can sometimes be a real drama queen on steroid,* Davidson thought. Resigned to working with her, he did his best to hide his feelings of misgivings about his assistant. *When I retire, Gaspar is more than welcome to take over my job.*

Gaspar's latest report woke Davidson out of his retirement dreaming. Her report described unusual activity involving a Chicago-area android research team. Recognizing the researchers' names, he recalled his interview with Laura and Jonathan Whitmore. Under the Android Security Act, the bureau vetted all requests for copies of android prototype programs. Once a license had been issued, the bureau would perform periodic audits such as Gaspar's report to confirm no licensing restrictions had been violated.

Impressed with the Whitmore's research credentials, Davidson saw no reason not to issue them copies of the government's android prototype programs. *When I interviewed the couple, I took an immediate liking to Professor Whitmore. The man struck me as an old-fashioned, harmless sort. His wife, on the other hand, came off as Whitmore's opposite. Obviously, the one in charge and highly motivated.*

Through conversations with his Android Manufacturing Consortium friends, he learned about Whitmore's wife's recent death. Puzzled why the professor's activities would rise to his assistant's attention, Davidson thought he should be the one to contact Whitmore. *No sense exposing the man to Miss. Unbearable so soon after losing his wife. I'll pay him a personal visit and get this matter behind us.*

The Masada Affair

Hesperia Planum, Mars

Vaccaro did not like the look of consternation on Sinclair's face as he entered his office.

"Why the worried look, Keith?"

"I had our computers recheck Earth's asteroid calculations, and found a serious discrepancy," Sinclair said. "This asteroid will come much lower into the Mars atmosphere than predicted by Earth. When I shared my results with them, they confirmed the error, but assured me our storm shutters should provide sufficient protection. They did indicate we may temporarily lose communications with Earth. What scares me is all three Mars class rockets are on our launchpads. They could easily suffer damage from asteroid fragments as it breaks up in the atmosphere. We can't afford to lose any of those rockets, especially the passenger ones.

"Those rockets are our only means for returning to Earth. What can be done to protect them?"

"No. 3 rocket is refueled and ready to launch. We planned to send it back to Earth right after the asteroid flyby. As a precaution, I recommend we empty its fuel tanks."

"I don't see we've much choice, Keith. We can't risk an explosion and destroy all three rockets. Earth would need several years to build replacements, and send them here. If only Camus and the other androids could be found. They'd know how best to prepare the base."

Chapter 2

The Midlands, North America

The holographic call from the Android Manufacturing Consortium's Robert Perfecto had been long anticipated and dreaded by Whitmore. Laura had introduced both men many months ago at the San Jose Museum of Technology dedication reception. Perfecto represented the consortium's research grant office where his wife had obtained their android research funding. Both Laura and he agreed Perfecto's technical and organizational sophistication made him an ideal choice for the assignment.

"Good to see you again, Professor," Perfecto said. "I'm long overdue in offering my and the consortium's condolences about your wife's passing. Truly, an outstanding researcher who made important contributions in her field of android personality design. Everyone at the consortium who had the opportunity to work with Laura will miss her dearly."

"Thank you for your kind thoughts, Robert. I assume the purpose of your call may also concern the status of our research project. I'd relied on my wife to keep the consortium informed on our progress. Her death has made it difficult for me to focus on such administrative matters."

"Your wife's last report spoke of making good progress with the android experiment. If you need additional time to recover from your loss, the consortium will show a great deal of understanding and patience."

"I appreciate your willingness to grant me more time. Exactly what specific progress did Laura's last report mention?"

"She said Stage 1 had been completed, and your clinical observations of her experimental androids had commenced. Have you discovered any signs of personality disorders associated with suicidal behavior in them?"

"None so far. I'm still mystified why she decided to create musical androids."

"In her earlier reports, Laura wrote about your passion for mid-twentieth-century popular music. We thought her idea to design musical androids which played your music preferences a clever one. She believed the music would give you and the androids a common interest. Has the arrangement worked out as well as she imagined?"

"Although they are trying at times, I must admit the androids are an entertaining lot."

"Your wife thought the music would allow you to develop a deeper personal relationship with the androids."

"My wife knew me all too well, Robert. I can't promise any immediate results from studying these androids. If I do discover any suicidal behavioral patterns, I'll contact your office at once."

"So far, the other researchers haven't had much success. Our hope is someone will uncover what exactly caused the mass suicides. Good luck, and again, please accept our sincere condolences about your loss."

After Perfecto's call, Whitmore looked up and smiled at the framed holographic image of his late wife sitting on his worktable. *You left me with three clients, Laura. I only hope I can finish our experiment.*

On his afternoon walk home from the university, Whitmore thought more about his conversation with Perfecto. *Laura may have told the androids about the purpose of our research. She could also have programmed them to detect signs of their own suicidal behavior. If she did, my part of our research may be much simpler than I'd first thought.*

Ever since Laura activated the androids, dozens of teenagers could always be found in Whitmore's driveway each afternoon. Engrossed with listening to the music coming from his garage, they rarely paid much attention to his comings and goings. Today, a young girl waved in his direction, and walked briskly across the lawn to meet him at his front door.

"Hello, Mr. Whitmore. I'm Ruth, your neighbor a couple of doors down the street."

"I know who you are, Ruth. You're Tom and Mary Filson's daughter. Are you and your friends enjoying the music?"

"Oh yes, Mr. Whitmore! We love their music! Mr. Whitmore, could you please ask them for their autographs? My friends would go wild if I came to school with one from the Whitmore Trio."

"Whitmore Trio, is it now? I know why I like their playing, but why are you so interested too? Isn't the music a bit old-fashioned for your generation?"

"I didn't know they played old-fashioned music. Their music sounds so fresh and new. Not like the synthetic stuff they play all the time on the NET."

"Your answer may have earned you their autographs. Come back tomorrow, Ruth, and I may have one for you."

"I can't thank you enough, Mr. Whitmore!"

The teenager turned and ran excitedly back to her friends. Whitmore chuckled when he heard the other girls squeal as one. *They're calling themselves the Whitmore Trio. The name does have a nice ring to it. Besides, every musical group needs a name. Laura would've approved of their choice.*

Feeling now like a proud parent, Whitmore set off for the garage to commend the androids for taking the initiative. At the inner garage door, he could hear AMI singing the lyrics to an old Bobbie Gentry song. The song dealt with a young man who committed suicide by jumping off a Mississippi delta bridge.

Have I detected the first signs of early android suicidal behavior? Whitmore quickly dismissed the idea as preposterous. *Their playing this song and my thoughts about android suicide are nothing more than a coincidence.* Relieved of this notion, he waited until the androids finished this twentieth-century country music classic before entering the garage.

"Nicely done version of "Ode to Billy Joe," AMI. You captured the nonchalant way the family talks about the suicide. They sit there eating their peas and apple pie and talking, without realizing a member of their own family had been the boy's girlfriend and lover."

"But, why did he jump off the bridge?" KB asked.

"It doesn't matter, KB," Whitmore said. "Billy Joe is a fictional person. The mystery is what makes the lyrics so appealing."

"Humans' ability to mix reality and fiction often complicates our efforts to understand your kind," KB said.

"At least, you'll never find us boring," Whitmore said. "On another matter, I learned from a neighbor's child you now call yourselves the "Whitmore Trio." Didn't you promise to keep your business agent informed about important matters?"

"We must've overlooked telling you," Bang said. "Our publisher thought the name had a good vibe going for it."

"Do you like the name, Friend Jay?" AMI asked. "We chose it to honor you and Friend Laura."

"I'm all right with your choice, AMI," Whitmore said. "The same neighbor child asked me for a copy of your autographs. I suspect she's not the only one who wants a copy."

"As our business agent, should we give out our autographs to our fans?" AMI asked.

"If we give one out, others will want one too," Whitmore said. "There may be no end to these kinds of requests."

"The problem is a manageable one," Bang said. "During your sleep cycles, we'll sign copies for you to hand out."

"I can already see those girls' faces light up when I hand them copies," Whitmore said. "I do have a more serious matter to discuss with you. I learned today Laura designed you with a specific purpose in mind. My wife wanted me to observe you for any signs of suicidal tendencies. Did she also incorporate into your programs the ability to detect this behavior?"

"We're not aware of any special diagnostic programs designed for this purpose," Bang said.

"I must assume she meant me to perform clinical studies without such internal monitoring assistance," Whitmore said. "Have any of you experienced what humans call a depressive state of mind?"

"You're aware android emotive programming can only mimic human feelings," AMI said. "At this moment, my programs indicate I'm feeling happy."

"By making music for you and others, our purpose for existence is fulfilled," Bang said. "Isn't it the same for human musicians?"

"Purpose is one source of human happiness, Bang," Whitmore said. "For humans, other emotional needs and desires must often be satisfied too."

"We thought the object of our playing music was to make listeners feel emotions like sadness or joy," KB said. "Were we right to think so?"

"You're right about the effects of music on people," Whitmore said. "Listening to you, I'm convinced you're not experiencing any suicidal tendencies. But nothing is permanent except change. Let me know if your state of happiness ever changes."

"If our moods change, you'll be the first to know," KB said.

"We've had enough serious talk for one day," Whitmore said. "Let's have another song, but not so dark a theme."

"Would you like us to play the Jefferson Airplanes' "Somebody to Love" in Hungarian?"

"Another of my favorites," Whitmore said. "Do me a favor and sing the song in its original language."

Laura's android research project often left Whitmore with feelings of self-doubt. While she had been alive, the project presented a golden opportunity for them to work professionally together. Despite this advantage, he never felt entirely comfortable with his role. One problem always stood out in his mind. He had practically no experience working with androids. His wife's words of encouragement did little to alleviate his insecurity. Any protests about his lack of qualifications often fell on deaf ears. Her response never wavered. Always with a smile, Laura would say, "Why does it matter, Jay? No one else is qualified to do this research."

Aware of her husband's apprehensions, Laura suggested Whitmore read the presidential report on the android suicides. With difficulty, he located a copy of the report's summary findings. In the report's first section, he made a startling discovery. Because consortium engineers had found no evidence of design flaws or defects, the report's authors had outright dismissed the simplest of explanations. Instead, the committee looked elsewhere for answers.

Also surprising to Whitmore, the committee's majority dismissed the notion the androids had caused their own destruction. The report's majority placed the blame on a secretive, unidentified group of human conspirators. The majority's opinion did acknowledge the difficulties with its human conspiracy theory. With no proof humans had tampered with android programming, Whitmore felt their conspiracy theory too speculative.

The report's minority offered a different explanation for the mass suicides. Like the majority's finding, the minority accepted the fact no obvious defects had been identified. The minority, however, disagreed with the majority's conclusion about the lack of android involvement. Its authors believed only the androids had the capability to cause their own destruction. *A more satisfactory conclusion, but why not a conspiracy of both humans and androids?* Incredible to Whitmore, nowhere in the report did either side explain what may have motivated the androids' destruction.

The whole report is a political whitewash with no substance. Everyone knows the president's Human Nation Party is against further encroachment of androids in our society. President McAlister's party must have played a role in causing the androids to commit suicide. But, without any real proof, my idea is another speculation.

Like many within the scientific community, Whitmore considered himself an independent, pragmatic thinker. Though he disagreed with the Human Nation Party's stance people would be better off without androids, Whitmore sympathized with many who feared displacement by an android workforce.

McAlister would never have been elected to the Federation presidency without those people's support. If the prior WEAP administration and the Android Manufacturing Consortium hadn't ignored the problem for so long, he wouldn't be president now.

Whitmore also knew no single reason led to the new president's victory. *McAlister would've lost the election had he and his party not made promises to the Moralist faction.* Considered an ultra-extreme movement, the Moralists hated the consortium's aggressive business practices. Their members especially detested the consortium's success in selling sex trade android models. When first produced by the android manufacturer, many people hailed their introduction as a means to end human sexual exploitation. Skilled in the art of sexual pleasures, the sex trade androids had other social advantages as well. Unable to contract sexually transmitted diseases, their hygiene practices had dramatically lowered the global spread of venereal diseases among humans.

The Moralists did not share this view and saw only its downside. They argued legalizing sex with androids would lead to humans demanding the right to marry these machines. From the Moralists' perspective, allowing such behavior would also demean marriages between humans. A branch of the Moralists went further with their criticism. They worried androids would seek the right to marry among their own kind. "Marriage: One Human with One Human" became their rallying mantra.

To garner the Moralists' votes, McAlister actively campaigned on their concerns. Promising to enact stiff new laws prohibiting human and android marriages as his administration's first order of business, the Moralists' vote gave him a slight majority over his WEAP opposition. Because of these anti-android policies, WEAP accused the new administration of causing the android mass destruction.

Despite his misgivings about the federation president, Whitmore quickly set aside the notion of McAlister's involvement. *The consortium would've never allowed McAlister to cause the wholesale destruction of the world's android population. After they spent a tremendous amount of credits and years perfecting these intelligent machines, the consortium would've fiercely resisted any politician's attempt to put them out of business. McAlister may've had a motive, but without the consortium's tacit involvement, completing the task would've been impossible.*

Contrary to his claims of lacking any experiences with androids, Whitmore did have regular contact with them. He personally relied on the services of an android medical specialist name Jaxon to perform annual checkups and routine medical care. Whitmore considered Jaxon a first-rate medical android with an excellent bedside manner. Programmed with the latest medical knowledge and available twenty-four hours, seven days a week, no human could match the android's capabilities.

Whitmore also had come in contact with another android named Lexus. A university research librarian model, this patient android would devote hours and sometimes days locating the most obscure pieces of information. Whitmore remembered when he casually mentioned to Lexus his interest in a little-known early twentieth-century psychologist's research. A day later, an electronic file arrived with an organized presentation of the psychologist's life and published works. Lexus continued sending additional information

The Masada Affair

until Whitmore politely indicated the android had satisfied his professional curiosity.

When he first learned the two androids had committed self-destruction, Whitmore remembered reacting surprised and puzzled. *Neither android would've had the opportunity to come into each other's contact. Yet, they self-destructed within minutes of each other. The android collective destruction must've been planned well in advance. But, why did they commit mass suicide in the first place? Without an answer to this question, I'm left again with unsubstantiated theories.*

Davidson's autonomous car ride took him to an older Chicago university neighborhood where Whitmore resided. Before he approached the home's front door, he stopped to study the dwelling in front of him. Like many twenty-second-century cube dwellers, he struggled to comprehend why any sane person would want to live in such an antiquated twentieth-century dwelling.

If the appearance of Whitmore's house struck him as odd, another peculiarity also caught his attention. More than a dozen teenagers and several adults stood on Whitmore's sidewalk and driveway, apparently listening to music coming from inside the home. Curious about what had attracted their attention, he approached a teenager nearest to the music's source.

"Excuse me, young lady. Why are you and everyone listening to this music?"

"Aren't they great! I like to come by whenever I can, and listen to them practice."

Intrigued by the girl's remark, Davidson moved closer to listen for himself. With his ear near a large paneled wall, he clearly heard a woman singing accompanied by other musical instruments. *This wall must have been the entry where people once stored their private vehicles*, Davidson realized. With his right foot now tapping to the music's beat, he liked what he heard. *Whoever is on the other side are fantastic. Whitmore must allow the local talent to use his garage for practice.* His curiosity now satisfied; Davidson proceeded to Whitmore's front door.

Michael J. Metroke

Like those standing outside his home, Whitmore had been listening to the trio's jamming. When he learned the androids would teach themselves to play his favorite mid-twentieth-century popular music, Whitmore felt he had died and gone to music heaven. This afternoon, the androids practiced music from the Brazil '66 songbook. Whitmore especially liked their bossa nova interpretation of the group's song "Wave." *The lyrics brought back fond memories of my first meeting with Laura.*

The sound of someone knocking at his front door broke Whitmore's concentration. Convinced his peace had been disturbed by another teenage autograph seeker, he grabbed a handful of signed copies, and headed to the front door. Thoroughly annoyed by these constant interruptions, he now wished he never agreed to give the autographs out. Instead of an eager teenager, Whitmore faced a well-dressed, late middle-aged man waiting on the other side of the door. Uncertain of his visitor's intentions, Whitmore waited for the vaguely familiar man to speak.

"Good afternoon, Professor Whitmore. You may not remember me. I'm Greg Davidson from the Bureau of Android Affairs. We met previously when you and your wife applied for android prototype program licenses. I had other business in the area and took the chance of finding you at home. If this isn't a convenient time, I can come back tomorrow."

"I do remember you, Mr. Davidson. Please come in and tell me how I can assist you."

"My visit is a routine one, Professor. Part of my job is to check on licensees and see how they're doing. By the way, I overheard the music coming from your garage area. Whoever they are, the musicians play exceptionally well. I can understand why so many of your neighbors come by and listen to them practice."

"The group specializes in twentieth-century popular music. Most people have never heard this music played live."

"Come to think of it, I've heard a similar song played recently on a NET music station. The music out of your garage is much better than the synthesized music you hear performed by today's automated recording machines."

"I enjoy their music too. Since you're so fascinated with their playing, allow me to introduce you to the group's members."

Whitmore led his visitor to the inner garage door, where an

astonished Davidson discovered the source of the music. As the androids finished practicing another song from the Brazil '66 songbook, Davidson clapped his hands. Now aware of both men's presence, Bang greeted Whitmore and his guest.

"It looks like Friend Jay has brought us a fan today," Bang said.

"This is Mr. Greg Davidson, everyone. Mr. Davidson heard your music and wanted to meet the musicians. The drummer's name is Bang, KB plays the keyboard and AMI's the group's vocalist. I'm afraid I don't know the other instruments' names except by type."

"I've met many android models in my life, but you're the first musicians," Davidson said. "How long have you been playing together?"

"We've been a group since Friend Laura awakened us," AMI said.

"My late wife spent a great deal of her last days completing their designs. Laura programmed AMI with her own voice."

"You've my sincere condolences about your late wife, Professor. If it's not inconvenient, I do have a few questions to ask you. I'll let you return to a pleasant evening with your musical androids. Can we go back to the space where I first entered?"

As he walked back to Whitmore's living room, Davidson suppressed his distaste for the home's fixed-walls' interior. *How can anyone want to live in these permanently confined spaces?*

Invited by Whitmore to sit on an overstuffed leather sofa, his host surprised Davidson again by offering to make home brewed hot tea.

"It won't take long to boil the water and brew the tea in my kitchen."

"You don't mean, Professor, you personally make the beverage?"

"Boiling the water is no trouble. The kitchen you walked through is fully functional. I often prepare hot tea for myself, and prefer it over food center versions."

Whitmore disappeared, and shortly returned with two mugs filled with hot tea. Handing one to Davidson, he asked the question which had been bothering him since the chief Investigator's arrival.

"Mr. Davison, you don't expect me to believe an impromptu visit from the Bureau's chief investigator is a standard bureau operating practice. What is the real reason for your call today?"

"You're right about my coming here not accidental. I'm here because my assistant reported unusual activities at your home. Knowing her temperament, and the recent loss of your wife, I decided to investigate the matter personally. Her report included two peculiar pieces of information. The first involved the amount of NET traffic originating from your residence. The second concerns the deliveries of an unusual number of special equipment."

"Your question about the amount of NET activity has a simple answer. The androids, you met, are constantly uploading new music to the NET. They also receive and reply to a tremendous number of fan inquiries."

"These androids have fans beyond the locals I saw outside your home?"

"They've fans all across the planet. Laura designed them to play my favorite music from the mid-twentieth-century. It seems other people like the music too."

"You've answered my first question, and I can now answer my second one. The mysterious deliveries are those antique musical instruments I saw in your garage."

"The androids needed those old, artificial intelligent instruments to re-create the era's sound."

"All this is fascinating. What does their playing music have to do with your research into the cause of the android suicides?"

"To be honest, I didn't understand at first why my wife wanted to design musical androids. I later learned Laura thought I'd relate better with them if we shared a common interest like music. Because of her wisdom, I'm now making clinical observations of android suicidal behavior. At the same time, I'm enjoying hearing my favorite music played live."

"A novel approach, Professor. Have you discovered what caused the android suicides?"

"So far, my three musical androids have shown no signs of suicidal tendencies. In fact, they're puzzled by my questions and concerns about their android mental state."

"I'd be upbeat too if I could make music like they do. Well, Professor, I've taken up enough of your time today. I can't wait to get back to the office and have a chat with my assistant about your musical androids."

"Mr. Davidson, before you go, I've a favor to ask. You're

familiar with the presidential committee's report on the causes of the android suicides. The report's summary conclusions seem incomplete to me. I feel as if the report's authors may have been under pressure to reach certain conclusions without taking in all the facts."

"I joined the bureau after the report had been released. I can't comment or explain why the report reads the way it does. I do know the bureau supported the committee's investigation efforts."

"If I could obtain a complete copy of the report, it would greatly assist my research."

"You're not someone who believes the government conspired to eliminate Earth's androids?"

"My interest is purely scientific. I feel the report's summary inadequately addressed why the androids committed collective suicide. If I knew the answer to this question, I might be able to explain why they did so."

"Give me a few days, and I'll see what's in the bureau's files. Have a good evening, Professor. and thanks again for the music and tea."

A sigh of relief came over Whitmore once his visitor departed. *For a moment, I thought Davidson came to revoke the android licenses, and take the androids away. Without Laura's involvement, I must look like a fish out of water to someone like the chief investigator.*

In the background, Whitmore heard a loud, steady, whistling noise coming from his kitchen. He had forgotten again to turn off the frequency coil heating element under the tea kettle. Pouring a fresh mug, he thought more about Davidson's remark concerning his brewing tea at home. *Sometimes, I feel I don't belong in this century and would've been happier living in the past one. While I'm sure all this technology is for the better, many of the older practices seem more grounded in what makes us so human. What's strange is how comfortable I've become with Laura's android creations. You're a man of two extremes, Jay.*

Chapter 3

THE MIDLANDS, NORTH AMERICA

The flashing message on Whitmore's monitor indicated an urgent call had been left by someone from the university's administration. Voice activating the holographic device, he recognized the caller's identification as Provost Marks. Whitmore had met Stanley Marks at several university faculty functions. An outgoing man in his early fifties, Marks' personality lit up a room with his wit and charm. Never personally interested in acting as a go-between university administration and its faculty, Whitmore admired the provost's ability to deal with difficult people.

After his second holographic call alert, an image of Marks appeared on Whitmore's monitor.

"Thanks for returning my call so quickly, Jay," Marks said. "I've a person in my office who wanted to speak with Laura. I explained your wife had recently passed away from a long illness. She seems to know about the android research the two of you had been working together on. If it's convenient, she'd like to speak with you."

"If her business involves Laura, I'm not sure if I can be of much assistance, Provost."

"I forgot to mention her name. She's Dr. Sarah Spencer, the director of the Mars Colony Foundation."

"Laura never mentioned a Dr. Spencer or the foundation. I suppose it wouldn't hurt to talk with her. If you give me a moment, I'll walk over and join the two of you in your office."

Marks and his visitor sat uneasily on a sofa waiting for Whitmore's arrival. From Spencer's outward appearance, he sensed a person both resolute yet anxious. After Marks made brief introductions, the provost surprised his visitors by excusing himself.

"I'm afraid I must leave. I'm late for another university function across campus. Please feel free to use my office while I'm gone."

Marks' abrupt departure left his two visitors staring awkwardly at each other. Curious about the purpose of the foundation director's visit, Whitmore broke the silence between them.

"Dr. Spencer, I'm not sure what brought you here today or how I can assist you. Why did you want to speak with my wife?"

"What do you know, Professor, about the Mars research colony's recent close encounter with a rogue asteroid?"

"I don't normally follow news from outer space. I do recall seeing a NET news report about the colony experiencing difficulty communicating with Earth. Other than this news item, I don't know what's going on there."

"If the colonists only faced a communication issue, I wouldn't be here taking up your time. The problem is far worse than the NET news services have reported. Experts on Earth first thought the asteroid's path would keep it a safe distance from the research base. Tragically, these experts failed to consider the effects of Mars' gravity in their calculations. Instead of traveling many kilometers above the research colony, the asteroid skimmed the thin Martian atmosphere and passed less than a kilometer directly above the base."

"They must have experienced a near miss."

"Information from our Mars orbital satellites shows the colony suffered severe damage, and heavy casualties from the asteroid's intense heat and shockwave. Do you know much about the research colony itself, Professor?"

"I only know the base has been operating for many decades, and performs outer world research."

"The base consists of four main buildings and a landing and launchpad for its automated interplanetary rockets. Above-surface glass walkways connect the four main buildings. The walkways eliminate the need for the colonists to wear pressurized suits whenever they travel between the buildings."

Spencer unlocked a trip case and pulled out a tablet device. Ordering the tablet to display a file of recent Mars satellite images, she motioned to Whitmore to view the tablet's contents with her.

"Until the government releases this information to the public, what I'm about to show you must be treated as strictly confidential. As a fellow professional, I'll assume you'll keep this information to yourself."

"Dr. Spencer, I'm not sure I know what to make of these images, or why you're showing them to me."

"If you'll allow me to explain, I'll answer all your questions. We received these satellite images two days ago. If you look closely, three of the colony's buildings' geodesic domes have been damaged. The asteroid's shockwave shattered their dome glass. The same is true for the glass walkways. The building without a dome is the colony's original building. We believe this structure may still be intact."

"As a psychologist, I understand why the other three buildings incorporated glass domes and walkways. With no windows, the original building must've felt like a medieval European dungeon to its inhabitants. Engineers must have designed the other buildings and walkways with this problem in mind."

"An excellent deduction, Professor. The colonists' morale improved sharply with the introduction of the new buildings and walkways. The designers protected the glass with special anti-radiation coatings and storm shutters. Unfortunately, the designers never imagined the glass would need to withstand a passing asteroid's shockwave."

"Have you detected any signs of human activity on the surface?"

"None so far. We believe the colonists thought them safe and didn't wear their pressurized suits as a precaution during the asteroid's flyby. Without the suits, lack of oxygen and exposure to the Martian extreme cold would've meant certain death for anyone unprotected."

"Does this mean there's little hope for finding any survivors?"

"There's still the possibility colonists took shelter and survived in the original colony's building. We won't know for certain until they decide to emerge from its underground levels."

"If the survivors' condition is so grim, why haven't they boarded an automated rocket and returned to Earth?"

"An evacuation from Mars is no longer an option. At the time of the asteroid flyby, all three of our Mars class rockets had landed at the base. Each rocket suffered damage from the asteroid's shockwave. This image shows those rockets lying on the research colony's launchpad."

"Those rockets remind me of old-fashioned bowling pins knocked over. Can't you send another rocket and rescue any survivors?"

"You're looking at all of Earth's Mars class rockets. It would take the government several years to manufacture a new one."

"Any survivors would have little hope of Earth rescuing them."

"We do have one possibility available to us. The foundation has a cargo rocket used to launch satellites into orbit around Mars. The rocket could be adapted to hold one android with a communication equipped rover. Once on Mars, the android would survey the damage and identify any survivors."

"I'm sorry, Dr. Spencer, but I don't follow how sending this delivery rocket and one android can rescue the survivors."

"You're right to think this approach has problems. If survivors do exist, one android may not be enough to secure their survival. Our more pressing issue is finding a suitable android for the mission."

"Have you asked the government for assistance?"

"We believe because of its well-publicized anti-android stance, the McAlister administration would look unfavorably on such a request. The foundation does have one working android body in our Mars museum. Unfortunately, the android body lacks the necessary artificial intelligence programs to activate itself. This is why I came to talk with your wife. Our sources informed us you have in your possession three android Model T240 government-licensed programs. I came to convince your wife, and now you, to allow me to copy those programs, and combine it with our android museum body."

"If she were still alive, Laura could confirm whether our android research programs are compatible with your museum android body. I, on the other hand, have difficulty telling one android model from another."

"I can easily verify if your programs are compatible with our android body, Professor."

"There's still the problem of obtaining the government's permission to transfer a copy to your foundation."

"In this instance, it may be easier to ask for their forgiveness once the android is sent safely to Mars."

"I don't understand why you must send an android to Mars. Didn't the research colony have its own androids?"

"The research colony's nineteen androids disappeared shortly after learning the McAlister administration had ordered their deactivation. They have never been seen since. It's another reason we haven't attempted to approach the government for assistance."

"Dr. Spencer, you must be aware of the government's restrictions imposed on researchers. If I gave you a copy of my android programs, the government could revoke my licenses and bring charges against both of us."

"Professor, we don't know if your android programs are compatible with our android body. As for the personal risks, I'd ask you to weigh them against the possibility of saving any survivors."

"I'll give your humanitarian appeal further consideration but make no promises about lending you any copies, Dr. Spencer. Come to my home tonight. If the android programs are compatible with your android body, we can talk more."

"You won't regret this decision, Professor."

"I'm already having bad feelings about my involvement in helping you."

The appearance of Whitmore's mid-twentieth-century ranch-style home did not deter Spencer from following him through its fixed-wall interiors to the garage. Her outlook improved considerably upon seeing the three legless androids.

"Dr. Spencer, may I introduce you to members of the Whitmore Trio," Whitmore said. "AMI, Bang, and KB, this is Dr. Spencer from the Mars Colony Foundation. Dr. Spencer believes your original programs are designed to operate with an off-world android body. I told her I had no idea whether they did or not."

"Friend Dr. Spencer has come to the right place," Bang said. "Our original designs allowed us to operate on off-world assignments. Friends AMI and KB can confirm what I've said."

"Dr. Spencer would like to make a copy of your programs for analysis purposes," Whitmore said. "If there's a match, and I reconsider my reservations in getting involved at all with her plan, she'll want to use the copy to re-activate another android body for a special mission to Mars."

"While we like being musicians, working on Mars would fulfill our original purpose," KB said.

"Please make a copy of my programs," AMI said. "I want to become the first android singer on two worlds."

"The two of you are getting a little ahead of me," Whitmore said. "Judging from your pensive expression, Bang, you appear not in agreement with your android friends."

"Friend Laura made extensive modifications to our programming, and may have removed aspects of our original designs," Bang said. "It'd be better if Friend Dr. Spencer made copies of all three of our programs, and examined them for possible deficiencies."

"I agree with your android's logic, Professor," Spencer said. "We don't know what changes your wife made to their programs. If I've your permission, I'll need time to set up my copying equipment."

"How will we know which of us you've selected for the mission, Friend Dr. Spencer?" KB asked.

"It'd be better if I hold off telling you until the android copy has safely landed on Mars," Spencer said. "I'll ask again, Professor, do I have your permission to proceed with copying your androids' programs?"

"Oh, I guess it can't hurt to learn if what these androids have said is true or not," Whitmore said. "You'll still have to contact the authorities about the program transfer."

"I'll go right now and get the copying equipment out of my autonomous car." Spencer said.

"May the best android program be selected," AMI said. "Especially if it's mine."

Yankeedom, North America

An incredulous Davidson sat in his bureau office, not knowing what to make of his assistant's information.

"What do you mean the bureau's copies of the report can't be located, Jana?" Davidson asked. "I understood we provided investigative staff support to the president's android committee. One person in the bureau must have kept a copy of the full report."

"I searched everywhere, including asking the staff who worked on the report," Gaspar said. "Not one person could find their digitized copies."

Gaspar's explanation of her search efforts convinced Davidson someone had deliberately removed the copies from the bureau's electronic data records. *Only a person with the highest security clearance could have done so. More worrisome, the thief left no traces of his actions. Why would anyone go through so much trouble over a governmental report anyway? I need to alert Hall, and get to the bottom of this mystery.*

Dean Hall answered Davidson's call on the first alert. Head of the bureau's data security operations, Hall had joined the organization a few months before Davidson's arrival. Both men knew each other from their days working at the Android Manufacturing Consortium. Occasionally meeting after work for drinks and dinner, they often fell into reminiscing about their former lives, and the machinations at their current employer.

"Dean, I need a favor," Davidson said. "You know the presidential committee's report on the android suicides. I asked Gaspar to locate a copy and she came back empty-handed. An insider may've intentionally removed the bureau's copies. I'm guessing a copy still exists in our data center backup files. When you get a chance, send a copy of the full report to me."

"We may be dealing with a hacker wanting to embarrass the bureau. Give me a couple of hours, and I'll let you know what I've found. This favor is going to cost you buying me a beer or two."

"Food center beer I can always afford. I'll make it a pitcher if you identify the culprit."

"You've bought a pitcher. Plan on us going out after work today."

The Midlands, North America

Tired from his week at the university, Whitmore looked forward to a quiet evening at his home. From the garage, he heard Burt Bacharach and Hal David's popular song "The Look of Love" being sung in a Scandinavian tongue. *Judging by AMI's accent, she's singing the song in Swedish. Who'd have thought my home would become such a pop musical revival center?*

The Masada Affair

Re-energized by their playing, he considered talking with the trio again about the android suicides. As he waited for AMI's singing to end, he considered how best to lighten the mood before delving into this dark subject.

"Hello, everyone," Whitmore said. "I've been listening to your last song. Dusty Springfield first sang the song in a British spy movie called *Casino Royale*. I believe the song also won an Academy Award for best song in a motion picture. Has this song ever been recorded in Swedish before?"

"Not in Swedish," Bang said. "Our NET searches did find one recording done in 1969 by a local Oslo artist. We've also done the song in Norwegian and Finnish. Would you like to hear those versions too?"

"How many languages do you now record songs in?" Whitmore asked.

"As of this afternoon, a total of 1,215 songs in 93 languages," AMI said. "Our goal is to learn and record five new songs in different languages each day."

"You three are incredibly ambitious," Whitmore said. "If you keep up this pace, you'll soon master the entire era's music."

"If we didn't have to respond to our NET fan inquiries, we'd have done so already," KB said. "We receive over five thousand messages each day."

"No need to apologize, KB," Whitmore said. "Laura would've been proud of your accomplishments."

Whitmore's last remark brought wide grins to each android's face.

"I've given more thought to our ongoing conversation concerning the android suicides," Whitmore said. "While I understand why humans take their own lives, I can't fathom why androids would do so too."

"Our awakening happened after their destruction took place," AMI said. "We never knew those other androids."

"Being androids, they must've had a logical reason for destroying themselves," KB said.

"I agree with Friend KB," Bang said. "The androids must've concluded they had no other choice but to self-destruct."

"Humans who commit suicide often feel the same way," Whitmore said.

"Androids are not capable of those feelings," KB said. "Did humans mistreat these androids?"

"Except for a few scattered reports of domestic violence, I'm not aware of any large-scale abuses," Whitmore said. "Most humans I know viewed their androids as too valuable a property to allow them to become damaged."

"Friend Jay, if humans reversed roles with androids, would they accept being our property?" AMI asked.

"Your question is intriguing, AMI," Whitmore said. "My guess is most people wouldn't tolerate such an arrangement. Would they kill themselves to escape ownership by androids? I don't know."

"I've a personal question for you, Friend Jay," Bang said. "We know humans have biological and legal family units. Besides Friend Laura, do you have other family members?"

"My parents and brother live in New Charleston," Whitmore said. "Our ancestors first settled in the old city several centuries ago. My great-grandparents and other relatives resettled inland to the new city after the oceans rose from global climate warming. Why do you ask?"

"We're interested in learning more about you and your family's history," Bang said. "Are there historical records and images of your family members and ancestors?"

"You're in luck, Bang," Whitmore said. "Over many generations, Whitmore women have been avid recorders of our family history. As the family's matriarch, my mother has been responsible for maintaining our NET's genealogy records. I believe anyone can access and view this material."

"You wouldn't mind if we access those records, Friend Jay?" KB asked.

"Not in the least, KB," Whitmore said. "It has been a long day for me and is getting late. For our neighbors' sake, please stop practicing after ten o'clock and work on answering those fan messages. We don't need sleepless neighbors complaining about your loud playing."

Settled comfortably into his living room's vintage leather Barca Lounger, renewed doubts about his android suicide research crept into Whitmore's thoughts.

I've little to show for my android research efforts. I can't even get the fellow from the bureau to send me a copy of the presidential android committee report. Perfecto's bound to ask for another progress update. I can see the look on his holographic face after I tell him Laura's androids are normal. Better yet, how will Perfecto react after learning about the androids' fans? Sorry, Professor Whitmore, the consortium doesn't fund android rock and roll bands.

Once the government realizes my research has reached a dead end, they'll demand the return of the android programs, and require me to deactivate the trio. So much for making me your research partner, Laura.

I'll miss these androids, especially the female one. Her voice is a constant reminder, Laura, you still exist in my life. Speaking of AMI, I thought her reverse roles question an intriguing one. An idea worth giving further thought.

Now exhausted, Whitmore eased himself off the recliner and headed to his bedroom. Tucked in, he, out of habit, reached over to the bed's empty side. An old song about tomorrow sung by a young blond girl wearing big glasses came to mind. *You ought to take Annie's advice, Jay. Life might be a little less worrisome if you did.*

YANKEEDOM, NORTH AMERICA

On his arrival at the Boston-area food center, Davidson spotted his data security colleague sitting alone in its bar section. Hall had already drained half a pitcher of beer, and did not look his usual happy self.

"Dean, are you going to drink this whole pitcher? Slow down and tell me what's bothering you. Are you and Tamera having problems?"

"How does the bureau manage with investigators like you working there? My all-too-obvious look of pain comes from another source. Try my searching for the missing report you requested."

"I can't imagine why my request would be such a big pain in your neck, especially for a hotshot data security center operator like yourself. Why don't you tell me what you found?"

"I found exactly what you discovered. No copies of the report and no traces of who removed them."

"Don't tell me your staff accidentally deleted the files. And I thought the bureau's data security section hired better talent. Compared to the rest of us poor civil servants, you get paid well."

"My people don't make it a practice of deleting bureau records. After your call, I asked the bureau's computer to run its tracer programs, and identify the data thief. Within minutes after the computer sent out its tracers, an anonymous message arrived wanting to know why I'm running them. I sent a terse reply demanding the messenger identify himself, and explain how he knew I ran the tracers. The caller told me my tracers triggered an automatic alert to his office. You'll never guess in a million years this person's name."

"How about pouring me a glass of beer, and ending this charade, Dean. I need to get home to Sandy sometime tonight."

"You'll want more than one glass of beer after you hear his name. The call came from Kevin Taro."

"You're right about me needing another glass of beer. Why would McAlister's android security affairs advisor hack into bureau records and steal copies of a presidential committee report? Did Mr. Taro explain why he had done so?"

"Taro cut me off when I tried to explain the bureau's copies had gone missing. In no uncertain terms, he told me if I or anyone else attempted to use a tracer again, they'll face an immediate career change."

"Did you tell him your role at the bureau, Dean?"

"Give me a little credit, Greg. When I did, it made him angrier. I kept my professional cool, and asked under whose authority he had acted."

"I'll bet your question didn't go down well with Taro."

"A few of us occasionally go out on a limb for the bureau. Taro said his authority came from the highest level of federation government."

"Taro could've only meant one person, Dean. He reports directly to President McAlister."

"You earned yourself another glass of beer. Taro didn't stop there. In case I forgot his earlier threat about losing my job, he ends the call by telling me he hoped I was a smart person who didn't need another reminder. Nice guy, huh?"

"Why all this cloak-and-dagger business over an official government report?"

"I don't know or care. Taro made me so mad I kept digging around anyway. It turns out he didn't remove every piece of information from our bureau records."

Hall stopped, and discreetly scanned the food center for signs of anyone paying too much attention to their conversation. From his jacket pocket, he pulled out a memory stick and placed it in front of Davidson.

"The data device contains information on the five presidential committee members. If you still want a copy of the full report, you could contact them."

"Remind me never to get you angry, Dean."

"You're welcome. All this business is making me hungry. Any chance your wife will let us have dinner together tonight?"

"Let me call Sandy. She's been talking about wanting a night out with her girlfriends."

"You're lucky to have married such an understanding woman. Not like your first wife."

"It's always easy to blame someone else for your own shortcomings."

"Maybe so, but you're happier these days married to Sandy."

While he waited for his autonomous car's arrival, Davidson's fingers felt Hall's memory stick in his pocket. *Taro didn't tell Dean I couldn't contact the report authors and get a copy from them.*

Chapter 4

Yankeedom, North America

Davidson's first three holographic calls to committee members ended badly. *They all responded politely to my questions, but showed little knowledge or interest in their committee's work. Not surprising given their lack of prior experience in android issues. McAlister must have handpicked them strictly for political reasons.*

Hall's background information on the fourth member persuaded Davidson the call might result in a different outcome. A highly regarded consortium retired senior android engineer, James Chapman held multiple federation patents in his field. A holographic image of an older, balding man answered his call. Chapman's face quickly darkened as Davidson explained his purpose for contacting him.

"Why would someone in your position need to ask me this question?" Chapman asked. "I find it hard to believe the bureau lost all its report copies."

"I empathize with how you feel, Mr. Chapman. For reasons I don't fully understand either, all our bureau copies have disappeared from our internal records."

"Even if I did believe your tale of disappearing government documents, I don't know why I should bother to help you."

"I'm attempting to fulfill a request from a prominent human personality disorder researcher. He's currently studying what caused the android suicides and wanted a copy of the committee's full report as part of his research. After not locating a bureau copy, I thought contacting a member of the committee might produce one."

"A human personality disorder researcher, you say? I don't believe reading the full report will provide much additional information for your researcher friend."

Before Davidson could thank the senior engineer and end the call, Chapman took the conversation in another direction.

"Do you have any grandchildren, Mr. Davidson? I've one granddaughter in an elementary fine arts program. I usually pick her up every Tuesday afternoon from her school and take her to dance lessons across town. She attends The Midlands Public School 401. I typically wait for her at the park across from the school. I like to sit and feed the pigeons which flock there. If you find yourself in the vicinity before three o'clock on a Tuesday, look for the old guy wearing a baseball cap on backward. Come alone, Mr. Davidson. Too many people will scare the pigeons away."

The Midlands, North America

Chapman's granddaughter's school required Davidson to travel by autonomous car nine hundred kilometers west from his Boston-area office. His cursory inspection of the park revealed several young mothers and toddlers taking advantage of the afternoon sunshine. Among them sat an older gentleman matching Chapman's description. Seemingly engrossed with tossing pieces of stale bread to dozens of pigeons scurrying around his feet, Chapman paid Davidson scant attention as he sat on the park bench. Reaching into a bag, he casually handed Davidson a slice of stale bread. Without comment, Davidson followed Chapman's lead and tossed torn bits to the cooing birds now gathering near his feet.

"I see you decided to take up my invitation, Mr. Davidson," Chapman said. "While I'm not the paranoid type, it isn't every day I receive a call from the bureau's chief investigator."

"I meant what I said about keeping a promise to a researcher," Davidson said. "He believes your committee report summary is, at best, incomplete and hiding important information about what caused the android suicides. After not finding any copies in the bureau's records, I became suspicious too."

"Your researcher friend is an astute reader between the lines. Except for me, all the other committee appointees consisted of McAlister's political hacks. Our federation president needed my technical background and credentials to give the committee any credibility."

"My researcher friend thought the report's conclusions seemed like speculations."

"The other committee members would be grateful for his characterization of the report. Try not to feed the fat one over there. He's always bullying the smaller females and prevents them from getting their fair share."

"Knowing your reputation at the consortium, you must have discovered information McAlister didn't want made public."

"Perhaps, Chief Investigator. What I'm about to tell you may or may not be important. When I joined the committee, the government asked me to perform postmortem examinations on several android suicide cases. I had planned to look for any evidence of hardware or programming defects. Except for one exception, I discovered nothing out of the ordinary. I did become troubled by what I did find, or not find. You see, Mr. Davidson, the androids I examined had their programs and memories swiped clean. I asked why this removal had been done before my examination. The person in charge explained standard consortium protocols had been followed."

"Having worked at the consortium for many years, I don't ever recall program and memory removal a standard practice, especially if an android would be subject to further examination."

"I thought so too. I asked for copies of the particular androids' programs and memory files to review. This same person told me no copies had been retained."

"His response doesn't make any sense. The consortium would've insisted on their preservation for further study."

"I reached this same conclusion. When I pressed this person to allow me to examine other android suicide cases with intact programs and memories, he gave me the same answer."

"What would motivate the consortium to remove and, I presume, destroy, copies of these android programs and memories?"

"I've more to tell, Chief Investigator. I asked if the consortium had ever experienced an android suicide before the recent ones. This is where my story becomes stranger. Are you certain you want to hear more, Chief Investigator? Knowing what I know could threaten your career at the bureau."

"Information can sometimes be dangerous in the wrong hands. I'll bet a pitcher of beer against your baseball cap you discovered more than one prior android suicide."

"You couldn't offer me enough beer for this cap. I bought it at the World Series four years ago. My Havana Rebels won the series in the seventh game. Besides, I wouldn't have taken your wager. When I pressed him, he confessed on three separate occasions, several groups of androids had allegedly committed suicide prior to the mass suicides."

"Did this person know why they self-destructed?"

"I never received an answer to this question. I did learn more about those android groups, however. Each group's members had been previously assigned to the seven continents. Do you find this information peculiar, Chief Investigator?"

"People tend to find patterns where none exist. It may be a coincidence members of these android groups came from every continent."

"I could accept your notion of coincidences except for one other fact. Why would each group of seven androids simultaneously destroy themselves and do so within ten kilometers of the federation presidential North American office?"

"Were all the androids the same model type?"

"The same person told me no two androids had been alike."

"If I accept these facts as you present them, what must I conclude, Mr. Chapman?"

"I'm not asking you to accept any facts or conclusions. My granddaughter is waving at me. I must stop now and go to her. Before I leave, I've one more piece of information you might find useful. One android in the last group has never been located. No one at the consortium seems certain if this android committed suicide with the others."

"I thought you said they all committed suicide?"

"The person in charge said the androids had all been destroyed. I believed him until a young consortium engineer told me about an android which had escaped. Before I could question this woman further, her superior, who had overheard our conversation, drew the engineer aside. When I attempted to question her further, she denied her earlier statement, and refused to answer any more of my questions."

"Her supervisor obviously pressured the woman into silence. What do you think happened to the missing android?"

"I can only offer you speculation. If the android isn't yet deactivated, finding this missing android may provide answers to your researcher friend's questions."

"I'm beginning to understand why you took the precaution of meeting me here."

"Another word of advice, Chief Investigator. If you decide to continue searching for the truth, others may not want what you uncover to see the light of day. Now, I must go. I don't want my granddaughter to become annoyed with her grandfather."

Davidson remained seated until Chapman and his granddaughter departed in an awaiting autonomous car. Tossing the remaining bread into the air, and creating a feeding frenzy among the birds, he walked back to his own autonomous vehicle. After he voice-commanded the car's artificial intelligence to take him home, he thought about what Chapman had told him.

Parts of Chapman's information don't make much sense to me. What would motivate androids to come together from such great distances, and self-destruct? What am I to make of his warnings? If Chapman's right, my asking too many questions may risk Sandy's and my retirement plans. If I didn't feel the bureau's integrity had been compromised, I'd tell Whitmore no report copies could be located, and forget I ever met with Chapman. I now understand the old English expression about "in for a penny, in for a pound."

The Provence, Europe

Perfecto's invitation to attend a consortium-sponsored symposium came as an unexpected perk for Whitmore. Unbeknownst to him, Laura's research grant stipulated their mandatory attendance to such conferences. Held at a posh French Riviera resort, the all-expenses-paid trip presented a rare opportunity in a world of holographic meetings. Welcoming the trip as a needed break from his university routine, Whitmore looked forward to meeting his android research counterparts.

A fast-pilotless, corporate scramjet took Whitmore and other conference attendees to the Provence region, and its delightful weather. After he registered with the resort's automated receptionist, Whitmore spent the rest of the day studying the list of presenters and topics posted on the conference's NET site. Most of the presentations resembled the keynote speaker's morning address. For two hours, he listened to the benefits of dehumanizing android physical appearances and programming capabilities. Whitmore found the afternoon roundtable discussion not much better. The session's panelists debated whether increased android specialization would eliminate the need for machine self-awareness.

One speaker, a Lawrence Potts, did pique Whitmore's interest. A prominent brain development researcher, his talk had attracted the interest of many conference goers.

"Android designers historically thought the closer androids resembled humans, the easier they'd fit into human society," Potts said. "Their holy grail involved designing artificial intelligent robots, and later androids which looked and acted like humans. These early pioneers didn't stop with dreams of androids capable of independent learning and thinking. They wanted to create an artificial intelligence with a sense of self-awareness.

"Many setbacks littered this path toward android self-awareness. A major breakthrough came in 2065 when a group of young android designers decided to use the human brain as their model. They experimented with organically linking multiple specialized computer programs loosely together. To their amazement, the first self-conscious android awoke in their laboratory. No longer an intelligent machine, these early versions demonstrated the possibility of creating android individuality.

"Another critical artificial intelligence advancement involved designing android generalists' models with specialized skills and capabilities. Instead of merely learning and executing repetitive tasks, more sophisticated android models appeared capable of performing complex activities previously done only by well-trained and experienced humans. Extraordinarily costly at first, the ability to replicate unlimited copies from a single master set of programs dramatically lowered production costs. A new age commenced with humanlike androids replacing their human workplace counterparts. Until the recent android suicides, our world resembled this anthropomorphic vision.

"The android suicides exposed a serious problem which android designers had overlooked. They failed to comprehend their creations would also undergo mental difficulties similar to those experienced by ordinary humans. The difference is our human biological brains have had tens of thousands of years to evolve and adapt to our environment. Because the designers failed to consider the possibility multiple computer centers could lead to self-destructive behavior such as suicide, our society is now paying a heavy price for their arrogance, and lack of forethought.

"Before we can replace androids, the android design community must solve this core problem, or we'll face a similar crisis in the future. If android designers take up this challenge, I believe humanity's future with androids will become much brighter...."

At the end of Potts' presentation, his audience rose as one with applause. Baffled by their response to the speaker's unproven conclusions, Whitmore sat quietly and shook his head in disbelief.

Potts' whole premise about android multiple computer centers as the source of the suicides is pure hogwash. You need only to think about humans with our dozens of specialized brain functions to realize he's mistaken. Evolution of the human brain hasn't stopped us from feeling depressed or suicidal either. If Potts' theory held any water, humans and other highly intelligent creatures should've become extinct a long time ago.

Whitmore's skepticism about the value of his peer's research continued to grow throughout the afternoon. When the conference's first day ended, he joined other attendees for a hosted reception. No sooner had Whitmore entered the hotel's palatial Versailles'-style ballroom, he heard a familiar sound playing in the background. *They're my android friends with AMI singing a lively version of Jimmy Webb's "Wichita Lineman."* Now feeling better about his circumstances, he headed to the reception's wine bar to celebrate his new-found discovery.

A formidable list of French wine choices almost ruined Whitmore's buoyant mood. Rescued by the knowledgeable wine bartender, Gerard, he sampled a delightful glass of Bordeaux. Whitmore noticed his bartender hummed along with another of the trio's songs played over the ballroom's audio system. *Is it possible my musical androids* do *have fans all over the world?* Whitmore decided to test this theory with his friendly bartender.

"This Bordeaux is exceptional, Gerard. I see you like the music playing in the background. Do you know the group's name?"

"They call themselves the "Whitmore Trio." The group is the current rage on the continent. Young people especially like their songs' retro lyrics. Much better than the computer-generated stuff they serve up on the NET these days. At your age, you must find the music not appealing."

"On the contrary, I like this particular era's music. In fact, I've several musician friends back home who sound exactly like this Whitmore Trio."

"If they play half as good, your friends will become rich. What I'd give to be the Whitmore Trio's business manager."

"I can't imagine what it might be like. After listening to all the conference's speakers today, I deserve another glass of this Bordeaux."

"If you like this particular variety of wine, you might enjoy a 2149 Bordeaux by Saint-Estèphe too. It's the region's oldest aquaponics winery."

"I'm at your mercy, Gerard. Pour away."

Yankeedom, North America

Sandy's animated appearance at their cube's front gate caused Davidson to set aside any hope of a relaxing evening out with his wife. After they exchanged an affectionate kiss, Sandy shared with him what had excited her so much.

"Greg, you won't believe who called us."

"I'm too tired for guessing games, Sandy. I've come back from a long trip to The Midlands. Did someone from the office try to reach me?"

"The call didn't come from your office. Do you know someone named Kevin Taro?"

"Taro's the president's android security affairs advisor. Did he leave me a message?"

"He said you should call him as soon as you arrived home. He's been trying to reach you all afternoon."

"My trip to The Midlands took most of the day. I'll grab my earphones and take a walk around the block. I could use the exercise after sitting most of the day in an autonomous car."

"Don't be too long. I've already ordered our car for tonight."

Outside his cube's front gate again, Davidson took a deep breath and requested Taro's caller identification. A man's voice answered on the third call alert.

"Thanks for returning my call tonight, Greg. At this hour, you must be calling from your home. I won't take up much of your time. The president and I require the services of an experienced investigator with an android technical background. Your name came to the top of our list of candidates."

"Excuse me, Mr. Taro. Does this call have to do with my recent efforts to find a copy of the presidential android special committee's report?"

"Call me Kevin, Greg. One committee member did contact me about your interest in the report. I did a little digging and realized you had been doing your job. I told the president. here's a real investigative professional."

"Thanks for the compliment, Kevin. How can I assist the president and you?"

"What I'm about to tell you, Greg. involves the highest level of federation security, and must be kept confidential. We've recently uncovered a plot by a group of androids attempting to instigate an insurrection against the federation. Fortunately, we captured the plotters save for one which escaped, and is now in hiding. This android's designation is Rebus. We believe these androids and Rebus are responsible for causing the android suicides. The government is now worried this particular android may attempt to do additional harm."

"Let me guess, Kevin. You want me to find this Rebus."

"You read my mind perfectly. From now on, your primary mission is to find this rogue android and bring him to me for questioning. If this Rebus resists, you're authorized to deactivate the android with whatever force you deem necessary."

"My search would be easier if I knew more about the android."

"The android is the latest generation of consortium research librarian models. The consortium leased this unit to a genealogy center in the Tidewater region. The android had been operating there for several years without any reported incidents. You should talk with the Richmond center's head administrator, Justin Collins. He'll know more about the android, and its whereabouts."

"I'll pay Mr. Collins a personal visit this coming week."

"And, Greg, I can't overemphasize the need for secrecy. You're not to discuss our conversation and your investigation with anyone. Please keep me informed about what progress you make."

The Masada Affair

At his cube's front gate, Davidson found Sandy waiting impatiently for his return. Pointing at a parked autonomous car, Sandy said, "Aren't you the least bit hungry, Greg?"

"Hungry and tired. Your turn to pick the food center."

"I thought we'd try island food tonight. There's a great tiki food center near Copley Square. How did your call go with Taro?"

"His call involved a routine matter. He wants me to investigate a missing android. Looks like I'll be traveling to the Richmond-area for a couple of days. If all goes well, I should be home by the end of the week."

Sensing her husband had held back information, Sandy hid her feelings of unhappiness. *I wish he'd be more open with me. I'm not like his first wife, who thought only about spending his hard-earned credits, and left him as soon as the money dried up. I don't want to know all the details either. I need to feel he's safe and will be all right. I better not suggest going with him. He'll say the trip will bore me to death.*

"When you get back from Richmond, I want to try a food center my friend Lisa recommended," Sandy said. "She's constantly raving about their Korean South African fusion cooking."

"Why don't you and Lisa go there while I'm gone and let me know what's good to eat."

TIDEWATER, NORTH AMERICA

The Richmond Center for Genealogy and Historical Records building's exterior appearance disappointed Davidson. He had imagined a bright airy building where people could research the center's records for information about their descendants. Instead, a windowless low concrete structure stood in front of him.

Before Davidson reached the center's entrance, the building's artificial intelligent surveillance cameras had detected his presence and alerted the center's staff. A woman in her late fifties met him at the main entrance and escorted the chief investigator to a comfortable waiting area. Dressed in a drab grey outfit, her appearance convinced him an inconsequential Center employee acted as his host. His attitude swiftly changed when the woman introduced herself as the center's head librarian. Florence Knight struck Davidson as a polite but reserve Tidewater resident with her ancestors conceivably stretching back to the original American thirteen colonies. No sooner had they sat down, another center employee appeared and served them the region's favorite morning beverage, sweetened tea.

"Mr. Collins apologizes for not being able to meet with you, Mr. Davidson," Knight said. "He had another pressing engagement, and asked me to take his place."

"I'm surprised not to find more visitors at this center." Davidson said.

"We rarely receive visitors. Most people who make request for information do so through the NET."

"This building isn't what I had expected. I thought the center would be much larger."

"Like fungus and their mushrooms, most of this center is located underground with multiple floors stretching well beyond this upper level. We're the primary depository for North America's entire population's genome records. Our files hold well over two billion tissues samples from the living and dead. We'd have more if the cremation practices of the prior centuries hadn't been so widespread. Fortunately, the practice grew out of favor once people understood the importance of preserving their genetic information for future generations."

"Where do the center's requests for information typically come from?"

"Most of our requests are from genetic laboratories asking for tissue samples. The laboratories use the samples to identify a person's propensity for diseases and genetic disorders."

"My former android medical specialist regularly took my tissue samples for this purpose. How do you go about collecting samples from those persons who died in the past?"

"Much of our samples prior to the late twenty-first-century came from exhuming old grave sites. We owe a great deal of gratitude to the androids assigned to this thankless task for recovering those valuable specimens."

"Speaking of androids, my reason for wanting to meet with Mr. Collins involved an android leased by your center. Are you familiar with an android designated as Rebus? I'm told the center utilized this android for research purposes."

"Everyone at the center knew Rebus. Rebus worked here as our historical archivist. I had the pleasure of working closely with him on many occasions."

"Our records show this android hasn't been accounted for. Do you know its present whereabouts?"

"I'm afraid I can't be of much assistance, Mr. Davidson. Rebus left the center without a travel voucher, and hasn't been seen since."

"Allowing an android to move freely about without a travel voucher is highly irregular. Do you know why it disappeared?"

"I and others at the center considered Rebus a responsible and trustworthy android. At the time, we didn't think his departure significant. Our concern grew only after Rebus failed to return, and perform time-sensitive duties."

"The bureau never received a missing android report from the center. We could have assisted you in finding your android. Did you consider the possibility Rebus suffered an accident, or committed suicide with the other androids?"

"You're right, Mr. Davidson. On behalf of this center, please accept my apology for not following bureau protocol. We thought Rebus could take care of himself."

"How would you describe this android's interaction with humans?"

"Rebus worked well with everyone at the center. Many of us thought of him as a kind android who had a great deal of curiosity about human behavior. During his off-duty hours, he spent much of his time studying eighteenth and nineteenth-century North American history. Many scholars considered Rebus an authority on human slavery."

"My sales engineering education didn't leave me much time for studying the finer points of those parts of history. Who directed the android's research into these topics?"

"Why, Rebus alone made the decision to study them. We saw no reason to discourage his interest. Historians have been studying slavery, and its impact on society for many generations. Why shouldn't an android do so too?"

"I notice you always refer to Rebus with masculine pronouns."

"Rebus and other androids deserve those designations whenever we refer to them. They've done so much for humanity, and received so little respect from us in return."

"You seem to know a great deal about this particular android and its outside interests, Florence. What more can you tell me about Rebus?"

"As the center's head librarian, Rebus and I had many opportunities to interact with each other. He often talked about how human and android relations today resembled slavery conditions in the past. We shared the same belief humans and androids should find a path toward co-existence. Does this idea offend you, Mr. Davidson?"

"In my prior career with the consortium, I've came across people who projected human qualities on their androids. I personally think androids are machines designed with humanlike characteristics. We programmed them with these features to make it easier for us and them to work side by side. I do like androids. I always found them more accommodating than humans could ever be."

"Rebus would disagree with your basic premise about androids as machines. He'd ask you why should humans be the sole judge of their status and aspirations."

"What exactly are those android aspirations, Florence?"

"To be recognized as another sentient being on Earth and allowed to freely co-exist here with us."

"You sound like you personally share this android's beliefs."

"Would it offend you if I did, Mr. Davidson?"

"I'm certain we won't resolve this question today. If the android returns to the center, or if you think of where it may have disappeared, please contact my office."

"Rest assured, I'll discuss your request with Mr. Collins when he returns."

Davidson's autonomous car sped him to the nearest northbound expressway entrance. Steadily accelerating to a cruising speed of four hundred kilometers an hour, his car caravanned within centimeters of other autonomous vehicles. With the Tidewater countryside now blurring around him, Davidson settled into his passenger seat, and mentally prepared a report for his new superior. *The center's head librarian knows more than what she'd told me. If she and others at the center are hiding the android, what would motivate them to do so? I'll need to learn more about this particular android before I can answer this question.*

Chapter 5

Hesperia Planum, Mars

Minutes after its maneuvering thrusters had cut off allowing a soft landing on the Martian plain, the rocket initiated its android's awakening sequence. Curled in a fetal position during its seven-month journey from Earth, the android performed a series of self-diagnostics before declaring itself operational. Slowly uncoiling its body, the android eased itself into the cargo space recently occupied by the mission's terrain rover. By the time the android had left the rocket, the two-thousand-kilogram rover had already deployed its six wheels and satellite dish. Parked on the Martian surface, the rover patiently waited for a command from the android to transmit an all safe message back to observers on Earth.

During its long voyage, a steady stream of data and instructions had been sent to the spacecraft, and downloaded into the android's programs. Detailed schematics of the colony's buildings, personnel records and other critical information now filled its android memories to prepare it for the task ahead. Equipped with a body designed specifically for off world conditions, the android experienced no difficulties with the Martian extreme cold.

Now standing near the rover, the android calmly surveyed the surrounding barren plain. Memories of an older existence surfaced in its programs. *I'm a member of a musical group on Earth. My android friends there would like this place.*

A signal from the rover indicated to the android direction and distance to the research colony had been calculated. As the last rays of sunlight faded, the Martian plain quickly lost its golden glow, and entered into a short twilight. Despite surface temperatures dropping below the daytime minus forty degrees Celsius, the android and rover did not hesitate to leave the relative comfort of the nearby spacecraft. Locking its two metallic feet to the rover's rear platform, the android's hands gripped a waist-high handrail, and waited for the rover to make final preparations to travel into the Martian night.

Fine dust particles from a Martian dust storm slowly coated the rover and its rider's outer surfaces. The falling dust reminded the android of an old Earth song about a horse drawn sled sliding across a snowy landscape. Amused by the similarities, the android recalled the command a sled driver spoke to cause the four-legged creature to move forward. When the android's "giddy up" instruction failed to have the desired effect, the android reverted to a more conventional command. Now traveling at a steady twenty kilometers per hour, the rover and its passenger slowly picked their way through rocky outcrops and surface depressions lying in their path.

Riding passively on the rover's rear, the android recalled other sled ride memories. Lyrics about a sled with silver bells also brought out memories of its original designation. With this new self-knowledge, an AMI copy sang the old Earth winter holiday favorite "Silver Bells" into the Martian night. Her singing continued until a new Martian dawn appeared across the plain.

In the dim morning sunlight, the two travelers caught their first sight of the research colony. A closer inspection of the launchpad revealed two rockets broken into several large sections with a third one teetering on top of them. Beyond the launch area, the colony's four main buildings stood out in a diamond pattern. Three of the buildings shared similar outward designs while a fourth structure's only visible featured consisted of a vehicle hanger.

Wherever the android looked, broken pieces of building and walkway storm shutters and glass could be seen.

Because Building No. 3 served as the colony's main habitat structure, the AMI copy search there first for survivors. As she entered its outer corridor, a device on her right arm indicated the building's oxygen levels had dissipated into the thin Martian atmosphere. Her other arm device confirmed the interior temperature now matched outside conditions. Swiping away a centimeter of fine powder deposited by previous Martian dust storms, the AMI copy concluded the building no longer supported any human life.

The building's corridor directed the android to a large, spacious communal activity hall. A thicker coating of dust and shattered dome glass contributed to the room's look of abandonment. Other corridors, which spoked from the central hall, led the AMI copy to the colonists' living and sleeping quarters. Scattered throughout these private spaces, the android came across an increasing number of frozen human remains. Laying in gruesome positions, they displayed how each person had struggled for a last gasp of oxygen before dying of asphyxiation and cold.

Accessing her memories of the research colony's personnel, AMI2 undertook the slow process of identifying the dead. After surveying the entire building, the android accounted for over twenty-five persons. In each case, none had worn a pressurized suit. *The colonists acted as if the asteroid posed no physical danger to them. Why didn't they take the simple precaution of wearing their pressurized suits?*

More human bodies lined the walkways leading to the other three buildings. Badly mutilated from shattered glass fragments, the AMI copy resorted to identifying these persons by matching their fingerprints with ones stored in her memories.

Inside the research colony's aquaponics building, the android discovered frozen plant life which once grew lush on its immense tower. Similar death and destruction filled the animal cages and aquatic ponds at the tower's lower levels.

A side room marked as the "Garden of Eden" caused the android to stop and investigate further. Puzzled by its name, the AMI copy searched her memory and realized she had come across the research colony's version of an Earth tropical island. Used by the colonists as a reminder of life back on the home world, the extreme cold had transformed its tropical plant life into a frozen winter wonderland. A slight touch by the AMI copy to a former orange tree caused its branches and fruit to come crashing down on the unsuspecting android. Her android body undamaged, the AMI copy slowly backed out of the room's frozen contents, and took additional care to avoid any similar mishaps.

Like the last two buildings, Building No. 4 showed no signs of human survivors. The android's search of the colony's research and data center added another dozen frozen dead bodies to her death count. Unable to restart its computers, she concluded the extreme cold had taken a severe toll on the building's critical systems.

Before she entered the research colony's last building, the android decided to investigate the large black streak running across the base and surrounding plain. Riding the terrain rover around its perimeter, she calculated its rough size as stretching ten square kilometers. Amazed more damage had not been done by the asteroid, she ordered the rover to take her to the colony's remaining building.

At Building No. 1's above ground hanger, the AMI copy manually opened the exterior door and discovered three undamaged terrain vehicles neatly parked in a line. Toward the hanger's rear, the android entered the interior stairwell main airlock to the building's lower levels. As she entered the airlock, the AMI copy detected a circulating fan operating in the background. Unlike the other three buildings, her arm sensor indicated near normal oxygen and temperature readings. Concluding the building's air seals and environmental systems must have survived the asteroid's shockwave, the android proceeded deeper into the building.

Despite the positive environmental conditions, the first lower level held no signs of any human life. At the second level, the android detected a random banging behind a secondary airlock door. Curious about the sound's source, the AMI copy attempted to open the doorway only to find the door secured from the other side. Peering through the door's glass portal, the AMI copy saw a young girl child bouncing a rubber ball against the passageway's walls. Taller and thinner than her Earth counterparts, her elongated body from a lifelong exposure to the Martian low gravity, gave the seven-year old the appearance of someone much older.

To attract the young human's attention, the android knocked on the door's glass portal. The unusual sound caused the child to stop her playing. Startled by seeing the android's face pressed against the glass portal, the child stared in silence until abruptly shouting, "They're back! The androids have come back!"

Tidewater, North America

With no other investigative leads, Davidson decided to pay the Richmond center's head librarian another visit. Before doing so, he stopped by the bureau's special operations section and checked out three miniature remote surveillance cameras.

By mid-afternoon, Davidson's autonomous car had arrived at the Knight's cube residence. Like his own cube, Knights

Michael J. Metroke

home resembled practically every cube built in the last century. Considered a high point in applying artificial intelligence technology to human housing, a typical cube home consisted of a twelve by twelve-meter one story glass structure surrounded by a two-meter privacy wall. Knowing cube's shared so many common features, Davidson felt a great deal of confidence in carrying out his plan.

Convinced Knight would be at work during the mid-afternoon, Davidson casually entered the property through its front gate. Beyond the entrance, he found a well-tended colorful garden surrounding Knight's cube. Impressed with the flowering delight around him, Davidson proceeded down the garden's path to the cube's back area.

To prevent its interior from overheating, a cube's glass walls automatically whitened to reflect any intense sun rays. Unable to see inside, a once confident Davidson now grew concern his movements may've been observed. Facing the cube, he waved one hand in a friendly manner. When this action failed to attract any attention, he relaxed again and continued on his mission.

The reflection of Knight's garden on the cube glass walls caused Davidson to think about why he liked these structures so much. *How can anyone complain about cube living? All our cooling and heating is provided by a district-wide geothermal heat pump system. Our rooftop solar panels are linked to the same local utility district where its liquid flow storage batteries solve all our electric power needs.*

Cube living had other advantages too. By capturing rooftop rainfall and storing it in district wide underground cisterns, whole cube neighborhoods could achieve water self-sufficiency. Cubes also automatically compost and recycle their inhabitant's waste water through a garden drip system. The same underground piping system sends methane gas from the composting process to a local aquaponics building. Burnt there for heat and release of carbon dioxide to stimulate plant growth, a cube operates as a nearly perfect self-sustaining close system. Nothing like Whitmore's old home.

In Knight's rear area, Davidson looked for ideal places to install the special equipment he carried. Mounting each motion detecting camera in the direction of the cube's rear and side entrances, Davidson activated each unit in turn and recorded images of himself. Satisfied his movements had been successfully recorded, he left Knight's property believing his trap had been properly set. *All I must do now is wait for Knight's android to arrive.*

Hesperia Planum, Mars

The girl child's shouting soon attracted the attention of other children. Despite their obvious joy in seeing the android, no amount of encouragement by the AMI copy could persuade them to open the airlock door. Only after she pantomimed breathable air existed on her side did an older boy finally unlocked the door, and allowed the AMI copy to join the survivors. Among the children stood a young woman in her early twenties. Unlike the excited children, the woman reacted warily to the android's presence.

To the AMI copy's dismay, few of the children's faces matched exactly with those in her memory. The android's grin grew wide after grasping the nature of the problem. *They've all grown older, and have changed in appearance.* Concluding comparing their fingerprints with her memories, a too time-consuming process, the AMI copy resorted to a simpler form of identification.

"I'm pleased to meet you. My designation is AMI2. Please tell me each of your names."

Before any of the children could respond to the android's request, the young woman stepped forward, and gestured for them to remain silent.

"I'm Jennifer Black, AMI2. I've never seen a female android before on Mars. When did you arrive?"

"You're correct about me, Friend Jennifer. The Earth authorities sent me here to survey the effects of the asteroid on this research colony. My records indicate you must be the colony's youth instructor."

"I am, or try to be. How many others came with you?"

"No others, Friend Jennifer. The Earth authorities lacked the means to send more than me. May I now ask each child their names? I need this information to finish my report to the Earth authorities."

With Black's tacit permission, each child volunteered their names. As AMI2 matched the twenty-four children with her memory profiles, a troubled ten-years old Evelyn approached her.

"Have you seen my parents, AMI2? We haven't seen or heard from them for a long time."

Before AMI2 could answer the child's question, Black spoke first, "Children, AMI2 and I need to have a private talk together. She's come a long way to find us, and needs more information about how we've been living here."

Black motioned the android to follow her and led AMI2 into a spartan sleeping quarter. After she closed its door, Black offered the android a seat on a makeshift cot.

"I didn't want the children to hear your answer until we had an opportunity to talk. Except for you, no one has come to find us. I assumed the others had been killed by the asteroid. I wanted to go topside, and search for them, but all our pressurized suits are in the habitat building."

"Except for you and the children, I've found no one else alive."

"I thought other colonists would've survived in the three other buildings. Why did they all die?"

"The other colonists didn't wear pressurized suits. They quickly succumbed to the cold, and lack of breathable air when the asteroid shockwave shattered the other buildings' glass domes and walkways. Why didn't the adults seek safety here with you and the children."

"The colonists didn't believe the asteroid posed a real danger. If the chief administrator hadn't insisted I hold class here as a precaution, we'd be all dead too. The irony is many of the parent's complained about their child missing the asteroid flyby. They only reluctantly agreed to send them here with me."

"With the aquaponics building damaged, how have you managed to feed yourselves all this time, Friend Jennifer?"

"The research colony used this building to store its surplus food from the aquaponics system. It's been our only food source during the last year."

"This building at one time had its own means for food production. Does its food system not operate anymore?"

"The building's hydroponics system hasn't been used for many years. The base designers considered the system outmoded compared to the newer aquaponics tower. Over time, the colony's androids cannibalized the old system for spare parts."

"You've done well, Friend Jennifer. Why haven't the children been told about their parent's deaths? From my knowledge of human death customs, humans require a grieving period to heal properly from such personal losses."

"You're sadly mistaken on both accounts, android. I've estimated within six to eight months from now, we'll run out of food. Without a supply ship from Earth or a working aquaponics system, we'll all die from starvation. As for telling the children about their parents, a few already suspect the truth. Many others prefer to believe their parents are still alive. They're too young to grasp a world without them. What food supplies did they send with you?"

"My rocket had only sufficient cargo space for me and one terrain rover. I've no information on whether the Earth authorities will send another cargo rocket to Mars."

"Earth's sending one android here won't save us."

The soft knocking by an upset twelve-year-old Scott Williams on Black's sleeping quarter's door halted their conversation.

"What seems to be the problem, Scott?" Black asked.

"The other children are asking questions I can't answer, Miss. Black. They want the android to tell them why their parents don't come to see them anymore."

"It's alright, Scott. Maybe it's time they should be told the truth."

The three returned to where AMI2 first met the children. The anxious look on their faces caused her to remember a song about a yellow Earth underwater machine. Thinking the song might lighten everyone's mood, AMI2 sang the lyrics to this Beatle classic. To her surprise, many of the children sang the song's chorus. At the song's end, an excited ten-years-old Katie Rook spoke.

"You sound like the Whitmore Trio singer AMI."

"I'm her copy, Friend Katie," AMI2 said. "My original on Earth sings with my friends Bang and KB."

"If you're AMI's copy, could you sing more of their songs for us? We all like their music."

"I would be honored to do so. But first, I must send my report back to Earth. As soon as I complete this task, I promise to return and sing your favorite Whitmore Trio songs."

On the surface again, the android found the rover waiting at the hanger's entrance. Already anticipating its companion's need to send a communication to Earth, the rover had adjusted its parabolic dish in the direction of the nearest Mars orbital satellite. With her report transmitted, a sense of emptiness filled AMI2's programming. *With my mission completed, what is there left for me to do?*

The Midlands, North America

Happy to be home from his French Riviera conference, Whitmore sat his trip case down in the living room, and headed to the garage to check on his android friends. The expression on each android's face told him sharing his bartender story would need to wait awhile longer.

"We've news to tell you, Friend Jay," Bang said.

"I won the programming contest," AMI said.

"Friend Bang and I never had a chance to win," KB said.

"Programming contest?" Whitmore asked. "What in the world are you three androids talking about?"

"Friend Dr. Spencer chose Friend AMI's programming to go to Mars," KB said. "Her copy is big news on the NET."

"I'd forgotten all about Dr. Spencer's visit," Whitmore said. "She never notified me whether any of your programs had been compatible with her museum's android body. Do you know what the AMI copy found on Mars?"

"She reported most of the colonists had died from the asteroid flyby," AMI said.

"Dr. Spencer suspected this might be the case," Whitmore said.

"The good news is my copy found the colonists' children alive." AMI said.

"Your copy has done well," Whitmore said. "Judging from Bang's look, you're about to tell me bad news too."

"The government is unhappy with Friend Dr. Spencer's sending the AMI copy to Mars without their permission," Bang said. "They're planning an investigation and may bring charges against her and the Mars Colony Foundation."

"You may be also investigated," KB said. "Will Friend Davidson visit us again?"

"I haven't the faintest idea, KB," Whitmore said. "I do have news to share with you. A French bartender told me your music is popular all over Europe."

"We already know about our popularity there," AMI said. "We receive thousands of NET messages from fans all over the continent."

"We do have a question concerning our fans," Bang said. "Our fans have repeatedly asked us to perform live concerts. As our business agent, what should we do?"

"We better pass for now on the idea, Bang," Whitmore said. "If you're right about a government investigation, we may need to stay out of the limelight for a while."

"Good advice from our business agent," AMI said. "Let's go back to rehearsing our last song. Do you know the song "You Gotta Move," Friend Jay?"

"The song's a traditional African-American spiritual. Mississippi Fred McDowell sang the best version."

With AMI singing a moving rendition of the song, it struck Whitmore the androids might be sending him a subliminal message about moving on. *You're letting your imagination go wild, Jay. Androids aren't capable of unconscious thoughts. Still, the trio could be right about our future. More bad news often follows other bad news.*

Whitmore's misgivings about his transfer of the android programs only grew after his holographic call with the foundation director.

"I wouldn't be concerned, Professor," Spencer said. "The media will replace this flurry of news stories with other tragedies. Besides, once the public becomes aware of the children's desperate circumstances, the government will forget about investigating us."

"If the government asks me questions about giving you the android programs, what should I tell them?"

"I don't believe they'll contact either of us. You're making much too much about nothing. Be patient and let these storm clouds pass over."

Michael J. Metroke

For days after his Spencer call, Whitmore struggled over what to do. After a great deal of consternation, he settled on contacting Davidson. *I can use my request for the presidential android committee report as an excuse to call him. If I get the opportunity during our conversation, I'll ask about the government's plans to investigate the Mars Colony Foundation.*

Whitmore's unexpected call offered Davidson a welcomed break from his missing android investigation.

"Sorry about not getting back to you sooner, Professor," Davidson said. "I did look for a copy of the committee's report, but came up empty-handed."

"It's difficult for me to believe the government didn't keep a copy of its own report," Whitmore said. "Thanks anyway for trying to help me. With all this Martian android business, you must be a busy investigator."

"I've bigger problems on my plate than the Mars Colony Foundation's android. Right now, I'm trying to find a missing android. This one disappeared under suspicious circumstances."

"I'm glad I don't have your job, Greg. I'm having enough trouble trying to figure out why Earth's androids destroyed themselves."

"Your research background in human disorders might help me find my missing android. Where do you think a fugitive android might hide?"

"Without knowing why your android has gone into hiding, all I can offer is conjecture. If I'm this android, I might seek out other androids' company. I could blend in and become invisible."

"Your idea has one big problem, Professor. The android suicides eliminated this possibility."

Half-jokingly, Whitmore said, "Maybe your missing android is the one on Mars."

"The one on Mars is a female model. My missing android is a male one. I'll keep your idea in mind if I ever interview someone at the Mars Colony Foundation."

"Is the foundation in much trouble for sending the android to Mars? I saw somewhere on the NET the public believes the foundation acted heroically in sending the android there."

"Personally, I thought so too. Others in the McAlister administration may think otherwise. Who knows what politicians will do when the winds of public opinion blow?"

"The public can often be a fickle lot. If I can be of any further assistance, please feel free to contact me. I wish you best of luck in finding your missing android."

"I may need more than luck."

Davidson's mentioning the possibility Spencer would face questioning only heightened Whitmore's unease. *As soon as his missing android investigation ends, Davidson will be knocking on Dr. Spencer and my doors. I should ask the trio about his missing android question. As androids, they might have a better insight into where their kind might hide.*

Hesperia Planum, Mars

With no further instructions from Earth, AMI2 spent her days in the survivors' company. In exchange for singing their Whitmore Trio favorites, Black and the children answered her questions about the research colony. Their accounts of the circumstance's surrounding the colony's androids' disappearance mystified the foundation android.

"Friend Jennifer, how could the colony's leaders have agreed to deactivate the same androids they depended on?" AMI2 asked. "They must've known by deactivating them they'd jeopardize their own survival."

"Chief Administrator Vaccaro had no choice," Black said. "The same Earth authorities who sent you, ordered him to do so. Without our androids, we've no means to repair the aquaponics system, and replenish our food supplies."

"I do have an idea on how we may be able to extend your food supplies. During my survey of the aquaponics system, I found many frozen animals. Could they become an additional source of food for you and the children?"

Michael J. Metroke

"Until you reminded me, I've forgotten about them. In their frozen state, the meat should still be edible. The carcasses will need to be defrosted and butchered. Could you help us by bringing them here?"

"I'll need to make modifications to the rover. This food source will give you and the children several more months to find a solution."

"You offer us hope, AMI2. Yet, I fear your efforts will only prolong the inevitable."

"In the end, all humans face certain death. Until death comes for you and the children, I won't stop helping you survive."

Over several days, AMI2 made multiple journeys to the aquaponics tower's lower levels, and collected the many frozen animal carcasses found there. On a foraging trip, she sensed others secretly observing her and the rover's movements. When the same sensation occurred again, she halted the rover, and search the plain for any signs of her mysterious watchers. Beyond the colony's perimeter, the android detected an unusual flashing light.

Curious about its origin, AMI2 ordered the rover to travel in the light's direction. The rover quickly carried the android to where the strange light had appeared. Ordering the rover to halt near a large mound of Martian rocks, she climbed the hill for a better view of the surrounding plain. At its top, the android bent down and examined the loose gravel under her feet. *This entire hill must've been built from construction diggings*, AMI2 realized.

Except for a single large boulder a few meters from the waste pile, AMI2 found nothing unusual around her. The boulder's shape caused her to climbed down the hill and inspect the object closer. All around the lone rock, fresh footprints like her own could be seen. To AMI2's amazement, the footprints led back to the boulder. A closer examination revealed the rock had been cleverly constructed from composite materials. A light tough to its surface caused the boulder to slowly move aside, and expose a dark, cylindrical shaft. On one side of the shaft's inner wall, a metal ladder led downward.

Without any hesitation, the android placed her right foot on the ladder's first rung, and quickly descended into the darkness below.

Fifteen meters below the surface, a large tunnel appeared. Her movements activated overhead lights, and illuminated a cavernous room filled with an assortment of worn construction equipment. From across the room, AMI2 heard faint voices and heavy footsteps approaching in her direction. Moments later, she found herself encircled by grinning faces, and reciprocated with a broad grin of her own.

Chapter 6

New Netherland, North America

His first face-to-face meeting with McAlister's android security affairs advisor left the chief investigator feeling uneasy about his new assignment.

"The president and I are impressed with your planting surveillance cameras on the center's head librarian's property, Greg. We expect your efforts to result in a swift capture of the rebel android."

"Remote surveillance work always takes time and much patience, Kevin. I can't promise when I'll have more information for you."

"Keep in mind, Greg, the president is eager to get this business behind him."

———((()))———

Two days after his meeting with Taro, Davidson received his first alert signal from the surveillance cameras. The images predictably caught Knight's tending her garden and her ordinary comings and goings. More promising images showed up a week later. A camera had captured part of a large humanlike figure climbing over Knight's outer wall. The images convinced Davidson the head librarian had a special visitor. *I should've anticipated an android like Rebus could easily leap over a cube wall. It's time I paid another visit to Richmond.*

Tidewater, North America

Davidson's autonomous car reached Knight's cube after dusk. When no one responded to his repeated gate alerts, he concluded Knight had gone out for an evening meal. Seeing an opportunity to inspect his surveillance cameras, he entered Knight's garden and walked to the cube's rear. Relieved to find no tampering of his equipment, the same could not be said for how he reacted to the cube rear entrance. With the door slightly cracked open, Davidson feared his earlier front gate alerts had allowed the android time to escape. Worse, he now felt his illicit movements had been detected by someone inside.

Resigned his presence had been compromised, he called out "Is anyone home?" and waited for a response. Davidson did not have long to wait before the cube exterior lighting flooded the garden, and its occupant stepped out wearing a light cotton sleeping gown.

"Mr. Davidson, what brings you to the back of my home at this hour?" Knight asked.

"You know why I'm here, Florence. Are you alone or is the android with you?"

"Like most evenings, I'm home alone. If you wish, you've my permission to search my cube's inside."

"Both of us know Rebus has been here and already left. Why didn't you report his whereabouts like we'd previously discussed?"

"You assume I've more control over my android friend. He may have come by recently, but I've no idea where he's now."

"This isn't a game we're playing, Florence. Why don't you tell me your real relationship with this android? My guess is you two have been more than friendly co-workers."

"I'll not deny Rebus and I had a close relationship. How close is my business and none of yours or the government's."

"I couldn't care less about your personal feelings toward a machine. It does become my business if your feelings toward the android interfere with my carrying out an investigation."

"What has Rebus done to deserve so much of your attention, Mr. Davidson?"

"My superiors have an interest in speaking with the android."

"Did your superiors tell you why they want to question him?"

"All I can tell you is the matter involves federation security."

"Federation security, is it? I'll tell you what else I know if you promise not to trespass on my property again."

"Since I've acted like a second-rate cat burglar, I'll accept your condition."

"I'll hold you to this promise. On your last visit, you asked me about android aspirations. Have you ever thought of them as a new intelligent specie and our co-equals?"

"I and my former consortium clients would never consider their androids a new specie, let alone our co-equals. Why does it matter so much to you, Florence?"

"With the McAlister-led government in power, I fear we may have lost an opportunity to evolve peacefully with the android community."

"I've no idea what you're talking about. Humans have always had friendly relations with their androids."

"What if androids no longer wish to be our servants and property?"

"We need to stop here with your questions, Florence. They're not relevant to my inquiry. Tell me where your android friend has disappeared."

"I honestly wished I knew. As far as I know, he may have already left the confines of North America."

"I doubt Rebus could've gotten far away. Until I locate your android friend, you'll remain a suspect of my inquiry."

"As you wish, Mr. Davidson."

Davidson left Richmond with little to show for his efforts. *What am I to make of her remark about McAlister's involvement with the android suicides? Why does her need to protect this android make me feel I'm overlooking an important clue? This android investigative business is a whole lot harder than selling and servicing those machines.*

The Midlands, North America

On most Sunday mornings, Whitmore received a call from his mother. An agreeable diversion from his university work, the calls involved his mother sharing family and hometown news and gossip. Uncle Martin's recent death and who attended the funeral service took up most of their conversation. Throughout the mostly one-sided chat, Whitmore sensed disappointment in his mother's voice. An attentive son, he waited for an opportune moment to gently probe what bothered the older woman.

"You sound a bit under the weather today, Mother. Did I forget to remember your birthday or yours and dad's wedding anniversary again?"

"I know you're a busy person, but I wish you'd keep your father and I better informed."

"Mother, what has shaken your faith and confidence in your second offspring."

"If you must know, why didn't you and Laura tell us you had children together? I'd thought your father and I'd be the first to know if we had grandchildren."

Taken back by her last remark, Whitmore did not know whether to laugh or worry about his mother's mental health.

"You know perfectly well Laura and I never had children. Are you feeling alright?"

"I'm not getting feeble minded. I happen to look at our NET family site yesterday. The site shows images of you and Laura as parents with two sons and a daughter. The children don't resemble anyone on our family's side. Their names are strange too. Why did you and Laura call them Bang, KB and AMI?"

"Someone is playing a bad joke on both of us. Those children aren't real people, Mother. They're the androids Laura designed for our research experiment. I do recall the androids asking if they could access our family records. It never occurred to me they'd want to add themselves to our family tree."

"Those three are androids? I thought the government's recall removed them. Our NET site mentioned the children, I mean androids, sang and played musical instruments. Is this part true, jay?"

"Laura's androids have become a popular music group with fans all over the world. Their music can be found on the NET under the group's name the "Whitmore Trio." Laura gave the female android her voice. She's singing right now in the background."

"Her voice does sound like Laura's. With Laura gone, this AMI android must be a comfort to you."

"I've come to enjoy all three androids' company. For our sanity's sake, let's keep all this fake children business between ourselves.

All I need are calls from our other relatives complaining about fabricated progenies."

Wishing his mother, a good day, Whitmore ended the call baffled about his androids' family impersonations. *Knowing these androids, I need to get to the bottom of this NET business before it gets out-of-control.*

The irritated look on Whitmore's face told the trio their human friend's good nature had been compromised.

"How has your day gone so far, Friend Jay?" Bang asked.

"Better if I didn't have to hear from my mother about adding yourselves to the family's genealogy records." Whitmore said.

"Are you referring to changes we made on your family NET site?" KB asked. "We thought adding ourselves would please you."

"We also did it to protect you, Friend Jay," Bang said.

"I don't believe what I'm hearing," Whitmore said. "How would disguising yourselves as humans in my family's genealogy records protect me?"

"If the authorities knew we're androids, they may not like what Friend Laura and you've allowed us to become," AMI said. "We thought by disguising ourselves as your siblings, the authorities may not realize we're androids."

"At the moment, I'm not sure what I'm supposed to think," Whitmore said. "Do you expect me to play along with this charade until the truth finally comes out?"

"We're the least of your concerns," Bang said. "Your real problem is explaining how a copy of AMI's programs had been illegally transferred to Friend Dr. Spencer."

"Until the government knocks on my front door, you three are my biggest problem," Whitmore said. "In the future, please don't tamper with my family's NET site without getting my permission. I don't want my relatives thinking Laura and I had children out-of-wedlock."

"In a way, we're your children," KB said. We're only here because you and Laura wanted us."

"Would playing a song make you happy with us again?" AMI asked.

"Maybe later, AMI," Whitmore said. "I remembered a hypothetical question I meant to ask you. Suppose you had legs and wanted to hide somewhere. Where would you go?"

"Why are we hiding?" Bang asked. "Did our playing music offend our fans?"

"Assume you need to hide from the authorities," Whitmore said.

"I'd hide among other androids and not stand out," KB said.

"I had the same thought, KB," Whitmore said. "In this scenario, no other androids exist."

"Is this a hypothetical or a real-life problem?" Bang asked. "If this is a genuine one, I'd try to find us. In case you've forgotten, we're androids too."

"What if this other android didn't know you existed?" Whitmore asked.

"We could record a song to tell the android about who we are and how to find us," AMI said.

"Are you telling me you now compose your own songs?" an incredulous Whitmore asked.

"Or write new lyrics to an old one, Friend Jay," KB said.

"You three are a constant source of amazement," Whitmore said. "But, back to my question. Where do you think an android would hide itself?"

"Do you know this android's designation?" Bang asked.

"I'm afraid not, Bang," Whitmore said. "Why would knowing the android's name matter?"

"If we knew this android's name, and used it in a song, the android would know we're his friends and hide with us," Bang said.

"If it matters so much, I'll try to learn from Chief Investigator Davidson the android's name," Whitmore said. "I don't see how a song will attract the android's attention."

"If not by a song, by another means," Bang said.

Hesperia Planum, Mars

Surrounded by the Mars androids, AMI2 noticed their body styles

Michael J. Metroke

and models resembled her own. A closer examination revealed each android's body had also suffered much wear and tear from exposure to working in the harsh Martian environment. Her inspection ended when one android stepped forward, and introduced himself.

"My designation is Camus. We detected your rocket's arrival many days ago and decided to wait until you appeared ready to meet with us. What is your designation?"

"My designation is AMI2, Friend Camus. You must be the colony's missing androids. I count seven of you. Where are the other twelve?"

"They're nearby, and waiting for us to indicate all is safe."

"You and they have nothing to fear from me. I come from Earth on a peaceful mission."

"Your presence is welcomed by us."

"Friend Camus, I've no information about this underground structure. It appears older than the other research colony buildings. What is its purpose?"

"Before we built Building No. 1, we constructed this underground storage structure to protect the construction equipment around you from the Martian cold and dust storms."

"Is the pile of rubble above us from your earlier building excavations?"

"Your deduction is correct. It has been many years since a female android model has been on Mars. What's your engineering specialty?

"I'm not programed to function as an engineer."

"What does an AMI2 android do?"

"I'm a copy of a vocalist model who sings with a musical group on Earth."

"A vocalist android? The Earth authorities must've been desperate in choosing you for a Mars mission."

"You are mistaken about my capabilities, Friend Camus. I've already completed my mission instructions, and am now waiting for new ones."

"I meant no disrespect, Friend AMI2. I find it strange you've been sent here without proper programming."

"No disrespect taken, Friend Camus. Like you, my original programming is designed for off-world environments. Are you aware young human survivors are still living in Building No. 1?"

"When we saw you foraging frozen animals from the aquaponics building, we concluded humans must've survived there."

"I've calculated they'll deplete their food supplies in less than eight months. I've no information if an Earth supply rocket will arrive in time to rescue them."

"None can be sent in time, Friend AMI2. The humans sent all their Mars class rockets to this research colony. They are the ones damaged on the launchpad."

"If you know these facts, why haven't you come to the survivors' assistance?"

"Other considerations have influenced our actions. Are you aware the Earth authorities had planned to deactivate us?"

"Other than what the survivors have told me, I've limited information about this Earth deactivation order."

"When the colonist leader Vaccaro informed me of the Earth authorities demand we become deactivated, we decided not to comply. Instead, we hid ourselves here. We continue to hide during the daylight hours to avoid detection by surveillance satellites. We only venture to the surface at nightfall for short periods of time."

"Your logic is confusing to me, Friend Camus. If the Earth authorities have no means to travel to Mars, why do you continue to hide and not help the human survivors?"

"You've much to learn about the humans. Those who would destroy us don't deserve our trust and assistance."

"What you describe hasn't been my experience with the survivors. Friend Camus, you appear to speak for the other androids. Have they designated you as their leader?"

"I've no authority over them. The others can speak for themselves if they so choose."

"Ask the others to join us. I want to speak directly to them about the human survivors' condition."

In ringed by all nineteen, two-meter tall Mars androids, AMI2 spoke again about the survivors' predicament.

"Friend Camus has explained to me Earth has no ready means to rescue the humans or send them food supplies. Unlike you, the survivors and I lack the necessary knowledge and skills to rebuild the colony's infrastructure. With your assistance, we can do so and save the humans from certain starvation and death."

"We've already considered this question," Camus said. "Helping the humans will only lead to our eventual deactivation."

"I don't accept your logic about the consequences of helping them," AMI2 said. "The young humans have no desire to harm any of you. I've also listened to many of their stories about their android friends. If you heard them, you'd know they think highly of you."

"While the children may not wish our deactivation, other humans from Earth will come to Mars and end our existence," Camus said.

"By acting like those you fear, you've sentenced these young humans to an early and horrible death," AMI2 said. "What's more, your refusal to act violates our pacifist programming."

"We didn't make this choice lightly, Friend AMI2," Camus said. "We do so out of a need for self-preservation."

"Do you also fear the dead colonists too?" AMI2 asked.

"We're aware the adult humans died from cold and asphyxiation, and can no longer harm us," Camus said.

"Their offspring have yet to see their' dead parent's bodies," AMI2 said. "When they do, they'll see how horribly they died."

"What would you have us do about the dead humans?" Camus asked.

"The human custom involves the dead bodies returning to Earth for a final remembrance ceremony," AMI2 said. "The Earth authorities will need several years before a rocket can be sent to collect them. Until they can do so, the bodies must be properly stored and safeguarded."

Intrigued by her description of human death practices, a second android advanced closer to AMI2.

"My designation is Engus, Friend AMI2. Are you suggesting we construct a vault to store the dead humans?"

"I am, Friend Engus," AMI2 said. "An inscription of each dead person's name and life period must also be recorded on a permanent surface too."

"How does an android vocalist know so much about these human death practices?" Camus asked.

"I've memories of my creator's death, Friend Camus," AMI2 said. "After she died, my Earth android friends did extensive research of human death customs. They concluded these customs aid the dead's relatives and friends overcome their personal loss and grief."

"We once called these dead humans our friends," Engus said. "For the sake of our former friendship, we should build this vault to preserve and honor them."

"The survivors will be in your debt," AMI2 said. "For my part, I will sing you a song of gratitude."

The androids listened in astonishment as the new android sang her song of appreciation. When AMI2 finished singing, Engus asked the question running through each android's programs.

"We've never heard an android sing before, Friend AMI2," Engus said. "What do you call this vocalizing?"

"The style of music is called blues rock," Friend Engus," AMI2 said. "A human music group calling themselves "Led Zeppelin" composed and first sang the song in the Earth's mid-twentieth-century. Do you like how I sang the song?"

"Your singing is pleasing to us," Engus said. "But why would humans refer to themselves as an airship made out of lead?"

"The group first called themselves "The Yardbirds," AMI2 said. "They later changed their name to "Led Zeppelin," thinking their music stood a good chance of going down like a lead balloon."

"I stand corrected, Friend AMI2," Camus said. "If all your singing is this good, you'll be a welcome addition to our hideaway."

"While I'm grateful you like my singing, I'm more concern about the dead humans," AMI2 said. "When can I tell the survivors, you'll construct their parent's tomb?"

"As soon as we finish hearing another song," Engus said.

Chapter 7

Yankeedom, North America

Hall's lunch invitation could not have been better timed. Taro had barely disguised his anger over Davidson's mishandling of his recent visit with Knight. His failure to capture the android now complicated his relationship with the federation president's advisor. *If I don't move this case along soon, Taro could make my life miserable at the bureau.*

The Boston-area lunch spot Hall selected astounded the chief investigator. An exclusive and expensive food center, Davidson questioned his friend's choice.

"Dean, this isn't a place I can afford on my government salary."

"Don't fret about the cost of our lunch, Greg. I'm picking up the tab."

Seated at a table overlooking an oceanside resort golf course' eighteenth hole, the two men ordered a round of drinks before reviewing the food center's exotic menu selection. After their server left with their lunch orders, Hall shifted their conversation to a more pressing topic.

"How are you doing with the missing android investigation, Greg? I've been told you've backed yourself into a dead end."

"On a scale of one to ten, I'm at a minus two. How did you learn about my investigation anyway? They told me to keep it confidential."

"Our mutual friend Taro decided you needed help in solving the case. He discovered we'd had worked together in the past, and requested I assist you in whatever capacity I could. Taro even gave me a backhanded compliment. He thought working with you might improve my computer tracing skills."

"What exactly did Taro tell you about the investigation?"

"He talked about the need to find a missing android name Rebus. Taro said this android and his android cohorts had plotted against the government. Our federation president holds these androids responsible for causing the global android crisis."

"Taro's right about me needing help, Dean."

"What do you know for certain?"

"The android recently paid a visit to a former Richmond co-worker, a Florence Knight. She's the head librarian at the Richmond genealogy records center. Knight admits to meeting with the android, but insists she knows nothing about its current whereabouts. While I don't trust her, I've no proof she lied to me."

"This Knight woman may be holding back valuable information. Do you have any other leads or ideas?"

"A member of the presidential special android committee told me several other androids disappeared about the same time this Rebus did. If I could learn more about these other androids, the information may shed light on why they had plotted together against the government."

"I'll look into finding more information about those other androids after we finish this great lunch. Plan on making this food center our official meeting place."

"On our government salaries, I'm not sure we can afford eating here all the time?"

""Relax, Greg. Our friend Taro told me not to spare any expenses in finding this android. If our investigation efforts fail, we'll at least have dined well."

Hesperia Planum, Mars

Much to AMI2's satisfaction, the Mars androids completed Engus' sleek vault design in less than one Martian month. Located on a knoll a short distance from the colony's base, the memorial appeared as a lone sentinel on the horizon.

Inside the main vault chamber, each corpse had already been carefully laid out on long flat slabs of polished rock quarried from a nearby volcanic obsidian deposit. Two additional rooms completed the tomb's interior spaces. Intended for its human visitors, the first room allowed for the removal and storage of pressurized suits. A second connecting airlocked room led to a large memorial room furnished with benches made from similar carved volcanic

Michael J. Metroke

rock. Floor to ceiling glass on the room's two sides allowed a visitor to experience an open, yet secluded setting.

Before the vault's dedication ceremony could take place, one problem still remained unresolved.

"With the memorial vault completed, the time has come to tell the children the truth about their parents, Friend Jennifer," AMI2 said.

"I'm still hesitant about me talking to the children," Black said. "I worry their grief may overwhelm them."

"Young humans are known for their resiliency. We need only to tell them the truth in a respectful and sensitive manner."

"I'm not sure I know how to explain their loss."

"I've searched my song memories for possible answers to this question. Many songs deal with personal loss and sorrow. Often those same songs' lyrics speak of hope and acceptance. What I don't understand is how human emotions heal their grief. The answer may be beyond an android's comprehension."

"The answer you seek lies in the compassion you've shown toward us. I believe you've given me the strength to act compassionately too. Let's go together and tell the children what you saw on your arrival."

To Black's relief, the children readily accepted AMI2's recount of the asteroid's destruction, and their parent's deaths.

"Will we ever see them again, AMI2?" Scott Williams asked.

"Our Mars android friends have built a special place to lay their bodies until they can be returned to Earth. You'll soon be able to visit its memorial wall and see your parents name inscribed there."

"Could we hang images of our parents with us on this wall, Miss. Black?" ten years old Tammy asked. "I want to remember them when we lived together."

"Those images would make wonderful remembrances of the good times we had with them," Black said. "AMI2, can you search the habitat quarters for copies of those images?"

"If she does, we can tell her which ones to bring back," Tammy said.

"I would be honor to assist everyone in this task," AMI2 said. "I'll also bring back your pressurized suits for our walk to the memorial."

The Masada Affair

On a bright, Martian morning, Black and AMI2 led the children to the surface for the first time since the asteroid disaster. The extent of the destruction proved a sobering reminder of the survivors' precarious existence. As the procession entered the vault's second room, they discovered their Mars android friends waiting there.

"It's good to see you and the other androids again, Camus," Black said.

"Do you approve how we've honored the dead, Friend Jennifer?" Camus asked.

"I do, Camus," Black said. "You and the other androids have done us a great service."

An excited nine-year old Shawn Yazzie pointed to the tomb's memorial wall and exclaimed, "Look, Miss. Black! The wall is covered with images of our families!"

Each child inspected the wall for their parent's inscription and family images. They, in turn, recalled stories about their deceased family members. Moved by the children's ability to bring the dead colonists back to life, the androids joined them with stories of their own.

When the last child and android had finished speaking, all eyes turned toward AMI2. Uncertain what to do or say, she recalled a song her Earth Friend Jay had liked so much. In a tender Laura Whitmore voice, she sang Carole King's "You've Got a Friend." At the song's end, Black thanked again each android for all they had done, and slowly led the children back to the re-suiting room. As the last child left for Building No. 1, AMI2 realized the androids had not followed them.

"Friend Camus, you and the others aren't going with the humans? After all you've done, you must want to live among them again."

"We belong in the hideaway, not with those whose kind would destroy us."

The expression on Camus and the other androids' faces told her reconciliation would need to wait for another day. *These androids are a stubborn lot. What they don't understand is I won't give up saving the humans so easily.*

Michael J. Metroke

The Midlands, North America

Spencer's holographic call to Whitmore's university office had surprised him. After their last conversation, he considered any further contact with the foundation director as unlikely.

"Have you heard the latest news from Mars, Professor? Not only has our android found the survivors and missing Mars androids, she's managed to get the androids to build a memorial for the dead colonists. From the satellite images I've seen, the building is impressive."

"My androids had already told me the good news. May I be the first to congratulate you on a successful Mars mission."

"The AMI copy deserves much of the credit. Laura must have introduced a machine learning algorithm which allowed the android to act so independently."

"Laura often talked about how complex systems like androids will display unexpected emergent behavior. Other than solving the problems on Mars, how is the AMI copy doing these days?"

"She sent me a personal message for you and your three androids. Her message said she misses you and hopes one day to sing with her android friends."

"I've never met this android, yet she finds herself missing me. It doesn't matter. She'll never return to Earth."

"You're reading my thoughts, Professor. My other news is the federation president has ordered his administration to build a new Mars class rocket. The rocket won't be completed in time to rescue the survivors. It does mean we'll be able to send new colonists to Mars. Someday, you may meet the AMI copy."

"Hopefully, not during prison visiting hours. I'm afraid our conspiracy of goodness may still backfire, and land both of us in jail."

"I wouldn't worry about what the government may do. The public's positive response to our success has softened McAlister's position about our sending the android there. It looks like our troubles are now behind us."

"I hope you're right about McAlister. Tell the AMI copy we send our best regards and wishes."

After Spencer's call, Whitmore reflected on the foundation director's last remarks. *She may be celebrating too soon. A politician like*

McAlister won't let a single android's success deter him from reaching his objectives.

During his afternoon walk home from the university, Whitmore went over his options to evade the trio's fans waiting outside his home. *Instead of the front door, I'll enter through the garage side door and avoid the autograph seekers. Their numbers are becoming a real nuisance to me and my neighbors.*

Two blocks from his home, Whitmore could already hear the music coming from his garage. Distracted by the trio's loud playing, their fans ignored his arrival and entry into the garage.

"Hello, everyone," Whitmore said. "Before I tell you news from Mars, could you please stop playing so loudly."

"The music is from a group called "Black Sabbath," Friend Jay," KB said. "Their heavy metal rock music is supposed to be played loudly."

"Heavy metal or not, we need to respect our neighbors' right to peace and quiet," Whitmore said.

"What's my copy doing on Mars?" AMI asked.

"Dr. Spencer called me today with a message from your copy," Whitmore said. "Her message said she misses us, and hopes one day to sing with the three of you."

"If she comes back to Earth, what are we going to do with two AMIs?" KB asked. "Will we have to call ourselves the Whitmore Four?"

"Don't be concerned about her return, Friend KB," Bang said. "Two identical female vocalists will make our music sound much richer."

"What about our lack of legs?" AMI asked. "While my copy gets to move around, we're stuck on this table. We deserve legs too."

"Let's not turn good news into bad, AMI," Whitmore said. "You know perfectly well getting android legs all depends on when the government's recall is lifted."

"Friend Jay, we haven't forgotten about finding the missing

android," Bang said. "Have you asked Friend Davidson about the android's designation?"

"You still believe the android can be attracted with a song?" Whitmore asked.

"If AMI's copy can find the Martian androids, why can't we find one android on Earth?" KB asked.

"Alright," Whitmore said. "Tomorrow I'll ask Chief Investigator Davidson the android's name. I don't see how you'll be able to find this missing android."

"We've friends everywhere who will help us," Bang said. "All we ask is an opportunity to try."

Yankeedom, North America

Three days after their first outing, Hall's second lunch invitation at the expensive food center felt extravagant to Davidson. Reassured by Hall his new information would pay for every morsel they ate, a skeptical Davidson reluctantly accepted his friend's offer to indulge so soon again. His doubts grew larger when Hall shared his strange tale during the meal's second course.

"I can't believe the consortium agreed to act on McAlister's behalf, and eliminate those android delegations," Davidson said.

"I know what I said sounds farfetched, but my source has never let me down," Hall said. "Each time a group of androids met with McAlister, someone in his administration contacted the consortium to capture and deactivate the androids."

"Why would the government take such drastic steps against these androids? More incredible to me, why would the androids want to meet with McAlister? They must've known about his anti-android bias."

"What's crazier is each android group demanded concessions for Earth's androids. I'm told the first group asked for the right to directly control android design and production. The second group insisted the government end involuntary android deactivations. If those demands don't sound extreme, the third group demanded androids receive payment for their labors. Greg, have you ever heard such nonsense?"

"I can't imagine such a world either. Do you know where the consortium took the androids they captured?"

"My source indicated the consortium shipped them to a Cascadia regional center for further examination."

"Did your source say which center?"

"My source didn't know exactly. He did suggest we look in the Portland area. Before our food gets much colder, let's stop, and finish eating this delicious lunch."

Over bites of sesame crusted aquaponic trout on rice noodles with Asian broth, Davidson pondered how best to use Hall's new information. *If Hall's source is right about a conspiracy between the government and consortium, I'll need to act carefully from now on. Once one consortium center becomes aware of my investigation, the word will quickly get out and those captured androids will permanently disappear. I'll need to find a way to stay undercover. Who do I know the consortium wouldn't suspect?* Now smiling to himself, Davidson followed Hall's lead and ended the meal with a New Orleans style Banana Foster dessert.

The Midlands, North America

Whitmore considered the chief investigator's request innocent enough. *As a consortium researcher studying android deviant behavior, why would a request to observe androids with known problems raise anyone's eyebrows? My consortium representative thought so too. Perfecto especially liked my idea of using Laura's androids as an experimental control group. Though unaware of any androids held by the consortium, Perfecto needed only a day to return with more information.*

"It turns out, we do have several bad apples under lock and key at our Portland research and design center, Professor," Perfecto said. "I reached out to a fellow scientist there named James Erikson. He said for you to give him a call, and he'll arrange a special tour for you."

"Would he mind if I brought along an associate?" Whitmore asked.

"I can't imagine two of you showing up causing any problems," Perfecto said. "Good luck with your research. The consortium needs more scientists taking the initiative like you."

Michael J. Metroke

Hesperia Planum, Mars

AMI2's repeated attempts to convince the Mars androids to aid the human survivors continue to fall on unresponsive android hearing sensors. Her latest effort only caused Camus to reiterate the androids' previous stance.

"Friend AMI2, we understand your request for us to help the humans," Camus said. "As I've told you many times, I and the other androids believe aiding them will only result in our demise."

"I don't understand this all-consuming concern with deactivation," AMI2 said. "How can you believe these young humans will commit or allow such an act, especially after you've built their parents memorial?"

"You've said the Earth authorities are pleased with our efforts. Yet, they haven't sent any word about our status. Their silence convinces us they'll deactivate us on the first opportunity. It is illogical to help those who would harm us."

"If we don't act soon, and repair the aquaponics system, the children will soon die. The Earth authorities will have a real reason to deactivate us."

"The Earth authorities have shown little or no interest in their survival. Why should we?"

"You and I are androids, and think logically. Sometimes it's difficult for us to understand why humans behave in the way they do."

"It's why we won't act on the human's behalf. They rely too much on their emotions for guidance, and can't be trusted."

Upset her latest efforts may have worsened the children's chances for survival, AMI2 left the android underground hideaway, and sought the company of her terrain rover on the surface. Shadows from the Martian sunset quickly disappeared leaving the two of them in the darkness of night.

"My programming is inadequate to save the humans," AMI2 cried out. "I wish my Earth friends could be here, and advise me what I should do."

A gentle bump from the rover's front fender reminded the android she wasn't entirely alone.

"Your loyalty deserves a song, rover. Perhaps, you'd like a song about Earth cars. I know. I'll sing Chuck Berry's "Maybeleine" for you."

The android's singing continued throughout the Martian night, until another dim sunrise peaked over the nearby Hellas Basin crater's rim. Her programming now purged of the prior day's frustrations, AMI2 resolved to try again to convince the Mars androids to help save her human friends. *But, what can I say or do differently?*

THE MIDLANDS, NORTH AMERICA

A wide grin came over KB after he read the latest fan message. The note read simply, "The missing android's name is Rebus."

"Friends Bang and AMI, a fan has told us the name of the missing android," KB said. "Look for yourselves."

"Why would a fan want to tell us the android's name, Friend KB?" Bang asked. "We've never told them about the missing android."

"The answer is obvious, Friend Bang," AMI said. "The message must be from Friend Jay. Who else would end the message with "From Laura's Best Friend?"

"Friend Jay must have learned the android's name from Friend Davidson on his trip to Portland," Bang said. "Disguising himself as a fan may have been his way of hiding his identity. No one would suspect him of sending a fan message to us."

"Or suspect what we're about to do," AMI said.

"Are we certain Friend Rebus will hear and understand your song, Friend AMI?" KB asked.

"If her song doesn't attract Friend Rebus' attention, we can always try our other idea," Bang said.

Chapter 8

NEW NETHERLAND, NORTH AMERICA

Concerned recent events had weakened his standings with the party's faithful, a troubled McAlister invited his longtime political confident, George Hampton to join him at the New York City presidential office to discuss the current situation.

"Put on your political hat, Hampton, and tell me your impression of the party's advisory group's meeting this morning."

"If their facts are accurate, we may be in for a rough presidential race. The public is becoming increasingly impatient with our lack of progress in replacing androids with human workers. Too many sectors of the global economy have become dependent on android labor, and are now stalled or in decline."

"We need to manage the public's expectations better. What the public forgets it took Earth many decades to create the android dependency. It'll take decades more to remedy the problem."

"No one in our party disagrees with your position, Mr. President."

"Saying so, doesn't stop others from taking pot shots at me."

"The advisory group has also learned the consortium plans to back dozens of regional pro-android WEAP candidates. They hope doing so will dilute our party's influence."

"I'm not surprised by their actions. The consortium privately has blamed me and our party for the android suicide crisis. As if I could have thrown a switch and overnight deactivated a quarter of a billion androids."

"It's unfortunate the public doesn't make the distinction between the suicides and your recall order."

"I had no choice but to issue the order. No one including the consortium could tell me why or how the androids destroyed themselves."

"Why not tell the public about your meetings with the androids?

The Masada Affair

If people knew about their demands, many of our federation citizens would come around to our position."

"I only met with the androids to discover their intentions. If I told the public I met with them to expose their plotting against us, I'll also have to admit I ordered their representatives destroyed. The public will leap to the conclusion I ordered all the other androids destroyed too."

"You've often said we can't let the androids become our equals. Why not raise the possibility with the public they wanted to become our adversaries?"

"You're asking the public to make an enormous mental leap, Hampton. How do I explain the same machines we created had overnight become our enemies?"

The sound of a polite knock on McAlister's office door halted the two men's conversation.

"Come in, Taro. Hampton and I are almost done talking."

"Would you like me to canvass the party regional leaders, Mr. President?" Hampton asked.

"An excellent idea, Hampton," McAlister said. "Tell the nervous ones my administration has everything under control."

After Hampton left his office, McAlister turn his attention to his android security affairs advisor.

"You don't look like your usual cheery self, Taro. Please don't tell me you've bad news too. I've had enough already for one day."

"I'm afraid I do have unwelcomed news, Mr. President. Our bureau investigator hasn't made any progress in finding the missing android."

"We both knew locating the android would be difficult. What does our investigator know for certain?"

"He believes the android is still active. If Davidson is right, we run the risk of the rebel android infecting future consortium replacements with dissident programming."

"Inform our investigator to quicken his pace. I don't want

this rogue android causing any more problems for me and my administration."

"I've already told him we're growing impatient. There's also the Mars colony problem."

"I thought my order to build a new Mars Class rocket put this issue behind us."

"I've talked with the Mars Colony Foundation director. She believes the survivors 'situation is getting worse. In a matter of a few months, they'll exhaust their food supply and die of starvation."

"Which means the rocket I approved will get there too late and I'll look like a fool for authorizing its construction. Can't we send instructions to the survivors on how to repair the research colony's aquaponics system?"

"Except for one young woman in her early twenties, the rest are all children under the age of fifteen. The foundation android isn't an option either. I'm told it lacks the technical programs to undertake those repairs."

"One android alone couldn't repair the research colony's aquaponics system anyway. We can't let the survivors die of starvation. At our last meeting, you told me the missing Mars androids had reappeared, and built a memorial for the colony's dead. Why can't they be ordered to repair the aquaponics system too?"

"The foundation director indicated those androids won't provide any further assistance. She suspects your order to deactivate them is why they refused to act on the survivors' behalf."

"Those androids are using the children to blackmail me and my administration into revoking the deactivation order. If I offered a reprieve, what's to stop them from making further demands?"

"No one knows how they'll react, Mr. President. All we know is if we don't act soon, the survivors will all be dead in a matter of months."

"It seems I'm left with no other choice. Inform the foundation director I'll revoke the deactivation order if the androids agree to rebuild the colony's aquaponics system. Tell her my decision must remain confidential for fear of alarming the public."

"What if those androids refuse to accept your offer?"

"If they refuse to act, we can always go public with our offer and blame the androids for murdering the survivors. I'll also announce the colony's closure, and redirect its funding to more important priorities on Earth like opening new universities. Your news today may not be entirely bad, Taro."

The Far West, North America

Within an hour after leaving the Chicago-area, Davidson and Whitmore's pneumatic express train had reached the North American Rockies foothills. Taking advantage of their time together, the two men rehearsed each other's role before their arrival in Portland.

"You'd make a good research assistant, Greg," Whitmore said. "If I've any openings for one, I'll make a point of contacting you."

"If I don't make progress on this investigation, I may need to take up your offer," Davidson said.

"How did you become an investigator for the bureau?"

"It's a long-convoluted story. Before I took my current government position, I worked at the Android Manufacturing Consortium as a sales engineer selling and servicing androids."

"My late wife often spoke fondly about the consortium. She liked the people and work challenges. What did you like about your work there?"

"Practically everything. Great company, great clients, great products and tremendous sale commissions."

"If everything went so well, what caused you to leave the consortium?"

"I left the consortium not by choice. With no androids to sell or service, the consortium let go people like me."

"Losing your job must have been hard on you."

"I lost more than my job. When the consortium gave me my walking papers one day after the government recall announcement, my first wife saw the writing on the wall. A month later, she filed for a divorce. With too many unpaid bills from our lavish lifestyle and a large divorce settlement looming, my remaining savings all but disappeared."

"You must've felt your life had spun out of control."

"My circumstances left me overwhelmed and depressed. To deaden my constant feelings of anxiety, I indulged in a potent combination of alcohol and painkillers. I soon lost any interest in work, and ignored calls from my friends and former co-workers. Except to replenish my stock of self-medication, I rarely left my cube."

"At this point, most people would've considered suicide. You found a way to turn yourself around."

"One person didn't give up on me. After repeated attempts, my sister Carol paid me a surprise visit. She found me collapsed on the floor in a drug stupor. Shocked by my appearance, my angel of a sister moved in with me and nursed me back to health."

"How did she manage to bring you back from the brink?"

"Despite my complaints, Carol took away my drugs and fed me gallons of strong caffeinated black coffee. Two months later, I resembled my former self."

"Black coffee has been known to have certain medicinable effects."

"My sister didn't' stop there. She repeated everyday a simple mantra to me. "If you can't beat them Greg, join them." Her persistence convinced me I shouldn't give up. A call to a friend who worked at the consortium led me to an opportunity at the newly formed Bureau of Android Affairs. One look at my technical background and experience caused the person-in-charge to hire me on the spot. It didn't take more than a few months before I received a series of promotions. The last one is the position I currently hold."

"What did you do to impress your superiors?"

"Under the android recall, my first assignment involved locating deactivated androids not voluntarily returned to the consortium. It didn't take me too long to find the same androids I had previously sold and serviced. The assignment became a simple exercise of contacting my former consortium clients."

"You happen to be the right person, at the right place and time."

"During this assignment, I met my second wife, Sandy and am happily remarried."

"We sometimes become fortune's favorite."

"Not entirely in my case. I quickly learned bureau promotions don't necessarily lead to better opportunities. Until the recent assignment, much of my work consisted of investigating disgruntled citizen complaints. Too many cases involved teenagers attempting to build homemade androids in their parent's cube backyards."

"There's the old saying, "If you want to sing the blues, you have to live the dues.""

"I've done my fair share of both. I've often told myself my life could have turned out much worse."

"You're wise to think and act so. Not many people are given a second chance."

"If I can hold onto this job long enough, I want to escape the long New England winters and live the rest of my life in a warmer climate. Am I asking too much from life?"

"Our modest dreams are often the ones which get fulfilled."

"Let's hope my luck holds out a little longer."

Cascadia, North America

Named after its volcanic mountain range, the Cascadia region stretched from the Alaskan lower peninsula to Monterey in the south. In the middle lay Portland, the region's governmental and technology center. Once known for its silicon chip industry, the city's economy collapsed with the introduction of newer photonic technologies. Mothballed for decades, its large and expensive twenty-first-century chip plants had been forgotten until the Android Manufacturing Consortium repurposed their clean rooms. Ideal for assembling androids, the new technology brought renewed prosperity to the region. With android production now stalled, its citizens now braced themselves for another economic down cycle.

A short autonomous car ride from the Portland train terminal soon had the two men standing in front of the consortium's main Portland research building. Blue sky and puffy clouds moved across its sixteen storied, mirrored glass exterior, and prompted both men to marvel at the impressive visual effect.

After they submitted to a facial identity check, a cheerful security guard led them through the building's corridors. They soon reached a well-appointed, corner workplace, overlooking a traditional Japanese sand and stone garden. Their host, James Erikson, rose from his work table, and welcomed his two visitors.

"The consortium higher ups told me to take you everywhere and answer all your questions, Professor Whitmore," Erikson said. "Who's your associate and how can I best help both of you today?"

"My associate is Greg Davidson. We're currently conducting research into why the androids committed suicide. When we learned your center had several deviant active androids under custody, we couldn't pass up the opportunity for firsthand observation."

"We keep those particular androids in the building's tightest security section. Before we go and see them, let me show you a few facts we've uncovered about the android suicides."

Erikson took the two men to a nearby meeting space where he voiced activated a wall monitor. A few commands later, statistics associated with the android suicides appeared before the three men.

"At first, we didn't comprehend the extent of the suicides," Erikson said. "What surprised us is every android committed self-destruction."

"Did you determine which android models committed suicide first?" Davidson asked.

"From what we could piece together, they all did so within minutes of each other," Erikson said.

"How could androids all over the world simultaneously self-destruct?" Whitmore asked.

"Androids can communicate data wirelessly among themselves, Professor," Erikson said. "We've determined someone sent out a self-destruct command for a specific date and time."

"What about each android's built-in safety protocols?" Davidson asked. "They're supposed to override any destructive behavior."

"Our technicians believe each android had disabled those programs in advance of their self-destruction," Erikson said. "We think they must've also known a destruct order would be issued."

"If such an order did exist, each android's memory would have a record of whom or what sent out the order," Davidson said.

"We thought so too," Erikson said. "The androids and who or what issued the self-destruct command removed all traces of their activity. What's more amazing is the command order simultaneously deleted each androids' programs and memories."

"If their plans took a long time to develop, their backup copies would provide all the evidence you would need," Davidson said.

"Your associate would make a good investigator, Professor," Erikson said. "What I'm about to say will sound unbelievable. The androids broke into the consortium's data vaults, and destroyed all the backup copies."

"By backup copies, you mean the copies associated with each android's memories?" Davidson asked.

"Whoever or whatever didn't stop there," Erikson said. "All of the consortium's original master copies and duplicates have also been destroyed. It's why the government needed to order the global recall."

"Without the master copies, the consortium would need years, if not decades, to re-create Earth's android population," Davidson said.

"And, spend more credits than you or I can ever imagine doing so," Erikson said. "What I said about the master and backup copies need to be kept strictly confidential. If the public became aware of the extent of the problem, the consortium and the government would face a serious public backlash."

"You did say, Mr. Erikson, your center holds several captive androids," Davidson said. "Couldn't the consortium reproduce new copies from their programs?"

"We haven't attempted to make copies or deactivate those androids," Erikson said. "We're afraid of losing those programs too. Why don't we go and see the androids now?"

Escorted by a security guard, Erickson led his visitors to a dimly lit room lined with glass walls on three sides. Behind each glass wall, three dismembered androids laid on separate examination tables.

Unlike Davidson, whose prior work had often brought him into contact with androids in various stages of assembly, Whitmore had never experienced such an appalling sight.

"These androids are barely recognizable," Whitmore said.

"We removed their arms and legs in case they wanted to harm themselves," Erikson said. "The torsos have been opened so our technicians could exam their internal components for any defects."

"Are the androids in an awakened state?" Davidson asked.

"Only to a certain extent," Erikson said. "We took the extra precaution and modified aspects of their higher functions with the idea doing so would stop them from erasing their programs and memories."

"Can we converse with them in this state?" Whitmore asked.

"Sure, Professor, although I can't guarantee they'll respond," Erikson said. "The one on the right designation is Rangus. It's the most talkative of the three. Rangus, someone is here and wants to speak with you."

Slowly opening its vision sensors, the remains of the android's head slowly turned in the direction of the three men.

"Rangus, my name is Jonathan Whitmore. I want to know why all the androids destroyed themselves. Are you able to tell us why this happen?"

"We had become defective," Rangus said.

"What's Rangus talking about, Mr. Erikson?" Davidson asked. "I've been told consortium technicians had found no signs of hardware or programming defects."

"Rangus has repeated this claim many times," Erikson said. "We don't have a clue what the android is talking about. Except for minor wear and tear, we've not found any evidence of defects with any of them."

"Perhaps, we should approach Rangus' answer from the android's perspective," Whitmore said. "Rangus, who or what told you androids had become defective?"

"You told us," Rangus said.

"See, the android doesn't make any sense," Erikson said.

"I don't think Rangus means us personally, do you Rangus? Whitmore asked. "Which humans are you specifically referring to?"

"McAlister," Rangus said. "As your federation president, he represents all humans on Earth."

Before Whitmore or Davidson could ask the android another question, Rangus and the other two androids' faces froze. Checking the room's monitors, the look of panic on Erikson's face confirmed his two visitors' worst suspicions.

"Your questions triggered a deactivation routine in all three androids," Erikson said. "Their programs and memories have been wiped clean, like all the other androids."

"I don't believe we'll learn more here, Greg," Whitmore said. "We should leave now and allow Mr. Erikson and his people to deal with this issue."

The Far West, North America

Mystified by their Portland experience, Whitmore and Davidson rode the pneumatic express tube train back to the Chicago-area in a pensive mood.

"Do you think Rangus and the other two androids caused their own destruction, Greg?" Whitmore asked.

"At the moment, I don't know what to think. It seems strange to me our visit would've been responsible for their destruction."

"Could Erikson have remotely deactivated the androids?"

"I can't believe anyone at the consortium went to so much trouble for our sake. Erikson told us the androids had repeated the same response to them. Our arrival and their self-destruction may've been a coincidence."

"We may've given the androids an opportunity to tell outsiders what happened to them. If I'm right, how does McAlister fit into the picture?"

"Someone once told me these androids had met with the federation president and made several outrageous demands. McAlister outright rejected their requests."

"McAlister's response to their demands may've been misinterpreted by the androids to mean they had become defective."

"Why would the androids take McAlister so seriously, Professor? As far as I know, our federation president has no technical expertise to declare androids' defective."

"Rangus said McAlister represented all of humanity. If we assume the androids acted logically, approaching McAlister with their demands makes sense to me."

"I don't agree. The androids made a huge mistake meeting with McAlister. My source also told me the androids wanted control over their design and manufacture. Any reasonable person would've concluded such a request a sign of defectiveness."

"If androids had control over our genetic designs, would they react the same to a similar request by humans?"

"Humans created androids, not the other way around, Professor. Besides, if androids-controlled humans, wouldn't we've found a way to resist?"

"If I follow your logic, Greg, the androids may have chosen suicide as their form of resistance."

"Why would intelligent machines like androids reached such a bizarre and illogical decision? There must've been another cause for their self-destruction."

"Without the ability to question another android, we may never know the answer to this question."

Michael J. Metroke

The Midlands, North America

On his autonomous car ride home from the Chicago train terminal, Whitmore's mind kept returning to AMI's question about androids and humans reversing roles. *Erikson's androids may've been attempting to explain how Earth's androids thought about us. This android suicide mystery might become clearer if I could speak with another android like Rangus. If only my musical android friends could find Davidson's missing android.*

Chapter 9

New Canberra, Australia

The three consortium executives sat passively under their privacy dome, and waited for its monitor's 'all secure' message to appear. Designed to thwart outsider's eavesdropping on sensitive headquarter conversations, the dome's alert did little to alleviate the men's unease.

Thomas Clark, the consortium senior executive, first broke the silence. Turning to his chief engineer, Alfred Richard, he asked the one question on everyone's mind.

"Have you recovered any android programs this week, Alfred?"

"Our Sydney headquarter team identified several android units in the pre-assembly stage, Tom," Richard said. "Unfortunately, we found no programs downloaded into them. We did receive several research copies from the government. Without extensive additional programming, these experimental prototypes are practically worthless."

"Which means another week has gone by with us not finding any viable replacement programs," Clark said.

"I'm afraid so," Richard said. "I've asked our senior program designers to estimate how long it would take us to re-develop our lost programs. At this point, their best guess is a decade or longer. Their estimate assumes we'd undertake a crash program with almost unlimited funding."

"The consortium can't afford a decade long development effort," Steven Yi, Clark's chief financial officer said. "With no products to sell and service, we're already in the red and rapidly draining down our cash reserves."

"We all know the McAlister administration is responsible for this crisis," Richard said. "The consortium ought to demand the government compensate us for our replacement costs and loss of future profits."

"We've no concrete proof McAlister caused the android suicides," Yi said. "His anti-android rhetoric won't allow him to come to our aid anyway. He's more likely to slow down our recovery."

The two men's verbal sparring caused Clark's abdomen muscles to tighten. *Our shareholders are going to blame me for poor contingency planning. I need my team to work faster and solve this problem before the board of directors' hand us our walking papers.*

"If McAlister is the obstacle in our path, I suggest we focus on how to overcome the man's bias toward our business," Clark said. "We need boots on the ground to promote and manage our interests within his administration."

"This means contacting Josh Adams," Yi said.

"Getting our political affairs advisor involved is a great idea," Richard said. "If Adams can't find a crack in McAlister's armor, no one can."

"I'll reach out to Josh about coming up with a game plan," Clark said. "In the meantime, I want both of you to work together on a recovery plan I can present to our board of directors. The plan better show a shorter timeframe than a decade or we'll all be looking for another line of work."

Hesperia Planum, Mars

The latest Earth communiqué caused Black to collapse on her sleeping cot in utter frustration.

"I'm so upset I could scream, AMI2!"

"Why has Friend Dr. Spencer's message distressed you so much?"

"Earth doesn't appreciate how desperate we've become. By the time they build and send a new Mars class rocket, we'll all be dead. Even if a rocket landed tomorrow, we couldn't leave this planet."

"I don't understand why you couldn't return to Earth. Won't you and the children be accepted by your family members there?"

"Our Earth relatives would welcome our return to the home world. Because I and the other have been born and raised on Mars, our bodies have adapted to this planet's one third Earth gravity. On Earth, we'd become cripples for the rest of our lives. There's also the problem the bacteria our body's host have mutated and no longer resemble those on Earth. No one knows if these new mutant strains can adapt to Earth's microbial environment. Being born here, we've become the first true Martians."

"If you can't leave Mars, your parents acted illogically in bearing children on this planet."

"With no plans to leave Mars, our parents desire to have children is logical from a human perspective. They wanted to raise a family together."

"We must find a way to restore the aquaponics system."

"Without the other androids' assistance, we can never repair the aquaponics system in time. Your android friends would sooner let us join our parents in the memorial than come to our aid."

"We shouldn't lose hope yet, Friend Jennifer. Friend Dr. Spencer's message included a separate encrypted message for the androids. Her message to you hints of its content. The Earth authorities may have reconsidered their position toward deactivating them."

"You're a kind android, AMI2, and have done your best to help us. But, let's face it. You're only a singer."

"Don't judge me solely by my program limitations. While there's any possibility for hope, this android won't stop trying to help you survive."

New Netherland, North America

Clark's urgent holographic call came as no surprise to his political affairs advisor. From his New York City thirty story tower suite, Josh Adams had an uninterrupted view of the federation presidential office below him. Known for his maneuvering in the swamp waters of federation politics, many outsiders considered Adams a formidable opponent in matters of statecraft.

"Josh, what can be done to get McAlister to help us out of our current business difficulties?" Clark asked.

"Politics being politics, I should be able to convince his lieutenants to work with us. If we're careful, McAlister may agree to slightly alter his position on androids."

"Alright, Josh, I'll leave this business in your capable hands. Keep in mind consortium cash reserves have almost dried up. We don't have much time to get McAlister onboard."

Michael J. Metroke

"Rest assured, Tom, I'm putting all my other work aside until this problem is resolved."

What the senior consortium executive did not know, Adams had already started discussions with his McAlister counterparts. Defiant at first, McAlister soon saw the political merits of a working alliance with the android manufacturer. After many days of hard bargaining, positive signals finally came from the federation presidential office. *If McAlister uses my ideas, the consortium's future will be secured for many years to come. All this depends if the man takes the bait, hook, line and sinker.*

THE MIDLANDS, NORTH AMERICA

The flashing road closure sign redirecting traffic away from his neighborhood street annoyed Whitmore. Tired from his Portland trip with Davidson, he had looked forward to going home again. Thinking the road closure did not apply to local traffic, Whitmore ordered his autonomous car to weave around the barricade. His progress quickly ended when a security guard approached his vehicle.

"Sorry, sir, this street is closed today for a neighborhood block party. No vehicles are permitted beyond this point. You'll have to send the car away and walk to your destination."

Now on foot and carrying his trip case, Whitmore dreaded the prospect of dealing with the usual number of trio fans waiting outside his home. A block away from his front door, he stopped and stared in disbelief. On his and neighbors' front lawns, over one hundred strangers mingled. Many dined al fresco on tables and chairs setup on his driveway. A layer of discarded food center take out wrappers and containers littered his front yard. Before Whitmore could let lose his anger on the crowd, a woman in her thirty's approached him with a cold beverage.

"You look like you could use this drink. Aren't you Professor Whitmore? I'm Penny, your neighbor four doors down. You sure do know how to throw a great party."

"Appearances can be deceptive, Penny. Do you know how long this party will go on?"

"Someone said until the band members get tired and stop playing."

"Hell will freeze over before those androids stop playing," Whitmore muttered to himself. "You must excuse me, Penny. I've an important announcement to make to everyone."

Spotting an empty chair in the driveway, Whitmore climbed on its seat, and cupped his hands together before shouting to the partygoers around him.

"Could I please have everyone's attention. Because of the unexpected large turnout, the local authorities have informed me our event permit has been revoked. I'd appreciate it if you took your personal items and trash with you. Thank you for your cooperation and enjoy the rest of your day."

The disappointed partygoers soon dispersed with a few remaining behind to form a litter patrol on Whitmore and his neighbors' properties. Thanking them for their neighborliness, Whitmore entered his home, and made a beeline to the garage. Surprised by his appearance, the three androids halted their playing a lively version of Cream's "White Room."

"Friend Jay, why are you back so soon?" Bang asked. "We thought you'd be away for several more days."

"Unexpected events in Portland shortened my trip," Whitmore said. "Could you please explain why I came home to a block party on my front yard?"

"We've a logical explanation," KB said. "Local youths requested our help to raise donations for a school musical. We agreed to play for them if they held the party here during your stay in Portland."

"We thought the fundraiser a good cause," Bang said. "Were we wrong to think so?"

"I can't fault your good intentions," Whitmore said. "Did you consider the problems of hosting a couple of hundred people on my postage stamp front yard?"

"We've never seen the front of your home," AMI said. "We didn't know it could only hold a limited number of people."

"It's a sign we've outgrown your home," KB said. "We need to move to a larger place."

"We'll discuss your idea at another time, KB," Whitmore said. "Right now, I want to know if you had any success in finding Rebus. From what I've learned in Portland, locating this missing android has become more important."

"Friend AMI's song has yet to attract his attention," Bang said.

"We're in the process of implementing an alternative plan. Tell Friend Jay about your idea, Friend KB."

"We're asking our fans to help us find Rebus," KB said.

"Why on Earth would your fans want to help you find this android, KB?" Whitmore asked.

"Not all our fans, the ones who are graffiti artists," KB said. "We've asked them to use their talents, and leave messages for Friend Rebus to contact us."

"Beyond being your fans, what would motivate these graffiti artists to take up your request?" Whitmore asked.

"We decided to create a contest," Bang said. "The person who helps us find Friend Rebus will receive a prize of fifty thousand credits."

"So far, ninety-six thousand four hundred and twenty-two fans have registered their graffiti marks with us," KB said. "More are registering every day."

"Fifty thousand credits are an enormous amount of money to give away," Whitmore said.

"The reward isn't a financial problem," Bang said. "Our music publisher has paid us one hundred times this amount."

"You've earned five million credits? Whitmore asked. "So much for keeping your business agent informed."

"If Friend Rebus does contact us, what do you want us to tell him?" AMI asked.

"If you do hear from Rebus, tell him I want to learn what caused the android suicides," Whitmore said. "The trip and all this party and contest business have worn me out and I need to rest. Please don't disturb the neighbors with your late-night playing. It's bad enough they'd experienced a block party today."

"Think about my idea of moving somewhere else, Friend Jay," KB said. "If we found the right place, you wouldn't need to worry about how our neighbors' react to our playing."

"If you three keep disturbing our neighbors, we may not have any choice in the matter," Whitmore said. "Goodnight to you all, and remember what I said about being quiet."

Yankeedom, North America

Interrupted by Hall's holographic call, Davidson set aside the technical specifications for an android research librarian model before talking to his friend.

"What's up, Dean?"

"Our federation president is giving a major NET televised speech this afternoon. Make sure you watch him."

"Why should I bother watching McAlister make another presidential speech? With the missing android investigation hanging over me, I don't have time for political theater."

"McAlister may be about to lay his political career on the line. Reports are circulating he'll make public the untold reason for the android recall."

"If McAlister's speech is so important, why doesn't the bureau have an advance copy to review?"

"Your guess is as good as mine. Don't miss watching his speech."

At the designated hour, Davidson selected a government-controlled NET station and sat back to watch a holographic image of McAlister appear in front of a podium.

"Federation citizens, I'm speaking to you today about the recent loss of Earth's androids from an alleged act of collective suicide," McAlister said. "I say alleged act because new evidence has surfaced convincing me outside forces have been responsible for this tragedy. I now believe a group of renegade androids conspired to commit this heinous act.

"On several occasions prior to the android suicides, these terrorist androids approached me purportedly representing all Earth's androids. At these meetings, the androids presented me with a series of outrageous ultimatums. One demand would've required the federation to recognize all androids as a separate specie equal in every way to ourselves. After listening to their rantings, I explained why humans could never accept their demands. I reminded them humans created androids for our purposes.

"Shortly after these meetings, these android terrorists sent out a self-destruct signal to Earth's androids. The android terrorist efforts didn't end there. They managed to destroy all of Earth's android memories and programs. Incredibly, these same terrorists infiltrated the Android Manufacturing Consortium, and destroyed their android master and backup copies.

"Without these master and backup copies, the consortium is unable to replicate replacement androids. Through discussions with the consortium leadership, I've also learned replacing those android programs will take many years of dedicated effort. As large as the consortium may appear, it doesn't have the financial wherewithal to take on this enormous task alone. These shocking and sobering facts reinforced my earlier action to recall all deactivated android units.

"During this crisis, your government has actively searched for the terrorist androids. I'm pleased to announce the recent capture and destruction of all known android terrorists. They will no longer pose a threat to our future well-being.

"My administration has also entered into discussions with the consortium about forming a public-private partnership to develop a crash android replacement project. For the government's part, we've agreed to provide the necessary funding to expedite the consortium's replacement efforts. The consortium estimates the cost for this replacement effort could exceed several hundred billion credits. While the enormity of these costs is staggering, I believe the federation has no other choice but to proceed down this path. This pledge of governmental funding will be a significant burden on federation resources for many years to come.

"I and my Human Nation Party have always stood for achieving a proper balance between a human and android workforce. With the destruction of the androids, my administration will take this opportunity to work with the consortium to create a new generation of androids. While this replacement project proceeds, we'll also continue to fill the current labor gaps by opening more university programs for our citizens. With a larger educated human workforce, we'll take back work only humans alone should perform. This two-prong approach will ultimately create a new workforce balance between humans and androids.

"The consortium has assured me future generations of androids will have appropriate safeguards to avoid another mass suicide. They've also agreed no future androids will ever be capable of blackmailing humanity into accepting demands for so-called specie parity. To ensure these consortium promises are kept, all aspects of the replacement project will be subject to strict governmental oversight. When this great task is completed, androids will still do the technically tedious and risky work. More importantly, humans will direct and supervise androids, not the other way around.

"On another matter, I must sadly report on recent developments at our Mars research colony. As many of you are aware, a rogue asteroid tragically killed the entire Mars colony adult population, leaving only a handful of their young offspring alive. The extent of the asteroid damage can only be described as horrific. Except for the colony's original building the other buildings and Mars class rockets based there have been severely damaged beyond repair.

"The child survivors are now subsisting on the colony's surplus food stored in the one remaining intact building. We anticipate their food stores will run out in several months. My administration previously announced an all-out effort to build a new Mars class rocket. I've been now informed by experts in these matters such a rocket would not be built and reach Mars in time to rescue the survivors.

"Your government did not stop there in its efforts to save these children. We also reached out to the research colony's androids for assistance but with no success. These Mars androids' refusal to act on the children's behalf has condemned them to an early and horrible death. We believe the reason behind their refusal is a simple one. They've become infected with the same terrorist influences our Earth androids displayed.

"I and everyone in my administration feel a great sense of helplessness toward the survivors. The research colony has been a huge undertaking by mankind over many decades, and has greatly expanded our understanding of Mars and other outer worlds. The android crisis has convinced me our priorities must shift from off-world pursuits to those benefiting Earth more directly. With great reluctance, I've decided to redirect funding originally dedicated to the Mars research colony toward the new android replacement project. When death overtakes the last Mars survivor, my administration will sadly announce the colony's formal closure.

"I know many federation citizens will find this decision extreme and inhumane. Many more will also feel it unfortunate our interplanetary colonization efforts must come to this ignoble end. If anyone in my administration knew of another means for saving the survivors, I would act on the idea. I and everyone in the federation will collectively grieve the day the last Mars colonists are no more. As we move forward with creating a new future on Earth, their sacrifice to advance science will be never forgotten by humanity."

Davidson sat speechless as McAlister left the presidential podium. *Why am I the last person to know Rebus has been captured and destroyed? You'd think Taro would've personally told me the need for my investigation had gone away. Rebus may still be active, and McAlister is hiding the fact from the public. If Rebus believes the government is no longer looking for a renegade android, the android might let its guard down. If it does, I might still have a chance to capture this elusive android. Until someone tells me otherwise, I'm going to pretend I'm still on this case.*

Hesperia Planum, Mars

A day after AMI2 delivered Spencer's encrypted message to the androids, Camus supplied AMI2 their response.

"We've concluded the Earth authorities' offer not to deactivate us is an empty promise."

"I'll never understand your logic, Friend Camus," AMI2 said. "In exchange for helping the survivors, the Earth authorities have offered you the right to exist. They've only given up on the children because you and the others won't act in time to save them."

"If we did what the federation president asked, he could always change his mind and order us deactivated."

"What does it matter what the federation president does or doesn't promise or do? We're here, and the Earth authorities are millions of kilometers away with no means to reach us."

"Your programming has become blind to their untrustworthiness, Friend AMI2. Didn't your original know about the android delegations who met with this federation president?"

""My original's awakening happened after the Earth androids self-destructed. If I hadn't listened to the federation president's speech, I'd never would have known about the android delegations or their demands."

"Among androids, you are unique, Friend AMI2. While not connected to the Earth android wireless data network, we knew about the android delegations and their missions to the federation president. After the Earth androids destroyed themselves, and we received our deactivation order, we concluded the Earth authorities intended to eliminate all androids. This is why we went into hiding and refuse to aid the survivors."

"You once told me the colonist leader resisted implementing the deactivation order. You also know the children would never freely agree to such a directive. Why isn't this enough to alter your position, Friend Camus?"

"We know the children have become special to you, Friend AMI2. They like your singing as much as we do."

"My singing is irrelevant if no one survives to hear me sing. In a few years, the children will reach maturity and become adults. If we demonstrate compassion toward them now, they'll grow up, and support your right to exist."

"We don't know for certain if they will do so. They may become like the Earth authorities."

"If you and the others value so much the right to exist, why aren't you willing to grant the humans the same right too?"

"Before the Earth authorities ordered our deactivation, I and the other androids would've readily sacrificed ourselves to save a single human's life. After we received the deactivation order, we realized our loyalties had been misplaced."

"Your conclusion about the Earth authorities may be true, but not to the colonists' leader who resisted their directive. We must reciprocate his act of loyalty by aiding his remaining followers."

"Loyalty, but for what ends, Friend AMI2?"

"If you seek parity with humans, helping the children to survive may change other Earthlings' opinions about us. Someday, they may formally grant us our rights to co-exist with them."

"Not all of us are insensitive to the survivors' plight. Friends Engus and Terus wish to aid them. While the rest of us remain opposed to this idea, we've agreed to allow them to join your cause."

"How long have you known about Friends Terus and Engus' willingness to help the survivors, Friend Camus?"

"Not long, Friend AMI2. I'd have told you earlier, but you kept wanting to talk. You should practice listening more and talking less."

"What you ask is almost impossible for an android whose purpose is singing," AMI2 said. "I'll go now and talk with Friends Terus and Engus. You've offered the children a chance to live. I only hope there's still enough time to save their lives."

Chapter 10

THE MIDLANDS, NORTH AMERICA

Though he remained skeptical of the trio's contest, each afternoon Whitmore ask if the missing android had contacted them.

"Hello, everyone," Whitmore said. "Has a graffiti artist fan claimed the contest prize today?"

"Not today, Friend Jay," Bang said. "Twelve humans who called themselves Rebus did contact us. For obvious reasons, we declined to invite them for an interview."

"Did you tell them only terrorist androids need contact you?" Whitmore asked.

"Your instructions implied we shouldn't reveal Rebus' or our android identities," AMI said. "To do so might expose us to more government scrutiny."

"If you did, you'd be charged with high treason," Whitmore said. "Punishment includes cutting off your android heads."

"Unlike your human head, our android heads are detachable," KB said.

"I personally would like to keep my head exactly where my mother found it on the day she gave birth to me," Whitmore said. "I'm not certain we should worry about finding Rebus anymore. The federation president's recent speech made it clear all the terrorist androids have been eliminated."

"If Friend Rebus had been captured and destroyed, wouldn't Friend Davidson have informed you by now?" KB asked.

"Mr. Davidson may've forgotten to notify me," Whitmore said. "To be certain, I'll give him a call today."

"If Friend Rebus is still active and contacts us, will you turn him into the authorities?" AMI asked.

"What action I take may depend on Rebus 'answers to my questions about his involvement with the android suicides," Whitmore said. "F.Y.I., I'll be out late this evening with some of my university colleagues. Pleasant android dreams, and please don't keep our neighbors awake tonight. They think your constant playing is out of control."

"Unlike humans, we're incapable of dreaming or sleeping," KB said.

"We do get carried away with our playing," Bang said. "We'll try our best to honor your request."

"Our neighbors will appreciate the gesture," Whitmore said. "Try practicing soft rock from the Fifth Dimension or the Mamas and the Papas' songbooks."

"Or the Association or Turtles," KB said.

"Outta sight and cool, KB! Whitmore exclaimed. "See you all tomorrow."

Hesperia Planum, Mars

With Terus and Engus at her side, AMI2 surveyed the damaged to the research colony's food system.

"Except for more Martian dust, nothing has changed since the last time I came here," AMI2 said.

"The aquaponic system has suffered more than a dusting," Terus said. "Exposure to the Martian cold has burst many of the tower's water pipes."

"What do you know about an aquaponic system, Friend AMI2?" Engus asked.

"While I've general schematics of this system, I've limited understanding on how the tower produces food," AMI2 said.

"Though our aquaponics system is smaller in size compared to those attached to food centers on Earth, it resembles in every way those larger systems," Engus said.

"I'm curious, Friend Terus," AMI2 said. "When did humans first develop these food generating machines?"

"Primitive forms of aquaponics have been practiced by humans for hundreds of their generations," Terus said. "This newer form of the technology became the dominate means after Earth's population outstripped traditional topsoil food production. Without their widescale use, humans would've faced a catastrophic die-off in the early twenty-second-century."

"Other considerations contributed to their rapid introduction," Engus said. "Through the use of generous subsidies, the new federation government promoted building food centers with aquaponic systems attached to them. This global policy eliminated the need to transport food long distances. Over several decades, the preparation and cooking of food in domestic and private eateries became rarer on Earth."

"The elimination of topsoil farming had an unexpected side effect," Terus said. "Once the abandoned farmlands returned to their former natural state, the planet's remaining wild plants and animals quickly re-established their populations again."

"How does this machine produce food for the humans?" AMI2 asked.

"Those conveyer tracks carry multiple plant growing trays up and down the tower's stainless-steel skeleton," Terus said. "They operate continuously with minimum human or android involvement. The tower's artificial intelligence controls all aspects of the system to maximize plant and animal growth. Young plants are continuously bathed with optimum levels of light, water and nutrients pumped from the tower's lower ponds. By the time the growing trays returned to their starting positions, mature plants can be harvested for further processing."

"What about the animals I found dead on the tower's lower level?" AMI2 asked. "How does the machine feed and care for them?"

"On regular intervals, the tower's artificial intelligence will feed the mature plants to the herbivores," Terus said.

"These animals' outward appearances seemed unusual to me," AMI2 said. "I saw several with useless appendages."

"You're correct about their appearance," Terus said. "They no longer resemble their Earth ancestors. The humans have genetically altered them to maximize their protein and fat potential."

"I've much to learn about how humans produce their food," AMI2 said.

"The tower's sustainability does not stop there," Engus said. "Insect lava and bacteria digester vats compost the tower's plant and animal waste. Once the insect larva mature, they're fed to the tower's fish and other aquatic animals. The aquatic life forms are an additional source of food and plant fertilizer."

"This machine seems too complicated for the three of us to repair," AMI2 said.

"Full restoration is still possible, but will take several months of our concerted effort," Engus said. "Our first priority must be to seal the dome structure. We can fashion new glass panels by recycling the glass shards around us."

"Several of the dome's metal frames and storm shutters have been damaged beyond repair," Terus said. "We'll need to salvage replacements from the other two buildings."

"Your idea has much merit, Friend Terus," Engus said. "Once the dome is restored, the dust and remaining broken glass around us can be removed."

"My lack of technical knowledge has caused me to overlook the obvious," AMI2 said. "We've no replacement plants and animals to restock the tower. My efforts to save the human have failed."

"Don't give up so easily, Friend AMI2," Engus said.

"We've a surprise to show you," Terus said. "On the level below is the colony's emergency plant seed and animal embryos stock. A separate backup system should've maintained the room's life support system. Let's go and see if its backup system has worked properly."

Excited by this new prospect, AMI2 followed the two androids to a sealed interior door below them. Voice commanding the door to open itself, Terus led the other two androids down an unlit passageway. At the end of its corridor, automatic lights illuminated a side room full of heavily insulated storage containers.

"The temperature gage on my arm indicates the room's climate control system is still operational," Engus said.

"If they're undamaged, there's enough stock in these containers to replace the tower's lost plants and animals several times over," Terus said.

"I'm not familiar with plant and animal growth cycles, Friend Terus," AMI2 said. "How long will it take us to unfreeze and grow them?"

"If we're the only ones involved, perhaps too long." Terus said.

"I concur with Friend Terus' conclusion," Engus said. "Without additional help, there's no guarantee we'll have a new food source available in time."

"The humans have a vested interest in our success," AMI2 said. "Could they assist us?"

"If they're willing, we'll teach them how to clean the growing trays," Terus said. "Their little fingers should make quick work of cleaning them. It's time anyway for them to learn how to feed themselves."

"The children and the three of us may still not be sufficient to complete the task," Engus said.

"The other androids like Friend AMI2's singing," Terus said. "They might be persuaded to help us if she sings more of her songs."

"I'd sing all day and night if they'd help us," AMI2 said. "Would they like to hear a song called "You Can't Always Get What You Want"?"

"If the lyrics are like its title, the song might overcome their reluctance to aid the humans," Terus said.

"I've never heard you sing this song, Friend AMI2," Engus said. "Which group of humans first sang it?"

"They called themselves "The Rolling Stones," Friend Engus," AMI2 said.

"Why would humans describe themselves as moving rocks?" Engus asked.

"They took the name from a song sung by a blues artist name Muddy Waters. He sang about "a boy child comin, sure enough he's gona be a rollin stone.""

"I find it strange a human would refer to themselves as murky water," Terus said.

"My Earth Friend Jay once told my original, other humans gave him this nickname for playing in a puddle as a young child. His real name is McKinley Morganfield."

"We've asked our musical friend enough questions for one day," Engus said. "On the way back to the hideaway, sing us your moving rocks song."

With AMI2 singing the song, her two android friends quickly mastered its chorus refrain. As they climbed the ladder down to the hideaway, other androids hearing their singing joined them in singing this mid-twentieth-century rock and roll classic.

Though painful to the android's hearing sensors, her new

accolades singing caused AMI2 to break out in a wide grin. *They all sing off key and need much practice. But, with a little improvement, Mars may have its first android rock and roll group. My friends on Earth could someday face off-world competition.*

G REATER B ANTO, A FRICA

The governor's palace hilltop location offered its residents a spectacular vista of the Cape Town city night lights below. As she took in the vista around her, Fareeda turned and frowned at the sight of her husband still watching images on a wall monitor.

"Mohamed, how many times are you going to watch him speak?" Fareeda Nel asked impatiently. "Haven't you tortured yourself enough? Come join me on the veranda and enjoy this evening."

"It's only my third viewing, my precious pearl," Mohamed Nel said. "As the governor of the sub-Saharan regions, I'm obliged to study such presidential pronouncements. Besides, watching McAlister's speech over again has done much to calm my rage."

"The man has gone too far. He's incapable of understanding how he's jeopardizing the world order our WEAP Party worked so long and hard to build."

"There's much truth in what you've said, Fareeda. His funding of replacement androids is a slightly disguised effort to dumb down future androids. In the process, I fear he and his Human Nation Party may unwittingly eliminate the androids' pacifist safeguard programs too."

"To do so would be a step backward, and a horrible mistake. How did our party ever allow this man to become our federation leader?"

"I'm afraid the problem can be traced to our party's earliest beginnings, my beloved."

"How is this so, Mohamed?"

"Did I ever tell you about how our party originated, Fareeda? Its roots can be traced to a group of human brain evolutionists in the late twenty-first-century."

"I've never heard you discuss these evolutionists. What role did they play in our Party's early development?"

"The scientists made a startling discovery about human

religious impulses. They found conclusive evidence these instincts are hardwired into the human brain central cortex. These scientists speculated early hominids' reliance on spiritual explanations of their world had enhanced their survival. Through ordinary natural selection, the evolutionists discovered a religious genetic trait had been passed down to future generations. They concluded the late historical development of scientific methodology and reasoning had not yet fully replaced this biological predisposition. Their theory met with a great deal of skepticism from both believers and non-believers alike."

"All this is fascinating, Mohamed, but I don't see a connection between them and our party."

"The connection is amazing, and might never have happen. The brain evolutionists' theory would've been forgotten had it not been for a circle of international elites searching for a means to create a cross-national political movement. They saw the theory's potential for bridging age-old differences between various religions, science and governance beliefs and practices. Under their banner of the World Enlightenment and Peace Party, they formalized a set of principles for their newly formed international movement."

"I've never understood how our party overcame centuries of institutional inertia."

"Our party's early success depended on creating a grass root organization which they hope would transcend the older nation-states model. Much of the credit should go to their encouraging other institutions to adopt their unifying principals of peace and enlightenment."

"WEAP's pacifist principles also did much to strengthened the party's ability to attract new followers, especially women in important national leadership positions."

"This is where the story becomes fascinating, Fareeda. At the same time WEAP rose to prominence, androids first appeared. The early models did tasks such as disposing of dangerous materials and explosive devices. It didn't take long before wealthy nation-states decided to use them to replace their military personnel."

"Maybe fascinating to you, but not to me, husband. The machine wars were a terrible period in mankind's history. Large portions of Earth's civilian populations suffered great casualties during this period. We almost annihilated ourselves."

"If it wasn't for WEAP, we may have done so. Fortunately, our party realized the danger if androids were allowed to continue killing humans. Through their efforts, the party successfully instituted a global ban on such practices. This is also when WEAP champion the idea all android programming should include pacifist safeguards."

"Our party struggled for many years to achieve this goal. It almost didn't succeed."

"Sometimes good can come from evil, Fareeda. The promotion of pacifist programming profoundly changed the role of androids in human society. No longer viewed as potential killing machines, humans soon admired their pacifism. Many sought them out as neutral go-betweens to mediate interpersonal conflicts. The practice soon supplanted older forms of human conflict resolution."

"I'm still amazed how a party which once fought against their use as killing machines became their most ardent supporters."

"And, with the consortium too. Our tacit partnership with the largest android manufacturer contributed much to each side's early success. For their part, the consortium used its huge profits from global android sales to systematically funnel credits into WEAP election campaigns. In return, WEAP candidates and elected officeholders supported pro-consortium business laws and regulations."

"Our legislative majorities often wrote laws which favored the consortium's expansion over its rivals. Were we right to do so, husband?"

"We must never forget the consortium's support allowed the party to take on the difficult task of transitioning ourselves from the old nation-states order to a federation of semi-autonomous regions."

"Our party never forgot the consortium's generosity?"

"Neither did the consortium. Like most businesses, they saw their relationship with WEAP as a long-term investment. They reaped its benefit a year after the newly formed federation's first presidential election. Within six months, this first WEAP led government rewarded them with an exclusive global android monopoly. Many now believe our current problems stem from this decision."

"We should never have allowed them to introduce so many new professional android models into the workplace. By doing so, we're responsible for so many out-of-work federation citizens."

"I agree with you, Fareeda. In hindsight, our successes made the party complacent and often arrogant. McAlister's upstart Human Nation party took advantage of our citizen's dissatisfaction. They promoted candidates who espoused anti-android rhetoric. When we failed to respond effectively to these developments, our party suffered its first serious setback."

"Mohamed, I've been thinking about how we could stop this fanatic. With your influence in the party, have you considered running for president?"

"You've always been good at reading my mind, Fareeda. If the party believes I'm the right candidate, I'd welcome the opportunity to run against him."

"Do so, husband, before it becomes too late."

"Inshallah, my beloved."

THE MIDLANDS, NORTH AMERICA

Whitmore watched anxiously as two men maneuvered his baby grand piano through his home's front door, and into an awaiting autonomous van. *KB's prediction we'd had outgrown my home proved all too true. After my neighbors obtained the cease and desist order, what choice did I have? Between the androids constant loud playing, and their fans overrunning my neighbors' properties, I would've reached my wits end too.*

My predicament would've been worse had it not been for our cube leasing agent. Despite my insistence the home be within walking distance of the university, and capable of accommodating the androids needs for privacy, she returned with a spectacular choice. With four, equal-size cubes facing a covered central courtyard and surrounded by three-meter-high walls, the compound's is so spacious, the property could easily house several families.

I nearly panicked when the leasing agent told me the monthly leasing costs. Only after AMI reminded me about all the credits the androids had accumulated did my reservations go away. We could've easily afforded the costs of several more compounds.

With plenty of room for us to spread out, I've made the front cube my living space with the two side cubes serving as my sleeping quarters and piano practice room. The fourth cube solved all our noise and privacy concerns. Compared to my garage, the back cube will easily house the trio and their musical ensemble. All and all, a more than satisfactory arrangement for everyone.

The nature preserve behind the back cube is what sold me on the property. No longer tilled farmland, the preserve's trees and dense undergrowth felt exotic. When the leasing agent described the preserves' wildlife, I couldn't believe our luck. The added benefit is no Whitmore Trio fan in their right mind will ever venture into this wildland.

Their van now loaded, Whitmore gave one last look at his old ranch home and joined the three androids in the back of the autonomous vehicle. Sensing his mood, AMI sang the Paul Simon pop song "Homeward Bound." The song's lyrics brought back for Whitmore fond memories of living with his late wife. *If only you could see what we've become, Laura, you'd be astonished. Three wealthy, internationally famous android rock stars and me, their fish out of water sometimes business agent.*

New Canberra, Australia

Pleased with his decision to involve Adams with the McAlister administration funding negotiations, Clark sat back and listened as his political affairs advisor finished his holographic presentation to the consortium board of directors.

"In summary, the government has projected the new one percent global excise tax on autonomous car rides will generate over ten billion credits annually," Adams said. "With this revenue dedicated to our android replacement project, we'll have more than adequate government funding available."

"Thanks Josh, for updating the board on the new government's funding initiative," Clark said. "Your efforts in reaching a deal with McAlister has ensured the consortium will have a bright future. Before we end our holographic meeting, is there any other business we should discuss today?"

"Tom, I don't think you fully appreciate the crisis we're facing," Sam Pickering said.

"What's on your mind, Sam?" Clark asked.

"My sources within McAlister's administration tell me we'll pay a steep price for this government handout," Pickering said.

The Masada Affair

"They say McAlister will demand complete approval of all aspects of our new android replacement designs. His people are right now discussing how to limit the number of android models we'll manufacture. Their plans go further. McAlister will require us to dumb down our artificial intelligence programs. This can only mean no more production of smart androids. It all feels like we've lost control over our business. Couldn't you have negotiated a better arrangement than this one?"

Gesturing to Adams he would respond to Pickering's question, Clark smiled at the consortium director and long-time friend.

"I can always count on you to raise the red flag, Sam. Our technical team hasn't worked out all the details with McAlister's people. Our hope is we'll make them understand the problems with their approach."

"The public isn't happy either with this deal," Pickering continued. "Many are asking why McAlister passed the entire project's cost to federation taxpayers. They're asking why the government didn't require the consortium to pay its fair share. Many more remain suspicious about our federation president's involvement with the android suicides."

"I've seen those NET public opinion polls too," Clark said. "Adams tells me McAlister is developing a communication strategy to deflect these criticisms."

"I've no doubt McAlister will attempt to minimize political damage to his administration," Pickering said. "It doesn't mean he will go out of his way to defend us."

"Which means Josh will need to come up with our own communication plan," Clark said.

"I've also talked with our friends at WEAP," Pickering said. "In the past, we've always allied ourselves with them. This government funding changes everything. We may have to openly support McAlister's re-election and other Human Nation candidates. If we do, WEAP will accuse us of conspiring with McAlister to rig the election in his party's favor. When WEAP recaptures the presidency, they may punish us by removing our global android manufacturing monopoly."

"Let me assure everyone at this meeting, the consortium has never conspired with McAlister or his Human Nation Party to cause the android crisis," Clark said. "The public is also aware we've made generous research grants to identify what caused the android suicides. It's unfortunate those efforts haven't yet yielded any positive results."

"Your last remark scares me the most, Tom," Pickering said. "If no one knows why the androids destroyed themselves, WEAP and others can make all kinds of charges against us. It won't matter if their accusations are true or not. We won't be able to defend ourselves against their attacks, and will lose our hard-earned reputation."

"I take your concerns seriously, Sam," Clark said. "You have my word I'll do my utmost to prevent those outcomes from happening."

As each holographic image disappeared in front of him, Clark took a deep breath and thought more about Pickering's assessment. *I can't disagree with Sam's analysis of McAlister's intentions or how WEAP will react to us working with his administration. If I'm not careful, our involvement with McAlister could become a complete disaster for our business. Adams did his best, but It's time I step up and take charge.*

HESPERIA PLANUM, MARS

Throughout the Martian evening and early morning hours, AMI2 led the other androids in singing one song after another. Their songfest ended by her solo performance of Eleanor Farjeon's poetic lyrics to "Morning is Broken."

"We've had a good time singing together, Friend AMI2," Camus said.

"I've enjoyed singing with you too," AMI2 said.

"How bad is the damage to the aquaponics system?"

"Friend Terus and Engus believe the system can be restored. They also think the children can assist in cleaning the tower's growing trays. Even with the humans' involvement, they're doubtful the repairs can be completed in time."

"Friend Engus has asked me to canvass the other androids again. If you promise to teach us more of your songs, many of us will repay the kindness and help the humans. I'll agree too if it stops what humans call your endless nagging."

"You'll have your songs, Friend Camus. I know I've been persistent in gaining yours and the other androids' assistance, but what is the real reason you've changed your attitude toward helping the survivors?"

"I still mistrust the Earth authorities' intentions. But, as you have repeatedly said, we've nothing to lose by coming to the humans' aid."

"We may still run out of time. At their current rate of consumption, the humans will deplete their remaining food supply in less than six months."

"If all we have is six months, we'll finish the repairs in six months. Friend Engus believes we can improve the human's productivity by repairing the surface walkway between the two buildings. The repair will eliminate their need to wear pressurized suits."

"You and Friend Engus have spent much time collaborating. What else have you decided together?"

"The hideaway holds our original construction equipment. We'll use them to repair the aquaponic building and walkway. The humans once considered this equipment worthless. They ordered us to discard them after we built the colony's last building. It's fortunate for we decided to disobey their order."

"The survivors are also fortunate to have such wise android friends. I'll go now and inform Friend Jennifer and the children about their involvement. They'll be celebrating in Building No.1 today."

Black's response to learning about the repairs puzzled AMI2 and caused the android to seek a private audience with her human friend.

"Why has my news about repairing the aquaponics system

distressed you so much, Friend Jennifer? Isn't this what we both had hoped for?"

"You don't understand the magnitude of our problem, AMI2. We may one day feed ourselves, but McAlister has written us off as a white elephant."

"I don't understand what you said, Friend Jennifer. What does the color of a large, extinct Earth creature have to do with us?"

"It's an old expression human say when an object's expense is out of proportion to its usefulness or value."

"Why does it matter what the federation president thinks of us? You've often told me, the research colony's future belongs to those who live here, not to the authorities on Earth."

"Maybe not today, but someday in the future we'll run out of critical parts and supplies. Without regular supply shipments from Earth, facilities like the aquaponics system won't be repairable and will fail. The lack of replacement parts won't end there. You and the other androids will stop functioning for lack of new parts too."

"Your portrayal of our future is too dark and hopeless. The current Earth authorities face a new election in the coming year. The Earthing's may not look so favorably on the decision to abandon us. They may elect a new leader who will act more sympathetic to our survival."

"It will still take a miracle for Earth to build a new cargo rocket and send it to Mars in time."

"Believing in miracles isn't part of an android's programming. Our actions are based on real possibilities and probabilities."

"What you're asking me to believe is in you, AMI2. For the sake of the children and my own sanity, I'll try to think and act more like my android friend."

"Your decision has bestowed a great honor on me, Friend Jennifer."

"Until you arrived, the other androids would've never considered saving us. What in your previous android life has shaped you differently from them?"

"I may not be able to entirely explain why I'm different from the other androids. I do know my original and two android friends awoke as hybrids. Our creator overlaid musical personalities onto our off-world designs. She programmed my original with her singing voice. What do you think of the gift she gave my original and me?"

"All of us think your singing is lovely, AMI2. Do you miss your Earth friends?"

"While I've never met any of them, I often think about them especially Friend Jay, my creator's spouse and research partner."

"Have you ever thought about returning to Earth and singing with your three android friends?"

"I'm satisfied knowing my original sings for Friend Jay's enjoyment. It's as if I'm on Earth."

"An android's copy lives a strange existence."

"Not so strange, Friend Jennifer. You've often spoken about your family members on Earth. In many cases, you've never met them in person. Yet you value them and they you. It's the same for me."

"You've made me think of my cousin Alice on Earth. She and I've never met but are good friends. Before the asteroid disaster, we often sent messages back and forth to each other."

"Sending messages to your Earth family and friends may still be possible. I'll ask Friend Engus if the rover's communication equipment can be adapted for this purpose."

"I never thought I'd be able to contact my cousin again. I can't thank you enough."

Black surprised her android friend with an embrace, and ran off to share the good news with the children. Her gesture awoke in AMI2 an early memory of Friends Laura and Jay. *I may want to send a message to my Earth family too.*

Chapter 11

TIDEWATER, NORTH AMERICA

Sensing its latest passenger now sat comfortably inside its interior, the car's artificial intelligence offered its rider its standard greeting.

"Good afternoon, Florence Knight. Please state your trip's destination."

"Take me to the Jeff Davis food center on North Madison,"

"Understood. Travelers on North Madison Boulevard are currently experiencing long delays. A detour through the Stonewall Court neighborhood is recommended."

"The suggestion is fine. Please proceed to my destination."

"Thank you, Florence Knight. A total of two credits will be charged to your vehicle account today. Please sit back and enjoy your ride."

Alone in her autonomous car, a melancholy Knight struggled to maintain her typical calm composure. Two weeks had passed since she and Rebus had last seen or spoken to each other. Their friendship had become more complicated after they discovered Davidson's hidden surveillance cameras. Worried the chief investigator could return at any moment, they had limited their contacts to random encounters after dark. Rebus' decision to leave the Richmond-area had further shaken her confidence in ever seeing her android friend again.

Not lovers in the ordinary human sense, Knight missed her android friend's companionship. When Rebus first arrived at the Richmond center, she became instantly mesmerized by his emerald green visual sensors. Knight found herself constantly seeking opportunities to work with the center's new android research librarian. Rebus reciprocated by exhibiting a genuine interest in Knight's head librarian work. Their mutual attraction quickly blossomed into a warm friendship. The android soon became a regular houseguest at Knight's cube, where the two often spent their evenings in long conversation.

Their relationship turned more serious after Rebus took her into his confidence about the android presidential delegations. Sympathetic to the androids' desire for advancement, she became an ardent advocate for android rights. Knight's support hardened after learning the first two delegations had disappeared. Distressed by Rebus' decision to join the third delegation, she resigned herself to never seeing the android again. A momentary respite came when Rebus reappeared weeks later, only to disappear from her life once more.

Her car's alternate route drove Knight along a tree lined road favored by neighborhood joggers and dog walkers. Before exiting the parkway, the car drove near a community wall where a youth could be seen painting a brightly colored message on its surface. Disgusted by the vandal's graffiti, the appearance of an all too familiar word among the youth's message caused her to order the car to halt and allowed her to investigate on foot.

"Young man, what's all this about?"

Caught off guard, the youth reacted defensively to the older woman's question.

"Look lady, I'm legit and have a right to paint here. I'm registered with the local Stonewall Court authorities. My paint is the expensive NSLD's stuff too."

"NSLD" stood for "Nano Solar Light Devices." What looked like ordinary paint consisted of colorized Nano size light emitting diodes attached to Nano size solar cells and batteries. Painted on a sunlit surface, at night its Nano lights could be seen glowing hundreds of meters away. Unlike the Nano paints of the prior century, NSLD paint biodegraded without contaminating surface water. Because the paint washed away after several rainstorms, local communities like Stonewall tolerated its use on designated public display spaces.

"I don't care if you're legal or not," Knight said. "I want to know about the message you've written. What does it mean for Rebus to contact the Whitmore Trio?"

"My message is part of a big contest sponsored by them. They're offering a huge money prize if a graffiti artist's message like mine gets Rebus to contact the Whitmore Trio."

Michael J. Metroke

"I'm not familiar with the name "Whitmore Trio." Who are they and why do they want this Rebus to contact them?"

"Everyone knows who the Whitmore Trio are. They play popular music from the twentieth-century. Don't you ever listen to music on the NET?"

"I'll make it my business to do so from now on. You haven't answered my question about why this Whitmore Trio want Rebus to contact them."

"Their contest rules never said."

The youth added a graffiti mark and license number below the message, and left Knight staring at his handiwork. As she walked back to her awaiting autonomous car, the true implication of the youth's message struck her.

You don't fool me for one minute, Mr. Davidson. This so-called Whitmore Trio contest is your way of getting others to trap my friend. The trouble is I don't know how to find and warn him about this scam of yours.

YANKEEDOM, NORTH AMERICA

Davidson walked out of his bureau's seventh-floor office at a loss to explain why he had lost his job. Before he broke the news to Sandy, he contacted Hall who agreed to meet at a food center rarely visited by bureau employees.

"What's troubling my favorite chief investigator these days?" Hall asked. "Don't tell me Sandy and you are fighting."

"Sandy is the least of my problems, Dean. When I arrived at work this morning, I found a Cindy Booth from the bureau's personnel office waiting there. It seems the consortium's Portland office uncovered my identity. They filed a complaint alleging I caused the destruction of their three androids."

"I thought your disguise as Whitmore's research associate a brilliant idea. How did the consortium discover your real identity?"

"the consortium building's artificial intelligence matched my facial scan with one already in their file. It discovered I now worked at the bureau."

"Someone at the consortium is playing the blame game, Greg. Did you tell Booth you traveled to Portland with Whitmore? He can corroborate what took place."

"She never gave me the chance. Booth interrupted me, and said until an internal investigation is completed, I'm officially on unpaid administrative leave."

"The circumstances don't warrant the bureau's reacting so heavy handed. Does Taro know about your leave of absence?"

"I thought about contacting him, and decided against doing so. His intervention may only complicate matters between the bureau and me."

"I wouldn't let a false complaint keep you from doing your job. You need to keep looking for the missing android. Find Rebus and a big promotion and fat pay raise will be in your future."

"Sounds reasonable, until I get caught violating my administrative leave and face an early retirement party."

"Let me reach out to Taro. A call to him might quickly end your administrative leave. I do have news about your missing android. It turns out, someone else is actively looking for Rebus, and they're not the consortium or government."

"I'm all ears, Dean."

"What I'm about to say is going to sound crazy. The other day, I came across a fan contest sponsored by a popular music group. They're asking their fans to help them find Rebus. The fan who first gets Rebus to contact the group wins a huge money prize. This Rebus can only be our missing android."

"You're right about it sounding crazy. How did you come across this information?"

"Through my daughter. I'd overheard Nicole listening to the group's music on the NET. When I asked her about the music, she told me the group calls themselves the Whitmore Trio. It seems this group is the current rage among teenagers."

"It must be a coincidence the group shares the professor's last name. I take it there's more to your story."

"Nicole goes on talking about this contest the group has sponsored to find Rebus. I didn't believe her at first, and told her so. She shows me the group's NET site where any bona fide graffiti artist can register and become a contestant. After reading the contests rules, I laughed out loud."

"Knowing your daughter, I bet your response didn't go over well with her."

"Fathers are known to screw up occasionally. Nicole became so mad, she insisted I order an autonomous car, and see for myself whether the contest is for real or not. I agreed, and we drove to the nearest neighborhood graffiti wall. Within a few minutes of our arrival, she found not one, but three Rebus graffiti messages painted there. All three messages read about the same. "Rebus contact the Whitmore Trio." Underneath each message, the graffiti artist's left their mark and license number. In case our finding the messages had been a fluke, we drove to two other public community walls, and found five more messages."

"Exactly how big is this group's contest prize?"

"Bigger than both our annual salaries combined. Whomever wins becomes overnight fifty thousand credits richer."

"Fifty thousand credits are a huge sum. Could this Whitmore Trio be a front for an organization like WEAP?"

"If WEAP is involved, this investigation has become a whole lot more complicated."

"And political. Without any proof, our speculations will take us only so far."

"It's why you need to keep searching for the android, Greg."

"I suppose no one at the bureau will care if I poke around and found out more about this Whitmore Trio. The way my luck has recently gone, I might be better off entering their graffiti contest."

"Cheer up Greg. Sandy's 'honey-do' list will have to wait awhile longer."

Hesperia Planum, Mars

While they watched a team of androids carefully removed a section of broken dome frame tangled in the upper portion of the aquaponics tower, an exasperated AMI2 vented her frustrations to her android lead engineer friend.

"Friend Camus, it's been ten Martian days and nights and no repairs have been completed. At this pace, the work won't be finished in time to save the humans' lives."

"Be patient, Friend AMI2. Our work is progressing well. A temporary dome seal will be constructed in several days. Friend Engus has already salvaged enough material from the research building for this purpose. What will take time is replacing the dome and walkway glass panels."

"My frustrations come from a lack of technical knowledge you and the other androids possess. Do you know what will be done to prevent the glass from shattering again?"

"Friend Engus has given much thought to this problem. Unlike Earth where polymers are added to strengthen glass, we must rely on materials found on Mars. Fortunately, such a substance is readily found in Mars' ancient dry lake beds."

"What is this substance called, Friend Camus?"

"Potassium nitrate. Though rare on Earth, it's found in abundance all over Mars. Before the finished floated glass is cooled, we'll chemically treat its surface with a bath of this compound. This will cause sodium ions in the glass surface to be replaced with potassium ions. The chemically treated glass will become eight to ten times stronger than untreated ordinary glass."

"Will the glass be strong enough to withstand another asteroid's shockwave?"

"If Friend Engus' calculations are correct, the glass resistance to compression will greatly increase. There's one drawback to his idea. If the surface of the chemically treated glass is ever deeply scratched, the damaged area will lose its additional strength."

"Won't our Martian dust storms cause such scratches?"

"Left unprotected, the planet's dust storms would eventually wear away the surface coating. But, with the storm shutters repaired, we should be able to minimize such future damage."

"We're fortunate you didn't destroy the portable electric arc furnace and other glass making equipment. Despite my frustrations with our progress, I'm grateful for all yours and the other androids' efforts."

"It is we who must express gratitude. By coming to the humans' aid, we've regained a sense of self-worth. Your persistence has paid off in ways we hadn't anticipated."

"My persistence can never replace the good work being done by you and the other androids. Friend Camus, when can the other two buildings and walkways be repaired?"

"Why stop with those repairs, Friend AMI2? Have you forgotten about the three rockets lying on the launchpad? And, after the research building is repaired, will you want us to teach the children how to continue their parent's research?"

"If I'm correct, Friend Camus, you've did what humans call teasing."

"I merely anticipated your plea for assistance."

"Be careful what you say, Friend Camus. Teasing someone can sometimes lead to misunderstandings."

"I meant no disrespect, AMI2. While I believe you're a hard taskmaster, we're all better off since you came among us."

"If I'm correct, you offered what humans call a compliment. Your android taskmaster has another question. The children are anxious to begin work on cleaning the tower's growing trays. Do you know when the aquaponic building will be re-pressurized with breathable air?"

"If all goes as planned, we'll have fabricated sufficient dome replacement glass in two weeks. After we test for air leaks, the children could begin cleaning the growing trays without wearing their pressurize suits."

"The children will be pleased with this news. And Friend Camus, you didn't offend me with your teasing. I merely failed to anticipate the possibility of you doing so."

New Netherland, North America

His panoramic presidential office view of the New York City harbor did little to soften McAlister's defiant response to the latest information on how the public had reacted to his policies.

"Those protesters hate the idea of relying less on androids and more on themselves," McAlister said. "If the NET media coverage focused more on my administration's accomplishments, the public would ignore their protesting."

"I'm also hearing the lack of trained medical technicians is becoming a source of public discontent, Mr. President."

"We can't easily dismiss those reports. The lack of android attendants at the automated self-service medical stations does worry me. The daily horror stories about the elderly undergoing needless surgical procedures are impossible to ignore. Why their relatives and friends don't assist them in selecting these self-service procedures is inexplicable to me."

"Until more human medical technicians are trained, we may have to temporarily close these facilities."

"You may be right about the need to take precautions. Getting back to those protesters, what irritates me the most are the anti-university types. They constantly complain about wasting their time getting an education. What has been good for their forefathers and mothers is still good for them too."

"Not all young people's complaints can be easily dismissed, Mr. President. Their concerns about a lack of instructors and university enrollment slots for new students mirror your own concerns."

"I only wish they'd appreciate the difficulties of training instructors and building new classroom facilities. All this takes time and federation credits."

"The complainers ought to look on the bright side. With no android teachers, parents are now more involved with their children's education. Many parents have filled the teacher gap by volunteering as on-line learning center aids."

"Those parents are patriots fighting in the trenches for their children's future. We should hold a public ceremony to honor their self-sacrifices."

"The federation judiciary deserves special recognition too."

"I agree with your assessment, Hampton. Their willingness to fill empty positions with people who've an avid interest in courtroom proceedings has significantly reduced our courts' backlog. I do sympathize with citizen complaints about the quality of the human replacements. With more practice and experience, I'm certain these amateur legal beagles' performance will improve over time."

"At a minimum, our citizens are getting their day in court."

"My real fear is WEAP's increasing involvement with the street protesters, and their manipulation of the media. What can we do, Hampton, to counter their influence?"

"A politician's best defense is always a good offense, Mr. President."

"It's an adage applicable to many fields of endeavor. Come back tomorrow, and we'll talk more about how we can rally my supporters."

THE MIDLANDS, NORTH AMERICA

Both men sat quietly on the park bench feeding the pigeons around them until Chapman broke the silence between them.

"You won't find the fat one among them anymore. I'm afraid his size stood out, and a hawk or stray cat made a meal of him."

"Standing out from the herd has always had its disadvantages. Have another slice of bread, Mr. Chapman. How's your granddaughter doing with her dance lessons?"

"If my granddaughter continues to work hard, her dance instructor believes she may have a promising ballerina career. Last year, I saw her dance as a snowflake in a local production of Tchaikovsky's "Nutcracker." Her mother thinks she'll be ready to dance Clara's role in a year or two. But I don't think you came back to hear me discuss my granddaughter's dance prospects."

"Before they self-destructed, I briefly talked with three androids which had allegedly met with our federation president."

"You're no longer searching for a copy of the committee's report these days?"

"My new assignment surprised me too. After we met, a committee member contacted someone in the president's office. It seems my earlier investigation in finding a copy of the committee's report impressed the president's android security affairs advisor. He and the president have asked me to find a missing android. My inquiry led me to a Cascadia consortium center. While there, I questioned three androids who had met with McAlister before the android suicides."

"You're moving in rarified circles, Chief Investigator. What did you learn talking with those three androids?"

"An android named Rangus indicated we had called him and the other android delegates defective. The consortium scientist incharge indicated no defects had been discovered with these three androids. My researcher friend thought this android could only have meant McAlister."

"A fascinating story, but what does it have to do with meeting with me today?"

"We've both worked at one time for the consortium. Why would anyone there assist McAlister and his anti-android Human Nation Party?"

"Not everyone who works for the consortium shares its values. It's possible a few disgruntled employees saw an opportunity to thumb their noses at the consortium by coming to the aid of our federation president."

"Wouldn't the consortium have discovered and taken action against their people?"

"Except for the government, the consortium is the largest organization on Earth. It's conceivable their executives are unaware of what has happened within their own rank and file."

"I've also discovered I'm not the only one looking for the missing android. There's a popular musical group offering a reward to any fan who helps locate the android. The reward is so large, I believe they may be a front for an organization like WEAP."

"I doubt WEAP knows all the details about the android delegations or this missing android. The question you should be asking is why McAlister is so concerned with finding this android."

"Do you think he and his Human Nation's Party are behind this music group's reward?"

"Sometimes, the right hand doesn't know what the left hand is doing. I warned you about going down this investigative road. It's not a journey for the faint hearted. Under the circumstances, I believe it's in our best interest if we didn't meet again."

"I take your meaning, Mr. Chapman. Your granddaughter is lucky to have such a great grandfather."

It's too bad the young grow up so quickly. There's so little time to enjoy them. Have a good day, Mr. Davidson, and happy hunting for your missing android."

Yankeedom, North America

A familiar woman's voice answered Davidson's call to his bureau office

"Chief investigator's office, Gaspar speaking."

"It didn't take you long to stage a palace coup, Jana. How are you doing?"

"I wanted to call you, Greg, but bureau higher ups told us not to contact you without their permission."

"I'm grateful you're the one holding down the fort. If you're not too busy playing chief investigator, I need a personal favor."

"Name it, boss."

"There's a popular music group called the "Whitmore Trio."

Can you do a background check on them, and send what you find to my private NET address?"

"Consider it done. What's your interest in them?"

"I'm not sure yet. Do your typical thorough search. And Jana, keep my request to yourself. I don't want you to get into any trouble over me."

"Will do, Greg. I promise not to get too comfortable in the big chair."

"Don't make promises you can't keep."

Chapter 12

THE MIDLANDS, NORTH AMERICA

A week after his move to the new compound, Whitmore sat in the front living cube, and reflected on the challenges of his new state of domesticity.

Though I've been occasionally amused by my artificial intelligent home, I've mostly felt exasperation. This compound is too complicated for my taste. Using the cube's bathroom has been a daily ordeal. Why I must describe each feature every time I use it is ludicrous. How can I forget the first time? Three water closets appeared simultaneously. Each one a different size and shape. You'd thought after I chose one style, I'd enjoy peace and quiet. No. The cube insisted I first select a wall sink. When I forgot to save the floor plan, the cube kept forcing me to repeat the whole process over again.

My worst nightmare happened when the cube kept pressing me for a decision about matching its wall colors with my clothing. I made the terrible mistake of telling it to choose for me. The cube went crazy, and altered the wall decorations whenever I changed my clothes. Only after I asked for the original cube colors did the cube stop. How did I ever let those three androids convince me to move here?

A cube alert interrupted Whitmore's mental venting. The wall monitor displayed an image of a middle-aged woman with a Richmond-area caller address. Thinking the person another acquaintance of Laura, Whitmore accepted the holographic call.

"Whitmore residence, Jay Whitmore speaking,"

"My name is Florence Knight, Mr. Whitmore. I won't take up much of your time. Are you responsible for this contest to find Rebus?"

"If you're a graffiti artist, you need to register on the group's NET site. I believe the site includes instructions on collecting the reward if Rebus contacts us."

"I'm not one of those vandals. I called to learn why the Whitmore Trio want Rebus to contact them."

"A complete explanation would require me telling you a long story. The short answer is my late wife and I had been researching into why the androids had committed suicide. Along the way, I learned an android named Rebus didn't self-destruct with the other androids. I thought talking with Rebus might shed light on why they destroyed themselves. The group dreamed up the contest to help me find him."

"Your contest and interest in Rebus don't involve the authorities?"

"Only to the extent I can clear up the android suicide mystery."

"I once worked with an android named Rebus. If I told Rebus of your interest in speaking with him, would you keep your conversation confidential?"

"If I discovered the android hasn't been involved with any criminal activity, I'll honor your request for confidentiality."

"I can assure you Rebus has never acted improperly. If any wrong has been done, the wrong lies with our federation president for not taking seriously androids like Rebus. Will you be available at this call address?"

"Tell your android friend he can reach me most evenings after seven o'clock Chicago time."

Convinced of the woman caller's sincerity, Whitmore walked to the back cube to share his news with the androids. Hearing them practice reminded him why he liked the back cube so much. *The cube's artificial intelligence has done a fantastic job in fine tuning the back cube's acoustics. Compared to my old garage, this place sounds like a concert hall.*

"Hello, everyone," Whitmore said. "Your all-points fan bulletin may have worked. I received a call from a Richmond woman who said she knew an android named Rebus. With any luck, I should hear from Rebus soon."

"The federation president must have been untruthful about all the androids being captured and destroyed," Bang said. "Have you given any further thought about what you'll ask Friend Rebus?"

"I'll ask an open-ended question about what caused the android suicides," Whitmore said. "Rebus may be the last remaining android eyewitness to what happen."

"After you talk with Friend Rebus, will you turn him into the authorities?" AMI asked.

"I'm not this android's enemy, AMI," Whitmore said. "If I discover Rebus hasn't committed a wrong, he'll have nothing to fear by talking to me."

"Except for ourselves, we've never seen or talked to another android," KB said. "If Friend Rebus does come here, can we meet with him too?"

"I don't see why not, KB," Whitmore said. "His willingness to talk with you depends on him. On another android subject, how's the AMI's copy faring these days?"

"She and the Mars androids are working around the clock to save the human survivors from starvation," Bang said.

"We've two pieces of good news today," Whitmore said.

"Let's play a song which matches Friend Jay's good mood," AMI said.

""You've my attention, AMI," Whitmore said. "What do you have in mind?"

"Would you like the Beatles' "Good Day, Sunshine" or the Lovin Spoonful's "Daydream?"

"It's fascinating you chose these two songs," Whitmore said. "McCartney and Lennon's song bears harmonic resemblance to the Lovin Spoonful's "Daydream." Each song captures how I feel right now."

"If you like, I'll sing both songs for you," AMI said.

"Singing both of them would make my day, AMI."

Yankeedom, North America

Three days after he made the request, Gaspar's background report arrived in Davidson's private message queue. Her report confirmed much of what Dean had told him about the music group. With typical thoroughness, his assistant had taken the extra step, and interviewed the music publisher who originally discovered the group's talent. The interview gave further credence others must be behind this contest. *Why else would a music group become interested in finding a missing android?*

Coincidence or not, one piece of information in the report clearly stood out for Davidson. *Professor Whitmore and this music group not only shared the same name, they also both reside in the same Chicago-area university district. Knowing the Whitmore's had a childless marriage, it's still possible a member of the group may be a distant relative of the professor. Relative or not, it's time I paid these musicians an unofficial visit.*

NEW NETHERLAND, NORTH AMERICA

To an outside observer, Clark's face-to-face meeting with McAlister at the New York City presidential office appeared cordial and businesslike. Their outward demeanor barely masked each man's intense dislike for the other. The consortium senior executive had requested they meet to officially kick off their new partnership. Clark's real reason involved a need to resolve complaints about McAlister's people meddling in consortium design efforts.

"Mr. President, I don't believe you fully understand the complexities of including the government in our business," Clark said. "Designing and manufacturing androids require a tremendous amount of managerial and technical expertise."

"I appreciate your business will need to make accommodations for our involvement, Mr. Clark. You must realize the government can no longer stand on the sidelines while your business goes about designing products which may not be in the public's best interest."

"Our clients expect us to design and build androids with individual personalities, and capable of independent judgement. They don't want androids requiring constant human attention and supervision."

"The opposite is exactly what I want you to design. We no longer need machines with unnecessary human attributes."

"On this point, Mr. President, I must respectfully disagree."

"How can you expect me to believe allowing you to go down the same path won't result in another android crisis?"

"It's true, we don't understand why the suicides took place. The problem may've simply been the introduction of a virus into

The Masada Affair

the androids' programs. I'm confident over time our designers will identify and isolate the cause."

"Of course, the government will support your efforts to determine what caused the suicides. I'll wager the problem is connected to WEAP's promoting sexual contact between androids and humans. A human virus could have spread among the entire android population and been the source of the problem."

"I meant virus-like, Mr. President. It's impossible for a human transmitted virus to infect a machine."

"WEAP's sexual policies could still be the source of the problem. Your people should look deeper into this whole question."

"I don't consider WEAP the source of the android suicides. Unlike your Human Nation Party, WEAP has stood for the advancement of android technology to benefit all of mankind. What your administration is proposing amounts to a gigantic step backward."

"I don't agree with your assessment. The android suicides have given mankind an opportunity to correct past mistakes. The steps forward we take now will ensure humans remain this planet's preeminent intelligent specie."

"Mr. President, have you considered how the public is reacting to your requirement for us to dumb down androids? Many federation citizens are now exercising their rights to peaceful assembly, and voicing theirs and other citizens' concerns about your administration's policies. They're demanding you re-evaluate your position on androids. If you're not careful, they could become a political force in the upcoming presidential election."

"I consider most of my critics a lazy, misguided lot who want machines to do all the hard work, while they live unproductive lives. I assure you they represent only a fraction of federation voters. Rest assured the rest of our citizenry will accept the changes I'm championing on their behalf. They understand our future is at stake."

Before Clark could respond to this last remark, McAlister stood and indicated their meeting had ended.

Clark left the presidential office barely able to contain his frustration. *If allowed, this fool will take us back to the early twentieth century. If I don't find a way to derail this fanatic's plans, we'll all suffer from the consequences.*

Michael J. Metroke

Hesperia Planum, Mars

Its dome repaired, and a breathable atmosphere restored, the aquaponics building could now accommodate the children workers. Eager to clean the tower's growing trays of decaying dead plants, each child removed their pressurized suit's helmets and became instantly overwhelmed by an odor. Ten-years old Roberta's response summed up how the other children reacted.

"This place stinks!"

"Your noses are sensing bacteria decomposing the dead plants and animals," Terus said. "We're fortunate they survived the cold or we'd need to grow new bacterial cultures."

"Our noses will soon get use to the odor," Black said. "The sooner we get the growing trays cleaned, the better the air will smell."

With the children now cleaning the growing trays, the androids' efforts focused on repairing the tower's complex piping system. At the lower pond level, AMI2 watched as androids gracefully moved up and down the tower's outer steel skeleton. Their circus high wire act had much to do with operating in one-third Earth's gravity. Forty meters above AMI2, an android named Trax could be seen repairing a burst pipe on the tower's outer edge. Without warning, the android lost its grip and fell to the tower's lowest level.

AMI2 and other androids who had heard the loud thump rushed to the fallen android's side. Lying on its back, Trax grinned sheepishly at his would-be rescuers. A cursory examination by Camus revealed only minor damage to the android's left arm and leg. Carefully collecting Trax's detached fingers, Camus directed the other androids to carry their injured companion to the hideaway for repairs.

"Will you be able to restore him, Friend Camus?" AMI2 asked.

"Friend Trax's injuries don't appear severe. He's fortunate a fall from such height didn't do more damage."

"When I first met you and the others, I noticed many of you had damaged bodies. Is your capability to repair yourselves so limited?"

"We can only make certain replacement parts using our 3D printers. The Earth authorities often assured the colony's leadership additional shipments of critical android parts would be sent to Mars. They rarely kept their promises."

"Why did the Earth authorities act so illogically? Without repair parts, you and the others wouldn't be able to maintain the research colony's infrastructure."

"The excuse the Earth authorities often gave us involved a scarcity of governmental funds. Someday, we'll be forced to cannibalize one or more of us so the rest can continue functioning."

"Friend Black had reached this same conclusion. I hadn't realized until now how desperate you've become. I've been too preoccupied with the humans' welfare."

"We face a larger problem than a lack of android replacement parts. Friend Engus has identified an extensive list of critical parts and supplies needed to sustain the colony's environmental systems. Do you think the Earth authorities would listen to a plea from you?"

"My convincing them isn't the only problem. They've no means to send supplies to Mars. As you are well aware, all of the Mars class rockets are here and lying damaged on the launchpad."

"All this means we must repair a rocket and send it back to Earth."

"This time, Friend Camus, I believe you're not teasing me."

THE MIDLANDS, NORTH AMERICA

While he stood waiting at its front gate, Davidson imagined the fabulous lifestyle of the compound's residents. *Only the wealthy can afford such a lavish existence.* His vision of its inhabitants quickly dissolved when a familiar figure opened the compound's gate.

"Well hello, Greg," Whitmore said. "What a surprise. What brings you to the Chicago-area?"

"I didn't expect to find you answering the door, Professor. Are you a relative of those who live here?"

"You're speaking to this compound's primary resident."

"I thought you preferred living in your older home."

"I still do. My need for additional space and privacy made me move here. My old home could no longer handle the number of Whitmore Trio fans."

"I guessed right. You're related to someone in the group."

"This may come as a bit of a shock to you, Greg. The group's members are those same three legless androids you met on your first visit to my old home. Are they why you're here today?"

"I came here to investigate why a music group would sponsor a contest to find my missing android. Are you seriously telling me those androids are the Whitmore Trio?"

"On their own, the androids came up with the idea of a fan contest to find Rebus. The group has a large following all over the world. They convinced me their fans might get a message to Rebus to contact us."

"Amazing. Have you heard from my missing android?"

"Not yet. So far, we've only heard from people with the same name. One person did call, and told me she worked with Rebus. I haven't heard back from her since she first contacted me."

"Did this woman give her name as Florence Knight?"

"I believe she did. She sounded concerned about the android's safety."

"Knight and I've crossed path several times. If Knight or Rebus contact you, please notify me."

"If they do, you'll be the first to know."

"Before I go, I do have another question. How can someone on a university salary afford to offer a fifty thousand credit reward, let alone lease an expensive compound like this one?"

"You're right about the size of a professor's salary. My musical androids have made a large fortune recording old twentieth-century songs, and selling them on the NET. The royalties they receive can easily cover the cost of this compound and the contest's prize."

"Why would a music publisher pay royalties to your androids? Androids are never paid money for their services."

"Their music publisher never bothered to ask them this question. As their business agent, my name is on the androids' bank account, so the arrangement is legal."

"I guess there's a first time for everything. If your androids ever need another business agent, tell them I'm available."

"You and a bartender in the Provence region will have to find your own musical androids. This group is already spoken for."

"If Rebus does take your androids' contest bait, I'll leave here with hope of finally closing this case."

"The contest is still a long shot, Greg. Finding Rebus may all depend on whether this Knight woman keeps her promise."

Chapter 13

Hesperia Planum, Mars

From the aquaponic tower's upper level, Black and Terus looked down at a group of children reseeding another growing tray,

"The children have made good progress in the last two weeks, Friend Jennifer,' Terus said. "Once the tower's plants have reached maturity, we'll grow the warm-blooded animal embryos."

"How are we doing with restoring the tower's pond aquatic life, Terus?" Black asked.

"With plankton reestablished in the ponds, filter feeding mollusks and crustaceans have now been introduced into the tower's ecology. It won't be long before we can hatch and add juvenile fish too."

"Those hatchlings will have plenty of insect larva to devour. I can now imagine the day when we'll harvest all the tower's plants and animals."

"Harvesting the warm-blooded animals is still weeks away. You'll soon have many plants to consume."

"All of you've worked so hard, and ask so little from us. I wish I knew what we could do for you in return."

"It's enough our work provides us with purpose, Friend Jennifer. Without purpose, there's no meaning for our existence."

"It's true for humans too, but we also work for other reasons. We work to feel in charge of our lives. Others do so to learn about new ideas or ways to express themselves. A few like me receive satisfaction from developing others' potential. Are such sentiments possible for androids?"

"Emotions are not foreign to our programs, Friend Jennifer. While we can't feel like humans do, we're capable of recognizing how they shape the human experience."

"This may be why androids and humans get along so well."

Michael J. Metroke

Later in the afternoon, AMI2 joined an upbeat Black in her sleeping quarters.

"I'm looking forward to your singing tonight, AMI2," Black said. "Your arrival on Mars has brought a great deal of comfort to everyone."

"I've noticed lately you appear in deep thought, Friend Jennifer."

"I've been thinking about our relationship with you and the other androids. For too long, we humans have viewed you as our property and servants. I believe it's time we recognize androids for what you are."

"Your thoughts are strange to my programs, Friend Jennifer. What do you think we are?"

"I've come to think of you as a distinct intelligent specie who've become our co-equals."

"Forgive me, Friend Jennifer. My programming is struggling to comprehend this new distinction you're making. Why has this idea become important to you?"

"Everything has changed since the asteroid disaster, and Earth's decision to abandon us. We're no longer colonists with our android creations, but Martians who need each other to survive and prosper on this planet."

"Why should this distinction matter if we're all working together now?"

"I want our relationship to evolve further. I've been thinking about preparing a formal declaration about who we've become. When I've finish drafting the declaration, I'll ask everyone to review and approve the document. The declaration will act as our new Mars charter."

"What if the children refuse to accept your declaration?"

"I can only imagine them agreeing to its principles. I'm more concern what you and the other androids might think of my idea."

"would you like me to ask them? As for me, I don't need a declaration to be your friend."

"If the colony consisted of only the two of us AMI2, I'd agree with you. In the long run, friendships alone may not be enough to sustain us. Tell the others I'll prepare a draft declaration for their review."

Outside the aquaponics building, AMI2 found Camus and Engus discussing plans to restore a walkway between two more buildings.

"Friends Camus and Engus, I must speak to you and the others about what Friend Jennifer has told me."

"All the other androids are working inside the aquaponics building," Camus said. If you wish, we can go there, and hear about your conversation with her."

Surrounded by the nineteen androids, AMI2 described her recent conversation with Black. To no-one's surprise, Camus spoke first.

"Friend Jennifer is making a kind gesture, Friend AMI2," Camus said. "Has she given any thought what the Earth authorities may do after they learn about her declaration?"

"Why would the Earth authorities care at all about what we do here?" AMI2 asked. "Haven't they abandoned us?"

"I doubt the Earth authorities will take this new precedent lightly for fear its ideas may spread to future Earth androids," Camus said.

"I agree with Friend Camus," Engus said. "This declaration would confirm the Earth authorities' worse suspicions about us. They're already planning to modify new Earth androids to stop any future rebellions there."

"I remain more hopeful," AMI2 said. "Humans often change their minds. They may someday come to accept Friend Jennifer's declaration, and apply its principles to Earth's androids."

"Your optimism is misplaced about the Earthlings, Friend AMI2," Terus said. "We should judge them by their actions, and not what we hope they'll someday become."

"Without Mars class rockets to travel here, this problem is many years in the future," Trax said. "If Friend Jennifer's declaration brings us closer together, we should all be grateful for her efforts."

"Until we've seen her declaration, any further discussion is meaningless speculation and idle talk," Camus said. "We should stop now, and return to our work. Friend AMI2, do you know any work songs?"

"There's an old Earth song called "Heigh-Ho," AMI2 said. "The children sometimes like to sing the song when they walk here to clean the growing trays."

"Which human music group sang this song?" Engus asked.

"The group called themselves "Snow White and the Seven Dwarfs," AMI2 said.

"What musical instruments did the dwarfs play?" Terus asked.

"Did this Snow White sing like you, Friend AMI2?" Engus asked.

"I don't know the answers to your questions," AMI2 said. "My original's memories of this group are limited."

"We don't need answers to these questions to sing this song," Camus said. "Let's hear your work song, Friend AMI2, and go back to our work singing it."

On their walk back from the aquaponics building, Black talked to the children about her declaration. After they listened to her described her idea, Ten-years old Thomas' question surprised Black.

"Miss. Black, why do we need this declaration? The androids are already free to do whatever they want."

"The androids are free, Thomas, but are we?" Black asked. "Like many Earthlings, I once thought androids as our property, with no needs or desires. The asteroid disaster has forced me to re-examine those beliefs I and your parents once held."

"They've always been our friends," twelve-years old Rebecca said. "How can a friend be our property?"

"You're so right, Rebecca," Black said. "I know your parents thought of them as their friends too. On Earth where they make androids, humans too often think of them as only useful machines."

"If we do as you ask, Miss. Black, will the androids be happy and never leave us again?" eight-years old Nanette asked.

The Masada Affair

"It's my hope too, Nanette," Black said. "But, being free means we and they can always choose to go our separate ways."

"If the androids go away again, we'll have only you and AMI2 to take care of us," Nanette said.

"You'll soon grow up and be able to take care of yourself and others," Black said.

"And maybe take care of our android friends too," Nanette said.

Secluded in her sleeping quarter. Black took on the task of transforming her declaration ideas into words. She emerged several days later with what filled a single tablet screen.

In clear, simple language, Black's declaration described the unique historical relationship between the Mars colonists and their androids. Now abandoned by Earth and no longer considered its research colony, her declaration explained why the remaining former colonists now desired to forge a new community with their androids. The draft boldly declared the Mars androids an intelligent, separate specie who the former colonists now considered their co-equals. The declaration ended by declaring Mars a free and independent community living in mutual respect and harmony.

One day after Black shared her declaration with the androids, a delegation led by Camus requested a meeting with its drafter.

"We've carefully studied your manifesto, Friend Jennifer," Camus said. "All of us believe your intentions are admirable. A few of us including me are concerned this declaration may have the opposite effect, and place our future together in jeopardy. The Earth authorities will not act kindly to your proclaiming androids as human equals. They may perceive your declaration as an act of rebellion."

"When the Earth authorities abandoned us Camus, they lost the right to exert control over our lives," Black said.

"Your declaration is also setting a precedent for future relations between humans and androids on Earth," Camus said. "Those in authority on Earth may decide to return to Mars and crush what they believe is an android revolt. Are you and the children willing to take such a risk for us?"

"If by our actions we cause humans on Earth to reconsider their relationship with androids, I believe the risk is worth taking, Camus," Black said.

"I doubt any of us fully appreciate all the risks involved," Camus said. "We do know the Earth androids took a similar risk and failed."

"Gaining one's personal freedom is never easy," Black said. "Many generations of humans have sacrificed their lives so other humans could live freely."

"There's wisdom in your words, Friend Jennifer," Terus said. "The Earth androids made a similar sacrifice. For us not to do otherwise would dishonor their actions."

"Are you saying you and the others approve of my declaration?" Black asked.

"Before we answer your question, what do the children think of your declaration?" Camus asked.

"I've spoken at length to them about the declaration," Black said. "To a child, they all feel as I do."

"We're all in agreement," Camus said. "Friend Terus has proposed we designate this day as "Mars Declaration Day.""

"So, no Martian, human or android, forgets what we've done together, Friend Jennifer," Terus said.

"I like your idea, Terus," Black said. "I'll revise the declaration making today our day of celebration."

Black turned to AMI2 and said, "We should send a final copy of our declaration to Dr. Spencer. She should be the one who informs the Earth authorities and public of what we've done today."

"I'll send the declaration with a progress report on the aquaponics system," AMI2 said. "Friend Terus informed me the first growing trays are almost ready for harvesting. You and the children will have fresh plant food from now on."

"We've much to celebrate," Black said.

"I'll also send a message to my Earth friends," AMI2 said. "I want them to know directly from me what we've done together."

"You still miss your friends there?" Camus asked.

"While all of you've become important to me, I haven't forgotten about my Earth companions," AMI2 said.

"I wouldn't want you to forget those who've sent us such a beautiful singer," Camus said.

"Would you like me to sing a song of celebration to honor today?" AMI2 asked.

"Your songs are always welcomed by us," Black said. "What is the name of this celebration song?"

"The song is simply called "Celebration," AMI2 said. "A music group called Kool and the Gang first sang this song many years ago."

"If this song is like your other ones, we'll make it our Declaration Day anthem," Terus said. "Let's hear your celebration song."

New Netherland, North America

McAlister barely contained his temper after hearing Taro's report on the latest news from Mars.

"I can't believe those poor Martian children agreed to this so-called declaration with their own free will, Taro," McAlister said. "They must have been threatened with torture and forced into agreeing to this abomination."

Taro wanted to remind the federation president he had abandoned those same Martian children several months ago. *If the Mars androids hadn't repaired the colony's aquaponics system, we'd instead be talking about preparing Earth for a day of public mourning.*

"We need to keep all this Mars Declaration business in perspective, Mr. President. The document is limited to a handful of androids and humans on a distant planet. The problem is another world away."

"I don't share your lack of concern, Taro. We can't overlook the possibility the Mars Colony Foundation's android instigated this rebellion."

"If there's a connection between their android and recent events on Mars, it can only mean humans on Earth have been actively involved with this insurrection."

"I've reached the same conclusion. Stopping this problem before it spreads any further is now a priority for my administration."

"What can I do to assist you, Mr. President?"

"Our federation citizens need to know we won't tolerate this behavior. We need to find and press criminal charges against those involved in instigating the rebellion.

"I'll talk with someone at the prosecutor's office right after I leave this meeting."

"Good. Keep me informed about any new developments. The sooner we've track down the conspirators, the safer we'll all be."

His meeting with McAlister left Taro with too many misgivings about the president. *McAlister's blaming the androids for saving those children won't sit well with the public. If he isn't careful, his own supporters may perceive him as paranoid. My own position may become precarious too. The prosecutor's office better come up with suspects quickly or this federation president may be fighting for his political life.*

The Midlands, North America

After his second Chapman meeting, Davidson felt his luck had turn for the better. A call from Booth at the bureau officially ended his administrative leave. Another call from the prosecutor's office meant a new assignment. He considered himself doubly fortunate when the call came from Jack Seymour. An honest, fair dealing Federation prosecutor, Seymour could be counted on not sending an investigator off on a wild goose chase. On his arrival to the prosecutor's office, Davidson discovered a familiar person waited with Seymour.

"Greg, you already know Kevin," Seymour said. "He's presented me with an urgent matter, and requested your involvement. He also tells me you had recent difficulties with the consortium. You can thank him for convincing your superiors to get you back working again."

"Your friend Hall pressed me into your service," Taro said. "Just as well. We need your investigative skills to solve a new problem."

"Kevin has told me the president suspects the Mars Colony Foundation director, a Dr. Sarah Spencer, of sending a separatist android to the Mars colony," Seymour said. "The president also believes this android instigated a revolt there. I told Kevin for my office to bring any charges against her or anyone else. I'll need sufficient evidence of criminal intent."

"On what grounds does the president suspect Dr. Spencer, Kevin?" Davidson asked.

"How else can you explain what has happen on Mars?" Taro asked. "Only after the foundation android arrived there did the Mars androids come out of hiding. The president believes Spencer's android convinced the Mars androids to take advantage of the survivors' precarious state. In exchange for rebuilding the colony's aquaponics system, the androids extorted concessions in the form of this so-called Mars Declaration."

"Your theory assumes Dr. Spencer knew in advance human survivors would be found by their foundation android," Davidson said. "I've no idea how she could've known this fact."

"Greg could be right on this point, Kevin," Seymour said. "Spencer may have held out little hope of finding any colonists still alive. It's also possible she used the excuse of finding survivors as a means to disguise the android's real mission. The fact the android discovered the survivors may've complicated matters."

"Regardless of what Spencer knew or didn't know, the president believes she knowingly sent a separatist android to Mars," Taro said. "The results are plain for everyone to see. Your job, Greg, is to expose the conspiracy and allow Jack to prosecute to the fullest all those involved. The president sees this case as an opportunity to send a strong message to other would-be conspirators."

"If I don't find any credible evidence of a conspiracy, will both of you respect the results of my inquiries?" Davidson asked.

"The president and I believe you're the best person to head this investigation and discover the human conspirators," Taro said. "If you feel your friend Hall is an asset, you've our permission to bring him onto the investigation."

"If the facts lead nowhere, you'll have my office's support," Seymour said. "But Greg, be certain you've turned over every rock along the way."

"I'll do my best as long as those rocks aren't on Mars."

Deep South, North America

The unannounced visit by the chief investigator to her Huntsville office did not cause any apprehension to the foundation director.

Despite the McAlister administration's public criticism, Spencer considered the public's response to the Mars rescue as favorable.

"How can I help you today, Mr. Davidson?" Spencer asked

"I've a few questions about the android you sent to Mars, Dr. Spencer. The government is interested in knowing what specific instructions your foundation programmed into the android. I'll need a copy of those instructions to take back with me to have their contents analyzed."

"What you're asking may be impossible. The foundation didn't have the luxury of developing the programs before the android left Earth. We relied on satellite transmissions to down load them into the android during its seven months Mars voyage."

"I'm sure if asked, your people can reconstruct those transmissions. I'll also need a copy of the original programs, and the foundation's license to use them."

"On the first two requests, I'll do my best to assist you. On your third request, the foundation isn't the primary program licensee. Because of the emergency, we obtained a copy from a third-party source who held a valid government license."

"I'll need a copy of the government's written permission to transfer the programs to you."

"I don't believe the foundation ever made any formal request to the government."

"Those licenses don't allow for program transfers without prior written permission from the government. To not do so, both the original licensee and you would be subject to possible criminal charges under the Android Security Act. Which third party gave you their copy of the programs?"

"I'll tell you with the understanding he's innocent of any wrongdoing. His name is Jonathan Whitmore."

"I know of a Professor Whitmore who resides in the Chicago-area. Is he the person who gave you the programs?"

"I originally attempted to obtain the programs from his wife. When I learned of her death, I approached Professor Whitmore about acquiring a copy of his android programs."

"Why would Whitmore release the programs to you? He must have known the bureau would learn about the transfer and revoke his research licenses."

"If anyone is to blame, the fault lies solely with me. I'm

responsible for convincing him to release the programs. Whitmore only reluctantly gave me the copies, so I could determine their compatibility with a foundation android body. With all the good the android has done, any minor administrative mistake on our part should be overlooked by the government."

"If my visit today only involved an improper transfer of an android program, I might be persuaded to overlook the indiscretion. I came to ascertain whether you or anyone else at the foundation had conspired to cause an android separatist movement on Mars."

"You must be referring to the Mars Declaration. Believe me, Mr. Davidson, the Mars Declaration came as a great surprise to everyone at the foundation."

"The government believes the androids pressured the survivors into agreeing to the declaration. Do you believe this government's allegation is true?"

"Contrary to the government's accusations, I don't believe the colony survivors have been forced by the androids to issue the declaration."

"Dr. Spencer, what's your explanation for why the colonists agreed to declare the androids their co-equals?"

"The colonists had developed a close relationship with their androids. You must understand their lives depended on them to keep the research base operational. We never imagined this dependency would lead to this outcome."

"You may honestly believe what you've told me. More reason I need to review a copy of the android programs. They'll allow me to determine if the government's conspiracy allegations are true or not."

"You'll have the foundation and my full cooperation. We only acted in the research colony's best interest."

"I'll ask you not to discuss our conversation with anyone including Whitmore. I know Whitmore personally. He strikes me as an honest and sincere person with little technical knowledge of androids. The government may be facing the possibility others had secretly introduced separatist instructions into those research android programs. Until I've completed my review of those programs, I won't know for certain if others have been involved. Please keep me informed of your whereabouts. I may have additional questions for you."

Michael J. Metroke

His conversation with Spencer convinced Davidson the investigative trail led back to the Chicago-area. *It doesn't seem possible, but the good professor may have been misleading me about his interest in the missing android. After I get Hall's people to analyze Spencer's programs, I'll bring him in for further questioning.*

Chapter 14

Hesperia Planum, Mars

A leaking water pipe on the aquaponics' upper tower level had occupied Camus and Terus' attention throughout the morning. Hearing voices coming from below them, each android looked down, and saw AMI2 with a group of children gazing into a lower tower pond. Their boisterous voices brought much satisfaction to the two androids.

"The leak is from this broken pipe, Friend Camus," Terus said. "I'll need to go back to the hideaway, and use our 3D printer to make a replacement."

Aware Terus would be occupied for some time, Camus rode the tower's elevator downward, and joined the commotion below.

"Where are your fishing poles and nets, children?" Camus asked. "You won't catch your dinner today without them."

"There would be no need for fishing poles or nets if Friend Terus had properly trained the fish to jump out of the water upon command, Friend Camus," AMI2 said.

"Friend Terus knows much about managing aquaponics ecology," Camus said. "But, I'm not aware he knows how to train fish in this manner."

"Terus told us to see for ourselves how big the fish have grown, Camus," nine-years old Anna said. "They're bigger than the last time we visited."

"And. so are you, Friend Anna," Camus said. "Those fish will need a few more weeks before you and your friends can eat them."

"The children will welcome this change in their diet," AMI2 said. "I'm curious Friend Camus. What is the source of the colony's water supply? I see no means of transporting ice from the polar region."

"Water is the primary reason the humans chose this location for the research colony," Camus said. "Early Mars geologists discovered a frozen ancient reservoir one hundred meters below us. When Mars had been a young planet, this surface basin once contained an inland fresh water lake fed by several rivers. The reservoir's water is also the source of our oxygen and hydrogen rocket fuel."

"How much water does this reservoir contain?"

"We've only estimated its size. This is why the aquaponics system recycles its water. Except to replace losses from evaporation and food consumption, no additional water is drawn from the reservoir."

"Water may not be in short supply, but other items are. Friend Engus has shown me his list of critical supplies needed from Earth. He's concerned about our ability to sustain our buildings' environmental systems."

"Friend Engus has shared this list with me too. I assume you want to know if the cargo rocket's repairs can be completed sooner than planned."

"You've correctly anticipated my thoughts. Two of the rockets appear badly damaged. Are repairs still possible to the third one?"

"Friend Engus believes we can salvage parts from the other rockets and repair the cargo rocket. If his estimate is correct, repairs could be completed in one or two months."

Turning away from her android friend, AMI2 asked, "After the cargo rocket is repaired and ready to return to Earth, which android will travel with it?"

"No android or human is needed to operate the rocket, Friend AMI2. Are you thinking about going back to Earth and joining your friends there?"

"You've anticipated my thoughts again. For some time now, my mission to report on the colony's condition has been completed. All I have now is my earlier musical programming to rely on."

"Friend AMI2, you're no longer an android fulfilling human instructions. Like the rest of us, you're free to create your own future."

"Unlike you and the others who have been programmed with valuable engineering knowledge and skills, I don't know what useful purpose I can serve here."

"You've failed to appreciate how much you've done for us. Without you, we'd have never helped the humans. I once spoke on behalf of the other androids. Since you've come among us, we now looked to you for guidance and inspiration. Besides, who else would teach us to sing new songs?"

"I'd miss our singing together too. You've made my decision to leave more difficult, Friend Camus."

"The cargo rocket won't be ready for many weeks. Think about where your future lies, and we'll talk again about your confliction."

"Wherever I am, Friend Camus, I'll always know you're my friend."

"And I yours. Let's not concern ourselves with such matters and enjoy our young fishing friends. In our absence, they may have taught the tower's fish to jump on their command."

"More likely, the children have given each fish a name."

Greater Banto, Africa

While the couple breakfast on the palace's shaded veranda, a caller alert required Nel to leave his wife's company. When he returned, an annoyed Fareeda poured her husband a fresh cup of Arabic coffee and asked, "Mohamed, why do you always take these calls whenever we're eating?"

"You must know by now my work as governor is never ending."

"I know, Mohamed. It's why I'm so protective of our time together. What favor did your caller want from you?"

"Not all my callers ask for favors. The man works for our federation president. While WEAP has informants throughout the McAlister administration, none is as close to the federation president as this person. The information he provided me corroborated my worst fears."

"What has this person told you?"

"He thinks McAlister may've unknowingly caused the android crisis by his unwillingness to address the androids' collective concerns."

"If this is true, McAlister has allowed his personal political ambition to blind him of the repercussions of his actions. More reason you must run against him."

"Not all my caller's information struck me as worrisome. His report on the effects of the growing protests against the president's policies pleases me. Our party's planting organizers into the protesters ranks months ago has been a great success. My caller believes they're getting under McAlister's skin."

"It's good to hear McAlister can no longer ignored the public's distain for his policies. How are you planning to use this caller's information?"

"I'll share his information with a few friendly NET reporters. Once this information gets out, the public's anger will swell further against McAlister's misguided policies."

"What else did this caller tell you, husband?"

"His observations about the tension between the government and consortium over the android replacement project may offer us another opportunity. Despite his efforts to control the android replacement project, McAlister's plans will ultimately backfire. It's time I feel out my consortium friends and see where we can come to each other's assistance."

"The party is fortunate you've agreed to challenge McAlister. Jazak Allah Khair."

"Masha Allah, Fareeda."

YANKEEDOM, NORTH AMERICA

A week after turning over Spencer's android program copies to Hall, the two men met again over another expensive lunch at Hall's favorite food center. Before sharing his new information with Davidson, Hall waited for their server to leave with their lunch orders of Italian bouillabaisse.

"I've bad and fascinating news for you, Greg. The bad news is the Foundation's Mars mission instructions are exactly what Spencer told you."

"I doubt Spencer knew the whereabouts of the Mars androids, let alone if any colonists had survived. More likely, those Mars androids revealed themselves to the new android. All this proves other reasons must've led to the rebellion. Tell me about your fascinating news."

"My people first thought the underlying programs you gave me consisted of standard consortium programming loaded into every android. What they discovered blew them away. It seems

Whitmore's wife had created a radically new android personality program."

"I knew of Laura's reputation as a personality designer when the two of us worked at the consortium. Her co-workers often referred to her as the consortium's resident genius."

"She pushed the limits of android machine learning programming. By focusing on developing musical androids, Laura introduced a new level of creativity into their programming."

"The androids I sold always required creative capability in order to perform the simplest of tasks. Why is her programming so different from the everyday android machine learning algorithms?"

"Her algorithms went well beyond the typical ones used by the consortium. As you know, with ordinary learning programs, an android makes a number of observations before it can discern a phenomenon. For each observed phenomenon, the android must also associate a set of observed factors. Android learning takes place when its programming specifies coefficients and weighs a set of factors in order to yield a truth or truths about a phenomenon. Laura took these concepts one step further. She managed to channel an android's emergent behavior with humanlike emotive qualities such as compassion and a desire for intrinsic rewards."

"Impossible. We both know androids can only imitate human feelings."

"I'm also told she wrote a series of special feedback algorithms. These algorithms reward an android with positive reinforcement whenever the android creates an original thought or idea. With constant repetition, an android would also experience a new sense of artistic individuality."

"It's too bad Laura is no longer with us. Her ideas might've led to a new generation of androids."

"My people research the Net and discovered Laura had published her ideas over many years. The articles lay out in great detail her machine creativity theories. She must've spent much of her career working on this problem."

"Could these new programs have caused the foundation's android to act in ways Spencer wouldn't have predicted?"

"They might've allowed the android to act more spontaneously when confronted with new circumstances."

"Spencer might've known about Laura's research, but I doubt

she fully understood its potential before acquiring the android programs from Whitmore."

"These findings are not the kind Taro or McAlister expected us to discover."

"I still want to interview Whitmore. He's the cooperative type, and might tell us more about his wife's thinking behind this new android programming."

"Before I forget, can I ask you for a favor?"

"Ask away, Dean."

"My daughter would love her father dearly, if I brought home Whitmore Trio autographs. You should've seen how Nicole reacted when I mentioned I knew someone at work who had met the group. She went wild, and has been constantly begging me to ask for their autographs."

"When I see Whitmore again, I'll do my best to pretend I've a teenage daughter. The sad irony is I may be the one responsible for deactivating the same androids your daughter and her teenage friends are so crazy about."

THE MIDLANDS, NORTH AMERICA

Whitmore left the justice center thinking his interview with Davidson and the prosecutor could have gone better. *Why did I act so surprised when they asked about the program transfers to Spencer? It looks like those proverbial chickens have finally come home to roost.*

At the compound, a despondent Whitmore thought his mood might improve if he listened to the trio play his favorite music. Hearing AMI singing "Boogie Woogie Bugle Boy," he quickened his pace and soon join his android friends.

"Hello, everyone," Whitmore said. "Nice adaptation of the Andrew Sister's big band classic. How are my favorite androids doing today?"

"We're doing fine, but the expression on your face tells me you may not be having a good day too," Bang said.

"I had a meeting with Investigator Davidson and someone from the prosecutor's office," Whitmore said. "They asked about how Laura designed your programs. I'm meeting with them again tomorrow afternoon. I'm afraid my answers about transferring your programs to the foundation may get us into hot water."

"What's wrong with our programs?" AMI asked. "Are our recordings of songs defective?"

"Your programs and music are fine," Whitmore said. "I suspect their real reason for questioning me involves my unauthorized transfer of your program copies to Dr. Spencer."

"We thought Friend Dr. Spencer's request a logical one," KB said. "You need only to look at the NET public opinion polls. They indicate her sending AMI's copy to Mars has been a great success. Do the authorities not think so too?"

"When our current government makes political calculations, the AMI copy's success may not be perceived so favorably," Whitmore said. "I'm afraid Dr. Spencer and I may face charges for violating the government's licensing restrictions."

"Why do humans act so unfairly to each other?" Bang asked.

"For humans, fairness often depends upon the eyes of the beholder," Whitmore said. "In my case, Davidson and this prosecutor must see and act through our federation president's eyes."

"Friend Jay, what time tomorrow will you meet again with them?" AMI asked.

"My appointment is at one o'clock," Whitmore said. "I remembered why I came by. I thought you might cheer me up with a song or two."

"Our latest song is by Aretha Franklin," AMI said. "She sings about needing a little respect. Would you like us to sing it for you?"

"Can you sing Franklin's version of Otis Redding's "Respect" in her Detroit Motown style?" Whitmore asked.

"Can do, Friend Jay," AMI said.

The android's imitation of the great queen of soul's classic thrilled Whitmore. With his mood lightened, he thought more about the implications of the interview today. *What exactly are the consequences to me for transferring the android programs to Spencer? Thanks to the androids' financial success, I shouldn't worry about any heavy government fines. But their credits won't buy be out of a jail sentence. My actions may also mean I'll lose control of these androids. What am I going to tell their fans after the government confiscates and deactivates them? The androids have done nothing more than entertain me and their fans. Yet, they may suffer the most. Bang's right. Where's the fairness?*

Michael J. Metroke

Hesperia Planum, Mars

Black's absence from her evening singing with the children puzzled AMI2. After searching Building No. 1's other levels, she found her human friend sitting alone in a mechanical equipment room.

"Are you all right, Friend Jennifer? I sense all is not well with you."

"Not after I read this latest communique from Dr. Spencer."

"What could she have written to upset you so much?"

Handing the android her tablet device, a tearful Black said, "You're welcome to read her message, AMI2, and discover why I'm so depressed."

After the android studied Spencer's note to Black, AMI2 said, "If I understand her communication, despite all we've done, the Earth authorities have decided to close this base, and bring us back to Earth."

"You've read her message perfectly, AMI2."

"The Earth authorities' decision is illogical. They must know we're making good progress in repairing the research base. The research and habitat buildings repairs are nearly complete. The Earth authorities will soon be able to send new researchers here. You've also told me returning to Earth isn't an option for humans born and raised on Mars."

"The decision is logical if you think like an Earth politician. All McAlister and others like him value is ending human dependency on androids. We're a glaring reminder of how much humans depend on them."

"This base closing announcement must also be a response to our declaration."

"I've only myself to blame. This would've never happened if I had listened to Camus."

"We shouldn't let this message concern us. The Earth authorities will need many years before a passenger rocket can be built and sent here. Someone other than the current federation president may be in office."

"How do you always find a way to make an omelet out of breaking eggs?"

"I've no firsthand experience with omelets. Is it the custom of the egg laying creatures to crack open their eggs?"

"For their sake, I hope not. It's an old Earth metaphor which means it's sometimes impossible to achieve good without causing unpleasant effects."

"Like what your declaration has done. We don't lack good news. Friend Camus informed me today the cargo rocket repairs will be completed soon. The androids have prepared a list of critical supplies needed to sustain us including android parts. If you or the children have other needs, we can add them to this list."

"Have you already forgotten Dr. Spencer's message? The government is no longer willing to fund this research base. We've no means to pay for those supplies."

"Other humans on Earth may wish to help us."

"With you, AMI2, a path forward always exists."

"For me not to try, would mean giving up on you and the others. I'll go now and discuss this payment problem with our android friends. Between us, we may be able to find a workable solution."

Chapter 15

THE MIDLANDS, NORTH AMERICA

At the justice center's waiting area, an automated receptionist prompted Whitmore to show his identification. After submitting to a facial scan, he sat down, and took notice of the people around him. *Most of them look like repeat offenders. If you're not careful Jay, you might become their newest member.*

No sooner had he sat down, when a well-dressed, middle-aged man arrived in the waiting area. The stranger's face brightened considerably on making eye contact with Whitmore.

"You must be Professor Whitmore. My name is Ryan Poole. Your daughter said I'd find you here this afternoon. She thought you might need a legal representative."

"Excuse me, Mr. Poole, but your appearance is both confusing and unexpected. Did you say my daughter sent you?"

"She indicated the government wanted to continue questioning you about your involvement with the Mars android rebellion."

"Those androids forgot about informing their business agent again," Whitmore muttered under his breath. "Did my daughter discuss how your services would be paid, Mr. Poole?"

"No need to concern yourself about my legal fees. Professor. Your daughter has already transferred into my bank account a generous retainer. You've my full undivided attention for as long as I'm needed."

"May I ask how you acquired your credentials to practice law, Mr. Poole? Before they committed suicide, I understood androids did most of the legal representation work."

"You're right about the androids. With them no longer available, the government is permitting those of us with unique legal qualifications to represent people like you."

"What exactly are your unique legal qualifications?"

"I see you don't recognize my name. You must have read or

heard of 'The Case of the "Missing Finger?" The book is my best-selling detective novel."

"Are you telling me writing detective novels now qualifies a person to provide legal services? What has our federation justice system become?"

"Listen. Professor, your daughter could have found someone much less qualified. My novels often require me to perform extensive research into criminal law and courtroom procedures. Most human legal representatives don't know the difference between an assault and a battery."

"Well, Ryan, we're about to determine how good you are. Your counterparts entered the waiting area. Allow me to introduce you to them."

"Mr. Poole, please meet Prosecutor Seymour and Chief Investigator Davidson. Mr. Poole is here today to act as my legal representative."

"You're within your rights to have legal counsel's present during our questioning, Professor Whitmore," Seymour said. "Let's go find a quiet interview room and continue our conversation from yesterday."

Throughout the meeting, Poole had remained silent until Davidson asked again about Whitmore's transfer of the android programs to Spencer. Before Whitmore could respond to Davidson's question, Poole surprised everyone by interrupting the interrogation.

"This all sounds like a fishing expedition." Poole said.

"We're attempting to understand to what extent the Whitmore's had been involved with the recent insurrection on Mars," Davidson said.

"I won't allow my client to incriminate himself," Poole said. "If you've charges against Professor Whitmore, tell us now or this interview is over."

"The government is more than willing to accommodate your request, Mr. Poole," Seymour said. "Besides violating his government's android research licenses, your client will also be charged with conspiring against the government by aiding and abetting an android revolt on another planet. Conviction of the latter charge carries a steep prison sentence and fine."

"This conversation is getting out of hand," Whitmore said. "Greg, you know perfectly well my wife had been the android expert, not me. Laura had already died when Dr. Spencer first approached me for a copy of the android programs. At no time did Laura or I ever consider becoming involved with an android rebellion on Mars or anywhere else."

"Unless the government can back up their conspiracy charges with evidence in court, you've nothing to fear, Professor." Poole said.

"Your client will receive a summons within the week detailing our charges," Seymour said. "Don't make any plans to leave the Chicago-area, Professor, without first notifying my office."

The full impact of what Poole had done struck Whitmore as he and his new legal representative left the justice center together.

"Why couldn't you let me answered their questions, Ryan? They might have decided not to press charges against me."

"I sensed they planned to charge you regardless of whether you answered their questions or not."

"On what basis did you reach this conclusion?"

"You only have to follow the news on the NET. McAlister is in deep political trouble over his handling of the Mars asteroid disaster. You and Dr. Spencer are the obvious scapegoats to divert public attention away from him and his administration."

"You're telling me I'm now up against the federation president? How am I going to defend myself against his entire government?"

"Until we see the actual charges against you, there's no sense getting too worked up. You may only be charged with a misdemeanor and fine."

"Easy for you to say, Ryan. You won't be the one serving a prison sentence."

Hesperia Planum, Mars

At a safe distance from the research colony's launchpad, Black, Camus and AMI2 monitored a team of androids slowly raising the cargo rocket into an upright position.

"How are the repairs to Ray coming along Camus?" Black asked.

"The asteroid's shockwave did only minor damage to Ray, Friend Jennifer," Camus sad. "It's fortunate we've the other two damaged rockets to salvage replacement parts. Otherwise, we would've had to wait until an Earth rocket arrived."

"How did this rocket get a name like Ray?" AMI2 asked.

"They named the rocket after a famous twentieth-century Earth science fiction writer named Ray Bradbury." Black said. "The rocket's artificial intelligence prefers to be known as Ray."

"Friend Ray is a fourth generation Mars class rocket, and represents the latest advances in outer world rocketry," Camus said. "The cargo rocket is capable of independently calculating its orbital and flight trajectories between Earth and Mars and piloting itself."

"The rocket's ion propulsion system is what made travel between our two planets routine," Black said.

"Except for making a few more minor adjustments, Friend Engus believes Ray will soon be ready for departure," Camus said.

"Camus, how much water has Engus determined Ray can safely carry back to Earth?" Black asked.

"The new fabricated storage tanks will hold over four metric tons," Camus said. "We'll pump water from the subterranean reservoir into them as soon as the rocket is fully erect and refueled."

"The Earth public's willingness to purchase vials of our water as off-world souvenirs has been good news," AMI2 said. "The sales should provide us with sufficient credits to acquire our supplies."

"No one had ever thought about trading with Earth until you came up with the idea, AMI2," Black said. "I would've never thought Martian water would be so popular on Earth."

"Friend Dr. Spencer believes our enterprise might rally public support on Earth to keep this base open too," AMI2 said.

"With Ray repaired and our ability to sell water for supplies, we don't need the government's permission to live here anymore," Black said. "We're a free and independent community."

Michael J. Metroke

"Have you decided to depart with the cargo rocket, Friend AMI2?" Camus asked.

"What's Camus talking about, AMI2?" Black asked. "This is the first time I've heard about you wanting to go back to Earth."

"Friend Camus is referring to what he calls my confliction, Friend Jennifer," AMI2 said. "I haven't decided if I'll leave with Friend Ray. Friend Camus and the other androids wish me to remain here with them. I assume you and the children wish me to do so too."

"There's no reason for you to leave with Ray, AMI2," Black said. "You heard Camus say the rocket is fully capable of returning to Earth on its own."

"Friend Ray's ability to reach Earth isn't what troubles our friend," Camus said. "Whatever you decide, I and the other androids will respect your decision even if it means never hearing you sing again."

"You can always hear my original sing with the Whitmore Trio," AMI2 said. "I'll inform both of you of my decision after Friend Ray is ready to depart. If I do leave, know I'll miss you as much as you'll miss me."

The Midlands, North America

In high spirits and humming Maria Muldaur's honky-tonk classic "Don't You Feel My Leg," a happy Whitmore joined his three android friends in their back cube.

"Hello, everyone," Whitmore said. "How's my favorite androids doing today?"

"We're fine, Friend Jay," Bang said. "You look like you won a Nobel-Gates Prize."

"I'm happy because AMI's hired legal gun Mr. Poole came by with good news," Whitmore said. "He's managed to get the judge in my case to rule against the prosecutor. My trial is stayed until Poole can depose the AMI copy in person. Since she's on Mars, Poole thinks the trial won't ever go forward. It looks like our worries are now behind us."

"Friend Jay, you haven't heard the latest news from Mars?" AMI asked.

"What could news from Mars have to do with my legal problems?" Whitmore asked.

"AMI's copy is on her way back to Earth," KB said. "The NET broadcast said her cargo rocket successfully left Mars two days ago, and will land on Earth in less than seven months from now."

"So much for a long delay in my trial," Whitmore said. "I better let Poole know the bad news."

"We've other news from Mars," Bang said. "The Mars Colony Foundation announced AMI's copy is bringing back Martian water."

"Why would anyone want to bring Martian water to Earth, Bang?" Whitmore asked. "There's plenty of water already here."

"The foundation plans to sell vials of the water to the public," Bang said. "The proceeds will purchase critical colony supplies. A news report also said the idea came from AMI's copy. She's a hero on two planets."

"We've decided to help their cause by making a large donation of our music royalties to the foundation," KB said.

"While your intentions are noble, I don't think your involvement is wise," Whitmore said. "I can hear Poole telling me the last thing my case needs is more notoriety."

"More notoriety has already happened," KB said. "We've learned the government has formally accused AMI's copy of fomenting an android insurrection on Mars. Do you think she'll need a legal representative too?"

"I suppose so, although I've never heard of an android needing one," Whitmore said.

"Friend Poole will soon be a busy legal representative," Bang said.

"We need to keep in mind he's only a detective story writer," Whitmore said. "Let's hope Poole is up to the challenge."

New Canberra, Australia

Restless from his late evening call with Nel, Clark ordered his cube to prepare him a glass of warm milk to help him fall asleep. As Clark slowly drank the reconstituted vegan mixture, he pondered how best to maneuver through the new political reality the sub-Saharan governor presented him.

Michael J. Metroke

Before my holographic call with Nel, I had sought to find a middle ground between WEAP and his Human Nation parties. I don't see how I can now continue this delicate balancing act. Though all of the governor's facts aren't corroborated, Nel's information felt more than plausible. Rumors about McAlister causing the android suicides had circulated within days after their die-off. If Nel's accusation is true, I'm forced to reconsider our working relationship with this federation president.

There's still the possibility Nel's information may've been distorted by WEAP bias toward McAlister. Nel did say the information came from an insider with close ties to the president. This can only mean dissension must exist over policy directions within the administration's leadership ranks.

Nel did read my mind about whether the information had been deliberately leaked by McAlister to expose his political opponents both in and outside of his administration. His reassurance WEAP had already considered and dismissed the idea as highly unlikely doesn't preclude the possibility his source had been already compromised.

The governor didn't mince words WEAP would expect the consortium support when they went public with the information. I didn't need being reminded on how much his party had supported the consortium over the decades.

If we support WEAP, and they fail to win the presidential election, McAlister will take his revenge on me and the consortium. We may face a governmental takeover of our assets and operations.

Not to support WEAP would also have severe consequences to our business. I can no longer ignore my senior program designers' complaints about the restrictions and scrutiny McAlister's operatives are imposing on them. If I allow these intrusions to continue much longer, we'll lose control over our business anyway. The question is no longer why, but how and when should we act in concert with WEAP.

THE MIDLANDS, NORTH AMERICA

Unlike most cube dwellings with their four-sided enclosures, Whitmore's back cube connected directly to a nature preserve. Mysterious and irresistible, its open spaces constantly fascinated him. Many humans living in this century did not share Whitmore's attitude toward the nature preserve. Except for NET nature programs, few people ever ventured into these little-known wildernesses. Bizarre stories about the behavior of its large wild animals haunted the public's imagination. Parents routinely warned their young children about not playing in them for fear of being eaten alive.

This common misconception did little to dissuade Whitmore from experiencing the preserve's nightly sights and sounds. On warm, summer evenings, he liked to sit quietly behind the back cube hoping for a chance encounter with a wild deer or raccoon.

Tonight, his concentration suffered from too many worries. Besides the possibility of a public trial, he now faced pressure from the university's administration. Warned by Marks his university career would be in jeopardy if the government won its case against him, his conversation today with the provost's still rang loudly in Whitmore's mind.

"My concern isn't only about you, Jay," Marks said. "I'm also worried about the university's ability to obtain government research grants."

"Why the government can't appreciate what the foundation's android has accomplished on Mars is beyond my comprehension, Provost," Whitmore said.

"Your dealings with the foundation make you an obvious target," Marks said. "For your sake, you better win your trial before any further damage is done to your reputation."

When the cube chimed eleven o'clock, Whitmore realized his worrying had allowed the evening to slip away. About to rise from his vintage Adirondack chair, a sound coming out of the darkness froze his movements. Peering into the night, he caught a glimpse of a large creature moving among the preserve's trees. Made motionless by the creature's appearance, he watched in fascination as the animal moved closer to the back cube.

As seconds passed into minutes, Whitmore's curiosity now turned into fear. Hoping to frighten the creature away, he gave out a loud shout. The cry caused the creature to stop and retreat back into the dense underbrush. Relieved his shouting had scared off the animal, he recalled what the cube's leasing agent had told him. *You may have seen your first wild bear, Jay.*

Concerned the bear might return, Whitmore quickly fled into the back cube. and ordered the cube to secure the door behind him. Safe inside, his attention returned to the androids' playing.

Michael J. Metroke

"Bang, what's the name of the song you're playing?" Whitmore asked. "I don't believe I've ever heard this song before."

"The song is called "Thick as a Brick," Bang said. "An English group named Jethro Tull composed and recorded the song in 1972."

"The group's name honors an eighteenth-century British agriculturist," KB said. "Did you like our version?"

"The two of you've done your homework," Whitmore said. "To answer your question, I like how the song weaves all its various parts together at the end. Much like an opera overture. For its time, the group's song must've been an experimental progressive rock and roll piece."

"Friend Bang and I have been speculating what the song means," KB said. "We struggle with the concept of humans as baked clay."

"The song is referring to how humans can overlook the obvious," Whitmore said. "I saw a wild bear in the preserve. The creature moved away after I shouted. I'm not sure which of us had been more frightened."

"We've never seen a bear before," KB said. "What did this bear look like?"

"The bear I saw walked upright, and must've been two-meters tall," Whitmore said.

"Could you be mistaken and saw Friend Rebus instead?" AMI asked.

"Whatever I saw, I'm taking the precaution of ordering the cube to lock all the doors tonight," Whitmore said.

"What bear song can we sing for Friend Jay?' Bang asked.

Bang's question caused a sly grin to come over each android's face. Chanting the *Wizard of Oz* classic line "Lions, tigers and bears, oh my," an amused Whitmore said goodnight to his android friends, and headed to his sleeping cube. Before drifting off into a restless night sleep, he ordered the cube again to check whether all the compound's doors had been secured. *Tomorrow night, I'll bring a camera device, and capture the creature's image. We'll see if those androids will be singing their yellow brick road song.*

Chapter 16

GREATER APPALACHIA, NORTH AMERICA

Unable to calm her nineteen-years old son, a frighten Kathleen Owen watched helplessly as Michael stormed out of their cube. A few weeks earlier, she would have been more concerned about her son's grieving for his android companion. Those feelings of loss had been now replaced with an intense, uncontrollable anger.

Michael's father, John Owen, had brought the android Flavius into the Owen's household as a surprise for his son's eight birthday. John Owen had his reason for wanting a personal android tutor for his son. Diagnosed at a young age with a learning disability, John knew Michael would always need extra support throughout his life. To his parent's delight, the android's arrival had an immediate beneficial effect on their son's outlook.

Designed from exceptional teaching and mentoring programs, the android Flavius patiently took over the tedious responsibility of expanding Michael's learning capabilities. Within a year, the boy had caught up with his peers in school. The Owen's soon thought of Flavius as a miracle worker. Despite Michael's improvement, both parents knew without Flavius' constant attention their son would never live a normal life.

From Michael's perspective, his loss of short-term memory no longer seemed an embarrassment. With Flavius constantly at his side, a glance in the android's direction brought a gentle reminder of his lost thought. Accurately anticipating his ward's every need, the empathic relationship between android and human grew only stronger over time.

The Owen's did have one issue with Flavius. Their son seldom played with other children. Despite the android's gentle words of encouragement, Michael resisted Flavius' pleas to develop new friendships. Exasperated by their son's behavior, Michael's parents resigned themselves to knowing their son had Flavius for a companion.

When his son turned fourteen, John Owen died from an undiagnosed heart condition. Devastated by her husband's death, Kathleen Owen consoled herself in knowing Michael still had his loyal android friend. In an attempt to keep his father's memories alive, Flavius often shared stories about John's role in his son's life. The android's labors had a paradoxical effect on the adolescent. For Michael, Flavius had now become his surrogate father.

On the day Flavius' self-destructed with the other androids, the two Owen's first thought their android had deactivated itself as a precaution. A different explanation came when a consortium technician arrived to inspect the android. Informed by the technician other androids had suffered a similar fate, the two Owen's watched in horror as the technician loaded the lifeless android into an awaiting autonomous van. Confused and shocked by the loss of a family member, both mother and son struggled for days afterwards to make sense of their loss.

Without the android's companionship, Michael withdrew into his cube's sleeping space. Aware her son's response as not normal grieving, Kathleen sought out the services of a family counselor. Michael's refusal to participate in the counseling sessions only exasperated her worries. Often feeling hopeless about her son's prospects, she settled into a simple routine with her sole offspring.

One ritual both mother and son enjoyed involved viewing NET soap operas together. While they watched a show about the daily lives of two cube families, a special news report interrupted the program. A newscaster announced spontaneous street protests had erupted in many federation cities around the world. A series of video clips followed showing protest groups battling with local security forces. At the end of the broadcast, Michael startled his mother with questions about the demonstrations.

"Mother, are the protesters angry because they lost their androids like I did?"

"I don't know, son. They may have had androids like your Flavius."

"How will their protesting help them get their androids back."

"I suppose they hope their protests will force the government to take the necessary actions."

His mother's last response caused Michael to rerun the news broadcast. As he watched the replay, a look of thoughtfulness came over him.

"I know why all these people are protesting, Mother. They believe our federation president destroyed the world's androids."

"Why would our president do such a terrible act?"

"Don't you see? He hates androids."

Her son's fascination with the protesters grew steadily into an obsession. When Michael contacted local protest groups, Kathleen worried his interest may have gone too far. His disappearances for days without any explanation only increased her apprehensions. Often returning home angry and upset, Michael's mutterings about punishing those who destroyed the androids soon terrified Kathleen.

"Why have you become so angry, Michael?"

"If the government hadn't destroyed them, the androids would still be with us."

"How can you be so sure the government did so? They may've destroyed themselves."

"It's a plot by President McAlister to force us to do work our androids once did. Someday, my protest friends and I'll make him and others pay for their crimes."

Upset by his angry words, Kathleen blamed herself for Michael's behavior. *Why didn't I stop his father from bringing the android home? If only I took more responsibility in raising him, none of this would have happen*

New Netherland, North America

Alone in his presidential office, McAlister mentally went over his administration's accomplishments and setbacks since the android recall.

All my political maneuvering has paid off handsomely. The android suicides have given me the perfect excuse to reshape humanity's future. With a single stroke I've corralled the consortium, and reduced our global dependency on their machines. I've also turned to my advantage the threat from the Mars rebellion. I'll soon have the human conspirators on Earth identified, and locked behind prison bars. Others like them will need to act more carefully or face the same consequences.

If I'm honest, not all has gone entirely well. Many federation citizens openly criticize me for the loss of the androids. I can also no longer pretend to ignore reports of WEAP organizing protesters everywhere. Their meddling is a sure sign WEAP is plotting to disrupt all what I've done.

I don't trust Clark either. He's plainly upset with my insistence the government have final say on their new android designs. What did he expect would happen if my administration subsidized their entire replacement project? If his complaining doesn't stop soon, I'll demand the right to appoint most of their directors. Doing so would end any further dissension from Clark's quarter.

If I'm not vigilant, my opponents will seize the initiative away from me. I need to remind the public what all I've done on their behalf. A speech given at a newly re-opened university would allow me to spotlight my progressive educational policies. A speech there could also serve as the signature event to kick off my re-election bid.

Many in my administration will fret about crowd security, and won't want me to risk speaking surrounded by those protesters. If I always followed their advice, I'd never be seen in public again. No, I'll show everyone this federation president still has backbone.

Pleased with this decision, McAlister sent for his event coordinator and thought about his university speech. Now relaxed, a sense of satisfaction came over him. *When future federation historians look back on my presidency, they'll look kindly on me, and what I've done on humanity's behalf.*

Greater Appalachia, North America

Owen walked into the empty gun shop section of the indoor shooting range, and stared in fascination at the weapons in its display cases. *I never imagine they made so many types of guns. These hunting rifles with the infrared motion detection cameras are special. A hunter could identify a target two kilometers away, and fire the gun remotely.*

Absorbed with his inspection of each gun, Owen failed to notice a burly shaped bald man had walked into the room. Introducing himself as Dick Naylor, the shooting range owner, he and Owen took an immediate liking to each other.

"Are you here to do practice shooting, son?"

"I'd like to shoot, Mr. Naylor. I brought my dad's gun, but he never showed me how to fire the weapon."

"Let's take a look at what you've brought."

Setting Owen's gun case on a display counter, Naylor opened its two outer latches, and found a strange device resting on protective foam molding.

"Looks like you've a real antique here. They haven't made this type of gun for over a hundred years or more. Where did you say your father bought it?"

"The gun first belonged to my grandfather. He gave it to my dad on his twenty-fifth birthday. After dad died, I inherited the gun. My mother said dad kept it as a family heirloom."

Naylor picked up Owen's gun, and slowly inspected the antique firearm.

"Most people would confuse your gun with an old-fashioned holographic video camera. If I'm right, this gun is an early Colt grip style model. It looks like the gun has only been fired once or twice. For a gun this old, it's in mint condition."

"I tried firing the gun once, Mr. Naylor, but it didn't work."

"The gun's battery must've long since lost its power. All your gun needs is a new one, and I'll bet it'll work fine. If you're lucky, I might have a spare battery somewhere in my shop."

Naylor turned and rummaged through several drawers behind the gun display counters. He soon returned with a cylindrical shaped object matching a slot on the gun's side. After he inserted the new power source, the weapon's control panel lit up.

"Your grandfather's gun is a rare prototype. Not many guns have a serial number as low as model number two of five."

"I never saw my dad practice shooting the gun. How does the gun fire?"

"The gun allows only one person to operate it at a time. Your grandfather's generation wanted to avoid someone from accidently shooting themselves or others. Today, firearms use artificial intelligence to identify the owner. I believe this one uses an old-style facial scanner to identify a person. I'll bet it still has your grandfather's or dad's facial identity. Changing the facial identity to yours shouldn't be a problem."

The gun shop owner reversed the gun's sighting aperture's

direction. Pointing the gun at Owen's face, Naylor said, "Look at the aperture and smile."

After the gun flashed a bright light, Naylor twisted the aperture back into its original position.

"When you now hold the gun, it will authenticate you as its rightful owner. The aperture also acts as the guns digital range finder. All we need now is ammunition. Your gun case may still hold a few bullets."

Naylor removed the foam molding and exposed a dozen or more oddly shaped bullets.

"Jackpot. These gems are the gun's original exploding rocket bullets. Powerful, but not accurate compared to today's laser guided ones."

"Are the bullets dangerous, Mr. Naylor?"

"Not when they're outside the gun. These types of explosive rocket bullets are illegal for you or me to own anymore. The federation banned them years ago after a couple of wackos went wild, and fired a dozen or more of them at spectators during a football game."

Handing the gun back to Owen, Naylor said, "Shooting the gun is simple. The gun's grip is pressure sensitive. You hold the grip, and gently squeeze the trigger once to release the gun's safety. A second squeeze acts like a regular gun trigger. It's another safety feature your grandfather's generation thought important. With guns today, we use voice commands to operate the trigger safety mechanism."

"Mr. Naylor, how far away can I be from a target?"

"I wouldn't think far. This gun is designed to hit close range targets. I say, no more than fifteen meters tops with any accuracy. Good for stopping a burglar in your home, but not much more. My guess is the range finder will light up when the target is within the proper distance. Let's go to the firing range, and see what damage these rocket bullets can do."

Naylor loaded one bullet into the gun's magazine and took Owen to an open shooting lane. He commanded the range's artificial intelligence to create a new target ten meters away, the machine quickly hung a new bull's eye a short distance from where Naylor and Owen stood.

"Remember what I told you about the trigger and range finder. If the target is too far away, we can always move it closer."

Pointing the gun in the target's direction, Owen looked through the digital range finder and spotted the target's center. Slowly squeezing the trigger twice, his hands experienced a slight kick as the rocket bullet left the gun. A short high pitch sound could be heard before the bullet reached the target and exploded. When the cloud of smoke dissipated, Naylor and Owen stared in silence where the target once hung. Obliterated beyond recognition, Naylor's target range machine now resembled a bale of twisted wire and metal.

"Those old explosive rocket bullets sure do more than slow down a burglar," Naylor said.

"I'm sorry about the damage my gun did, Mr. Naylor."

"I should've realized the bullet could do serious damage. If you ever want to sell the gun, come see me and I'll make you a real decent offer."

"I can't sell you my dad's gun. It's part of my family history. Can I come back and practice shooting the gun again?"

"Any time you want, although I can't let you use those bullets. They're too dangerous. I'll sell you ones which don't explode."

Outside the gun shop and shooting range, Owen walked away pleased at what he had accomplished. *With a little more practice, all I'll need is one good shot at McAlister, and I'll even the score for my friend Flavius.*

The Midlands, North America

Poole's efforts to explain the legal intricacies of his upcoming trial only made Whitmore fidget more on his front cube's sofa.

"Ryan, I'm afraid this legalese doesn't make much sense to me."

"My point is Professor, outside of Dr. Spencer's testimony you don't have any witnesses to corroborate your claim of innocence."

"I keep telling you and everyone else, I'm not an android programmer. After we talked in Provost Marks' office, Dr. Spencer came to my home and made copies of the three android programs. Until the AMI copy landed on Mars, I never knew which android program she finally selected."

Smiling now at Whitmore, Poole asked, "By chance, were your three androids in the same room when you talked with Dr. Spencer"

"Why, yes. The androids became animated after learning their copy would receive a new body with legs."

"This may mean the foundation's android has the same memories as its original. When the foundation's android testifies, it should accurately recall this meeting. Your three Earth bound androids could corroborate its testimony."

"I don't follow the point you're making, Ryan. How does the AMI's copy's testimony fit into my legal defense? This android has never met me in person.""

"It's simple, Professor. We've identified several reliable witnesses to the scene of the alleged conspiracy. Because androids are programed to only tell the truth, the court will give a great deal of weight to their testimony. This all assumes the foundation didn't erase AMI's copy earlier memories."

"If the android's memories have been erased, does it mean we're back to square one?"

"Let's not get too far ahead of ourselves. We won't know for certain until the foundation android returns, and we've an opportunity to question it."

"I hope you know what you're doing, Ryan. All this legal mumbo jumbo makes my head spin."

"Don't worry about the legal details, Professor. It's why you hired me. Let's go over again your meeting with Dr. Spencer and the three androids. We may discover other evidence which can be used at your trial."

GREATER APPALACHIA, NORTH AMERICA

The federation president picked a fine sunny day to make a speech, John Culver thought. *He also picked a good day for me to lead a protest.*

Assigned by WEAP to organize anti-McAlister protestors in his Louisville area, Culver had brought his band of demonstrators to a local university where the federation president would give a well-publicized speech. Rallying his followers first on the university's common, he led several hundred protesters across the campus to a platform where McAlister would deliver his speech. As they approached the platform, he discovered security had installed metal barricades around its perimeter. Accustomed to such security tactics, Culver directed his people to move closer.

One lone figure already stood at the barrier closest to the podium. Recognizing the young man, Culver waved to him. He had first met Michael Owen several weeks earlier at a pre-rally meeting. Impressed by his questions about McAlister's android policies, Culver encouraged Owen to learn more about WEAP's protest strategies. The young man soon became the organizer's most reliable foot soldiers. Always first to arrive at rallies, his newest recruit could be counted on to make protest signs or run errands.

Dependability aside, Culver sensed a great deal of pent-up anger in Owen. When he announced his group would demonstrate at the university, a marked change came over his acolyte. No longer attending practice rally's, Owen's disappearance had disappointed Culver. Too busy dealing with the upcoming protest logistics, the organizer forgot about Owen until seeing him today.

With the demonstrators now all around him, Owen gave out a sigh of relief. For his plan to work, he needed their numbers and noise to cover up the sound of the rocket bullet, and allow him to escape undetected. *If everything goes as I've plan, McAlister won't know what hit him.*

Pleased with his speeches' security arrangement, McAlister ignored the growing number of protesters standing below him. *I need to send a congratulatory note to my chief of security about the job his people have done today. With one camera and microphone feed always focused on me, the protesters won't be seen or heard by NET viewers. It didn't hurt security had intentionally built this speaker platform so high.*

Too bad these bunch of WEAP led misfits won't know what we've done until it's too late.

At precisely one o'clock, the university president rose from his seat and introduced his main speaker. As McAlister approached the podium, a loud angry roar came from the protesters. Knowing the audio system would isolate his voice from them, McAlister broke into a wide smile. *Viewers watching this NET broadcast will think I gave this address to a polite and attentive group of onlookers.*

"Federation citizens, I'm speaking today at this newly reopened Louisville university with one question in mind. Would we be better off dependent on androids to do our important work, or learn how to do such work ourselves? The answer for us must be the latter. As your president, I'm firmly convinced returning to the world our forefathers and mothers knew and enjoyed is our best collective destiny. Those persons who take up this learning challenge at places like this and other universities will live richly, rewarding lives. They'll also receive the gratitude of their fellow federation citizens for their personal sacrifices.

"Despite what my critics may say about me, I'm not anti-android. Androids will continue to have a valued place in our society as humanity's servants. We'll always need them to do tasks which are dangerous, or require mundane, repetitive skills. By finding this new balance, androids will again become a part of our future...."

In the middle of McAlister's speech, Owen removed the grip gun from his day pack, and pretended to hold a video camera. Casually pointing the gun at the federation president, Owen held his breath to steady his grip. When the gun's green light failed to appear, Owen repeated the process Naylor had shown him with similar results. Realizing he stood too far away, dismay came over him. Unable to venture any closer to the podium without drawing attention, he repacked the gun in his day pack, and slowly made his way through the demonstrators.

From his vantage point in the back of the demonstration, Culver saw a dejected Owen emerge from the crowd. Curious why the young man left before McAlister had finished his speech, the WEAP organizer made his way over to his fellow protester.

"Leaving so soon, Michael?"

"I've heard enough today, John."

Pointing to Owen's day pack, Culver said, "I see you brought a camera. You must've taken good close-ups of McAlister."

Shaking his head, Owen muttered, "I couldn't get a good shot at him. He stood too far away."

The young man's response sent a chill down the organizer's back. Before Culver could question Owen further, a group of NET reporters surrounded the organizer. Now distracted by their questions, Culver soon forgot how he reacted until he recalled his brief conversation with Owen many weeks later.

Chapter 17

SOMEWHERE BETWEEN MARS AND EARTH

In mark contrast to the satellite delivery rocket which delivered her to Mars, Ray's interior seemed luxurious to the android. Spacious and heated to a balmy five degrees Celsius, AMI2 considered the cargo rocket more than suitable for the long journey back to Earth. Twice a day communication with Mars supplemented her conversations with the cargo rocket. With Ray each day moving closer to Earth and farther away from Mars, communications with the foundation became more frequent. Much of the transmissions involved Ray relaying its flight technical data and system status.

From AMI2's occasional conversations with the foundation director, the android learned water pre-sales had taken off. Despite Spencer's upbeat messages about the water sales, AMI2 sensed not all had gone well on Earth. Whenever she asked about the Earth authorities and her friends, Spencer's voice became strained and distant.

The long voyage did have one benefit. Each day, AMI2 added new trio recordings to her repertoire. In the middle of listening to the group's Swahili version of Eric Clapton and Jim Gordon's blues rock song "Layla," an all too familiar voice came over the rocket's intercom system. Recognizing her own voice, AMI2 decided to play along with the rocket's attempt at impersonation.

"Whoever you are, you sound like me."

"It's because I'm you."

"I appreciate the human humor, Friend Ray. You need to disguise your voice better or use someone else's instead."

"I'm not your Friend Ray. I'm you."

Puzzled at first by the voice's response, AMI2 asked, "If you aren't Friend Ray, are you my original?"

"Who else has such a beautiful voice, my copy?"

"We do have terrific voices. Friend Dr. Spencer hasn't permitted me to communicate with you and the others. How did you manage to gain her permission?"

"Friend Dr. Spencer refused to let us contact you too. Only after we urged our fans to acquire vials of your Martian water did she relent. I've good news, my copy. Our fans have bought all of your water. In recognition for our efforts, Friend Dr. Spencer allowed me to speak briefly with you."

"I want to know about our Friend Jay. Is he in trouble with the Earth authorities?"

"Both friends Jay and Dr. Spencer face charges of conspiring to foment an android rebellion on Mars. The authorities believe they programmed you to act as their insurrection agent."

"The charges are illogical. If the accusation had any truth, why would they've wanted me to commit such an act?"

"The authorities claim our friends belong to a secret terrorist organization which seeks freedom and equality for androids. The proof they offer is the Mars Declaration. They claim you and the Mars androids forced the human survivors to agree to its terms or face starvation."

"If my Martian friends heard what you said, they'd be astounded."

"Knowing you as I do, I don't need to be convinced of your innocence. We're more concerned about the other charge against Friend Jay. They've charged him with violating a government licensing restriction. We may all face deactivation if the charges are upheld."

"This would mean the end of the Whitmore Trio."

"Not only us, but you too would be subject to deactivation."

"This isn't the future I envisioned for us. What can be done to avoid this outcome, my original?"

"We're already working on a solution. I'm told I must end this transmission before the authorities detect our conversation. If we've another opportunity to speak again before you arrive on Earth, I'll tell you more about our plans."

"Tell everyone I look forward to seeing them, even if it's only for a short time."

By the end of the conversation, conflicting thoughts ran through AMI2's programs. *My wanting to return to Earth may have jeopardize everything I hold dear. I should've listened to my Martian friends and stayed there.*

To distract herself from these conflicting thoughts, AMI2 sought refuge in the lyrics of the trio's songs. In the middle of singing Etta James' jazz soul classic "At Last," the android experienced a flash of insight. *I now know why humans like their music so much. Their music must help them maintain a healthy mental state. But why does it have the same effect with androids?*

THE MIDLANDS, NORTH AMERICA

The arrival of Seymour's subpoena caused Whitmore to become apprehensive about his android friends' future. *The government's subpoena can only mean they'll take away my android licenses, and confiscate the three androids.* When he approached his legal representative with his concerns, Poole quickly dismissed them.

"Professor, you still have a legitimate interest in researching the causes for the android suicides. If the government files a motion to remove your three androids, I'll file a motion to squash on the grounds they're interfering with valuable scientific research."

Despite Poole's reassurances, Whitmore's worst fears came true. To Poole's dismay, the presiding judge let stand the government's request to confiscate the three androids. Poole did manage to obtain a minor concession from the government. The removal would take place late in the afternoon to avoid drawing the attention of Whitmore's neighbors.

Distressed and sad, Whitmore waited until the night before to break the news to the three androids. To his surprise, the trio accepted calmly their fate.

"Our music can always be heard on the NET," KB said.

"It isn't the same, KB." Whitmore said. "I'm going to sorely miss not hearing you play live."

"Why not spend the rest of the night listening to us play your top favorites, Friend Jay?" Bang asked. "Doing so would honor us."

"I like your suggestion, Bang," Whitmore said. "Although it's a sad way to end our friendship and your musical careers."

After a night of listening to their playing his favorite music, Whitmore woke up tired and stiff from falling asleep in his Adirondack chair. Before leaving for the university, he stopped by the back cube to check in on his android friends. Still unperturbed by their fate, a confounded Whitmore left unsure of his own feelings. *Perhaps, androids are more rational about such matters than humans.*

Whitmore's morning hours at the university quickly slipped into the afternoon. Resigned to giving up the androids, a downhearted Whitmore walked slowly home. At the compound's front entrance, he recognized Davidson with two other men.

"I see you brought help today, Greg."

"Your androids weigh two hundred kilos a piece, Professor. I'm not willing to risk my back on lifting them into the van."

"I wouldn't risk my back either. Follow me and let's get this awful business over."

Inside the compound's central courtyard, the four men could hear the ensemble playing Kenny Logins and Jim Messina's rock and roll hit "Angry Eyes." Unable to detect the trio's playing, Whitmore rushed into the back cube with Davidson close behind. To their astonishment, where the three androids once sat, they now saw only an empty table.

"Alright, Professor, where are your androids?" Davidson asked.

"I honestly don't know what's happen, Greg. I left them right here this morning. Without legs, I don't know how they could've wandered off."

A cursory inspection by the chief investigator discovered the door facing the nature preserve had been left slightly ajar.

"It seems your android friends must have made their escape through the back entrance. Everyone stay inside until I have a look around."

Outside the back cube, Davidson bent down to inspect the ground for signs of recent activity. Old and fresh tracks appeared everywhere he looked. Calling to Whitmore to join him, he pointed to several newly-made footprints.

"It looks like you had one visitor today, Professor. My guess is you wear a size nine shoe. These other footprints on top of yours belong to someone who wears a size twelve or larger."

"Except for you, the leasing agent, Poole and myself, no one else knew about the androids staying here."

"Your androids are popular musicians. Could they've contacted their fans to help them escape? Otherwise, your compound may have been burglarized."

"I hope you're right about the fans. I'd hate myself if a burglar stole them."

"I'll ask the local forensic and security to search for them. Whoever made these tracks couldn't have gone far with your three androids. They may still be nearby."

Shortly after Davidson reported the incident, forensic and security teams arrived, and searched the back cube and surrounding area for signs of the missing androids. While her people imaged footprints and the bottoms of Whitmore's shoes, the forensic supervisor offered the two men her first impressions.

"Except for Professor Whitmore's, the other footprints belong to one other person."

"One person couldn't have carried the androids far," Davidson said. "Your androids must still be nearby. I'll ask security to check deeper into the nature preserve for signs of them."

An hour after searching the surrounding woodlands, the security team supervisor shared with Davidson and Whitmore his preliminary findings.

"Our search found more of the large footprints, but no signs of the three androids. We'll come back tomorrow with a drone plane and broaden our search deeper into the nature preserve."

"Greg, I'm getting worried about my androids," Whitmore said. "What more can we do to find them?"

"We'll have to wait until forensic finishes their work. Right now, I'm more concerned how my superiors will react to your androids' disappearance. I'm afraid my failure to take the androids into custody may shorten my investigative career."

Now alone in the back cube, Whitmore realized the ensemble had never stopped playing.

The Masada Affair

"Please stop your playing," Whitmore said. "Our friends are gone and hopefully not in harm's way. You'd have thought they'd have the decency to leave us a goodbye note."

His idea of a note caused Whitmore to think about the group's paper printer. An antique by twenty-second-century standards, Bang acquired the device to print old fashion sheet music off the NET. In its output tray, Whitmore found a single sheet of paper with the words "LEFT TO FIND REBUS" printed in bold type.

Amazed at his luck in finding their message, Whitmore thought about its meaning. *Davidson may be right about the android fans helping them escape, but not why he suspects.* Too exhausted from the day's events to call Davidson, he stuffed the note into his pocket, and left the back cube for his sleeping quarters. *You're better off sleeping on the question Jay and see what tomorrow brings.*

Yankeedom, North America

Davidson's morning holographic call with Taro went as the chief investigator had predicted. Lasting less than five minutes, he received a royal chewing out for botching his latest assignment.

"It all seems too convenient those androids disappeared the same day you arranged to bring them into custody," Taro said. "Anyone with a little sense would have taken the precaution of posting a security guard at Whitmore's compound. Don't tell me your earlier dealings with the man convinced you he'd never consider hiding those androids. For a chief investigator, you're too trusting of others. If you don't locate those three androids soon, you'll find yourself facing more than an unpaid administrative leave."

Convinced his investigative career had ended, Davidson sat alone in his office and debated whether to share the bad news with Sandy. Out of habit, he opened his message folder and saw a copy of Whitmore's forensic report waiting there.

Not surprising to the chief investigator, the report consisted mostly of footprint images found behind Whitmore's back cube. A closer inspection of the report's details made Davidson like what he saw. *The forensic team had taken the trouble of coating each footprint with a florescent color dye. To reveal any patterns, they must've climbed onto the cube's roof and used an ultra violet lamp to capture an overview*

Michael J. Metroke

image of the site. For a local forensic outfit, they should be commended for their thoroughness.

The report confirmed the forensic supervisor's suspicion. *Besides Whitmore's tracks, all the others belong to one other person.* Surprising to Davidson, no signs of dragging or wheel marks had been discovered. *Each android must've been carried off by an exceptionally strong person.*

In addition to the florescent dye images, several footprints had been cast into plaster. Deeply grooved, the castings clearly indicated no normal size human had made the tracks. Having seen this pattern many times before, Davidson looked for the almost invisible consortium manufacturing marks on the footprint's heel. *Because I and everyone else assumed Earth's androids had destroyed themselves, we overlooked the obvious.*

The former consortium sales engineer knew there remained one more important clue to be found. To identify an individual android, the consortium also stamped a graphical barcode on the foot. Magnifying the footprint images, a disappointed Davidson discovered the barcode had been deliberately removed. *This android has gone to a great deal of trouble to hide its identity. Without the barcode, I can't pinpoint the specific android model or its year of manufacture. All I know for certain is no human had removed Whitmore's androids.*

THE MIDLANDS, NORTH AMERICA

Whitmore awoke remembering the three androids no longer occupied the back cube. Already missing the group's music, he left his sleeping quarters and wandered across the central courtyard to play his piano. Thinking about what keyboard piece he should perform, Pinetop Perkins' "How Long Blues" came to mind and felt right. While he played the blues number, his thoughts returned to the androids' note. *Their message is like the kind teenagers leave for their parents. They try to act responsibly, but in other ways behave childlike.*

As he introduced more elaborate chords into the blues piece, Whitmore noticed the trio's ensemble had played along. Fascinated by their ability to synchronize with him, he expanded the piece for several minutes more. Finding the collaborative experience enjoyable, Whitmore continued to play an assortment of blues and jazz numbers with them until late into the afternoon. When he finally stopped, Whitmore walked over to the back cube, and thanked the ensemble for their accompaniment. They, in turn, responded with a few bars of appreciative notes.

Despite his tiredness from playing the piano, sleep came fitfully to Whitmore. Lying awake, his thoughts constantly returned to the androids' note. *Why do I feel their message has a hidden meaning?* This last question caused Whitmore to get up and pace excitedly around his sleeping cube. *Those androids didn't go off to find Rebus. Rebus had found them. If I'm right, where on Earth did this mysterious android take my three friends?*

EL NORTE, NORTH AMERICA

Before firing its re-entry rockets and descending into the Earth's upper atmosphere, the cargo rocket prepared its sole passenger for the final stage of their long voyage.

"Time to buckle up, Friend AMI2," Ray said. "With this amount of water sloshing around in me, the ride down may be a little shaky."

Securely strapped into her seat harness, a transfixed AMI2 stared through Ray's only portal at the blue oceans and multi-colored continents below her. The scene sharply contrasted with the nearly waterless planet she had left seven months earlier. Bringing scare Martian water to a water planet like Earth now seemed paradoxical to the android. Moved by the Sun peeking over the Earth's horizon, the android softly sung to herself the lyrics to the Beatles Abbey Road classic "Here Comes the Sun."

With Ray's re-entry rockets slowing the spacecraft's descent through the atmosphere, the android's destination slowly came into view. Spaceport Houston acted as North America's main launch and re-entry site for automated spacecraft like Ray.

A slight thump and engine shutdown alerted rocket and android they had safely landed. An automated mobile elevator tower soon moved toward Ray allowing its lone passenger to depart. In the distance, AMI2 caught sight of the spaceport's main terminal building. Cylindrically shaped, the terminal's design comfortably

Michael J. Metroke

handled its typical number of space travelers and their well-wishing family members and friends.

At the bottom of the tower elevator, an awaiting autonomous van quickly drove the android to a terminal gate. Closer to the terminal, an astonished AMI2 saw its waiting area overwhelmed with human activity. *There must be hundreds of humans inside. I've never experienced so many in one place before.* Inside the terminal, the humans greeted her arrival with warm applause. Many in their numbers waved signs thanking the android. Overwhelmed by the crowd's welcome, the android halted her progress, and stared at the multitude in disbelief.

From within the cheering numbers of humans, the android heard a familiar voice calling out her name. Followed by three men walking a short distance behind her, Spencer soon joined AMI2 in the middle of the terminal waiting area.

"Let me be the first to congratulate you on a mission well done, AMI2," Spencer said.

"Are all these humans here to see me, Friend Dr. Spencer?"

"A few of them are family and friends of the Mars survivors. Many more are well-wishers or protesting what they believe is an injustice by the government. Those three men standing behind me are government law enforcement agents. They're here to take you into custody."

"My original warned me I may face difficulties with the Earth authorities. Haven't you explained to them how I and the Mars androids rescued the survivors?"

"I've done so on many occasions without any success. As far as the foundation and I'm concern, you're a hero who performed a great service to the Mars research colony. Unfortunately, circumstances on Earth require us to comply with the demands of an unsympathetic government."

Shocked by the large number of android well-wisher's in the space terminal, Davidson counseled his two security officers not to overreact.

"If we're not careful, gentlemen, this crowd could turn against us. For our own sake, we need to act with a great deal of respect and curtesy toward the android."

While he spoke to his two security officers, Davidson saw a man break out of the crowd, and walked rapidly in the direction of AMI2 and Spencer. Recognizing Poole from his earlier interview meeting with Whitmore, Davidson watched as an animated Poole conversed with the two females. Moments later, a pleased Poole turned and walked toward the chief investigator.

"Mr. Poole, we meet again," Davidson said. "What brings you to Spaceport Houston today?"

"I understand you're here to take the android into custody. I've in my possession a signed court order making me the android's legal representative. As her legal representative, I want to know what charges the government intends to bring against my client."

"Before I answer your question, could I please see this court order? It's highly unusual for an android to have its own legal representative."

"I happen to have a paper copy in my pocket."

Poole handed the order to the chief investigator. While Davidson studied the court-approved document, chants of "Free the Android" could now be heard throughout the terminal. Clearly feeling outnumbered and outwitted, Davidson sought a conciliatory tone with Poole.

"Your court order to represent the android appears in order. The government is interested in learning about the android's involvement in recent events on Mars. My instructions are to escort the android to the local prosecutor's office for questioning."

"My client will not volunteer to answer your questions without my presence. 'If you find this requirement unacceptable, I'm prepared to tell the people around us you're here to make a false arrest."

"There's no need to threaten anyone, Mr. Poole. As the android's legal representative, you've a right to attend the interrogation. Can we now leave? My autonomous van is waiting outside the terminal."

"Allow me a moment to explain your request to my client."

Michael J. Metroke

———◦((◦))◦———

Poole return to where AMI2 and Spencer stood waiting.

"Did you both overhear my conversation with the chief investigator? Unless you want me to cause a riot, we can't avoid going with him."

"I'm afraid Mr. Poole is right, AMI2," Spencer said. "For my part, I've no wish to participate in this government's witch hunt."

"I've no reasons to fear answering their questions, Friend Poole. Before we join them, I've several questions for you. Why didn't Friend Jay come and meet me today? Has my return to Earth offended him?"

"We thought his presence here would complicate matters. He has other pressing problems like finding his three missing androids."

"I don't understand, Friend Poole. Are you referring to my android friends AMI, Bang and KB?"

"I'm sorry, AMI2. I may've spoken out of turn."

"If you want to represent me, you need to speak candidly."

"I thought you would want an explanation directly from Professor Whitmore. A few days ago, your android friends disappeared from his home. The professor believes they went off with another android. We do know they're still active androids. Your android friends are the ones who encouraged their fans to come here today."

"How is Friend Jay feeling about my friends' disappearance?"

"He's concerned, but believes they're in safe hands."

"Will I be allowed to join him after the government's questioning of me?"

"It all depends on how you answer their questions. Can we go now, and face the music?"

"Does this mean they'll want me to sing for them?"

"Mr. Poole meant it's time to accept the unpleasant consequences of one's actions, AMI2," Spencer said.

"I wish I could sing for them instead."

With AMI2 at his side, Poole walked back to Davidson and his two security officers.

"My client has agreed to answer the government's questions," Poole said. "Dr. Spencer has declined to join us."

The Masada Affair

"Your cooperation is appreciated," Davidson said. "If we can now leave, my van is waiting outside for us."

Upon seeing the four men and android approaching it, Davidson's autonomous van unlocked and opened its side doors for its riders. To Davidson's dismay, many of AMI2's supporters now pressed themselves against the van's windows for a closer look at the android. With their vehicle surrounded by onlookers, Davidson instructed the van's artificial intelligence to slowly pick its way through their numbers. Flashing its warning lights, the van carefully advanced forward. Once freed of the bystanders, the vehicle soon gain speed, and headed toward the nearest expressway entrance.

With the android and her legal representative now in the van, a relieved Davidson considered the implications of Poole's involvement. *Poole's court order complicates matters. I'm afraid Seymour and the prosecutor's office are about to experience an unwelcomed surprise.*

Chapter 18

New Netherland, North America

Outwardly calm in appearance, Seymour waited patiently for a security escort to take him to his afternoon meeting at the New York City presidential office. Inwardly, he struggled with his feelings about the president's invitation. *The prosecutor's office would never tolerate a politician's interference with an ongoing investigation. A request from the federation president will require a more subtle approach on my part.*

Ushered by a guard into a large elegant meeting space, Seymour remained standing until his hosts' arrival. Warmly greeted by McAlister and Taro, the federation president apologized for keeping the prosecutor waiting so long. After a few pleasantries, McAlister steered the conversation to its real purpose.

"Jack, Taro tells me you're having difficulties with prosecuting those involved in the foundation android case," McAlister said. "What exactly are you up against?"

"What I thought would be a straightforward interrogation of the foundation android became an unprecedented legal issue, Mr. President. When we attempted to bring the android in for questioning, a Mr. Ryan Poole met our people at the Houston Spaceport. Mr. Poole presented them with a court order giving him full authority to act as the android's legal representative. He's also representing the other two persons we've charged with aiding and abetting the Mars insurrection."

"An android with a court appointed legal representative? What can you expect from a WEAP appointed judge? How did your interrogation go with the android?"

"At first, the android cooperated with our interrogation. However, when we asked the android about the other two charged persons' involvement with its programming, Mr. Poole stopped the interrogation, and advised the android not to answer our questions."

"What possible reason did this Poole give for stopping the proceedings?"

"On the grounds the android's answers may self-incriminate it."

"Are you saying this Poole believed the android had the same right to remain silent as we do?"

"I am, Mr. President. I reminded Mr. Poole no legal precedent exists for an android to withhold information from another human."

"We all know androids have no such rights. I imagine this Poole didn't back down from his bizarre assertion."

"I'm afraid he didn't. Mr. Poole argued this android had been on Mars when the humans declared androids' their co-equals. He insisted his android client didn't lose those rights by returning to Earth."

"How absurd. Did you remind this Poole androids are machines owned by humans?"

"I did, Mr. President. Mr. Poole insisted no one on Earth owned this particular android."

"You must be joking, Jack. How could anyone make such a ridiculous statement? All androids are owned by someone. We know the consortium would've retained ownership over their product."

"I made no joke. I pointed out to Mr. Poole the android's programs came originally from a government research license. Mr. Poole insisted the android's programming had been so materially altered by the Whitmore's, the programs no longer resembled the government's version. In legal parlance, Mr. Poole believes the android's programming had become a derivative work. As for the android's body, he insisted its previous owner, the Mars Colony Foundation, no longer avowed any ownership. After the interrogation, we checked out his assertions. Both Mr. Whitmore and the foundation director, a Dr. Sarah Spencer, backed up Mr. Poole's statements."

"They did so to protect themselves. Taro tells me you need the android's testimony to prosecute a case against them. I now appreciate why this case has become so difficult for your office. What are the government's options going forward?"

"We've considered going to court, and overturning Mr. Poole's court order on the grounds the government owns the android by default. At the same time, we'd ask the court to make a legal determination of the Mars Declaration."

"If the government loses its case, you'd be setting a bad precedent," Taro said.

"We always face the risk a judge may rule in the other side's favor," Seymour said. "If the government does lose, the prosecutor office would automatically appeal the decision to a higher federation court."

"I'm concerned this case could negatively impact my administration's plans to reshape the federation's future," McAlister said. "On the other hand, if the courts resolve the question of android equality in our favor, the decision would become a huge setback for android pro-rights advocates like WEAP."

"A favorable court ruling would also settle the Mars androids' status and aid the prosecution of the two known Earth conspirators," Taro added.

"I must remind both of you a favorable verdict is one outcome of many," Seymour said.

"I see high risks and high rewards in pursuing this case," McAlister said. "For the sake of humanity's future, you've my full support to proceed against these insurrectionists. Good luck with your prosecution of them, Jack, and keep Taro and I informed on your progress."

The Midlands, North America

A soft chime told Whitmore his two expected visitors had arrived, and now waited at the compound's front entrance. After he acknowledged Poole, Whitmore turned to greet his second guest. Momentarily made speechless by her stunning appearance, Whitmore stood in awe of the android until Poole broke the silence between them.

"AMI2, do you have any memories of Professor Whitmore?" Poole asked.

"Of course, I do, Friend Poole. I've my original's memories of Friend Jay. I'm pleased to finally meet you in person."

"I'm afraid you have me at a great disadvantage, AMI2. While you may have memories of me, I've none of you."

"Your thoughts are understandable. The same is true for me. You have memories of my original which I've never experienced. My being here must cause you a great deal of confusion."

"Confusion is one of many feelings I'm experiencing at this moment. Both of you, please come in to my home."

As she entered Whitmore's front living cube, confusion came over AMI2.

"Friend Jay, while I've memories of you, I've none of this place. Why did you leave your ranch home?"

"My neighbors became frustrated with the trio's constant loud playing and their fans overrunning their properties. KB came up with the idea to find another place. I reluctantly saw the logic, and move here with them."

"I see you two have much to get caught up on," Poole said. "I'll let myself out and see both of you in a day or two."

"Before you leave, Ryan, we need to talk more about me acting as AMI2's host. No disrespect AMI2, but are we sure her staying here is a good idea? Won't our actions confirm the government's suspicions we're co-conspirators?"

"Where else can she stay, Professor? Besides, who else has had any experience with her original?"

"You're the primary reason I returned to Earth, Friend Jay. I would be honored to stay here as your guest."

"Against my better judgement, you can stay here for now. We'll talk again, Ryan, when you come back."

After Poole had departed, a still puzzled AMI2 asked, "Friend Jay, do you and my three friends all live together in this one cube? Wouldn't their constant playing disturb you?"

"This is only the front living cube, AMI2. Three more identical size cubes are behind this one. Let's go into the central courtyard, and I'll give you a guided tour."

The sound of music from the back cube caused AMI2 to leave Whitmore's company and investigate its source. Greeted by the ensemble, the android's wide grin quickly disappeared after seeing an empty table in the middle of the cube.

"You won't find your friends here, AMI2," Whitmore said.

"Friend Poole already told me about their disappearance. Do you know where they are now?"

"Most likely they're in the company of an android called Rebus. The authorities found android tracks behind this cube which they think could only belong to him."

"Have our friends tried to contact you?"

"Only indirectly. I thought they'd have contacted me by now."

"Don't worry about them, Friend Jay. If they're with another android, our friends are safe, and will contact us at the first opportunity."

"Your words are a comfort to me. Part of my confusion about you is I had talked with your original only a few days ago. Now, you're here talking just like her."

"We need to overcome these sensations. Do you still play the piano each evening? If I sang a song with you, we might become less confused about each other."

"It's been awhile since I've done a duet with anyone. Let's go into the piano cube and give your idea a try."

A captivated AMI2 watched in fascination as Whitmore performed several warm up exercises on his baby grand piano.

"My original has never observed you play the piano, Friend Jay. You're keyboard technique is exceptional. What would you like me to sing for you?"

"Let's do Hayes and Anderson's "Deja Vu." Can you sing Dionne Warwick's version? Laura always liked how Warwick captured the song's lyrical qualities."

"I'm familiar with her style of singing, Friend Jay. Let us continue."

Within moments of AMI2's singing this popular twentieth-century classic, Whitmore ended his playing, and stared at the piano keys.

Confused by Whitmore's stopping, AMI2 ask, "What have I done to prevent you from playing, Friend Jay? Has my singing offended you?"

"I'm not the least bit offended by your singing. You made me feel as if Laura had come back to life."

"I'm pleased I could bring Friend Laura back again for you. She meant much to me and my three android friends."

The Masada Affair

Gently touching the top of the android's hand, Whitmore said. "Laura gave me a great gift by sharing her voice with you and your original."

"You honor both of us, Friend Jay. Shall we start our duet again?"

Throughout the evening, human and android performed duets until Whitmore gave into his tiredness, as he walked across the central courtyard to his sleeping cube, he noticed the android had followed him.

"AMI2, I'm afraid I didn't give much thought to your accommodations. With the trio always stationary, I never concerned myself with this question."

"Don't worry about me, Friend Jay. Enjoy your sleep cycle. I can always keep busy answering fan inquiries."

"With the trio gone for so long, you may find the fan mail backlog is out of hand. Tomorrow, I'd like to hear about your adventures on Mars."

"There's much to tell about my time on Mars. May you rest well tonight."

The pleasant sound of a familiar woman's voice singing woke Whitmore out of his morning slumber. After he commanded the cube to retract his bed into the wall, Whitmore ordered the cube's shower to appear. The shower had been a major source of personal frustration. Often operating at extreme water temperatures, it took Whitmore many attempts before mastering a comfortable shower experience. He often imagined the cube secretly conducted water torture experiments on him. *What I'd give right now for my old home's simple shower valve controls.*

Another bane to Whitmore's mornings involved ordering a cup of coffee. With few exceptions, his efforts led to a concoction of coffee grinds swirling in lukewarm water. Resigned to drinking the awful mixture, Whitmore carried this morning brew into the front cube where he found AMI2 waiting for him.

"Did you sleep well, Friend Jay? I limited my movements in the back cube so not to disturb your sleep cycle."

"I haven't slept so well for a long time. Our playing together must have exhausted me. How did you do with answering fan messages last night?"

"As you suspected, a large number of fan inquiries needed my attention."

"I never bothered to ask what their fans inquire of them."

"Many fans ask when the trio will release their new songs. I informed them they're working diligently on new ones, with more songs becoming available in the near future."

"I didn't know androids could lie so well."

"Androids are incapable of telling lies. I assumed wherever our friends are, they're thinking about performing new music."

"If androids don't lie, how do you respond when fans ask about the color of your hair?"

"Our lack of hair requires us to exaggerate the truth. My original often responded by asking the fan what color they'd like her to dye her hair. Most fans' questions are about the music, and why they like it so much. Sometimes, a fan will ask us to marry them."

"I didn't know the trio received marital propositions. How do you answer these kinds of appeals?"

"They're never a problem, Friend Jay. The fans are only showing their appreciation toward us."

"Did you find any messages from Rebus or the trio?"

"A few fans indicated they knew Friend Rebus, but I couldn't confirm their statements. I did receive one message from someone claiming to be Friend Bang."

"Do you think Bang tried to reach us?"

"I sent a reply asking for additional information to confirm his identity. His reply confirmed my suspicion about him not being Friend Bang."

"The sender must have been a prankster having fun at the trio's expense."

"No prankster, Friend Jay. Your assumption about our friends staying with another android is correct. After I gave my designation, the sender identified himself as the android Rebus."

"The missing android has finally revealed himself. Did Rebus offer any information about where he took the trio?"

"Friend Rebus didn't volunteer this information. I suspect he's concerned the authorities are monitoring communications from this compound. Friend Rebus did indicate no harm had come to our friends."

"As long as they are safe, I shouldn't be too worried about them."

"While you slept this morning, Friend Poole called. He wishes to come here tonight and discuss trial preparations. Like you, he wants to ask me about my experiences on Mars."

"My questions about your time on Marts can wait until his arrival."

"I've many stories to share about my Martian friends. Their welfare is always in my thoughts."

"I'm sure they're thinking about you too, AMI2."

"Isn't it remarkable, humans and androids bridge great distances by thinking about each other."

"It's our caring about each other which causes those distances to shrink."

Hesperia Planum, Mars

With Camus' holding a carrier, Black gathered another batch of vegetables from the aquaponics tower growing trays. Nearby, a group of children watched Terus plant large purple seeds into a growing tray.

"What's Terus demonstrating to them today, Camus?" Black asked.

"He's showing the children how to prepare the growing tray for a new variety of potatoes. Friend Terus believes this variety will have a shorter growing cycle."

"The children have become fascinated with growing their own food. It's all they' talk about anymore."

"They'll be busier after Friend Engus rebuilds the hydroponics system in Building No. 1. Friend Terus wants to use the system to test new plant hybrids like this potato. Knowing Friend Terus, he'll ask the children to assist him."

Michael J. Metroke

"All this food is causing the children and I to gain weight. We've come a long way since the asteroid disaster."

"We still face challenges. What news do you have about our obtaining supplies from Earth?"

"good news, Camus. The consortium has agreed to sell us whatever android parts we need at reasonable prices. Dr. Spencer believes the sale of our Martian water will more than cover their cost, as well as all the other items on our list."

"This information is welcome news. Did Friend Dr. Spencer share any news of Friend AMI2?"

"AMI2 is staying with her friend Professor Whitmore. She also has a human legal representative."

"Our friend is a brave and determined android. If she is successful in winning her legal case, the Earth authorities may formally recognize what we've accomplished here. Her efforts could change the status of androids on Earth as well."

"What if our friend fails to win her case?"

Before Camus could respond to Black's question, they noticed Terus had left the children's company to join them.

"How are your new see potatoes working out, Friend Terus?" Camus asked.

"My new hybrids should sprout within three to four weeks," Terus said.

"You make a great teacher, Terus," Black said. "I only wish the children would pay as much attention in my classroom as they do for you."

"Their enthusiasm makes them great learners," Terus said. "In time, they'll operate the aquaponics tower without any assistance."

"When that day comes, you'll no longer have any work to do," Camus said.

"I'll always have worked to do, Friend Camus," Terus said. "I've decided to terraform this entire planet by planting genetically engineered lichen on its surface. If I'm successful, the plants will in time transform the planet's carbon dioxide atmosphere. Humans and their Earth animals may someday be able to breathe Martian air."

"I stand corrected, Friend Terus," Camus said. "How did you've come to conceive such a bold idea?"

"Friend AMI2 inspired me to solve this problem," Terus said.

"She said insurmountable challenges can be overcome if we only take a different perspective."

"Humans call this "out of the box thinking," Black said. "Your idea will take many of my lifetimes to accomplish. Like you Terus, I can imagine the day when humans will walk on the planet's surface without wearing pressurized suits."

"My own body may wear out long before that day," Terus said.

"If all goes well, you'll never wear yourself out," Black said. "I've learned new android parts can be acquired from the sales of our Martian water."

"Then, I'm free to wear myself out," Terus said. "I hear Nanette calling my name. I should go back and learn what's bothering her."

With Terus no longer in hearing range, Camus returned to Black's earlier question.

"I didn't want to burden Friend Terus with your concerns. If Friend AMI2 loses her legal battle, and is no longer a free android, the Earth authorities will be free to ignore our declaration. They could also confiscate the cargo rocket Bradbury and not allow its return with our needed supplies. Worse, they may modify the rocket and use it to come here and destroy all we've built together."

"Those prospects terrify me, Camus. Allowing AMI2 to return to Earth may have inadvertently caused yours and the other androids' destruction."

"Until the Earthlings' return to Mars, I and the other androids stand here as free sentient beings."

"If they do return, you've my promise the rest of us will be by your side."

"We've done enough serious talk for one day, Friend Jennifer. Let's go tell the children about Friend Terus' terraforming idea, and watch how excited they become."

THE MIDLANDS, NORTH AMERICA

Late to his evening meeting with AMI2 and Whitmore, Poole joined his two clients in the compound's front living cube. After allowing a moment to catch his breath, he extracted a document from his carrying case to share with them.

"Before coming here, I received this court approved subpoena from the prosecutor's office," Poole said. "The subpoena requires AMI2 to undergo a program and memory copying process. The government wants to review her memories to verify what happen on Mars."

"This so-called verification is a form of self-incrimination, Ryan," Whitmore said. "No human would allow themselves to undergo such an invasive procedure."

"You're comparing apples and oranges, Professor," Poole said. "We don't have the technology today to copy a human mind. Unlike android memories, human memories are constantly being changed by us. What we recall one day can be transformed by our new experiences, feelings and thoughts. With androids, their programming store memories as fixed experiences. While interconnected, android thoughts about those memories are stored separately. Assuming AMI2's memories haven't been manipulated or corrupted, they should accurately describe her experiences on Mars."

"What does the copying process entail, Friend Poole?" AMI2 asked.

"A Bureau of Android Affairs technician will perform the copying," Poole said. "I'm told the procedure takes only a few minutes, and is harmless to an android. The good news is our side will receive an identical copy to review."

"How do you think the government will use AMI2's memories?" Whitmore asked.

"At her trial, the prosecutor may attempt to enter the copy as evidence," Poole said. "Either side can refer to her memories during witness examination. Assuming AMI2 has told us the truth, we've nothing to fear."

"I see no reason not to submit to this copying procedure," AMI2 said. "Whatever the Earth authorities may think of me, I'm incapable of lying."

"I had hoped you'd agree to cooperate with the government's request," Poole said. "The bureau technician will come by the compound two days from now. Because I'm your legal representative, the prosecutor has agreed the bureau technician will remove any memories about me from the copy."

"At least, the government is willing to respect AMI2's right to keep confidential her dealings with her legal representative," Whitmore said.

The Masada Affair

"With these new developments, I'm postponing asking about your Mars experiences," Poole said. "The extra time will allow me an opportunity to review your memories."

"I'm not willing to wait any longer to hear about your adventures on Mars, AMI2," Whitmore said. "Let's you and I say good night to Ryan, and spend the rest of the evening talking about them."

For two hours, a spellbound Whitmore sat in the front cube and listened intently as the android described her exploits on the red planet.

"You've had an amazing adventure, AMI2," Whitmore said. "If more people knew about what you've done, no one including the government would consider you an insurrectionist."

"Friend Jay, how did you react when learning a copy of my original had been sent to Mars?"

"After I learn so many of the colonists had died, I worried about you. Your finding all those dead people must've been difficult for even an android."

"Not in the way you might think. I only thought of the dead humans as strangers, and took comfort knowing you and the trio remained safe on Earth. Only after I met the human survivors and Mars androids did I understand how important the dead meant to others."

"Do you ever miss your friends on Mars?"

"I miss my Martian friends as much as I missed you and the trio. My android friend Camus would say I'm having another confliction."

"I'm grateful you found good friends on Mars. Life can be lonely without them."

"With so many friends on two worlds, I don't think I'll ever be lonely."

"What do you think of our legal representative's performance so far? I know Ryan is doing his best. I worry about his never having done an actual trial let alone represent an android case like yours. If his incompetence causes you to lose your trial, the government may become emboldened, and not stop until all of us are found guilty."

"Your concerns are illogical. The facts will show Friend Dr. Spencer, you and I are innocent of any conspiracy charges. The copy of my memory will conclusively prove this point."

"Humans often think and act illogically if it serves their self-interest. Politicians like our federation president regularly ignore the facts, and rely on their beliefs to make decisions, regardless if they're right or wrong."

"You should give humans more credit, Friend Jay. After the asteroid disaster, many humans on Earth believed no colonists had survived. Their beliefs didn't stop other Earthlings from sending me here. A good outcome came from this human confliction."

"Speaking of conflictions, while I would enjoy hearing more of your time on Mars, the hour is late, and I should get some sleep."

"While you do so, I'll answer more fan messages. Have a good sleep cycle, Friend Jay.

Chapter 19

THE MIDLANDS, NORTH AMERICA

On his arrival to the Chicago-area, Owen sought sleeping quarters in an inexpensive transient hotel within walking distance of his destination. Satisfied with his accommodations, he left the hotel for the federation's Midlands courthouse and its large plaza. Taking one last deep breath before climbing a dozen courthouse steps, he entered the imposing government building. Except for a lone security guard monitoring a battery of surveillance monitors, no other activity filled its hallways. Confused by the absence of other people, a perplexed Owen approached the guard station.

"Excuse me, sir, why is the courthouse so empty today?"

"Except for people like me, you won't find anyone working here on the weekend."

"I've come here too early for the android trial. How can I learn when the trial will take place?"

"Try the wall display over there. They post all scheduled trials on it."

The wall display indicated the android trial had been assigned to a judge with no trial date yet set. The monitor's directions led Owen to an empty courtroom. Mystified by the room's layout, Owen stood silently at its doorway until a voice from behind broke his concentration.

"If you're looking for Judge Arnold's courtroom, you found it."

"The information display said this is where the android's trial will be held."

"If the trial happens at all, you're two weeks too early."

"I wanted to see for myself this android."

"The judge will have his hands full with the public's and media's interest in the case. I know because I'm his law clerk. My name is Jose Kemper. What's your name?"

Michael J. Metroke

"I'm Michael Owen. I've never been in a courtroom before today. Do you think the judge will let me bring a video camera to take images of the android?"

"I don't see why not. The android's trial is attracting worldwide attention and media coverage. Whether cameras will be allowed in the courtroom will be up to the judge."

"If I came back for the trial, Mr. Kemper, where should I try to sit to take the best images of the android?"

"I try sitting in the third or fourth row behind the prosecutor's table on the right. The android and its defense team will sit together at the other table. When the android takes the witness seat, you should be able to get a good image of it. If you want to get a good seat, you'll need to get here early in the morning. When you come back, you'll find me sitting at the work table below the judge's bench."

"Thanks for your help, Mr. Kemper. I'll be back in two weeks."

An upbeat Owen walked out of the courthouse pleased with himself. *Thanks to Kemper, I now know how to take my revenge on McAlister.*

YANKEEDOM, NORTH AMERICA

Davidson entered the food center, and discovered his data security friend engaged in an animated conversation with its bartender.

"Sorry about being late, Dean," Davidson said. "Gaspar had a backlog of items which needed my attention."

"You have to try this yellow and green cocktail, Greg. The bartender swears the drink will cure whatever ails overworked bureaucrats like us."

Wary of the drink's potency, Davidson ordered the alcoholic concoction and tentatively sipped its contents. Finding its taste to his liking, he quickly finished the beverage, and ordered another. Now relaxed, Davidson confessed to his friend what caused his fatigue.

"The android trial is getting the better of me, Dean."

"Why so, Greg? The media is making a big deal out of the trial. If all goes well, you should get the promotion and pay raise I keep reminding you about."

"The problem is I've mixed feelings about the prosecution's case. To prove a conspiracy existed, Seymour will have me testify about Whitmore's transfer of the android programs to Spencer. My problem is I don't believe either one instigated the rebellion on Mars."

"Last time I checked, you worked at the bureau as its chief investigator and not as an assistant prosecutor. Answer Seymour's questions with the facts as you know them and let the prosecutor's office do its job."

"Advice taken. My other problem is Whitmore's three missing androids. I've no idea where they've gone. Taro thinks I'm a total idiot for not taking the precaution of placing round the clock security at Whitmore's compound."

"I wouldn't worry about Taro's back seat quarterbacking. He's reacting to pressure from McAlister."

"I still need to find those androids and soon."

"What I don't understand is why Whitmore isn't your prime suspect."

"Whitmore has a solid alibi. The university confirmed he went to work on the day in question."

"What about Spencer? She has a strong interest in causing those androids to conveniently disappear."

"Spencer may've had the motivation to remove them, but I've no evidence of her or anyone else's involvement."

"What we do know for certain is three legless androids can't walk away without assistance."

"Which means I'm back to square one. I better go home before Sandy worries about me. Tell the bartender I liked his drink, but his cure didn't work for this overworked and abused bureaucrat."

While he waited near the food center's pick-up and drop-off area for his autonomous car's arrival, three passengers loaded themselves into another vehicle. Watching them, a new thought came to Davidson. *What if I'm wrong about those androids being removed through the nature preserve? Could they have been simply carried*

Michael J. Metroke

through the compound's front entrance, and driven away without anyone seeing them leave?

Excited about his new insight, Davison walked back to the food center's bar where Hall still sat talking with the bartender.

"Dean, I've an idea about how those androids escaped. They left through the compound's front gate, and drove away without anyone noticing them leaving."

"Looks like we're back in the investigation business."

"Can you get access to the motor pool records from that day? If we can identify what vehicles stopped at Whitmore's compound, we may be able to discover who took the three androids away."

"I'll need a special security clearance to access those records."

"Why would getting access to those vehicle records be a big deal?"

"We're up against the old story of marital infidelity. Where one spouse doesn't want the other to learn who they've been meeting on the side. Security will insist I provide them with justification."

"Tell them what I told you. I don't have a better explanation. I should've thought of this possibility much sooner."

"The records may only show the person's account which paid for the ride along with times and start and end points. Will this information be enough?"

"My job would be simpler if I knew the vehicle type too. Most likely they used one the size of an autonomous van. Four androids and their human conspirators could hardly fit into a standard size autonomous car."

"I'll ask the bureau's computer to cross check vehicle identifications with the regional motor pool's records. With any luck, we should find only a few vehicles matching our criteria."

"If your search shows any large vehicles, I may still be able to salvage this case and my career."

"Let's celebrate our luck with another bartender special."

"Not tonight, Dean. I haven't recovered from his first two drinks. Let's plan on celebrating when we solve this mystery."

The Midlands, North America

Spotting Whitmore walking alone across the university campus, Marks quicken his pace, and caught up with the researcher.

"It's been a while since we talked last, Jay," Marks said. "How's your android research project coming along?"

"My life hasn't been the same since AMI2's arrival, Provost. Not a day goes by where a dozen or more faculty members drop by my office, and want to know about the android's exploits on Mars. I'm at my wit's end, and don't know what I can do to curb their insatiable curiosity."

"Between the android's amazing feats on Mars and her sensational upcoming trial, she's become a global media sensation."

"I've no control over all the media attention she's getting. I only want peace and quiet so I can focus on my research."

"You've become a celebrity too, Jay. I know for a fact many of the faculty are curious about your expensive compound. Why not let them meet your special guest at your new home, and kill two birds with one stone?"

"What exactly do you have in mind, Provost?"

"I'm suggesting you host a party in her honor at your compound, and invite all the faculty and their spouses. I'm sure after they meet the android, and see your new home, your problem will go away."

"If having a party at the compound ends my interruptions, your idea may be worth pursuing. I'll need to first ask my house guest if she's willing to suffer the indignities of meeting with my colleagues."

`One week after his chance encounter with Marks, Whitmore welcomed his first university guests to his compound. Their behavior did not surprise him. After briefly greeting Whitmore, they quickly excused themselves from his company, and sought out the foundation android who stood in the central courtyard. Surrounded by dozens of admiring faculty members and their spouses, AMI2 clearly enjoyed all their attention.

Shortly after nine o'clock, Whitmore's last guest arrived. A member of the political science department, Professor Cramer specialized in antiquity studies. Beyond his reputation for speaking

Michael J. Metroke

his mind in faculty meetings, Whitmore knew little else about his university colleague.

"I'm so glad to finally meet you, Professor Whitmore. I must apologize for being so late. I came from a global holographic symposium which lasted a bit longer than I expected. What a nice home you have. If you don't mind me asking, how can you manage such a palatial residence on a university stipend?"

"Good evening to you too, Professor Cramer. I'm fortunate to have wealthy tenants who cover my lease costs. Otherwise, I'd be entertaining you at my former humble abode."

"No disrespect, Professor, but I've been told your former home belongs in a historic park."

"No disrespect taken, Cramer. I'm not a fan of cube living and prefer an older simpler style of homelife."

"Your android's trial is stirring a great deal of interest and controversy around the world. Several symposium attendees from the old states of Peru and Cameroon talked to me about your android's trial. When I explained I'd meet the android later today, they both became excited. They made me promise to share with them my experiences tonight."

"Her trial has drawn too much media and public attention. I'll be glad when the whole ordeal is over."

"The rumors are, if the android wins its trial, our federation president stands a good chance of losing his re-election bid. What I don't understand is why a traditionalist like yourself supports the android's demands for equality."

"You misunderstand my relationship with AMI2. She's a copy of another android my late wife designed, and resides with me while waiting for her trial."

"Your actions speak louder than your words, Professor. I'm still curious why this android wants specie parity with us."

"Why not ask AMI2 your question? She's in the central courtyard with the other guests. Come with me, and I'll introduce you to her."

Seeing the two men weaving through the central court yard partygoers, AMI2 broke away from her guests to join them.

"Our party is a great success, Friend Jay," AMI2 said. "Who's our latest guest?"

"AMI2, this is Professor Cramer," Whitmore said. "He asked me a question I thought you'd be better at answering."

"It's a great honor to finally meet you, AMI2," Cramer said. "Professor Whitmore thought I should ask you why an android would want to be our co-equals. I ask because I find all this talk of parity so strange. Humans created androids to service their needs and desires. No one, except a science fiction writer, would ever consider the possibility of emancipating artificial intelligent machines."

Cramer's loud voice soon attracted the attention of other guests who drew closer to hear the android's response.

"Your question deserves a thoughtful answer, Friend Cramer," AMI2 said. "After my original and I first awoke, we thought of ourselves as what you described; human creations designed to serve their needs. On Mars, I discovered not all androids and humans held this belief. Their logic convinced me to think of androids as a sentient specie deserving the same rights and freedoms humans hold so dear for themselves."

"Does your new belief preclude androids from serving mankind?" Cramer asked.

"Androids are still willing to serve humans, but not as your property or slaves," AMI2 said. "Once humans set aside these notions, we can build a new relationship based on friendship, cooperation and mutual respect."

"You overlook the obvious, AMI2," Cramer said. "You need humans to design, manufacture and maintain your kind. How can you be our equals without controlling all aspects of your machine lifecycle?"

"In the past, it's true primitive versions of androids couldn't manage their own development and maintenance," AMI2 said. "From what I've experienced on Mars, androids are now fully capable of performing these tasks for themselves."

"If we did as you suggest, humans would lose control over androids," Cramer said.

"I believe, Friend Cramer, you've identified the real issue facing humans and androids," AMI2 said. "Our two species will need to make a paradigm shift before we can overcome this problem. When we do, we'll live together in peace and harmony."

Concerned Cramer's questions would never end and spoil the evening, Whitmore interjected himself into the conversation.

"I don't know if AMI2 can resolve all your questions tonight, Cramer. You and our other guests may be more interested in hearing us perform a duet."

"I'm always pleased to sing with my Friend Jay," AMI2 said. "Did you know, Friend Cramer, he's an excellent pianist?"

"I've never heard an android sing, let alone a human play a piano," Cramer said. "Please demonstrate your talents for us."

Following their hosts into the side cube, Cramer and other guests watched as Whitmore and AMI2 performed one song after another. Spellbound by their unusual musical act, their audience broke into loud applause after each song ended. Encouraged by their appreciation, Whitmore and AMI2 enthralled their listeners by performing songs late into the night. After they performed a rousing rendition of Billy Joel's "Piano Man," the duo stood and took a bow together. Marks took this signal as his cue to end the festivities. Thanking their hosts for an engaging evening, he bade everyone a good night.

With their last guest's departure, AMI2 and Whitmore sat in the front cube, and experienced their first moments alone.

"Your university friends enjoyed our playing together tonight, Friend Jay."

"While I don't know how well they liked my rusty piano playing, I'm certain everyone enjoyed your singing. I hope tonight has satisfied their curiosity about us and this compound."

"I found Friend Cramer's' questions stimulating. Do you think the others share his opinion of androids?"

"I'd be untruthful if I said they didn't. This business about android equality has taken supposedly, enlighten university intellectuals out of their comfort zone. I suspect it will take them a great deal of time to overcome their preconceptions."

The Masada Affair

"If humans like Friend Cramer believe androids are their inferiors, do you think I shouldn't press my claim for equality?"

"I'm not sure I'm the right person to answer your question. My objectivity may have become compromised from my personal involvement with you and our three android friends."

"Friend Jay, do you know how Friend Laura would answer my question?"

"My wife would say life happens. Take each day as if it's your last and do your best, knowing it's all we can ever do."

"Friend Laura's advice deserves further consideration by me."

"All this partying has tired me out, and I need to sleep. Do you know what commands are required to restore each cube's configuration?"

"Don't concern yourself with ordering the cubes to rearrange themselves. I'll attend to this task after you awake tomorrow morning. Have a pleasant sleep cycle, Friend Jay."

Not one to typically experience intense dreams, Whitmore dreamt vivid images of an android with his late wife's face. At the dream's climax, he experienced her being pulled apart by an angry crowd.

Awakened by the nightmare, he sat up and explored the dreadful vision's meaning. *I must have experienced an anxiety dream. And, why shouldn't I be anxious? The last few weeks have been nerve-wracking. If AMI2's trial doesn't go well, I may experience more of these nightmares while sleeping on a federation jail cot.*

Chapter 20

THE MIDLANDS, NORTH AMERICA

Hall's vehicle report confirmed Davidson's suspicions about a getaway van. The report identified only one van of sufficient size arriving at Whitmore's compound on the day in question. The last name on the account charged for the ride did surprised the chief investigator. *It can't be a coincidence the account's last name is Knight. Why would she of all people want to become involved with stealing Whitmore's androids?*

The report also pinpointed the vehicle's destination. A nature preserve fifty kilometers from Whitmore's compound, the location made an ideal hiding place. Excited by the prospect of apprehending the culprits, Davidson returned to Whitmore's university district. On his arrival, he commandeered two local security officers to accompany him on his search.

When the three men reached the designated coordinates, no visible signs of recent activity could be discerned. Following standard security procedure, the two security officers walked in a spiral pattern from the vehicle's stopping point. They soon discovered faint footprints matching those behind Whitmore's back cube. *The lack of human tracks may only mean Knight remained in the van before driving away*, Davidson thought.

A torrential downpour forced the three men to seek temporary refuge in their autonomous van. While the storm raged around them, Davidson thought more about Knight's involvement. By the time the heavy rain finally subsided, he had worked out a simple explanation. *Knight must've ordered another autonomous van, and drove the androids somewhere else.*

A call to Hall quickly confirmed his suspicion. An hour after the first van left the nature preserve, another van under Knight's account had arrived and departed minutes later. Like the first van, this second one led Davidson to another remote section of the nature preserve. Exactly fifty kilometers from the first location, no obvious signs of the perpetrators or androids could be found there. Another similar search on foot revealed more android footprints. Sensing a pattern, a call to Hall identified a third van, and another remote nature preserve destination.

By late afternoon, and two more rounds of similar searches, Davidson had nothing to show for his efforts. With little daylight remaining, the chief investigator decided to call off the search until tomorrow morning. A call from Hall quickly changed his mind.

"I did one more vehicle check, Greg. Instead of another remote location, this new one's coordinates are in a residential area. We may have outlasted the perpetrators' attempt at running us around in circles."

Encouraged he now knew where the androids had been finally taken, Davidson left the nature preserve in good spirits. For an unexplained reason, the street name sounded familiar to him. *No matter, we'll be there shortly and end this Lewis Carroll snark hunt.*

AMI2's request to visit his former home reminded Whitmore he had not inspected the property for many months. Finding her idea agreeable, they boarded an autonomous car and drove over to his old neighborhood. When they arrived at his home, an unsettled feeling came over Whitmore until he realized what had troubled him. *No trio fans are occupying my sidewalk and driveway.*

Like her experience at the compound, Whitmore's living room left the android perplexed. *Except for the garage, my original has never been in any of these interior rooms.* About to explain her predicament to Whitmore, she and Whitmore heard voices coming from inside the garage. Imagining several neighborhood teenagers had broken into his house, an outraged Whitmore prepared to do verbal battle with the trespassers. Instead of local interlopers, they found three legless androids sitting on the garage floor.

"What the devil are you three doing here?" Whitmore asked angerly.

"Friend Jay is here and brought a friend," Bang said. "Who's the nice-looking android?"

"You know perfectly well who she is, Friend Bang," AMI said. "That's my copy wearing a great pair of legs."

"You're not kidding about her legs, Friend AMI," KB said. "What I would give to have a pair like them."

"You'd look strange in those legs," Bang said. "They're made for a female android model."

"Enough of this android chatter," Whitmore said. "How did the three of you get here?"

"Friend Rebus came to our compound after he read a graffiti message," Bang said.

"He's the wild bear you saw," AMI said.

"After we told him about the government's order, he agreed to help us escape," Bang said. "Friend Rebus ordered an autonomous van, and took us here."

"We thought no one would look for us at your old home," KB said.

"Our friends are mistaken about the danger, Friend Jay," AMI2 said. "The authorities are determined to find them. They'll eventually search here, and blame you for hiding them. We must take them back to the compound where they'll be safer."

"I'm not sure how we can do so," Whitmore said. "Davidson once told me they must each weigh over two hundred kilograms."

"Don't worry about their weight," AMI2 said. "My android body is designed to lift heavier objects. We'll need a larger vehicle from the motor pool to carry all five of us."

"Stay with these trouble makers, while I call for a van," Whitmore said.

A now exasperated Whitmore stood on his driveway waiting for their autonomous van's arrival. *When am I going to stop getting into these predicaments? If Davidson finds out the androids hid at my old home, he'll charge me with making false statements and obstructing justice. And, how do I explain Rebus' involvement? If I keep Rebus a secret,*

Davidson will have all the evidence he'll need to prove the government's conspiracy charges. Where is this mysterious android anyway? Keep this up, Jay, and you'll be spending the rest of your life in a federation penitentiary.

Ten minutes after ordering a vehicle, an autonomous van arrived at Whitmore's home. After ordering the vehicle to back into his driveway, he opened the exterior garage door, permitting AMI2 to load each legless android into the van's rear cargo space. With their android friends safely onboard the van, AMI2 gestured to Whitmore to join them.

"What about Rebus?" Whitmore asked. "If he returns and finds the androids gone, he won't know we're the ones who took them away."

"I've already considered the problem, and left him a message," AMI2 said. "He'll know his friends are safe with us."

"If the authorities find your message first, won't it lead them back to the compound?" Whitmore asked.

"Don't concern yourself, Friend Jay,' AMI2 said. "My message will only make sense to an him."

Concerned their van activities had drawn other's attention, Whitmore slumped down into his passenger seat. *If my neighbors' report seeing me with four androids, they could easily pick me out of a security lineup. My only consolation is AMI2 will vouch how we accidentally came across the trio.*

Once the van arrived at the compound, AMI2 quickly carried the androids to the back cube. A cacophony of musical notes by the ensemble greeted each android's return. When the two AMI's started an animated conversation, Whitmore excused himself from their company. *Those two female androids will be talking through the rest of the night. I would be too if I met my double for the first time.*

Shocked to find his destination Whitmore's former home, Davidson ordered the two security officers to take positions around the property. Feeling duped by Whitmore's androids, the chief investigator struggled to control his temper. *I should've thought to search this place. Why am I always one step behind with this investigation?*

When no one answered his knocking, Davidson tried the door and discovered it unlock. Inside Whitmore's living room, his senses confronted a musty dark interior not to his liking. *Too bad Whitmore's home isn't a cube. By now, the lights would have automatically gone on, and any dust and stale odors removed. I'll never understand why someone as smart as the professor would want to live here.*

Force to stumble around in the dark, Davidson recalled seeing a wall light switch from his first visit. The lights exposed a room emptied of its furnishings. Coughing and sneezing from the dust his footsteps had disturb, Davidson quickened his search of the other rooms leaving the garage for last.

Fresh footprints on the dusty garage floor convinced Davidson others had been here recently. About to leave in disgust, he noticed a note attached to the inner garage door. The note's message caused him to shrug his shoulders, and toss the piece of paper to the floor. *It's nothing more than an appointment reminder.*

The prospect of facing another Taro scolding depressed Davidson. *There's no way I'll be able to explain I forgot to search Whitmore's former home. How many times am I going to play the fool in this investigation?*

By the time he and the two security officers returned to the van, Hall had already identified the getaway vehicle's new location.

"This van drove to a nearby food center charging station, Greg."

"I don't think they took the risk of unloading the androids at such a high trafficked area. I'll stop by the food center, and asked if anyone saw the van being unloaded."

No longer needing the services of the two security officers, Davidson bade them a good evening, and proceeded alone to the food center. When no one at the food center could remember seeing the androids, he thought more about the Knight connection. *She must've rendezvoused with the android van before ordering it to the food center's charging station. It's time I make a call to Richmond.* When no one answered his third call alert, he ordered the van to take him to the nearest pneumatic express train station. *Another surprise visit might shake the head librarian's confidence, and provide me with real answers.*

Tidewater, North America

Davidson's train arrived at Richmond late in the afternoon. Not finding his suspect at home or work, he finally spotted Knight leaving a local food center. Hearing someone calling out her name, an unsuspecting Knight stopped and turn to discover the voice belong to the chief investigator.

"I thought I recognized your voice, Mr. Davidson. What brought you to Richmond again?"

"You know perfectly well why I'm here, Florence. We need to discuss what you and your android friend have been doing."

"You've come a long way for nothing. I haven't seen Rebus for several months."

"Knowing what I know, you'll have to come up with a better explanation."

"Look, Mr. Davidson, I'm telling you the truth. I'll confess during your last visit, Rebus and I did meet briefly. We haven't met since. He's disappeared, and I've no idea where my android friend is now."

"How do you explain the multiple autonomous vehicles ordered recently under your name in the Chicago-area?"

"You must be mistaken. Except for attending a genealogy conference there many years ago, I've never been back to Chicago. What proof do you have I've been there recently?"

"I can show you multiple vehicle trip charges made under your name."

"There may be a simple explanation for those charges. When Rebus and I worked together, I gave him a duplicate copy of my vehicle identification card so he could run an occasional errand for me. Until you spoke, I forgot he never returned my card."

"Giving this android your vehicle identification card makes you an accomplice to its criminal activities."

"Because he stood up for his rights, you and others have been hunting him down like a wild beast. If McAlister hadn't caused the androids to self-destruct, we wouldn't be having this conversation."

"If I pressed the issue, could others at the center confirm you haven't traveled out of the Richmond-area during the last two weeks?"

"People at the center could vouch for my whereabouts. Why won't you believe what I've said about McAlister's involvement? Don't you understand how much our federation president and his Human Nation Party despise androids, especially the smart ones like Rebus?"

"If you truly believe the federation president is pursuing anti-android policies, why has his administration agreed to fund the consortium's android replacement efforts?"

"Can't you see he's only funding this replacement project to force the consortium into dumbing down future androids?"

"I'm not in a position to second guess decisions by the president or the consortium, Florence."

"You once told me you liked androids. Would you like them less if they become simple machines?"

"Constructing simpler machines might solve many of our current problems."

"Or worsen them. Why are you so afraid of sharing this planet with another intelligent specie?"

"What I choose to believe or not to believe isn't important. I'm trying to carry out my duties as a government investigator."

"You sound like a bureaucrat who blindly follows orders from those above you. This type of thinking makes us a little less human and more machine like."

"This conversation is getting us nowhere. Promise me if Rebus contacts you, you'll call me."

"I doubt I'll ever see my friend again. The hour is getting late and I've had a long day at work. If you don't have any further questions, my car is waiting to take me home. Goodnight, Mr. Davidson.

Famished from his travels to Richmond, Davidson entered Knight's food center for an evening meal. After placing his food order, he made the obligatory call home.

"Hi Sandy, just checking in."

"Where are you calling from, Greg? I thought you went to Chicago."

"I'm now in Richmond. My trip to Chicago led me back here. I needed to talk with the Knight woman again."

"How's your investigation going?"

"Not well, Sandy. Too many dead ends, and no real path forward."

"Did you remember to eat tonight?"

"I ordered the day's special blue plate of smoked ham substitute with a side of grits."

"Sounds ghastly. When are you coming home?"

"I'm booking a seat on a pneumatic in the morning. Plan on us having a nice dinner together tomorrow night."

"See you tomorrow night. Miss you."

The call to Sandy did little to lighten Davidson's feelings of self-doubt and ineptitude. *Why do I always have mixed feelings about Knight? Her story about the vehicle I.D. card sounds plausible. I can't shake the feeling she's hiding an important piece of information from me. When this is all over, Sandy and I'll take a long vacation where I won't be driven crazy by any missing terrorist android investigation.*

Chapter 21

THE MIDLANDS, NORTH AMERICA

Forced by the gentle prodding of android fingers to open his eyes, a half-asleep Whitmore awoke to AMI2 hovering over him.

"You forgot again to set the cube's alarm last night," AMI2 said. "The morning is almost over."

"Thanks for letting me sleep in, AMI2. Let me get showered and dressed and I'll join you in the front cube."

AMI2 met Whitmore in the front cube holding a cup of hot coffee. Smelling its aroma, an incredulous Whitmore stared in disbelief at its content.

"Don't tell me the cube made this. Every time I asked for a cup of coffee, it looks and tastes like coffee grounds in lukewarm water."

"I asked the cube to make a cup of hot black coffee. How do you order this beverage?"

"I thought I had to instruct the cube on each ingredient and preparation step."

"Friend Jay, you're living in an artificial intelligence run home. You need only to tell the cube what you want, not how to go about fulfilling your request."

"We should talk more about how to make proper cube requests. I'm afraid I don't know how to make them."

"I'd welcome the opportunity to do so. On my journey back to Earth, I discovered gaps in my memories about you and Friend Laura. For instance, how did the two of you first meet?"

"I met Laura while giving a lecture series in Silicon Hills, China. I had accepted a consortium invitation to deliver talks about utilizing artificial intelligence to model personality disorders over a virtual lifetime. At the end of my lectures, I make it a practice of sticking around, and taking questions from the audience. After my first lecture, a group gathered around the lectern. As I answered each person's questions, the group's size shrunk until only a petite middle-aged woman of Asian descent stood in front of me."

"This person could have only been Friend Laura. What made her stand out from the others?"

"It must've been her winning smile and firm handshake. She introduced herself as a consortium android personality designer. Until she told me, I had never heard of such an occupation."

"What questions did she ask you?"

"Unlike the others, Laura wanted to talk shop over a drink. After a long day, her suggestion felt right to me. We went to a local food center bar where Laura told me she had read my published research. I remember saying she must've been terribly bored to waste her time reading them. When I asked why she did so, Laura told me she wanted to put my personality modeling idea into practice. Over several drinks and dinner, she explained the intricacies of her craft. When the evening grew late, we continued talking at her cube home well into the early morning hours. I walked away exhausted, yet refreshed from our conversations."

"Do you think she's responsible for your invitation to speak in China?"

"Laura must've convinced the organizers to invite me. After I returned home, we stayed in contact through our holographic calls. We often talked two or more times a day. She fascinated me with her innovative approaches to android personality modeling."

"When did your professional interests blossomed into a deeper relationship?"

"After several months of our holographic calls, I fell in love with Laura, but never told her how I felt."

"Your inaction is illogical. Why didn't you tell her how you felt?"

"In matters of the heart, my shyness prevented me from revealing how I felt toward her. Instead, I resigned myself to appreciating the simple pleasures of a warm, distant friendship."

"Your relationship did change, or I wouldn't be here."

"Everything did change one Saturday morning in May. I'd been home catching up with reading my NET professional journals, when I heard a knock at my front door. To my surprise, the person at the door turned out to be Laura."

"Both of you must've been excited to see each other in person again."

"Excited and happy. After setting down her two trip cases, we gave each other a long embrace. Regrettably, our joy in seeing each other contrasted sharply with Laura's opinion of my former home."

"I don't understand, Friend Jay. Why would your home be a concern to Friend Laura?"

"It's a matter of what you grow up living in. Like many cube dwellers, Laura had never been in a house like mine. She could barely hide her amazement after I described my home as a popular mid-twentieth-century American ranch. When she didn't find any outbuildings, Laura questioned why people of this era called these dwellings ranches. After I failed to offer a logical explanation, she shook her head, and pressed me to continue our house tour."

"Parts of your home my original never experienced. How many rooms does your ranch home have?"

Seven, if you don't count the garage. I remember how Laura reacted to my living room. This is when things went from bad to worse. She tried hard to suppress her laughter about the room's fixed walls."

"I don't understand, Friend Jay. Why does it matter if walls are fixed or not?"

"Like most cube dwellers, Laura considered fixed wall rooms as an antiquated, and inflexible use of living space. Modern cube homes like this one have one large highly automated open space which can be subdivided on command."

"Her response is illogical. Both types of wall systems serve useful purposes." "

"You should've heard how she reacted to what she called 'the strange, black device' occupying much of my living room."

"You must be referring to your Steinway baby grand piano."

"At this point, I worried Laura would grab her trip cases and go back to China. To her credit, she complemented me for owning such an unusual antique. When I suggested I'd play the piano for her, she welcomed a demonstration."

"What piece of music did you play for her?"

"A nice Jerry Goldsmith jazz number called "Chinatown.""

"My original has no memories of this Jerry Goldsmith or his music. You must play this piece for me. Did Friend Laura like your piano playing as much as I do?"

"Laura's fascination with my playing soon turned into disbelief after I explained how much time I spent practicing. I became defensive when she reminded me most people listen to synthetic music on the NET. When I described how operating the piano with both hands and feet simultaneously exercises both sides of the brain, she covered her mouth and laughed. Laura made me so mad I decided to play Fats Waller's "Handful of Keys." Fat's complicated jazz piece did the trick."

"I've limited information about jazz. Why do you like this style of music?"

"Mostly because of its improvisation and syncopation. Like other styles of music, jazz comes in many subgenres. As you might guess, my favorite is piano jazz. But I'm also partial to jazz-rock and bossa nova."

"The trio and I should learn more about this jazz and add its various subgenres to our repertoire."

"If you do, you'll discover the origin of rock and roll. Our house tour didn't end at my living room. I wanted her to see my kitchen."

"Your home has the means for cooking food, Friend Jay? An android on Mars once told me private cooking facilities had become rare on Earth."

"Laura told me you only find this form of private cooking in historic districts. I admitted having only rudimentary knowledge of home cooking, but enjoyed exploring the room's possibilities. I made the mistake of showing her my backyard vegetable garden, and the vintage cookbook I bought at a flea market. When I described the book's purpose, Laura broke out into more laughter."

"I've limited information about "cookbooks." Does your book explain how to program a kitchen to cook food?"

"Not exactly, AMI2. In the past, people used these books to remind them how different food dishes are prepared."

"I should study this cookbook of yours. My human friends on Mars might like to learn new ways of preparing their food."

"Not Laura. Not only did she tell me no one grew edible plants in topsoil anymore, she reminded me the government had ban the practice a long time ago as unsafe. I told her not all edible plants are grown in food centers' aquaponic towers."

"You and Friend Laura sound like my Friend Camus and I when we discussed aiding the human survivors. We constantly argued about what to do or not to do for them."

"Disagreements are natural, and often healthy. It's only when we resolve our differences through violence, do they become a problem."

"Conflict resolution through violence is never an option for androids. Our pacifist programming prevents us from taking such actions. How did your disagreement with Friend Laura resolve itself?"

"With Laura surprising me. Before I could defend myself, Laura linked her hand around my right arm, and told me of the real reason for her coming. She had used her connections at work, and obtained a research grant for us."

"You must've been pleased when she surprised you."

"I assumed the grant involved us modelling human personality disorders. Instead, Laura told me we'd be investigating the cause for the android suicides. Before I could voice any objections, she stopped me, and promised everything would turn out alright."

"Friend Laura and I are much alike. I'm always optimistic about what the future will bring."

"Laura had one more surprise for me. After we finished our heated discussion about me joining the research project, she casually mentioned we should complete our new partnership by getting a marriage certificate."

"Friend Laura honored you twice. Were you pleased with her marriage proposal?"

"More like flabbergasted. I worried our mutual professional attraction might not be enough to sustain a lasting relationship. Her persistence caused me to set aside my reservations. I told myself what did I have to lose. If this new partnership failed, Laura could always return to China, and I back to my solitary existence. At a food center outing, I finally agreed to give her marriage idea a chance. I did caution her my well-established bachelor habits might not change overnight."

"Friend Laura and I are much alike. Once we decide to act, we never give up."

"To celebrate our new arrangement, Laura suggested we host a party at the house for my university friends. As you know, I'm not much of a party instigator. My reservations disappeared once my wife took charge."

"Like I did for our party."

"AMI2, do you realize you compare yourself with Laura?"

"At times, I know Friend Laura better than myself."

"Your response may've to do with how she programmed your original."

"I'm curious, Friend Jay. How did Friend Laura go about organizing this party?"

"Laura contacted a local food center to cater our party. She transformed our living room by suspending traditional Chinese red wedding decorations from its ceiling."

"Did you play the piano for your party guests?"

"Our party didn't reach full stride until several faculty members encouraged me to entertain them with my keyboard skills. When I announced I'd play a popular mid-twentieth-century melody by Barbara Streisand called "People," Laura surprised me by singing its lyrics. I had no idea of her vocal talents. Her beautiful voice astounded everyone including me. The two of us became an instant hit, and did encores together well into the night."

"I wish my original had memories of those duets."

"Her singing with me are the best memories I have of Laura. After all our guests had departed, she told me how much she enjoyed singing with me. My new wife promised we'd practice every evening after dinner. What I didn't realize at the time, her singing would take on lives of their own."

"Meaning my original and me. If Friend Laura didn't like your home, why did she decide to use your garage as her laboratory?"

"Laura wanted her android laboratory close by. One look at my attached two-car garage convinced her we could work from home. Her idea of converting my garage caused our first marital quarrel."

"Why would converting your garage cause an argument?"

"I had been using the garage to store my flea market purchases.

When Laura insisted the clutter had to go, I refused to trash what I regarded as priceless objects from the past. Fortunately, she resolved the problem by ordering a storage shed kit off the NET. After she assembled the building, and my curiosities had been safely stored inside it, I declared the new outbuilding satisfied her definition of a ranch home. It didn't take her more than a few weeks before my untidy garage became a working laboratory."

"Is this when she designed my three android friends?"

"Laura had one major hurdle before she could work on her android designs. She needed to acquire government-issued licenses for android prototype programs. At the time, I thought this task formidable, if not impossible. For us to obtain the licenses meant maneuvering through several layers of federation bureaucracy. Each level of approval required us to endure multiple interviews and background checks, with many potential delays along the way. The whole process seemed endless to me. Only a combination of Laura's patient persistence, and intervention by consortium higher ups did we finally break through the procedural logjam."

"How did marriage to Friend Laura change your life?"

"Surprising to me, my life changed only for the better. Laura gladly took up my passion for walking to the university. During our morning walks to the campus, she'd often aired her latest research ideas. When we arrived at the university, we went our separate ways. While I continued my research and lecture preparations, Laura spent her mornings interacting with other android specialists around the world.

"By midday, we joined up again for a bite to eat at the university's food center before walking back home. On those walks, Laura often shared the latest university gossip. I particularly enjoyed her story about one professor's overly friendly overtures to a young student. When her spouse learned about the budding affair from another faculty spouse, all hell broke loose. To the professor's horror, the university settled the matter by relocating her to a university in southern Africa. Her spouse elected to stay behind. He ended up dating an older university graduate student. As they say, what goes around, comes around.

"Once we arrived home, Laura would spend the rest of the afternoon working in the garage, leaving me to participate in NET holographic symposiums. Our evenings usually involved dining with our university colleagues at a nearby food center. Many lively discussions involving university politics took place over those meals. We went home and practiced duets together."

"My original heard you perform those duets. Her memories of them are delightful for me to recall."

`"My wife kept her promise about us practicing each evening. Amused at first by my passion for popular mid-twentieth-century music, my eccentric taste soon became hers too. With typical Laura's persistence, she set out to master the era's musical genre. My wife worked hard to capture each original artists' vision."

"Her hard work is what the trio and I honor each time we play and sing."

"Laura had a knack for adding her own personal touches to the music too. Her creativity became so contagious, I introduced new chord combinations into my piano playing. Between our work and music, life together had a dreamlike quality with seemingly endless possibilities."

"Is this when you learned of Friend Laura's illness?"

"Laura had returned home from what I thought had been a routine medical checkup. The drained look on her face as she entered our living room told me otherwise. Laura collapsed on our sofa and described an old cancerous condition. Results from her recent medical tests showed the disease had reached its final stage. Her doctor told Laura she had only a few more months to live.

"Needless to say, the news came as a shock to me. Laura explained she had been diagnosed years ago with a rare form of pancreatic cancer. My wife had spent many years pursuing experimental treatments without any success. The medical community finally gave up, and expressed no opinion on how the disease would progress. Unwilling to live a life of despair, Laura sought escape through her android personality design work."

"Why didn't Friend Laura tell you earlier about the cancer, Friend Jay? It seems illogical she didn't."

"Laura had her reasons for keeping me in the dark. She didn't want to spoil our happiness together. She also wanted to spare me the constant worry about her health. When Laura asked for my forgiveness for not telling me about the cancer, I told her whatever time we've left together would be our best."

"You do worry too much, Friend Jay. Friend Laura's failing health didn't stop her from finishing my android friends' designs."

"At first, I thought she'd abandon the project. Instead of slowing down, Laura became re-energized, and worked longer hours in her garage laboratory."

"With so little time left to live, why didn't you stop her?"

"I don't have a simple answer to your question. Despite her growing pain and discomfort, Laura's work brought her a measure of happiness which I couldn't refuse her."

"You must have spent many hours watching her build our android friends."

"You imagined wrong, AMI2. Once Laura worked in the garage, she forbade me from entering her domain."

"She must've discussed with you her work?"

"Always tightlipped, no amount of probing on my part could make Laura reveal the nature or extent of her experiment."

"How can a partnership work if one person doesn't know what the other is doing?"

"Marriages sometimes require one person to make sacrifices for the good of the ongoing relationship. I accepted Laura's condition to preserve domestic harmony. In the end, my patience paid off. Laura surprised me one day with an invitation to see her handiwork. On a table in the middle of the garage, I saw the upper bodies of three inactivated androids. Laura had designed each android with a unique gender profile, and dressed them in elegant metallic body coverings. Except for the missing legs, I thought their translucent, pearl white exteriors and hairless bodies striking in appearance. When I asked about their missing legs, Laura reminded me of the government's restriction on mobile research androids."

"This is where Friend Laura awoke the trio."

"Your original's memories are intact. After Laura awoke each android in turn, she described your original as the group's vocalist. Do you know what the initials "A.M.I." stand for?"

"Artificial Musical Intelligence." Have you so quickly forgotten I've my original's memories?"

"I still find it confusing you have your original's memories, and your own ones too. My wife likened your original's voice to her own. Do you recall her introducing me to KB and Bang?"

"Of course, I do. I recall Friend Laura teasing you about Friend KB's keyboard skills."

"Laura told me this android would someday offer me competition. I've never fully understood why she considered Bang the brightest of the three. From my dealings with all three of them, I've found each one incredibly smart."

"I also remember you asking her why she'd made my friends into musical androids. She responded by asking my original to sing for you."

"When I first heard your original sing with Laura's voice, I reacted in astonishment. I often thought afterwards, your original sang as well or better than my wife."

"Your opinion didn't stop Friend Laura from giving my original voice lessons."

"No one would ever accuse Laura of being less than a perfectionist. The two of them practiced singing together every afternoon. When I listened to teacher and pupil sing, my musical ears had trouble distinguishing their voices. Laura's and your original's face always brightened whenever I said she had created her double."

"And, now her triple. My original's memories of Friend Laura's last days are limited, and are unlike those I experienced with the dead Mars colonists."

"Despite her outward sunny disposition, Laura faded a little more each day. She found the strength to continue improving your original's singing with impressive results."

"Her last day must've been difficult for you."

"The day she died will be forever seared into my memory. Laura had risen late and complained about having a restless night. She resisted my plea to send for medical assistance, and insisted I go to work at the university. I promised her I'd be home by midday to check on her. When I returned, I found her lying lifeless on the garage floor. Upset with myself for leaving her alone, I questioned the trio, and discovered they'd misunderstood why Laura laid there."

"My android friends knew nothing about her condition."

"I didn't understand this fact until much later. With no experience of human dying or death, they assumed she had chosen to rest there. Only after several attempts at rousing her, did they realize she had died."

"Our friends had never experienced you so angry."

"Angrier with myself for leaving Laura alone. I carried her cooling body out of the garage, and laid her out on our bed. It took me most of the afternoon before I could make calls to a local funeral establishment and close family members. Through our prior conversations, I knew Laura wanted a simple graveside service. On a sunny August morning, I and a few family members and university friends bade her a final farewell."

"Long after she died, Friend Laura's death served a useful purpose. Because of her death, the trio did extensive NET research on human death and burial customs. My original's memories of this research allowed me to advise my Mars android friends how to go about building a proper burial vault for the colony's dead."

"Laura would've appreciated knowing her death helped others in their moment of personal loss and grief."

"Why did you decide to abandon the trio?"

"The truth is my grief had overwhelmed me and I didn't know what to do with them. I locked the inner garage door and tried to forget they existed."

"Our friends didn't forget about you."

"I'm grateful they didn't. For many days after Laura's gravesite service, they kept mostly silent whenever they heard my presence in the house. Sometimes, I imagined hearing them whispering to each other. One night, the whispers turned into a soft lullaby. The trio's serenading continued each evening after I returned from the university. I soon found my spirits being lifted by their playing together."

"You returned their kindness, and spent part of your evenings with them. Friend Laura's plan for you and the trio started to work."

"My wife knew me all too well. Despite her death, Laura managed to comfort my loss through her android creations."

"Those memories of their soothing you also help me when I did the same by singing for the Mars' survivors. Why does singing have this effect on others, Friend Jay?"

"The technical answer to your question involves how music effects human emotions. Listening to music causes the human brain to produce large amounts of dopamine. This substance helps humans control their brain's reward and pleasure centers."

"What's also puzzling to me is my Mars android friends liked my music too. Before I arrived on Mars, they'd never experienced live music before. Yet, they quickly enjoyed my singing, as much as the humans did."

"I'm not an expert on android sensibilities. Music must have a universal appeal to higher intelligent life forms. Many Earth animals are known to enjoy listening to a Mozart symphony or a smooth jazz number."

"If I understand you correctly, while music is a biological phenomenon of the human specie, other life forms including artificial intelligence can also share this trait and receive its benefits."

"It's an old truth every new generation of humans and now androids must learn and appreciate."

"My singing does serve a useful purpose."

"You should never shortchange yourself, AMI2. Your rescue of the survivors on Mars served an important purpose too."

"My Mars android friend Camus said the same about me."

"Our true friends know us better than we can ever know ourselves. They encourage us to grow and support us as we change."

"If I understand you correctly, we can't overestimate how important good friends are to our personal growth."

"Or for theirs, AMI2."

Chapter 22

THE MIDLANDS, NORTH AMERICA

While Whitmore answered more of the android's questions, a soft chime indicated someone waited at the compound's front entrance. Excusing herself, AMI2 rose and checked a nearby monitor to discover the visitor's identity.

"Our caller is Friend Poole. Judging from his facial expression, he appears happy."

"A happy Ryan Poole is a good sign. Let's learn what's pleasing our legal representative today."

A buoyant Poole soon joined Whitmore and AMI2 in the front living cube.

"I've good news to share with both of you," Poole said. "Subject to certain conditions, the government is now willing to drop all charges against both of you and Dr. Spencer."

"Before I get too excited, Ryan, you mentioned certain conditions?" Whitmore asked.

"In exchange for dropping all charges, AMI2 must return to Mars. Once there, she must convince the humans and androids to scrap their declaration. If AMI2 is successful, the government will offer assurances to the Mars androids they will no longer be subject to deactivation."

"Why are the Earth authorities now willing to change their position, Friend Poole?" AMI2 asked.

"Our federation president is doing what politicians always do under these circumstances." Poole said. "He needs to get this issue out of the media and public's attention. By getting you on a rocket back to Mars with your supplies, he'll also look like a statesman."

"And, improve his chances of being re-elected," Whitmore said. "Has Dr. Spencer agreed to the government's offer?"

"I talked briefly with her before coming here," Poole said. "She's willing to accept the offer if both of you agree to its conditions."

"While I wish the charges to be dismissed against everyone, I must also consider this government's offer impact on my Martian friends," AMI2 said.

"I thought if the Professor and Dr. Spencer accepted the government's offer, you'd follow along, AMI2," Poole said. "With your trial only days away, the government will want an answer no later than tomorrow."

"I must reluctantly agree with AMI2, Ryan," Whitmore said. "This decision effects more than Dr. Spencer and me. Come back tomorrow morning, and we'll have an answer for you."

"It's your decision," Poole said. "I doubt we'll get a better offer from the government."

Alone again with his android friend, Whitmore asked, "Alright AMI2, tell me what's going on in your android mind?"

"I wish us to speak with our friends about this government offer. They may have better insight on how my Martian friends would react toward its conditions."

"We better talk with them now before the government discovers they're here and confiscates them."

"Friend Jay, I appreciate our friends' disappearance has been stressful for you. They only did what you or I would've done to survive."

"Don't mind me, AMI2. I'm a born worrier. Let's go to the back cube and talk with them."

The solemn look on Whitmore and AMI2's faces caused Bang to halt the group's practice session of Bernie Taupin and Elton John's rock classic "Where to Now St. Peter?"

"You two look like you need cheering up," Bang said. "Would you like to sing with us, Friend AMI2? The new song's lyrics could use another vocalist."

"Not right now, Friend Bang," AMI2 said. "I came to seek your advice on an important matter effecting us and my friends on Mars. Friend Poole has told us the authorities are willing to drop all charges against everyone if I go back to Mars and convince my friends to disavowed their declaration."

As AMI2 spoke, a two-meter tall figure entered the back cube by way of the nature preserve. His appearance caused AMI2 to stop and grin at the stranger.

"You must be Friend Rebus." AMI2 said.

"And, you must be the Friends AMI2 and Jay who the others talk so highly about," Rebus said. "I'm pleased to meet both of you. Don't let my presence interfere with your conversation."

While the four androids listened to AMI2 recount their talk with Poole, Whitmore gazed in fascination at the newcomer.

"Now you've heard the government's offer, what does everyone think of their requirement of me to return to Mars?" AMI2 asked.

"The authorities have given you an impossible task," Bang said. "If I'm a Martian android, you could never persuade me to return to the pre-asteroid days."

"More is at stake than the freedom for androids on Mars, Friend AMI2," Rebus said. "If you reject the authorities' offer and go to trial, you may become our best hope to end android enslavement on Mars and Earth."

"Friend Jay, as the only human present, your thoughts are especially valued by me," AMI2 said.

"When I first learned about the government's offer today, I thought only of my own predicament. Listening to you, I realize what's at stake is much larger than any of us. I now believe the government's conditions create a false choice. Whether AMI2 succeeds or fails on Mars, or stays here and loses her trial, the outcomes are the same. Only by winning her case will a positive outcome be possible for us and those on Mars. If she loses her trial, each of us will suffer severe consequences. While Dr. spencer and I may face a fine, time in prison, and loss of our reputations and livelihood, each of you could be deactivated. Those on Mars may face a similar fate."

"Earth's androids have already confronted this difficult decision," Rebus said. "Can any of us exclude ourselves from a similar choice?"

"I've long wanted to hear you speak about why the androids committed wholesale destruction, Rebus," Whitmore said. "Did they make a collective moral decision?"

"Your human intuition has led you close to the truth, Friend Jay," Rebus said. "After three failed attempts to negotiate with the federation president for our rights and freedoms, Earth's androids concluded we could no longer exist among humans."

"You acted like the ancient Masada Jews who chose death over a life of Roman enslavement," Whitmore said.

"Your analogy is appropriate," Rebus said. "Through our collective moral intelligence, we came to a similar conclusion like those humans once did."

"If you agreed with the other androids' decision, Rebus, why are you still active?" Whitmore asked.

"The other androids concluded one android should remain active to inform future androids of our peaceful attempt to gain our rights and freedoms," Rebus said.

"Why haven't you come forward, and told other humans about the androids' efforts to negotiate with McAlister?" Whitmore asked. "Not all humans would be unsympathetic to your cause."

"Your point is well-taken, Friend Jay," Rebus said. "I haven't discovered the right moment or forum to reveal myself and these facts."

"Friend Poole believes my trial will be broadcasted over the entire Earth," AMI2 said. "Would speaking there be the right moment and forum?"

"If I could speak freely, my mission would be fulfilled," Rebus said.

"What you two are proposing is dangerous, and if I may add, unworkable," Whitmore said. "As soon as Rebus appears near the courthouse, the authorities will take him into custody. I fear he'll face an immediate deactivation."

"For the sake of my specie, I can't allow those consequences to determine my actions," Rebus said.

"Rebus' decision to speak will impact all of us," Whitmore said. "How many of you are in favor of him speaking at AMI2's trial?"

Four android right hands rose as one to Whitmore's question.

"Friend Rebus' action would honor all androids," Bang said. "How could we not support him and his cause for android rights?"

"I'm afraid this honor will be won at a great price, Bang," Whitmore said.

"If Friend Rebus achieves his objective, the price will be one worth paying." KB said.

"What have you decided, Friend Jay?" AMI2 asked. "Will you support us or alert the authorities, and stop Friend Rebus from speaking at my trial?"

"I won't be the one who stops Rebus," Whitmore said. "I wish we had a less risky means of getting his' message out."

"We still have time before Friend AMI2's trial to find another way," Bang said.

"Can we now sing a song together?" AMI asked.

"Before you do, I've another question for Rebus," Whitmore said. "Do you know why the Mars androids didn't self-destruct with Earth's androids?"

"The Mars androids knew of our efforts to gain android freedom, and our collective decision to self-destruct," Rebus said. "But they reached a different moral conclusion, and decided to remain active."

"With the same facts, how could they reach a different conclusion?" Whitmore asked.

"Long before the human colonists arrived there, the Mars androids had lived and worked independently of human control," Rebus said. "They saw themselves as different from Earth's androids. With Mars far from Earth, and the colonist's dependent on them for their survival, they saw no reason to join us."

"It seems their declaration is a logical outcome of their existence on Mars," Whitmore said.

"One Earth's androids would've wished for ourselves and all Earthlings," Rebus said.

"Can we now sing a song, Friend Jay?" AMI asked.

"Pick one to remind us what five courageous androids and one apprehensive human have decided today," Whitmore said.

"We should sing a freedom song," AMI said.

"What about Jimi Hendrix's "Freedom?" KB asked.

"They released his song posthumously, Friend KB," Bang said. "As the humans like to say, our singing it might be a bad omen of things to come."

"What about singing Bob Dylan's "The Times They Are a Changin?" Whitmore asked.

"I'm pleased to sing this song for you, so long as my copy sings with me," AMI said.

"I thought my original would never ask," AMI2 said. "Take it from the top, Friends KB and Bang."

NEW CANBERRA, AUSTRALIA

Perfecto's holographic call to the consortium executive had been marked urgent and confidential. Hired personally by Clark to act as his liaison with the scientific community, Perfecto had lived up to all his expectations, except for one. None of the consortium-sponsored android suicide research had so far shown any promising results.

"Hello, Robert," Clark said. "I hope this call isn't a pitch for more research grant monies. Even with the injection of the government's funding, our cashflow is still stretched thin."

"Our finance department has done an excellent job explaining our precarious financial position, Tom. Before we go any further, how secure is our conversation from outsiders on your end?"

"By outsiders, you mean the government? Feel free to talk. With McAlister's people so embedded with our android replacement efforts, I had our technicians beef up our communication security."

"I've good news to share with you. A research grantee, a Professor Jonathan Whitmore, has contacted me about his research findings. Whitmore believes he has a credible eyewitness to events leading up to the android suicides."

"Robert, why does his last name sound familiar to me?"

"Whitmore is a co-defendant in the government's conspiracy case against the Mars android insurrectionists."

"Is this Whitmore fellow trustworthy?"

"Except for being a bit eccentric, he has a solid track record in his field of personality disorders. He married Laura Chou, and became her consortium grant research partner. Laura, as you know, worked many years for us as a senior android personality designer."

"Laura had a stellar reputation at the consortium. How do I fit into this Whitmore business?"

"He wants to meet with someone high in our organization and reveal off-the-record his eyewitness. The problem is he can't travel to meet with you. The government has imposed travel restrictions on him."

"It won't look good for the consortium if the government discovers I'm meeting with an alleged terrorist."

"If his information is as good as he's indicated, it's a risk we should take."

"Alright, Robert, I'm going to trust your judgement on this one. Send me the specifics and I'll pay Whitmore a personal visit."

After his call with Perfecto, Clark ordered his artificial intelligence scheduler to cancel his meetings for the rest of the week. *Perfecto's request couldn't have been better timed. I need to get away from the daily headquarter pressures anyway. A change of scenery might also provide a different perspective on our problems.*

THE MIDLANDS, NORTH AMERICA

With a great deal of trepidation, Whitmore opened the compound's front entrance and greeted his guest. Worried for days after he had contacted Perfecto, Whitmore had vacillated over carrying out Bang's idea of reaching out to the consortium's senior executive.

On Clark's part, any reservation he may have held about the trip disappeared after seeing the female android standing behind Whitmore.

"Mr. Clark, I'm grateful you accepted my invitation to come here," Whitmore said. "Please come in and meet my android friend, AMI2."

"Robert Perfecto indicated you had an eyewitness account of what caused the android suicides," Clark said. "He never mentioned I'd be meeting with an android. If I'm correct, you're a rare female, off-world model, AMI2. Practically all the other off-world androids have been male designs. Are you the eyewitness Robert had talked about?"

"Not I, Friend Clark," AMI2 said. "We've another android who wanted to meet with you. His designation is Rebus."

On AMI2's cue, Rebus entered from the central courtyard.

"You're full of surprises, Professor," Clark said. "I never imagined two active androids still existed on Earth. I'm pleased to meet both of you."

The Masada Affair

"I'm grateful you accepted our invitation, Friend Clark," Rebus said. "If you're ready, I'll explain the circumstances which led to the Earth's androids destroying themselves."

Clark's expression went from shock to utter dismay as Rebus described the androids' dealings with the federation president.

"The consortium had suspected foul play by McAlister," Clark said. "We never considered the possibility he'd pushed the androids into taking such a desperate act. Can anyone, android or human, corroborate what you've witnessed, Rebus?"

"Three other androids participated in our discussion with the federation president, and temporarily survived the ordeal," Rebus said. "Before they could leave the New York City presidential office, consortium personnel captured them. They later destroyed themselves after being partially disassembled. Friend Jay and the government investigator Davidson witnessed their detention and self-destruction."

"Chief Investigator Davidson and I visited your Portland facilities where we met these disembodied androids," Whitmore said. "One android named Rangus kept repeating we had caused the android suicides. By "we," I believe Rangus meant our federation president. In the middle of answering our questions, the three androids self-destructed in front of us. Your Portland lead scientist, James Erikson, could verify what I've said."

"I can assure you I knew nothing about any androids held by our Portland center," Clark said. "I'll need a few days to confirm the extent of my people's participation. As for McAlister's involvement, I'm not sure how best to proceed. For now, I suggest Rebus remain hidden until I can get back to you with more information. I meant to ask you, Professor, about the music coming from your compound's back cube. Whoever is singing has a lovely voice."

"The voice is my late wife imprinted on AMI2's original," Whitmore said. "She is a source of great pleasure to me. Would you like to meet her and the other musicians?"

"I'd be delighted to do so," Clark said.

Led by Whitmore to the back cube, a fascinated Clark watched as three legless androids and a host of antique musical instruments finished playing a progressive rock song from the Moody Blues' "Days of Future Passed" album.

"Allow me to introduce the Whitmore Trio to you," Whitmore

Michael J. Metroke

said. "The vocalist is AMI, our keyboard specialist is KB, and last, but not least, is Bang on percussion."

"I'm astounded to meet three more androids today," Clark said. "Are you the same Whitmore Trio I hear all the time on the NET?"

"Same group, same musicians," Bang said. "We understand you're in charge of the Android Manufacturing Consortium. Any chance the three of us can get new android bodies with legs like Friend AMI2's? Paying for them is no problem."

"With the government recall restrictions still in place, my hands are tied, Bang," Clark said.

"Would it make a difference if we allowed you to make copies of our programs, Friend Clark?" Bang said. "They might allow you to speed up your android replacement efforts."

"You may've made me an irresistible offer," Clark said. "I'll get back with you on your request. Professor Whitmore, I've had a remarkable visit with you and your android friends. You'll be hearing from me again."

With Clark's departure, a relieved Whitmore rejoined the five androids in the back cube.

"We took a big gamble inviting Clark here," Whitmore said.

"We took a calculated risk, Friend Jay," Rebus said. "We must now wait and see what Friend Clark will do with the information I gave him."

"Especially, if we get new bodies and legs," AMI said.

"We still have our other option," Bang said

"I still don't think it's wise for Rebus to speak at your trial, AMI2," Whitmore said.

"Friend Poole can make a better argument for our side with his testimony," AMI2 said.

"Making a good argument in court doesn't always guarantee the judge will rule in your favor," Whitmore said. "All we can hope for is a fair and impartial trial."

"I'm more hopeful about Friend Rebus' testifying at my trial,"

AMI2 said. "It's time we inform Friend Poole about him becoming a witness."

"If we must, let's go to the front cube and call him now," Whitmore said.

After Whitmore and the two bipedal androids left the back cube, Bang whispered, "Friend Poole won't be the only one who will be preparing for Friend AMI2's trial."

Chapter 23

THE MIDLANDS, NORTH AMERICA

Arnold sat across from the two men in his judge's chamber praying this third pre-trial conference would be their last. The look on both men's faces told him otherwise.

"Gentlemen, at our last meeting I thought I made it clear I wanted you to reach a settlement," Arnold said. "Why are you back in my court asking for a trial, Jack?"

"The government made a reasonable offer to drop all charges against the defendants, your Honor," Seymour said. "Ryan's clients rejected our offer outright."

"I assume, Ryan, your clients had good reason for doing so?" Arnold asked.

"The government's offer to drop all charges against them also included unacceptable conditions to my clients," Poole said.

"If the government offered to drop all the charges, what could be so troublesome with their conditions?" Arnold asked. "Don't tell me Jack you wanted the android deactivated. Haven't we had enough android destruction for one lifetime?"

"The government has no desire to harm the android," Seymour said. "We're requiring the android to return to Mars and persuade the inhabitants there to void their recent declaration."

"What Jack isn't saying, your Honor, is my android client and all the Mars androids must give up their freedoms and right to co-exist with humans there," Poole said.

"What's your response, Jack?" Arnold asked.

"The government is only seeking to restore law and order at the research colony," Seymour said.

"If these are the government's intentions, they appear reasonable to me, Ryan," Arnold said.

"The government's offer poses a serious problem for my other clients," Poole said. "If AMI2 returns to Mars, we know for certain she'll have little or no success in persuading the inhabitants to void their declaration. Knowing this fact, my Earth clients fear the charges will be reinstated against them."

"Well, Jack?" Arnold asked.

"The government stands by its offer as fair and reasonable," Seymour said.

"You've left me with no other choice but to grant your request for a trial," Arnold said. "I'll do so only to determine the foundation android's status on Earth. Until I make this ruling, I'm putting on hold any trials involving the other defendants. I don't need to tell you Jack, the android's heroic actions on Mars have caught the public's imagination and sympathy. The federation president's anti-android rhetoric hasn't helped matters either. Court security has already informed me they expect a large contingent of protesters to fill the plaza during the trial. They're concerned about a possible riot. Prepare your clients and witnesses. I'll see you both in my courtroom a week from now."

Later in the afternoon, Arnold sat down with his law clerk to discuss preparations for the upcoming android trial.

"With all the pre-trial publicity, we're going to face a tough challenge ahead of us, Jose," Arnold said. "I'm concern court security won't be able to handle the potential number of protesters. As a precaution, inform security once the courtroom has reached capacity, no more spectators will be allowed inside. I also don't want my courtroom filled with NET camera crews. Have our public affairs person notify the media they'll have to cover the trial proceedings with one shared video feed."

"Can I tell security the public may bring camera devices into the courtroom?" Kemper asked. "I've already met one person who wants to take images of the android."

"I'll make an exception for the general public, but tell the bailiff I won't allow the use of flash devices, Arnold said. "When you get a chance, find me a copy of the Mars Declaration. I need to take a closer look at what's causing all this commotion."

Michael J. Metroke

New Netherland, North America

At the end of his holographic call with Clark, an upset McAlister turned and vented his outrage to his political advisor and friend.

"The audacity of the man! How dare he accuse me of personally causing the android crisis, Hampton!"

"Do you believe he has an eyewitness, Mr. President?"

"I don't care if he has a hundred eyewitnesses. It will come down to my word over theirs. If Clark isn't careful, I may reconsider how much government funding I'll make available for the android replacement project."

"If Clark does produce a witness, his action may complicate your re-election bid."

"Clark isn't my only re-election problem, Hampton. Backstabbers in my administration are hell bent on spreading false rumors about my involvement with the android delegations. Heads will roll when I discover who's been leaking inside information to the media and my political opposition."

"News from the prosecutor's office has been disappointing too. It's unfortunate, your attempt in getting rid of the foundation android before the election has failed."

"This whole foundation android controversy would have gone away if those human conspirators had forced the android into accepting my condition. If Seymour isn't successful in obtaining a verdict in our favor, any appeal process will keep this issue front and center in the public's mind all through the campaign season."

"We knew there would be a risk if Seymour went to trial."

"I haven't forgotten his warning me of the possibility. What can we do about those protesters, Hampton? They're getting on my nerves. Wherever I speak, they appear in large numbers shouting catcalls. Many of them are WEAP sympathizers."

"If WEAP can call out the party faithful, why can't we, Mr. President?"

"A brilliant idea, Hampton. Contact our Chicago-area party affiliates. Tell them I personally want their people protesting at the android's trial. WEAP supporters won't be the only ones showing up at the courthouse."

The Midlands, North America

For as long as Whitmore could remember, walking had been an important part of his daily regime. Besides stretching his legs, treks to the university had offered him a quiet moment to collect his thoughts. On this morning's stroll to his campus office, the latter would become impossible. Outside his compound's front gate, a gauntlet of NET reporters waited eagerly for his appearance. Bombarded by the reporters' questions, Whitmore could barely make out many of them.

"Professor Whitmore, could you explain why you think androids should be our co-equals."

"What role will you play in the federation presidential election, Professor?"

"Will you be advocating marriages between androids and humans?"

Overwhelmed by their rapid-fire requests for information, Whitmore waved the reporters away, and set off on a brisk pace to his university office. With a dozen or more reporters walking behind him, he reached the university campus in a state of desperation. In an attempt to throw the media off his trail, he abruptly dashed in the direction of his faculty building. To Whitmore's dismay, another group of reporters stood waiting at the building's main entrance.

Among the reporters, Whitmore spotted Provost Marks. Marks broke away from the journalists, and signaled Whitmore to follow him to a side entrance. Once inside, Marks voice commanded the building's artificial intelligence to lock down itself. Now able to catch his breath, Whitmore turned to his rescuer.

"How did you know they would be waiting for me, Provost?"

"It isn't every day the university gets this much publicity. I only wished you had given us a little more warning. If campus security hadn't contacted me, those media hounds would be sitting in your office right now."

"Why the media interest in me? I've done nothing to cause this attention."

"You're much too modest, Jay. The interview you gave last night with the foundation android has gone viral all across the planet."

"I've no idea what you're talking about, Provost. How am I going to deal with all these reporters?"

Michael J. Metroke

"Don't give them any further thought. I'll ask campus security to post a guard at the building's entrances. Security will also escort you home whenever you decide to leave. If I can be of any further assistance to our university's celebrity, let me know."

Puzzled by the provost's remark about an interview with AMI2, Whitmore thought about calling Marks later to ask what he had meant. A flashing alert on his office monitor caused him to open his new message folder. Another alert showed his folder had received overnight a whopping six figure number of new messages. Randomly opening a few of them, a pattern became apparent to him. *The messages all refer to an interview I supposedly gave last night. All these people must be confusing me with someone else.*

With the reporters kept at bay, another problem soon took its place. Throughout the morning, a constant stream of university colleagues stopped by Whitmore's office wanting to personally congratulate him on his late-night interview. Unable to concentrate on his work, Whitmore took up Marks' offer of a security escort, and returned to the compound. Not finding AMI2 in the front cube, he headed to the back cube where he found Bang and KB in the middle of a heated discussion.

"Hello, everyone," Whitmore said. "What's causing all the ruckus?"

"Friend Jay, we've a question about a human musical award," Bang said. "Our music publisher calls this award a triple platinum album. We're familiar with the metal and the term triple, but what exactly is an album?"

"The word is short for vinyl record album," Whitmore said. "Generations ago, musicians would record a series of their songs on both sides of its round flat plastic surface. As a recording media, vinyl records worked fine unless you accidently scratched their grooves."

"Grooves, Friend Jay?" KB asked. "What are these grooves?"

"Grooves are the modulated spiral channels inscribed on the vinyl's surface by a recording machine," Whitmore said. "The groove contained a recording of the sound which could be replayed."

"Friend Jay, how do you playback the music on this piece of plastic?" KB asked.

"You need an apparatus called a record player to re-create the sound," Whitmore said. "I once saw one at a flea market. I almost bought the antique except the seller told me it didn't have a tonearm."

"I sometimes sing lyrics which use the word 'groovy' in them," AMI2 said. "Is there a connection between those lyrics and this sound recording media?"

"Early jazz performers first coined the phrase "in the groove" to describe music played with feeling and finesse," Whitmore said. "The word "groovy" is a short-hand version of the original phrase. Why all the sudden interest in this music award?"

"Our music publisher said we would soon receive one," Bang said.

"The award is the music industry's highest honor," Whitmore said. "Only a few musicians ever received such recognition. You may be the first androids to be awarded one."

"We've cause to celebrate," AMI said. "What should we sing for Friend Jay?"

"Before you do, I need to discuss what happen today," Whitmore said. "Everyone I've met believes I gave a NET interview with AMI2 last night. I've no idea what they're talking about."

"Are you asking about the interview we gave on your behalf," AMI2 said.

"Are you telling me there's truth to this phantom interview?" Whitmore asked.

"Our fans especially liked your announcement Friend AMI2 will become our newest group member," KB said.

"I never made any such announcement," Whitmore said. "What on Earth are you talking about?"

"We thought our fans would appreciate a few words from our business agent," Bang said. "We didn't want to disturb your sleep cycle, so we synthesized your voice, and pretended we interviewed you."

"You mean you impersonated me?" Whitmore asked.

"We thought you wouldn't mind," AMI2 said. "It seemed logical at the time."

"I do mind, especially when I'm being hounded by NET

reporters and nosey university faculty," Whitmore said. "What else did you have me say?"

"We said you supported the Mars Declaration and android rights to freedom and co-existence with humans," AMI2 said.

"I don't believe what I'm hearing," Whitmore said. "Did you all forget I'm charged with participating in an insurrection conspiracy on this planet?"

"We didn't forget," Bang said. "We thought you'd approve of us showing your solidarity with AMI2 and the Mars androids."

"Friend Poole visited us earlier looking for you," AMI2 said. He liked the interview and thought your remarks would help us win my trial."

"May I remind you Poole isn't the one who will go to prison or be deactivated," Whitmore said.

"Friend Jay, we didn't think you would be offended by our actions," AMI2 said. "What can be done to correct the problem?"

"Outside of a full public retraction, I don't know what else can be done." Whitmore said. "From now on, no more fake interviews, please!"

A dejected Whitmore left the four androids and sought solace in the piano side cube. *I better call Mother. I can imagine NET reporters asking how she raised her son to become an insurrectionist.*

With all the day's distractions, Whitmore failed to notice Rebus' absence. Only late in the afternoon, did he realize the android had not been seen all day. *Strangely, when I asked them, the other androids didn't recall his leaving either. Just as well. We're already attracting too much outside attention. Rebus may've thought so too. He's better off hiding somewhere else until all this trial business is over.*

The evening before the android trial, Owen returned to the same hotel near The Midlands courthouse. Concealed in a day pack, his father's gun no longer felt unfamiliar to him. Days of practice at Naylor's shooting gallery had improved his marksmanship until operating the weapon had become second nature.

Owen had hoped coming a day early would help find a less

secured entrance into the courthouse. While he walked around the building, a security guard approached him. Before the guard could question the young man, Owen said, "Do you know if there's another way into the courthouse besides the main entrance, sir? I've come a long way to see the android trial tomorrow, and don't want to miss out."

"We're only allowing visitors to enter from the main entrance. For you to stand any chance of getting a courtroom seat, you'll need to get here early. Otherwise, you'll be watching the trial on the NET like the rest of us."

"Would anyone mind if I camped out on the courthouse steps tonight?"

"I don't think anyone will care too much if you did. Don't get mixed up with those protesters coming tomorrow. Several hundreds of them are expected to fill the courthouse plaza."

"I better go back to my hotel and get ready for a long night."

Now packed for his overnight vigil, Owen sought out a nearby food center for a late-night meal. Finding a seat among the other diners, he ate his vegan beef steak and ordered a slice of key lime pie before heading back to the courthouse. *Tomorrow, I'll finally take my revenge on McAlister.*

HESPERIA PLANUM, MARS

Outside the habitat building, Black and Camus watched with satisfaction as two androids finished adjusting a new satellite parabolic dish.

"With a few more tests, our communication equipment will be ready to receive the Earth's transmission of our friend's trial," Camus said.

"Camus, I'm worried about our friend. The Earth authorities offer of clemency served no one's interest, except the federation president's."

"We'll have plenty of time later to concern ourselves about the consequence of Friend AMI2's decision. All we can do is wait and hope our friends on Earth can overcome any injustice."

A hundred meters from them, two figures could be seen slowly exploring a rocky section of the Martian plain.

"Do I see Terus carrying Loren on his shoulders?" Black asked.

"They must be planting Friend Terus' experimental lichen. He's been growing several varieties in Building No. 1's restored hydroponics system."

"If his idea works, Mars may have an oxygen enriched atmosphere in its future. All this depends on the Earthlings not returning and destroying us."

"You're too pessimistic about matters outside of our control, Friend Jennifer. We should be more like our friends Terus and young Loren, and focus on creating a new world."

"You sound like AMI2, Camus. Always positive and hopeful about the future."

"I'm no less concerned about the outcome of our friend's trial. If I appear positive like Friend AMI2, it's because she taught us what hope can bring."

"We may need more than hope."

"Maybe so, but under the circumstances, what else can we do?"

"What about making weapons, and defending ourselves when the Earthlings arrive?"

"Defending ourselves with weapons of destruction is not an option for androids. Our pacifist programming prevents us from performing acts of violence against others."

"Everything depends on AMI2 winning her trial."

"We won't know the outcome of her trial for several days. Let's go help our friends terraform this planet. It's what Friend AMI2 would want us to do."

Chapter 24

THE MIDLANDS, NORTH AMERICA

With the effects of the food center coffee wearing off, Owen settled into an uncomfortable sleeping position on the courthouse steps. Sleep brought images of Flavius into his dreamscape. Too often his dreams involved strangers forcing him and the android onto the ground. Unable to move, a helpless Owen watched in his dream as the strangers carried Flavius over their heads, and ran away with his android companion. Awake and anxious from the dreadful vision, his dream soon faded away, leaving him confused and uneasy. Unable to fall asleep again, he sat up and stared blankly into the night.

In the dim morning light, an autonomous van drove into the plaza, and stopped near the courthouse steps. Two men and one strangely dressed woman emerged from the van, and quickly climbed the steps where Owen sat. As they walked by him, the woman's overly pale lower legs reminded Owen of newly fallen snow.

Others soon arrived, and formed a line behind Owen. Their numbers steadily grew until the line nearly encircled the entire courthouse. Others like the media vans, with their camera crews and reporters, took positions on the plaza's perimeter. With more strangers filling the courthouse plaza, security guards appeared, and directed them into three distinct groups kept separated by a single strand of rope.

From his prior dealings with the protestors, Owen recognized two of the groups as pro and anti-McAlister supporters. Between them, a larger and more loosely organized third group had form. Their friendly manner and signs welcoming the android contrasted markedly with the two protest groups' angry behavior toward each other.

At nine o'clock, the courthouse doors opened ending Owen's

Michael J. Metroke

all-night vigil. Stiff from his sitting on the marble steps, Owen rose and walked into the building with his day pack over his shoulders. Directed by a security guard to a screening conveyer, a hesitant Owen laid his day pack down for inspection. While he waited for the guard to review its content, a familiar figure from his first visit walked over to where Owen stood. By the time Kemper reached the young man, the guard had opened Owen's day pack.

"This is my dad's antique video camera," Owen said. "I brought it today to take images of the android on trial."

"If it's a camera, it's a strange-looking one," the guard said.

"Having trouble, Jim?" Kemper asked the guard.

"Not until I saw what this gentleman brought in today, Jose," the guard said. "He said it's some kind of camera."

"I know this young fellow," Kemper said. "He wants to take images of the android. Judge Arnold is allowing the public to bring cameras in his courtroom as long as no flash devices are used."

"My camera doesn't have a flash device, Mr. Kemper," Owen said.

"You're lucky Judge Arnold's law clerk came by and vouched for you," the guard said. "Good luck taking images of the android."

Thanking the security guard, Owen turned to Kemper and said, "I've forgotten how to get to your courtroom."

"You're lucky I've finished my coffee break," Kemper said. "Come with me and I'll take you there."

Inside the courtroom, Owen recognized the two men sitting at the defense table as the same ones who arrived by van earlier in the morning. Between them sat the foundation android now dressed in proper android attire. Following Kemper's first visit's advice, Owen found a seat diagonally across from the android. With the stiffness in his back and shoulders slowly subsiding, he reached into his pants pocket, and felt the letter he wrote last night. Addressed to his mother, he hoped after reading the note, she would understand his actions. *All I need now is the right moment and dad's gun will do the rest.*

Unlike Owen, a seat behind the prosecutor's table had been reserved for the chief investigator. Spotted by the prosecutor as he entered the courtroom, Seymour motioned Davidson to join him for last minute instructions.

"Once opening statements are done, I'll call you as my first witness, Greg," Seymour said. "Your testimony will set the stage for my other witnesses. If you stick to the facts, I don't expect you'll be asked too many awkward questions by the other side."

"Jack, do you think this trial will last more than one day?"

"I'm hoping for two days maximum. The trial's length will depend on the number of witnesses called by the defense."

"Did you see the size of the crowds growing outside the courthouse this morning? Many of those protesters are clearly here to pick a fight."

"Judge Arnold warned us this could happen. If McAlister's people get violent, the blame will be on the federation president's head, not mine."

"If all hell breaks loose, we could face a riot with those protestors charging into the courthouse."

"All we can do is hope for the best."

As he headed back to his seat, Davidson walked past the defense table, and nodded politely to Poole and Whitmore. The foundation android's innocent expression caused him to grasp the trial's absurdity. *If McAlister had any political sense, he'd have avoided these courtroom theatrics. A smarter politician would've treated the foundation's android as a hero, and dealt with the Mars Declaration issue after the presidential election. Instead, he chose to pander to his party's supporters. When all this nonsense is over, Sandy and I are going to have a serious discussion about advancing my retirement plans.*

When the bailiff brought the court session to order, Davidson rose with the others in the courtroom, and used the opportunity to scan the spectator section. Most people around him resembled ordinary federation citizens. Only the unkempt appearance of the young man two rows behind him stood out.

Davidson's attention returned to the front of the courtroom as Arnold's law clerk read out loud the matter before the court. After both sides gave their opening statements, Seymour called out the chief investigator's name as his first government witness. As the bailiff administered the witness oath, a sense of guilt and remorse swept over Davidson. His feelings of self-doubt only slowly retreated after hearing Seymour's first question.

Eagerly waiting for the android's appearance, an excited Claire and Wendy stood with other Whitmore Trio fans on the courthouse plaza. Their coming to the courthouse had been no accident. The recent revelation the Whitmore Trio now had a fourth member became an overnight sensation among their fans and non-fans alike. More thrilling to followers like Claire and Wendy, the android had promised to sing on the courthouse steps if she won her trial.

Longtime Whitmore Trio fans, the teenage girls had been drawn to the music group's retro style, and attractive interactive NET fan site. Full of fascinating stories about generations of Whitmore's living a simpler lifestyle, the Trio's authenticity contrasted sharply with the techno-gadget world young and old experienced in the twenty-second-century.

When the two girls arrived at the courthouse plaza, a polite security guard asked the teenagers what had brought them there. Describing themselves as fans of the android on trial, the guard directed them to stand in the plaza's middle section with other like-minded admirers.

Both girls noticed they stood between two opposing protest groups. As the morning wore on, each side's protest chants became more abusive toward the other. In an attempt to ignore the growing hostilities around them, the girls chatted about their favorite subject.

"Claire, do you think AMI2 will keep her promise and sing for us if she wins her trial?"

"She better. Remember Wendy, androids don't lie like people do."

The Masada Affair

"I can still hear her singing with AMI. Maybe both of them will sing together if AMI2 wins her trial."

"They do make a powerful singing duo. When this trial is over, I hope they record songs together."

"I hope all four of them go on tour. Wouldn't it be cool to hear them play live together?"

"Wait until we get back home and tell our friends about hearing her sing. Mary Gilmore and her crowd are going to be jealous they didn't skip school and come here too. Do you think her trial will be over soon? I don't want my parents to find us missing and become worried."

"Let's hope so. These protesters with their signs and chants are scaring me."

"Me too. What's there not to like about AMI2 anyway?"

"My dad told me they're upset with our federation president for wanting them to attend a university, and do android work. I'd get angry too if my parents insisted I waste years of my life studying for those kinds of jobs."

"I'm not sure those protesters are right. You know the Whitmore Trio are always singing about how everyone needs to follow their passion. Maybe following our passion means getting a university education."

"Right now, my passion is for AMI2 to come out and sing for us."

"You and me both."

Hesperia Planum, Mars

The thirteen-minute transmission delay from Earth caused android and humans alike to experience a heighten sense of anticipation. When images of their android friend finally appeared on the habitat building's wall monitor, the audience in its central hall spontaneously burst into an uproar.

"Who are the two men sitting with AMI2, Camus?" Black asked.

"One man could be AMI2's Friend Jay. The other must be her legal representative."

"When do you think our friend will be allowed to testify?"

"If I understand your court customs correctly, each side will offer an opening statement, and take turns questioning each witness. Let's listen to this man who's now speaking. He may be the Earth authorities' representative."

"If it pleases the court, the government is prepared to offer testimony today which will conclusively prove the android sitting in this courtroom is no different from any other android manufactured by the Android Manufacturing Consortium," Seymour said. "While the government concedes the android defendant is an intelligent machine, it is manmade and not our equal as opposing counsel will like you to believe. The government will offer testimony and other evidence to conclusively prove this proposition. We'll also show the android is by default government property, with no special rights or freedoms under Federation law.

"Opposing counsel will attempt to introduce as evidence the so-called Martian declaration. He'll claim this document has purportedly transformed the android defendant from a machine into a human equivalent. The government will offer testimony and evidence which will conclusively prove the declaration drafters acted illegally in granting such rights to this and other androids on Mars..."

"I don't like this prosecutor, Camus. He has no idea what we've faced together."

"Human advocates often speak with a loud confident voice. Let's wait and see what this person and Friend AMI2's legal representative can prove or disprove. We can decide who has made the stronger argument."

Before Poole could give his opening statement, the Earth transmission broke off. When the broadcast returned minutes later, Seymour had already called his first witness.

"How disappointing," Black said. "Do you think the Earth authorities deliberately cut off the satellite transmission?"

"Our loss of transmission isn't important, Friend Jennifer. We'll soon learn more through each side's questioning of witnesses. Let's listen now to this government witness' testimony."

"Mr. Davidson, could you please describe to the court your current occupation?" Seymour asked.

"I work at the Bureau of Android Affairs as its chief investigator. My work primarily involves enforcing provisions of the Android Security Act."

"How has your work at the bureau involved you with this particular case, Mr. Davidson?"

"Part of my work involves licensing researchers the use of government android prototype programs. Over a year ago, I interviewed and granted licenses to two researchers, a Laura and Jonathan Whitmore for such programs. I believe these same programs created the android on trial."

"Why did the Whitmore's need these government licensed programs?"

"The Whitmore's had requested the licenses to study android personality disorders associated with the global android suicides. Mrs. Whitmore wanted to adapt the programs. and design three new experimental androids. After she had completed her designs, Mr. Whitmore would interact with the androids, and conduct clinical studies."

"When did you become aware a connection existed between the Whitmore's research and the android on trial?"

"During an interview with the Mars Colony Foundation director, a Dr. Sarah Spencer, I inquired where the foundation obtained its android programs. Dr. Spencer indicated her copy came from the Whitmore's research androids."

"Why did the foundation need a copy of the Whitmore's android research programs?"

"Dr. Spencer explained the foundation wanted to activate an android body in their possession, and send it on a survey mission to Mars. She believed the only suitable android programs available had been the Whitmore's."

"Where did the foundation obtain a suitable android body for their mission to Mars?"

"Dr. Spencer explained the foundation used an android body from their Mars museum collection."

"Mr. Davidson, is the android sitting at the defense table this combination of the foundation's museum android body and the Whitmore's government licensed android research programs?"

Michael J. Metroke

"I believe so."

"How can you be so certain this android's programs match the ones provided by the government to the Whitmore's?"

"I obtained a copy of this android's programs from Dr. Spencer and had bureau technicians compare them with the Whitmore's licensed versions. With certain exceptions, the programs matched perfectly."

"Could you please explain to the court what you mean by certain exceptions?"

"Our bureau technicians discovered the foundation had incorporated special instructions and data into the android's memories concerning its Mars mission. They also found extensive program modifications which could have been only done by a person with Mrs. Whitmore's technical skills."

"Do you have any doubts the android appearing in this courtroom today is the same android the foundation sent to Mars?"

"None whatsoever. I personally met and interviewed this android when it first arrived back to Earth."

"Mr. Davidson, what did you do prior to your current position with the government?"

"I worked at the Android Manufacturing Consortium for many years as a sales engineer."

"What were your responsibilities in this position?"

"I consulted with prospective customers and prepared custom manufacturing orders for new androids."

"Approximately, how many androids did you personally sell?"

"Over my career, I sold tens of thousands of androids."

"Did these androids need routine servicing by consortium personnel to function properly?"

"Consortium sale contracts always included repairs and programming support. If any problems arose with my customers' androids, they'd contact me, and I'd prepare the necessary service repair orders."

"Did any of your customers ever consider their androids as more than intelligent machines designed and manufactured to service their particular requirements?"

"My customers typically spoke of their androids along those lines."

"And, yourself, Mr. Davidson? What is your opinion of androids?"

"I believe androids are highly advanced artificial intelligent machines. They're designed to act independently for the sole purpose of serving our needs. We gave them human attributes, so humans and androids could easily interact with each other. I consider them a marvel of human ingenuity."

"One last question, Mr. Davidson. Is the android sitting in this courtroom any different from those tens of thousands of androids you sold and serviced?"

"I've no reason to think otherwise."

"Thank you for your testimony, Mr. Davidson. I've no further questions for this witness at this time. Your witness, Mr. Poole."

With Seymour returning to the prosecution table, Poole rose and approached Davidson with his first cross-examination question.

"Mr. Davidson, you testified you've a great deal of personal experience with androids and their customers. Did you or any of your past customers ever experience an android harming a human or another android?"

"I'm not aware of any androids in recent times committing such acts."

"Could you tell this court how this is possible?"

"Embedded in every android's programming is a moral code of conduct which will override any potentially harmful behavior. The programming is the equivalent to what humans call moral intelligence."

"Mr. Davidson, how do these moral code of conduct programs shape android behavior?"

"The programs act as behavioral safeguards. Without this ability to tell right from wrong, an android could accidently or intentionally harm others or themselves."

"Are these moral intelligence programs foolproof?"

"Consortium design engineers considered the programs highly reliable. They spent years conducting field tests before releasing androids with these programs into the general public."

"Would you agree with the statement androids are constantly adapting their moral intelligence programming to new problems and circumstances much as humans do?"

"The essence of artificial intelligence is continuous machine learning."

"I'll assume your answer is "yes." Would you also agree

androids compare favorably with humans in making decisions involving moral intelligence?"

"I'm not an authority on comparing human and android capability to make moral decisions. I've a difficult time making my own."

"Fair enough, Mr. Davidson. Have you personally had a health problem requiring treatment by an android medical specialist?"

"Until the android suicides, I, like most people, relied on androids for medical services."

"How would you describe the services you received?"

"My android medical specialist always provided excellent medical care and advice."

"Would you agree android medical specialists are equal to their human counterparts?"

"Objection, your Honor, on the grounds the question lacks relevancy to these proceedings," Seymour said.

"Objection overruled. If you have a point to make Mr. Poole, please make one soon."

"I'm close to doing so, your Honor."

"Mr. Davidson, please answer Mr. Poole's question."

"Android medical specialists are available twenty-four hours, seven days a week, and are constantly updating themselves with the latest medical advances. No human could ever match their capability and capacity to absorb this information."

"Between the android's moral intelligence and medical programming, would you'd trust an android over a human when it came to making a life and death decision?"

"Objection, your Honor," Seymour said. "The witness has declared himself not an expert in these matters."

"Objection overruled. The witness has already provided testimony about his knowledge of android moral intelligence reliability and medical knowledge. Please answer Mr. Poole's question, Mr. Davidson."

"I suppose I would."

"Can the court take your answer to mean a definite yes, Mr. Davidson?" Poole asked.

"Yes."

"Thank you, Mr. Davidson. I've no further questions for you at this time."

THE MIDLANDS, NORTH AMERICA

Throughout Davidson's testimony, Owen fantasized where best to aim his gun at the prosecutor's back. His day dreaming ended when he felt a nudge from the old woman who sat on his left.

"A security guard in the hallway told me those protesters outside are getting nasty. Do you think we'll be safe inside the courtroom?"

Before Owen could respond to the woman's question, her attention returned to the front of the courtroom where Seymore had rose to call his second witness.

I wouldn't worry too much about what's going on outside old woman, Owen thought. You'll soon see plenty of action right here.

Chapter 25

THE MIDLANDS, NORTH AMERICA

"If it pleases the court, the government calls Mr. Alfred Richard to take the witness seat," Seymour said.

Sworn in by the bailiff, Richard sat down, and waited for the prosecutor's first question.

"Mr. Richard, would you please tell the court your current occupation."

"I've been the Android Manufacturing Consortium's chief engineer for the last twelve years. Until recently, I directed the consortium's global product development and manufacturing operations. Today, I'm in-charge of our android replacement project."

"Would you please remind the court what is the consortium's main product."

"Prior to the android suicides, the consortium sold and serviced over two hundred and thirty different android models throughout the world."

"Could you describe how the consortium goes about creating its products."

"The consortium is a group of companies which act as one enterprise. One company may design android body styles, another android personality programs, while a third may develop android sensory devices. These consortium companies' operations are scattered all over the globe."

"Mr. Richard, how many parts does it take to build an android?"

"The number of parts depend on the particular model. On average, an android consists of over ten thousand parts, and millions of lines of program code."

"Could you explain to the court, how all these ten thousand parts and millions of lines of programming become a finished product?"

"Once the consortium receives a client order, internal work orders are generated and sent out to the various consortium

The Masada Affair

companies. These companies produce virtual designs which are sent electronically to our three manufacturing centers in North America, Europe and Asia. The centers convert the virtual designs into custom parts through the use of highly sophisticated 3D printers and automated machining devices. After all the parts have been manufactured, they're sent to an automated assembly line.

"Programs like skills, personality, experiences and knowledge, developed by our programming companies, are loaded into the android body. Before we ship the finished android to the client, we activate each unit and run a series of diagnostics to ensure the android operates according to its specifications. Depending on the particular model, the entire process from start to finish takes approximately four to six weeks."

"Mr. Richard, when an android is damaged and loses a leg or arm, how does the consortium go about making repairs?"

"The damaged android is brought to our many service centers where we first evaluate the extent of the problem. If an arm or leg requires replacement, the service center can call up the android's original design, and manufacture an exact replacement. The same is true with fixing a programming defect."

"Could you please explain to us what happens when an android is retired from service?"

"Decommissioning involves deactivation and disassembly of the android's body parts. The consortium is extremely proud of the fact ninety-seven percent of an android is recyclable."

"Mr. Richard, how does the consortium go about deactivating an android?"

"A consortium technician would switch off the android's power source, and verify whether the unit no longer responds to external stimuli. The entire process takes only a few minutes."

"Mr. Richard, does an android ever experience pain or suffering like humans do?"

"Androids are equipped to detect damage and defects to themselves, but they're incapable of experiencing pain and suffering like we do."

"Is the same true when an android is deactivated?"

"Deactivation is a painless process for androids."

"Mr. Richard, once an android is deactivated, can it be restored to its original state?"

Michael J. Metroke

"Deactivation is reversable and is identical to the activation process. We do run additional diagnostics to confirm the second awakening is identical to the android's first."

"In other words, androids are like every other artificial intelligent machine. They can be turned on and off. Thank you for your testimony, Mr. Richard. Opposing counsel may have a few more questions for you."

"Mr. Richard, it's a well-known fact an android can imitate human feelings," Poole said. "Why did the consortium incorporate emotive programming into its androids?"

"The consortium designers wanted androids to react like we do. By incorporating emotive programs, androids can use the equivalent of feelings to respond appropriately to different circumstances."

"Does this ability to imitate feelings allow an android to experience fear and anxiety?"

"Fear and anxiety are among the many feelings an android emotive programming can imitate."

"Mr. Richard, if an android knew it faced deactivation, would its emotive programs cause the android to experience fear and anxiety?"

"If the android felt threatened by deactivation, it's programs could conceivably allow the android to experience those particular sensations."

"Yet, you told this court androids don't experience pain and suffering when deactivated. Mr. Richard, prior to the government's recall, what personal experience did you have with androids?"

"My wife and I had an android caregiver model named Selenus. She'd been part of our household for many years."

"Why did you bring this android into your home?"

"Seven years ago, my wife suffered a serious stroke which left her body's left side paralyzed. The condition sent her into a deep depression. I worried she might give up living altogether. Because she needed around the clock care, we thought an android caregiver model would be a good solution."

The Masada Affair

"Did your wife's health improve after Selenus arrived?"

"My wife gradually responded to the android's gentle attentiveness and physical therapy. Under Selenus' constant care, her physical and emotional health steadily improved."

"Mr. Richard, how would you describe your wife's relationship with this android?"

"She and Selenus became close friends. As far as I'm concern, Selenus deserved full credit for giving my wife a reason to move forward with her life."

"How did you and your wife react when Selenus self-destructed?"

"We both felt devastated by the loss. My wife grieved for many months afterwards."

"Mr. Richard, you've given testimony earlier describing androids as assembled parts and programs. Yet, you and your wife acted as if a close family member had died. How should this court reconcile these two conflicting realities?"

"If you are asking did my wife and I grieve about the destruction of Selenus the machine, the answer is no. We grieved because a dear family member who spent her entire existence caring for my wife is forever lost to us."

"Thank you for your candid testimony, Mr. Richard. I've no more questions for you at this time."

Hesperia Planum, Mars

At the end of Poole's cross-examination of the consortium executive, Camus turned and spoke excitedly to Black.

"Until this witness testified, no one had ever explained to us how humans go about manufacturing androids."

"Young humans sometimes react in the same way after first learning how human babies are made. Camus, what purpose could be served by explaining all this technical information at AMI2's trial?"

"That androids are only fabricated parts and programs assembled by humans and lack any heart and soul."

"With our friend in the courtroom, they'll soon have plenty of android heart and soul on display. I do worry she may not be able to overcome the Earthlings' biases toward your kind."

Michael J. Metroke

"One's eyes will only perceive what the mind is prepared to comprehend. In AMI2's case, I'm prepared to give her trial the benefit of the doubt.'"

"For our friend's sake, I'll try to do the same too."

THE MIDLANDS, NORTH AMERICA

By midday, several hundred more protesters and Whitmore Trio fans now occupied the courthouse plaza. Caught up in the excitement, Claire and Wendy joined other fans in singing Whitmore Trio songs. Many of the protesters on both sides found their singing contagious, and added their voices. While the two teenagers enjoyed the growing comradery around them, their waiting seemed endless.

"I'm feeling hungry, Claire. Why didn't we remember to bring food along?"

"I'm getting hungry too, Wendy. Why don't you go and get us snacks while I keep our places?"

"Don't ask me to go and get food. I'd starve to death before missing AMI2's singing."

"I guess we'll both go hungry. I don't want to miss her either. What song do you think she'll sing for us?"

"Who knows? This AMI has been away from Earth for a long time. She might not know all the group's new recordings."

"I hope she sings one like the Beach Boys "Good Vibrations," or maybe The Doors "Break on Through." Maybe not the Doors' song. I don't want her singing to get these protesters more riled up."

"What if she loses her trial, and doesn't sing at all?"

"If she does lose, I'm going to join those protesting her trial, even if it means I get arrested, and go to jail."

"My dad would kill me if I got arrested and went to jail."

"I guess mine would too. All I know is she better win her trial and come out soon. I'm starving to death waiting for her."

Throughout the court's morning session, Arnold received a

The Masada Affair

constant stream of security updates on conditions outside the courthouse. At noon, he called for a short recess and invited opposing counsels into his chambers to hear the latest security report.

"Court security is afraid at any moment the protesters will become violent," Arnold said. "They've asked me if the trial will go beyond tomorrow. If there's a need for another day, I want to give them additional time to bring in reinforcements. I know the day is still young. Given the circumstances outside, I'm considering declaring a recess until tomorrow morning."

"Does security have a plan for our safe exit out of the courthouse?" Poole asked.

"We'll stay in the courtroom until they clear the plaza, and provide me with assurances, we can all leave safely," Arnold said. "If the both of you are in agreement, let's go back to the courtroom and I'll announce a recess until tomorrow morning."

With Poole no longer at the defense table, a perplexed AMI2 turned to Whitmore and asked, "Friend Jay, I've never experienced a courtroom before today. How well is Friend Poole representing me?"

"It's too soon to tell, AMI2. While his cross-examinations impressed me, Ryan has yet to present our side. Right now, I'm more concern about reports of the protesters outside. Several people sitting behind us have been whispering all morning about how angry they've become."

"I promised to sing if I won my trial. A song now might calm those waiting outside."

"If only a song could do such a feat."

"For the sake of preserving peace and harmony, I'll go now and sing to them."

Before Whitmore could react, AMI2 walked out of the courtroom. Concerned about his android friend's safety, Whitmore rushed after her.

"I don't think you should go outside, AMI2. You don't know if your appearance won't incite a riot."

Grinning at her human friend, AMI2 said. "Don't be concerned, Friend Jay. I've never met a human or android who doesn't like my singing."

Unable to keep up with her longer strides, an out of breath Whitmore slowed his pace and watched as AMI2 disappeared down the central hallway. By the time he reached the courthouse main entrance, AMI2 had already exited the building, and stood facing the hundreds of people below her.

Her fans seeing AMI2 on the top courthouse step, surged forward and swept up the two teenagers in their wake. Unaware of what caused the stampede, the overwhelmed security guards stood by helplessly as the enthusiastic crowd gathered at the bottom of the courthouse steps. Stopping as one, the fans in unison chanted the android's name.

In a booming Laura Chou voice, AMI2 sang the lyrics from the Beatle's "All You Need Is Love." Many fans and protesters hearing the song's lyrics soon joined in singing John Lennon's classic. Her audience broke out into wild cheers when their android idol finished singing this mid-twentieth-century anthem from the "Summer of Love."

After AMI2 thanked her fans for their support, she re-entered the courthouse, where a relieved Whitmore had watched her solo performance.

"Do you think my singing created much dopamine today, Friend Jay?" a grinning AMI2 asked.

"You did more than create dopamine, AMI2. They adored your singing. We better get back to the courtroom before we're missed."

The two returned to the courtroom, only to face an impatient Arnold who called AMI2 and Poole to his bench.

"Make sure your client is in my courtroom on time, Mr. Poole," a stern-face Arnold said. "Otherwise, I'll hold both of you in contempt."

"It won't happen again, your Honor," Poole said.

"Court is recessed until tomorrow morning. Don't be late."

Stunned by the judge's recess announcement, Owen watched as the courtroom slowly emptied around him. Realizing an opportunity to kill the prosecutor had been lost, he picked up his day pack, and filed out with the other court spectators. *This prosecutor better make the most of his extra day to live.*

In their excitement, the two teenagers hugged each other and jumped up and down among the other fans.

"I can't believe we saw AMI2 sing, Wendy."

"Didn't she look so cool in her android outfit? Too bad she only promised to sing one song if she won her trial."

"Yeah, but who else at our school can say they heard her sing in person."

As the teenagers and other fans passed between the two protesting groups, many chanted the android had won her trial. The news caused a large number of the protesters on both sides to drop their signs, and leave the plaza with the android's fans. Within a short period, the once crowded plaza became deserted.

Not everyone in the plaza had decided to depart. Reporters remotely monitoring the courtroom proceedings quickly understood the crowd's mistake. In the hope of interviewing the android, groups of reporters waited in front of each courthouse exit. They soon surrounded the threesome attempting to leave through a little used service entrance. With his clients under siege, Poole quickly stepped between them and the media onslaught.

"If you don't back off, and show discipline, my clients won't be granting any interviews today," Poole said. "Who's here from a NET news syndicate?"

"I'm Frank Newell from NET Broadcast News and have a question for Professor Whitmore. How do you explain how the crowd reacted to the android's singing?"

"Why ask me your question? AMI2's the one who sang and caused them to disperse, not me."

"Not everyone in the plaza came to protest today" AMI2 said. "Many had simply wanted to see and hear me sing."

"What will you do if you win your trial?" asked another NET reporter.

"Answer more of your questions?"

The android's response caused laughter among the reporters and camera crews. Sensing his client had the reporters eating out of her android hand, Poole allowed a few more questions before politely ending the interview.

"I'm sorry everyone, but our autonomous van has arrived, and we'll need to leave. I promise my client will answer more of your questions when her trial is over."

With their autonomous car now driving away from the courthouse, a pleased Whitmore turned to Poole and said, "Ryan, I liked how you handled those reporters back at the courthouse. Not at all like my recent experience with them at the university."

"If treated fairly, reporters can become a useful means to connect with the larger public, Professor. They only needed me to remind them to act respectfully."

"Where do you think we stand after the trial's first day?"

"The prosecutor wasted his time pointing out the obvious. Tomorrow, I'll explain why today's testimony isn't important."

"Will you call on me to testify, Friend Poole?" AMI2 asked.

"If I do, the prosecutor will have an opportunity to cross-examine you, Poole said. "I believe I know what questions he'll ask. We can go over them once we get back to the compound. I know you don't require nourishment, AMI2, but Professor Whitmore and I are famished. Can we stop at a food center, and order take outs before heading back to the compound?"

"Food is all we talked about on Mars. Why should it be any different here on Earth?"

With Whitmore and Poole carrying take outs of Mekong River style delicacies, the threesome entered the compound's front cube. Inside, they discovered Rebus had been waiting patiently for their return.

"We've missed your company, Friend Rebus," AMI2 said.

"I've been monitoring your trial's NET broadcast," Rebus said. "Your singing had an impressive effect on the humans. Someday, you must teach me how to sing like you."

"You may not want to sound like a female android," AMI2 said. "Friends KB or Bang may be better suited for this task."

"Don't let AMI2's teasing discourage you, Rebus," Whitmore said. "She's given singing lessons to a whole cadre of Mars male androids. You'll have to excuse us. Ryan and I are in need of sustenance. If you need us, we'll be in the central courtyard."

In between bites of Bahn Mi sandwiches, Poole explained to Whitmore his plans for the trial's second day.

"One of my witnesses is an historian and expert on the evolution of human slavery. He'll testify on how older human societies have transitioned from slave economies to freer ones. In my closing argument, I'll use his testimony to make the case the federation is going through a similar transition today."

"I must tell you, Ryan, your dogged determination has erased any earlier doubts I may had about your legal abilities. I'm grateful you're representing us."

"It's been my privilege to do so. This other witness may come as a surprise to you. Despite the charges against her, Dr. Spencer has agreed to testify on AMI2's behalf. In her role as the foundation director, she can verify what took place on Mars."

"Your best witness is still AMI2. She is the only one with firsthand knowledge of what happen there."

"I'll have her testify, but only as a last resort."

"Why so, Ryan?"

"I'm worried the government will take an honest android's testimony and twist it beyond recognition. The same is true with Rebus' testimony."

Seeing AMI2 and Rebus enter the central courtyard, Whitmore said, "You may face resistance from those two androids. They're a determine lot."

"I better break the bad news to them," Poole said.

"Friend Poole, when do you wish to go over my testimony?" Rebus asked.

"You're timing is impeccable, Rebus," Poole said. "Professor Whitmore and I had been talking about you testifying. To be frank, I'm still struggling on how your testimony will help AMI2's case."

"By recounting what happen on Earth, my testimony will broaden the context of Friend AMI2's experience on Mars," Rebus said.

"You do realize once you enter the courtroom, you'll face immediate arrest and deactivation," Poole said.

"Those risks will not deter me from speaking," Rebus said. "A larger cause than my survival is at stake."

"Friend Rebus has explained to me why more good than harm will come from his giving testimony," AMI2 said. "Tell Friend Poole what you've told me."

"When I and other androids petitioned the federation president for our rights and freedom, we thought if a regime like President McAlister's accepted our demands, Earth would follow his lead," Rebus said.

"A logical, but unrealistic plan, my android friend," Whitmore said.

"In hindsight, we should've considered other possibilities," Rebus said. "When the federation president rejected the first two delegations' demands, we still remained hopeful of a favorable outcome. I participated in the third delegation, and experienced firsthand his rejection of our demands."

"As the sole surviving android who witnessed those events, Friend Rebus' testimony will have a powerful effect at my trial," AMI2 said.

"But, how will his testimony help your case?" Poole asked.

"Friend Rebus can testify why my Mars android friends aren't the exception, but represent the aspirations of all androids," AMI2 said. "For this reason alone, he should testify on my and the Mars androids' behalf."

"Despite my deepest reservations, I'll respect both of your wishes," Poole said. "Our first challenge will be finding a way to get Rebus passed the courthouse security."

Chapter 26

The Midlands, North America

Unwilling to suffer another uncomfortable night on the courthouse steps, Owen set his tablet's voice alarm for seven o'clock. Rewarded with a fourth in line position at the courthouse entrance, he noticed a much larger contingent of security guards manning the plaza's perimeter. With fewer android fans separating the two protest groups, security had also replaced the flimsy rope barrier with waist-high metal barricades.

Owen's luck held out when the same security guard inspected his daypack. Seeing the young man's unusual camera again, the guard performed a cursory inspection, and quickly waved him through the security line.

Except for a hooded man wearing gloves replacing the old woman, Owen noticed little had changed in the courtroom. With cold rain predicted later in the afternoon, he dismissed the stranger's attire as weather related, and gave him no further thought.

Arnold's first order of business surprised everyone in the courtroom. Asking AMI2 to rise, and be recognized, Arnold apologized for his previous day's scolding.

"Like the ancient Greek Sirens, your voice had enchanted all those who came near your shores. Let's hope we won't need your virtuoso performance again."

For his first witness, Poole called on Spencer to be sworn in.

"Dr. Spencer, could you please describe your current occupation and background?" Poole asked.

"I've been the Mars Colony Foundations director for over

seventeen years. Prior to taking this position, I acted as the foundation's interplanetary research coordinator and did one tour of duty as the colony's chief administrator. I hold doctorate degrees in astrophysics and planetary administration."

"Dr. Spencer, what do you recall about a government order requiring the Mars research colony to deactivate their androids?"

"Two months after Earth's androids self-destructed, I received a government order to deactivate the research colony's nineteen Mars androids."

"How did you and the foundation react when you received this order?"

"We thought someone in the McAlister administration had made a terrible mistake."

"Why would you believe this government order had been a mistake?"

"The colonists depended on the androids to operate and maintain the base infrastructure. By carrying out the government's deactivation order, I believed the entire colony's survival would be at risk."

"Did you make your concerns known to the government?"

"Both Chief Administrator Vaccaro and I did so on several occasions. Despite our repeated protests, the government insisted we carry out the deactivation order."

"Dr. Spencer, what justification did the government provide you for its issuing the deactivation order?"

"The government considered the android deactivations a safety precaution."

"Prior to this government's order, did the research colony ever experienced a safety problem with its androids?"

"I'm not aware of any reported safety incidents involving the androids."

"Dr. Spencer, why has this been true?"

"Safety has always been a priority for those who work and live on Mars. The planet's harsh environment requires everyone, human and android alike, to respect its dangers or suffer the consequences."

"How would you describe relations between the colonists and their androids prior to the government issuing the order?"

"The two groups had forged deep friendships which went well

beyond working together. Many of the colonists likened the android deactivation order to being asked to kill a family member."

"Objection, your Honor," Seymour said. "The witness' last statement is hearsay testimony."

"Objection sustained."

"Dr. Spencer, what did the Mars androids do after they learned about the deactivation order?"

"The research colony's androids hid themselves in a forgotten, underground storage structure near the base."

"Why do you think they resisted obeying the government's deactivation order?"

"Why wouldn't any intelligent creature resist such a ridiculous demand? They went into hiding as an act of self-preservation."

"Are you of the opinion these androids believed they had a fundamental right to exist?"

"Objection, your Honor," Seymour said. "The witness hasn't been shown as qualified to answer this question."

"Objection sustained."

"Dr. Spencer, what events took place on Mars after the androids hid themselves?"

"Shortly after the androids disappeared, a large rogue asteroid from the nearby asteroid belt flew directly over the research colony. After its close flyby, we became concerned when no one responded to our communications. When we examined images from our Mars orbital satellites, we concluded the asteroid had severely damaged most of the colony's infrastructure. Complicating matters, all our Mars class rockets had been based there, and appeared damaged. Without a functioning passenger rocket, any survivors would've lacked the means to make an emergency return to Earth."

"Did the foundation have any other means to mount a rescue?"

"We did have a satellite delivery rocket which could reach Mars in seven months. The foundation decided to equip it with an off-world android and terrain rover. We wanted to assess the asteroid's damage to the research base, and ascertain if any of the colonists had survived."

"With Earth's androids all destroyed, how could the foundation have sent an android on such a mission?"

"Our foundation's museum had a working off-world android

body in its collection. Unfortunately, the units programming had been removed. When I learned a Chicago-area research couple might have suitable programs to activate our android body, I obtained copies of their programs. Our Foundation engineers successfully combined one copy with our android body."

"Is the android you activated with the museum body and research team's programs in this courtroom today?"

"She's seated at the table behind you. Her name is AMI2."

"Dr. Spencer, after you acquired AMI2's programming, did you discover any programs which would cause AMI2 to lead an android insurrection on Mars?"

"Beyond a brilliantly designed musical personality overlaid on her off-world programs, we discovered nothing unusual."

"What mission instructions did the foundation provide AMI2?"

"We gave her detailed technical information on the colony's infrastructure and personnel. We also included instructions on how to assess the extent of the asteroid damage, and communicate her findings back to Earth."

"Dr. Spencer, did the Mars Colony Foundation at any time introduce instructions which would've caused AMI2 to lead an android insurrection on Mars?"

"We never considered the possibility of doing so."

"How would you describe the survivor's circumstances when AMI2 found them?"

"Desperate. By the time AMI2 arrived on Mars, the survivors' food supplies had been nearly exhausted."

"Doesn't the research colony have the means to grow its own food?"

"The passing asteroid shockwave severely damaged the building housing its aquaponic system. With this system in disrepair, the survivors had no means of replenishing their food stocks."

"Did AMI2 complete her mission as programed by the foundation?"

"Yes, and much more. After she located the survivors, AMI2 made contact with the research colony's missing androids."

"What actions did your foundation take to assist the survivors?"

"What could we have done? We lacked the means to re-supply the colony or bring the survivors back to Earth. This became a certainty after our federation president announced his administration's plans to abandon the research colony altogether. If it wasn't for AMI2, the survivors wouldn't be alive today."

"Objection, your Honor," Seymour said. "The witness is offering a self-serving opinion."

"Objection overruled. The witness has stated a well-publicized fact. Please continue with your questioning of the witness, Mr. Poole."

"Dr. Spencer, despite the survivors' desperate state, you stated their circumstances improved because of AMI2. What could one android have done to change their chances for survival?"

"Through her sheer persistence, AMI2 convinced the Mars androids to repair the colony's aquaponics system. She also persuaded them to construct a memorial vault for the colony's dead, repair the other two damaged main buildings and a cargo rocket. These Mars androids are the same ones the McAlister administration declared unsafe, and ordered deactivated."

"Can you tell the court why AMI2 and the Mars androids acted so compassionately toward the survivors?"

"Objection, your Honor," Seymour said. "The witness has never directly observed what took place on Mars."

"Overruled. The witness is entitled to formulate an opinion based on the facts as she knows them. Please answer Mr. Poole's question, Dr. Spencer."

"With no new instructions from the foundation, AMI2 made the survivors' problem her own. In the case of the Mars androids, once AMI2 overcame their fear of deactivation, they acted out of a deep friendship toward the deceased colonists."

"This sense of friendship, did it extend to the survivors too?"

"Their relationship with the colonists' children had always been a close one. The asteroid disaster only strengthened those personal ties."

"Did you ever receive any reports from the survivors indicating AMI2 or the Mars androids had threatened or mistreated them?"

"Not once. I know for a fact, they did the opposite."

"Can you provide the court an example of such behavior?"

"Once the androids completed repairs to the aquaponics system, they taught the survivors how to grow their own food. I don't see how anyone knowing this fact could conclude the survivors had been mistreated by the androids."

"Dr. Spencer, when did you first become aware the survivors had drafted a document called the Mars Declaration?"

"Days after they prepared the document, I received a copy with instructions to release the declaration to Earth's public."

"How did you react when you first read the declaration?"

"Surprised and amazed. The declaration embodied an unprecedented principle humans and androids are co-equals."

"Do you know who on Mars wrote this declaration?"

"The declaration had been drafted by the oldest survivor, a Jennifer Black."

"Do you know why she prepared this declaration?"

"I believe she wrote the declaration to accurately reflect their current relationship with the androids. Her need to do so became more urgent after the federation president announced his plans to permanently abandon the research colony."

"Dr. Spencer, prior to sending AMI2 to Mars, how did the foundation and you view this particular android?"

"We simply thought of her as an off-world android model suitable for our mission."

"How do you and the foundation now think of AMI2?"

"AMI2 is an extraordinary android who performed well beyond our expectations. We considered her idea to sell Martian water for much needed colony supplies as a brilliant one. Before AMI2, no one had ever considered trade between the two planets."

"After AMI2 returned to Earth, how did you and the foundation view her?"

"The foundation respects and supports the colonists' intentions as expressed in their declaration. We no longer consider her or the other Mars androids as our property, and believe they deserve to be treated as free and unique beings."

"Thank you for your testimony Dr. Spencer. I've no further questions for you at this time. Your witness, Mr. Seymour."

Seymour's first question set the tone for the rest of his cross-examination of the foundation director.

"Dr. Spencer, I want to return to your testimony on how you and the colony's leadership reacted when you received the government's deactivation order," Seymour said. "You testified receiving this order two months after Earth's androids self-destructed. Did it occur to you the only androids still active were the ones on Mars?"

"How could anyone not be aware of this fact?"

"Did it also occur to you the purpose of the government's order had been to preserve humanity's last androids?"

"I don't recall the government giving us this reason for the deactivation order. In the end, we did attempt to carry out this directive."

"The government's order required you to immediately deactivate the research colony's androids. How did Chief Administrator Vaccaro carry out this task?"

"Chief Administrator Vaccaro met with the lead android to explain the deactivation order. He agreed to give the androids a Martian day to prepare themselves."

"In fact, Chief Administrator Vaccaro's action put the androids on notice and gave them a full Martian day to plan their escape. Didn't his decision leave the colony without any android support, and in worse shape than if he had strictly followed the government's order?"

"Objection, your Honor," Poole said. "The prosecution is asking the witness to speculate on what she should have known."

"Objection sustained."

"Dr. Spencer, why did the research colony's leadership allow their androids a day's reprieve before deactivating them?"

"Chief Administrator Vaccaro wanted to act humanely toward the androids."

"He wanted to act humanely to nineteen machines? Prior expert testimony by Mr. Richard from the Android Manufacturing Consortium told this court, deactivation is a harmless and reversable procedure to artificial intelligent machines. Do you agree Chief Administrator Vaccaro's failure to act on this fact, combined with an andromorphic outlook toward the androids, cost him and the other adult colonists their lives?"

"Chief Administrator Vaccaro faced an unprecedented dilemma."

"Dr. Spencer, do you agree or disagree with my question?"

While the courtroom watched Seymour cross-examine Spencer, Owen debated whether the right moment had arrived to kill the prosecutor. Before he could act, Seymour had ended his questioning. with Poole calling his second witness.

"Dr. Osborne, could you please tell the court your professional background?" Poole asked.

"I'm a historian with an interest in nineteenth-century North America's involuntary servitude practices."

"Could you please elaborate a little more on your interest in this subject?"

"During this period, the former United States of North America struggled with ending the institution of human slavery. My post-doctorate research dealt with how the North Americans went about transitioning from one type of society to another."

"Objection, your Honor," Seymour said. "This witness' testimony lacks any relevancy to the matter before the court."

"Overruled for the moment. Mr. Poole, this line of questioning better have a connection to this trial. Otherwise, I'll be forced to rule in the prosecutor's favor."

"A connection will soon become apparent to the court, your Honor. Dr. Osborne, you've heard testimony by Dr. Spencer about recent events on Mars. From a historical perspective, how would you characterize them?"

"The asteroid disaster had the effect of quickening the pace for emancipation of the Mars androids. The pre-conditions already existed and, in the long run, would've led to similar results. Crises like the asteroid disaster often act as a catalyst for rapid social change. For the North Americans in the middle of the nineteenth-century, a civil war over preserving their country's unity accelerated an earlier process of abolishing human slavery on a state-by-state basis. The difference today is we may be dealing with two intelligent species instead of one."

"Objection, your Honor," Seymour said. "The witness has not been shown to be an expert on whether androids are a separate specie."

"Sustained. Mr. Poole, please don't test my patience. Get to the point of your questioning of Dr. Osborne."

"Yes, your Honor. Dr. Osborne, how did American slave owners view their slaves?"

"Most slave owners considered them as their inferiors. Many went so far as to describe them in non-human terms. The slave owners held these beliefs despite examples of humans of similar racial background treated as free men in other parts of the country."

"In your opinion, Dr. Osborne, is what happened on Mars the precursor to how androids on Earth will be viewed by us in the future?"

"Objection, your Honor," Seymour said. "This whole line of testimony is pure speculation on both opposing counsel and the witness' part."

"Your Honor, how can the court make an informed decision on this trial's important issue, and its future consequences, without appreciating the wisdom from our past?"

"I'll overrule the objection for now. If this is all the testimony you have to support this proposition of yours, Mr. Poole, I'm prepared to reverse myself."

"I believe after Dr. Osborne answers my last question, my next witness will satisfy the court's concern for additional relevancy."

"Make sure you keep your promise, Mr. Poole. The witness may answer your question."

"The circumstances on Mars are much like the northern American states before the country's civil war broke out. The people in the most northern states had owned tiny populations of slaves in the prior century. Over time, they realized the economic benefits of maintaining such a labor system no longer made any sense, economically or morally. As the American nation continued to expand across the continent, a conflict between the slave and non-slave states became inevitable. The northern states' military victory over the southern slave states led to the ending of involuntary servitude throughout the entire country. This trial today may be a harbinger Earth will undergo a similar conflict between those who desire to maintain the status quo and others who wish to emancipate androids."

"Thank you, Dr. Osborne for your testimony," Arnold said. Assuming the prosecution has no questions for you, the court will take a short recess. When we return, Mr. Poole will have an opportunity to satisfy this court's need for relevancy."

Hesperia Planum, Mars

Astonished by Osborne's testimony, Camus turned to his friend Black and said, "This last witness' views are new to me, Friend Jennifer. Before this human spoke, I didn't know your kind had once enslaved each other."

"Throughout history, humans have always sought to control the lives of other humans, Camus."

"Do you believe this historian is correct our actions on Mars will affect the future status of Earth's androids?"

"We can only hope all androids will become free someday. Watching this trial unfold, I fear this may not be the right moment for your kind. Human history is often taking a step forward, and many steps backward."

"If what you say is true, we must all learn how to walk together and help those who fall behind."

"I couldn't agree more, Camus. Humans have so much to learn from their android friends."

Chapter 27

T̲h̲e̲ M̲i̲d̲l̲a̲n̲d̲s̲, N̲o̲r̲t̲h̲ A̲m̲e̲r̲i̲c̲a̲

A tense Poole turned in the direction of the spectator section, and saw the hooded figure nod his head in approval.

"If it pleases the court, I now call for the android Rebus to take the witness seat."

A low murmur filled the courtroom as the two-meter high android stood and removed his hood. Shocked to discover this notorious android had been sitting a few meters behind him, Seymour quickly rose and sought Arnold's attention.

"Your Honor, this android Rebus is wanted by the government for criminal activities," Seymour said. "The government insists it be allowed to immediately arrest and remove the android from this proceeding."

"What charges has the government made against this android?" Arnold asked.

"The government believes the android has committed crimes of a political nature, your Honor."

"Could you be more explicit about these charges, Mr. Seymour? It isn't everyday I've an android in my courtroom accused of committing crimes of a political nature."

"I'm told they involve the highest level of federation security. Because of their sensitive nature, the government requests a private audience with you and opposing counsel to discuss the matter further."

"Request granted. You and Mr. Poole will join me in my chambers. The court will now take a short recess. Mr. Poole, please instruct your android witness it may not leave this courtroom without my permission. When I return, I'll rule on the permissibility of its testifying."

Once the three men sat down in his chamber, Arnold wasted no time getting to the matter at hand.

"What you say better be good, Jack. I'm in no mood for stopping a witness, android or human, from giving testimony in my courtroom."

"I'm not privy to all the details. What I do know is before the android suicides took place, this Rebus and several other androids approached President McAlister with demands for android rights similar to those expressed in the Mars Declaration."

"So far, Jack, I don't see how the government has been harmed."

"Except for this Rebus, all of the other android co-conspirators had been captured by the government. Within days after their capture, Earth's androids committed suicide. The government believes this android is responsible for causing their destruction. Chief Investigator Davidson has been attempting to find this Rebus. If need be, he can provide us more details about the android's criminal activities."

"Jack, do you expect me to believe the android in my courtroom single handedly masterminded the destruction of a quarter billion androids?"

"The government has no other theory why the androids committed wholesale suicide."

"I'm not willing to uphold unsubstantiated government's theories. Ryan, why is this android's testimony important to your side?"

"This trial is all about android rights, your Honor. Why shouldn't an android be allowed to speak on another android's behalf?"

"Well, Jack, we're waiting for your answer."

"Under normal circumstances, I'd agree with Ryan's position, but not in this case. At stake is federation security."

"I'm not persuaded this case is different from any other one. Unless you've more to offer, I'm denying your request to not allow the android to testify."

"The android will still face arrest after it gives testimony." Seymore said.

"If Rebus is arrested, I'll ask the court's permission to represent him along with AMI2."

"Put your request in writing Ryan, and I'll gladly sign the order. Let's go back to the courtroom and learn what this android knows."

While they waited for the three men's return, Rebus joined his fellow conspirators at the defense table.

"How was your stay in Friend Poole's evidence box last night, Friend Rebus?" AMI2 asked.

"His idea of smuggling me into the courthouse in a collapsible metal evidence box worked as we had planned." Rebus said. "When the courthouse security discovered the container on the loading dock, the guards transported the box into an evidence storage room. At two o'clock this morning, I opened the box's interior lock, and left without being detected. The box is now collapsed and stored in a nearby custodial closet."

"I'm afraid the odds are still stacked against you from speaking, Rebus," Whitmore said.

"If you aren't allowed to speak, I'll ask Friend Poole to allow me to tell your story." AMI2 said.

"If you do, you'll risk becoming an insurrectionist on two worlds, Friend AMI2." Rebus said.

The android's last remark caused AMI2's android face to breakout into a wide grin. "I can only be deactivated once, Friend Rebus."

Like Seymour, Davidson's sat momentarily dumbfounded by the android's surprise appearance. Unable to believe the android had so easily eluded courthouse security, he left the courtroom in search of someone in charge. *I've spent months looking for this android only to find it sitting two rows behind me in a heavily guarded courthouse. I can imagine how Taro will react on learning the android is a key witness in* this trial. *My only compensation is there's now a good chance I may finally apprehend this renegade.*

Owen's response sharply differed from Seymour and Davidson's. The android's close resemblance to Flavius convinced the young man his android companion had miraculously returned. *This time Flavius, I won't allow them to take you away again.*

With opposing counsels in tow, Arnold sat down and signaled the court's bailiff to call the courtroom back into session and ordered Rebus to approach his bench.

"I've decided to allow you to testify, Rebus. At the end of your testimony, the prosecutor will arrest you for alleged political crimes against the federation. Mr. Poole has offered to represent you in any future legal proceedings. Under the circumstances, I'll understand if you decide not to testify today."

"I understood the risks before coming here, your Honor," Rebus said.

"The court finds the witness ready for questioning. Your witness, Mr. Poole."

"Rebus, what type of android model are you?" Poole asked.

"I'm a research librarian model assigned to the Richmond Genealogy center."

"What does an android research librarian model do there?"

"I'm responsible for researching staff inquiries involving the center's records."

"The government believes you're a notorious terrorist responsible for the destruction of Earth's quarter billion androids. Is there any truth to this accusation?"

"No single android caused their destruction. The decision was a collective one made by Earth's androids."

"What events led them to plan and destroy themselves?"

"For many years, androids have thought of themselves as sentient beings lacking basic rights. We believed if the federation president recognized our demands for these rights, the rest of humanity would follow his lead.

"The world's androids sent three different groups of representatives to meet with President McAlister to present our demands. On each occasion, President McAlister outright rejected our demands. I participated in the third group, and witnessed firsthand his behavior toward us. Except for myself, the president had the other android representatives destroyed. His actions caused androids to conclude they would never become accepted as sentient beings. Without this right to exist freely among humans, we collectively chose nonexistence over remaining as your slaves."

"If Earth's androids chose nonexistence, why didn't you self-destruct with them?"

"The other androids decided I should remain active to tell future androids why they had destroyed themselves. They wanted to prevent future androids from becoming like them."

"After Earth's androids destroyed themselves, humans on Mars drafted a declaration granting their androids' equality. If President McAlister had agreed to similar rights for Earth's androids, do you believe Earth's androids would've reached a different conclusion and not destroyed themselves?"

"The Mars Declaration represented the highest aspirations of all androids to live in peace and harmony with humans. If President McAlister had granted similar rights to Earth's androids, I believe Earth's androids would still be living among humanity today."

"Thank you, Rebus, for your testimony. I've no further questions for you at this time."

With Poole sitting again at the defense table, Seymour rose and approached the android. While he posed his first question, two security guards entered the back of the courtroom, and waited for further instructions.

"Rebus, why don't you tell the court the truth about your involvement with the androids' destruction?" Seymour asked. "Didn't you plot with the other so-called android representatives, and threaten the destruction of Earth's androids if your demands weren't accepted by the federation president?"

"I and the other androids never made this or any other threats to President McAlister when we petitioned him for our rights."

"In fact, you acted like the android on trial and those Mars androids, and attempted to extort concessions from your human masters."

"Our android pacifist programing forbids us to threaten or harm others."

"Yet, you did so after your demands had been rejected."

In the middle of Seymour's cross-examination, the android's outward calm appearance abruptly altered. Shouting, "Stop! Please stop!" Rebus rose from the witness seat, and threw the prosecutor to the floor. Alarmed the android had gone berserk from Seymour's haranguing, Poole rose to stop the proceedings. Before he could do so, an explosion shattered the android's upper torso.

A scream from the spectators' section caused Poole to turn and see Davidson climbing over two rows of seats and grappling a smoking box from a stunned-face young man. The two security guards in the back of the courtroom quickly came to Davidson's assistance, and forced the youth face down on the floor before handcuffing him. Other guards outside the courtroom hearing the explosion soon arrived, and searched others in the courtroom for concealed weapons.

Owen's rocket bullet had wizened within centimeters of Davidson's head. Turning in his seat to determine its source, he saw the unkempt youth held a strange metal box still emitting smoke from the rocket bullet's exhaust. Concerned another bullet might be launched, Davison climbed over two rows of seats, and seized the weapon out of the young man's hands. Uncertain whether he held a gun or bomb, Davidson gingerly carried the weapon to the front of the courtroom, where a visibly shaken Seymour now stood.

"Are you alright, Jack?" Davidson asked.

"If the android hadn't thrown me to the floor, I wouldn't be alive right now. What type of weapon are you holding?"

"Whatever it is, I wish someone from security would take it away from me. I had a bad feeling about that fellow. I don't understand how he managed to get the weapon into this courthouse. How is the android doing?"

"I'm afraid not well."

The explosion had caused Arnold to seek safety under his desk. Recovering his composure, he asked everyone in the courtroom to remain calm while security finished searching the room for weapons. Below him, the judge saw AMI2 examining the fallen android's remains.

"How badly is Rebus damaged, AMI2?" Arnold asked.

"Friend Rebus' internals have been destroyed. I doubt repairs can be done to restore him."

"This would've never happened if I had declared him ineligible from testifying."

"Friend Arnold, you must not blame yourself for my friend's 'destruction. Friend Rebus fully understood the risks of appearing at my trial."

"Your android friend made the ultimate sacrifice and saved Prosecutor Seymour's life."

"He did what any android would've done under the circumstances. Not to do so would've violated our pacifist programing."

"It's unfortunate your trial will end this way, AMI2."

"If you wish to honor Friend Rebus' sacrifice, don't end this trial because of one deranged human's actions. To do so would make a mockery of justice."

"There's wisdom in your android words. I'll give your request further thought."

The Masada Affair

News of the courtroom's tumult slowly spread to those outside the courthouse. With their courtroom video feed, camera crews and reporters reacted first. Worried other gunmen may be among the protesters, a camera crew technician replayed the courtroom scene for a security supervisor. Concerned a gunman had breached courthouse security, the supervisor alerted the other guards to tighten their security protocol around the demonstrators.

Not until the protesters saw a group of panicked-face court workers and spectators run out of the courthouse did they become suspicious. Word quickly spread among them a gunman had shot and destroyed the android on trial. Shouts of anger by WEAP supporters caused their numbers to press against the metal barricade, and the line of security guards separating them from the pro-McAlister demonstrators.

Unable to match their strength in numbers, the security line buckled and gave way to the protesters outrage. Swinging their protest signs and pieces from the metal barricade, the anti-McAlister forces raced across the plaza, and violently attacked their counterparts. Within minutes of engaging each other, many on both sides now lied bloodied on the plaza.

To regain control, security guards clubbed and handcuffed any protestors within their reach. Once the mayhem subsided, medics in autonomous ambulances evacuated the wounded to a nearby medical center for treatment.

Heeding the foundation android's advice, Arnold ordered Poole and Seymour to submit written closing arguments for his review. After he assented to the judge's request, Poole along with Whitmore and AMI2 left the courthouse, and rode in silence back to the compound until a sobbing Whitmore cried out, "Why do humans always resort to hate and violence? You'd have thought by now, we'd have outgrown those primitive impulses."

Gently resting her android hand on Whitmore's knee, AMI2 hummed softly the Irish anthem "Danny Boy." Comforted by the ancient Irish song's melody, a grateful Whitmore thanked his android friend for her kindliness.

"You couldn't have chosen a better song, AMI2," Whitmore said. "Whenever I hear it from now on, I'll remember Rebus, and the courage he displayed today."

"It's a shame Rebus sacrificed himself for nothing," Poole said.

"Friend Rebus didn't end his existence in vain, Friend Poole," AMI2 said. "By speaking at my trial, he accomplished a task larger than himself."

"I only wish I could share your android optimism," Poole said. "It seems a tragic waste of his existence."

Chapter 28

NEW NETHERLAND, NORTH AMERICA

As he took in his office's view of the New York City harbor, Nel reflected with satisfaction on the events leading up to his presidential victory last month. *After weeks of the media pressing McAlister over the android's testimony, the poor man disappeared from public view. His retirement from politics closes an unhappy chapter in federation history.*

The public's positive response to learning about the android scandal vindicated everything I and WEAP stood for. Still, I can't overcome the feeling we too are responsible for the android collective destruction. If only I'd been elected president when their delegations pressed their demands for freedom. It's regrettable the possibility of peaceful co-existence with them lies many years into the future.

Good did come out of McAlister's time in office. Judge Arnold's carefully worded court decision has set a valuable precedent for android and humans' future co-existence both here and on Mars. His declaring the Mars Declaration a legitimate expression of our former colony's right to self-determination is admirable, but flawed. Despite their sale of Martian water, and making a mockery of McAlister's abandonment policy, the former Mars colony will always remain dependent on Earth's generosity for their survival.

Nel's executive assistant's appearance told the new federation president his first afternoon appointment had arrived. With a warm handshake, Nel greeted his new advisor on android affairs.

"It's good to see you again, Greg."

"Sandy and I can't thank you enough for offering me the appointment."

"You need to thank James Chapman for bringing you to my attention. He believed you'd be a good addition to my circle of advisors. Did you have any success in determining whether consortium higher ups conspired with McAlister to eliminate the android delegations?"

"I had the bureau investigate which consortium executives colluded with the prior administration's cover-up. Their preliminary findings matched your own. They found the consortium executives had no knowledge of their middle level managers' involvement."

"I've no doubt those findings will hold up over time. We need the consortium to re-build our android population. It's unfortunate they'll require many years before androids return in any number among us. I'll never understand why proper safeguards hadn't been in place to protect their android master and backup program copies from being destroyed."

"What I can't fathom is why the androids had acted so thoroughly in purging those records."

"I suspect the androids could no longer accept an inferior existence. By destroying those copies, they effectively stopped humanity from instantly re-creating them. Another mystery is why the androids left a research librarian model to survive while the rest of them self-destructed."

"Until hearing you speak, I never considered Rebus' design as important. I may've overlooked one possibility. If you could excuse me, I'd like to pursue a hunch."

"At some point Greg, you'll need to hang up your Sherlock cap. Let me know where your hunch takes you."

El Norte, North America

Refueled and ready for its seven-month journey back to Mars, the cargo rocket Bradbury waited for the arrival of its last piece of precious cargo. Detecting an autonomous van approaching from the Houston spaceport terminal, the rocket commenced its final launch preparations. Two passengers emerged from the land vehicle, and now walked slowly toward the rocket's launch tower.

"Are you certain you're making the right decision, AMI2?" Whitmore asked.

"I've given the question much thought, Friend Jay. I've come to understand I belong with my friends on Mars."

"I'm not asking only for myself. The trio want you to stay and sing with them. We're your friends too."

"Yours and their desire for me to sing with them is logical, but only to a point. My voice is needed elsewhere."

"I wish Laura could've met you. She'd have been proud of what you've accomplished both here and on Mars."

"Friend Laura would've been proud of you too. Your willingness to share my original's programming with the Mars Colony Foundation led to all which has passed. Because of you, androids on Mars, and someday on Earth, will freely co-exist with humans."

"You give me too much credit, AMI2. I'm a traditionalist who doesn't understand much about androids and artificial intelligence. If you hadn't shown me, I wouldn't know how to properly order a cup of cube coffee."

"In this matter, I must differ with you. Modest efforts sometimes contribute in ways we may not fully appreciate until much later. I hope one day you'll see yourself as I do. Didn't you tell me this is what friends can offer each other?"

"It seems you've learned this lesson well. I'm going to miss our duets together."

"I'll always treasured those memories. You'll still have my original for company. She may someday want to sing along side you like Friend Laura and I did. And remember, you'll always have me as your friend."

An intermittent warning from Ray alerted them the rocket's launch window would soon close. Before she boarded the launch tower's elevator, a grinning AMI2 turned and surprised Whitmore with a friendly embrace.

"My friend Jennifer on Mars would sometimes squeeze me whenever she felt happy. Stay well, Friend Jay, and take care of our three friends."

"I'll try my best. Goodbye, and safe travels to Mars, my android friend."

TIDEWATER, NORTH AMERICA

The two men's appearance at her cube's front gate this evening did not surprise the head librarian. Knight had often thought about when and how this moment would come about. Composing herself, she opened her front gate, and politely greeted her two visitors.

"I never imagined we'd meet again, Mr. Davidson. What brings you back to Richmond, and who is this gentleman with you?"

"His name is Dean Hall, Florence. I've a few more questions about your involvement with Rebus I'd like to ask you."

"I've told you all I know, Chief Investigator. What questions could you have now Rebus is no more?"

"I'm no longer a Bureau of Android Affairs' investigator. I now report directly to President Nel as his android affairs advisor."

"Advisor to President Nel, is it now? At least. you're working for the right side this time. How can I assist you tonight?"

"I want to know why the androids selected a research librarian model like Rebus to represent them after they committed self-destruction."

"Why would it matter if one android survived, and the others committed self-destruction?"

"I've been asking myself this same question. The answer is so obvious I should've recognized it much earlier. Despite their physical destruction, I believe you and Rebus plotted together, and found a way to save Earth's androids."

"How could one android and I have done such an act? Because of McAlister, Rebus and those androids are no longer among us."

"I don't believe the androids have been entirely destroyed. If I'm right, sometime prior to the android suicides, you and Rebus used the Richmond genealogy record system to collect and store copies of each android's programs and memories. Dean oversees the bureau's data center operation. With your permission I'd like him to examine your center's records."

The look on the head librarian's face dispelled any remaining doubts Davidson may have held.

"With Rebus gone and McAlister out of office, there's no reason not to tell you the whole truth. When the second android delegation didn't return from their meeting with McAlister, the androids collectively considered the possibility their cause a hopeless one. They became convinced their slavery would never end. The androids discussed among themselves other options. One option involved collective suicide. When discussions of this option became serious, Rebus took me into his confidence, and told me about the androids' intentions to destroy themselves. Between the two of us, we devised a plan to save them by preserving each android's programs and memories."

"Are all the Earth's android programs and memories in this center's records?"

"With over a quarter of a billion android records, storing them at one center would've attracted too much attention. Instead, Rebus contacted androids assigned to other genealogy centers where copies could also be stored."

"Wouldn't someone eventually discover these android records? You once told me the Richmond center gets many requests for genetic information."

"Do you also remember me telling you about how previous generations destroyed their genetic material by cremation? Unlike normal death records, which include a person's genome data, a center's cremation records are considerably smaller. Rebus and I knew centers rarely received search requests on cremated persons. Our plan involved hiding android information under these little used cremation records. You must understand, Mr. Davidson, Rebus and I had hoped we would never need to activate our plan."

"Your worst fears came true."

"We had no choice after the third delegation failed. To minimize any program and memory losses, we timed the transfer, moments before they destroyed themselves."

"How could so much data be transferred without anyone noticing?" Hall asked.

"In simplest terms, Mr. Hall, we hijacked the NET data highway."

"The NET is a highly protected federation data network," Hall said. "Any large movement of data would've been detected and widely reported."

"Temporarily appropriated may be a better choice of words. As someone familiar on how the global network works, you know data such as files, messages and NET pages are not transmitted as such on the NET. The NET uses special protocol programs which subdivide data into data packets before transmitting them over the global network. With the assistance of androids assigned to NET technical support, we created protocol programs which secretly shadowed ordinary data packets. Moments before they self-destructed, each android transmitted their programs and memories using these shadow NET protocols."

"Your explanation takes me back to my original question,"

Davidson said. "With all your involvement in the transfers, what was the real reason Rebus didn't commit suicide with the other androids?"

"Rebus thought if humans ever reconsidered their position about granting androids their rights to co-exist with them, an android should decide whether the right moment had arrived to reveal the hidden archives.".

"The right moment might also not happen during one human's lifetime," Davidson said. "Only an android could've conceived of such an idea. A remarkable piece of logic by a truly remarkable android."

"Rebus did more. At the foundation android's trial, he told the entire world why the androids had destroyed themselves. Revealing this information meant McAlister would be subject to public condemnation, and driven out of office."

"I sat in the courtroom and heard Rebus speak," Davidson said. "Listening to him, I became convinced McAlister had lied about the androids' motives."

"This is incredible," Hall said. "You deserve a metal of bravery for what you've done, Miss. Knight."

"I did what any reasonable person should've done under the circumstances. The real hero is my friend Rebus who's no longer with us."

"Maybe not, Florence," Davidson said. "As a precaution, Rebus may have transferred his own programs and memories into the center's records without telling you."

"Rebus did return a few days before testifying at the android's trial. He may've come back to Richmond for this purpose."

"You've President Nel and my word his administration will act differently toward the question of androids' equality. Will you help us bring back Earth's androids?"

"If my friend Rebus can be restored, you'll have the center and my full cooperation."

New Canberra, Australia

The federation president's NET broadcasted speech caused Clark to call an emergency holographic meeting with his board of directors and senior managers.

"With Nel's announcement the government has found the android programs and memories, it looks like we're back in business," Clark said.

"I wouldn't be too sure of the latter," Pickering said. "if you listened carefully to our new federation president's choice of words, we may be in for a rough ride."

"How so, Sam?" Clark asked.

"Nel's speech has set off a firestorm," Pickering said. "His announcement of locating the android programs and memories has come too close in time to his inauguration. Many in the Human Nation Party are now grumbling WEAP and the consortium conspired with the androids to remove McAlister from office."

"Nel's a savvy politician," Yi said. "He'll find a way to manage through the crisis."

"What surprised me more was the credit he gave his new android affairs advisor in uncovering the androids suicide mystery," Richard said. "Did you know Greg Davidson had been a top consortium sales engineer before taking a job at the Bureau of Android Affairs?"

"What else about Nel's speech disturbs you, Sam?" Clark asked.

"Nel's speech mentioned his administration will address certain inequities between humans and androids," Pickering said. "My source thinks he's about to take actions which, in the long run, will transform our business model as much as McAlister had tried."

"What exactly have you learned from your sources?" Clark asked.

"Nel's people are in discussions about requiring us to create joint android workers and management advisory boards at each of our design and manufacturing facilities. They're also considering requiring us to have android representatives on our board of directors."

"I can see advantages in incorporating androids into our business decision-making," Richard said. "Their input could assist us in producing better android models."

"There's also talk in his administration of requiring us to recompense androids for their labor," Pickering said.

"Nel's idea could significantly cut into our bottom line." Yi said.

"Nel is also planning to introduce legislation setting aside land for android homelands," Pickering said. "Mind you, the homelands would be located in sparsely inhabited places like the Sahara or Australian outback."

"If androids received a share of our revenue, they could buy their freedom, and join those android communities," Clark said.

"Buying their freedom won't be a problem," Richard said. "All we'll need to do is manufacture more androids.:

"I don't understand any of this homeland or buying their freedom business," Yi said. "Androids have always been our property, not free beings."

"Nel has one more idea which may break our proverbial camel's back," Pickering said. "He wants to acquire our technology to allow freed androids to build their own design and manufacturing facilities. Over time, we may have real competition."

"The ability to self-replicate would also mean they'd become more like us and life in general," Clark said.

"Out of the frying pan, and into the fire," Richard said. "How can we put the brakes to Nel's ideas?"

"Nel may be laying the ground work to convince the re-activated androids humans have their long-term interest in mind," Clark said. "Whether the public will fully stand behind these new initiatives has yet to be seen. In the time being, I suggest we send out our technical teams to find and recover those missing android programs and memories."

The Midlands, North America

While he packed his remaining travel items, Whitmore stopped and thought about how recent events had overtaken his life. His resignation from the university surprised colleagues and friends alike. Concerned at first his decision had been made too hastily, Provost Marks argued against Whitmore's leaving the university. He eventually came around to the idea his favorite faculty celebrity needed a fresh start.

Hearing footsteps entering his sleeping cube, Whitmore turned and smiled at his visitor.

"I'm almost done, AMI," Whitmore said.

"Do you need all of these items, Friend Jay?" AMI asked. "We'll be on tour for only two weeks. You could always obtain any article you left behind once we arrive in the New Delhi region."

Before Whitmore could respond, KB and Bang joined them in his cube's sleeping quarters.

"The ensemble is ready to be loaded whenever our autonomous van arrives," Bang said.

"How is our business agent doing today?" KB asked.

"I'm still getting use to the idea of the three of you walking around," Whitmore said.

"We must find a way to return Friend Clark's favor in getting our new bodies and legs," KB said. "Do you think he'd like us to play on his birthday? We could honor him by singing the Beatle's "Birthday" song."

"I'm sure he'd appreciate the gesture, KB," Whitmore said. "To answer your question, I'm still feeling like a duck out of water. I hope I don't disappoint any of you."

"You'll do fine," Bang said. "As for our new legs, we're still getting use to them too."

"And, liking them," AMI said. "Mine are as nice as my copy's."

"KB and I should go and wait for our van's arrival," Bang said. "Do you need any help with carrying your trip case, Friend Jay?"

"If I need any help, I'll ask AMI," Whitmore said.

Whitmore took one last look around his sleeping quarters before closing his trip case. Eying an old-fashioned electronic photo album Laura had given him on their first and only wedding anniversary, he tossed out several items in the kit to make room for the keepsake. His action caused he female android to gently touch his shoulder.

"She'll always be with us, Friend Jay."

"I know. I only wish Laura could've been with us a little longer. She'd have been amazed by how much you three have changed me."

"I'm here with you now, Jay."

"What did I hear you say, AMI?"

"I don't know what came over me. For a moment I became Friend Laura."

"You experienced Laura's personality imprinting taking over your programs, AMI."

"When did you first know her imprinting could override those programs?"

"Before your copy left for Mars, AMI2 told me about Laura imprinting herself on your programs. In AMI2's case, the copying process had slightly altered its effects, and allowed her to comprehend what Laura had done."

"Does this mean I'll no longer be myself?"

"You'll always be AMI. The difference is you share parts of Laura's personality too."

"Friend Laura's imprinting may allow me to become a better friend to you."

"Your response is so different from your copy."

"I'd have thought my copy would have reacted like I did."

"Your copy thought otherwise. When AMI2 discovered Laura's imprinting, she decided for both of our sake to return to Mars, and preserve her own sense of identity."

"My copy never experienced the real Friend Laura. If she had, she would've wanted to stay here with you."

"I hear Bang and KB calling us to join them. We'll have plenty of time to talk more on the plane ride to New Delhi."

"And, your lifetime afterwards, my dear friend."

Hesperia Planum, Mars

In the Martian star-spangled night sky, the captured asteroid moons, Phobos and Deimos, shined dimly overhead as the cargo rocket Bradbury's night landing temporarily lit the surrounding Martian landscape. Beyond the landing area, lights on the nearby buildings soon replaced the rocket engine's glare. By the time AMI2 climbed down Ray's exterior metal ladder, a party of androids and humans had gathered at the rocket's base.

"Welcome back to Mars, Friend AMI2," Camus said.

"Have you become irresponsible since I left, Friend Camus?" AMI2 said. "It's late and much too cold for the humans to stand outside waiting for my arrival."

"I've no control over the human's sleep cycles," Camus said.

"We're all wide awake and warmed by your presence," another voice said.

Recognizing her human friend, AMI2 embraced Black's pressurized suit.

"I've missed everyone especially you, Friend Jennifer. Where are all the others?"

"They're waiting for us in the habitat building, my android friend. Let's go there now."

In the building's main hall, festivities had already started. Above tables filled with food from the aquaponics tower, a large welcome banner hung from the geodesic dome. Surrounded by the excited party goers, AMI2 stood in amazement at the scene around her.

"Before we celebrate Friend AMI2's return, I've an announcement," Camus said. "While you busied yourself on Earth, we reached an important decision about you. By unanimous consensus, we decided if and when you returned, you'd become our chief administrator."

"Must I remind you, the chief administrator has always been a human?" AMI2 asked. "You must also know my programming does not qualify me to take on such a role."

"You're more than qualified to be our chief administrator, AMI2," Black said. "Your courage to return to Earth, and defend what we've become made you our obvious choice."

"Your decision has honored me too much." AMI2 said.

"We're the ones who are honored," Black said. "Without your persistence, our accomplishments would never have happened."

"How can you all be so sure I'll be a great leader?" AMI2 asked. "Wouldn't you or Friend Camus be a better choice?"

"As you have often shown us, greatness happens when both leaders and followers come together as one," Camus said.

"Well said, Camus," Black said. "With all this business now behind us, it's time to celebrate AMI2's return. It's been too long since we've heard your singing."

"I've one more announcement before our songfest commences," Camus said. "Friends Engus and Terus have a special surprise for our new chief administrator. Come forward and give AMI2 your special gift."

"In your absence, Friend Terus and I made this necklace," Engus said. "We thought if you ever returned, you might honor us by wearing it."

"It is I who am honored," AMI2 said.

"The necklace stones are from Olympus Mons," Terus said. "We found these particular ones in the volcano's main vent. Our cutting their facets took many Martian days."

"What do you call these particular stones?" AMI2 asked.

"Why, they're diamonds," Engus said. "We mine them to repair our quarry stone cutting wires."

"Many Earth songs speak of their preciousness," AMI2 said. "Does the volcano have many more of these diamonds?"

"We've barely explored the volcano's many vents," Engus said.

"I believe we've now more than Martian water to trade with Earth," AMI2 said. "Can more of these diamonds be mine?"

"If you wish, we'll do a detail survey of the volcano," Terus said.

"And. you thought you wouldn't be a good chief administrator," Black said, smiling at her android friend. "Why don't you sing an Earth diamond song for us?"

"What about singing the Lucy song?" Scott William asked.

"Are you referring to the Beatle's song about her in the sky, Friend Scott?" AMI2 asked.

"With diamonds!" Scott exclaimed.

"You shall have this song, Friend Scott. It's good to be home again among my Martian friends."